BLOC
A 14th-Century Anglo-Saxon Resolution

Book two of the Blood and Brotherhood Duology

J W PHILLIPS

For permissions or inquiries, contact:
jwphillipsauthor@gmail.com

AUTHOR'S NOTE:

'Write about what you know,' they said. Fine – but I've never been a 14th-century English archer. By that logic, I shouldn't be writing a novel about one.

Then I got to thinking – I know history. I like to believe I have a grasp on human nature. And maybe it's not so black and white.

So, I wrote it anyway. Blood Settlement: A 14th-Century Anglo-Saxon Saga. Then I wrote another – this one – the finale of The Blood and Brotherhood Duology.

As before, I've kept the historical events as close to the recorded facts as possible. The horrors of medieval battle? I'll let you decide. I've written what my mind's eye saw. At times, it was harrowing. I make no apologies. More than once, I thought – people *really* lived through this.

Yet, even amidst the bloodshed, there were moments that showed humanity at its best – times when people came together, clinging to one another for comfort and love. Despite the relentless hardships of survival, life carried on. And here we are today – living proof.

But enough rambling – your time is precious.

Would I have liked to live back then? I've changed my answer.

Hell, yes.

CHAPTER 1

They came for my comrades first – dragging them from the pen, cutting each down like swine at slaughter. Cleavers hacked flesh, limbs wrenched apart, each piece tossed into the fire. Cries for mercy drowned beneath the butcher's laughter as fat sizzled like pork at a charter fair. It's funny what surfaces when you stare death in the face. As the last screams faded, my once-devout faith drained away. Where was God in this moment of need? Perhaps that's every condemned man's final thought before the light goes out. But in my case, He chose to intervene.

He took the form of a Scottish clan chief – Archibald Douglas, Duke of Touraine – a hulking brute with mud-caked red hair and crazed eyes burning above the wild beard shrouding his face. From his place by the fire, he turned and beckoned me forward. It was my turn to die. I prayed it would be quick.

Then he spoke.

'Bless me, Reverend Father, and grant me absolution.' His voice was calm as he dropped to his knees before me.

I met his gaze – cold, bloodshot.

'I will not ask again, Brother Michael,' he said.

I'd first set eyes on him that morning as part of a white-flagged envoy tasked with brokering a truce. His marauding Scots had swept through Northumberland, avenging a crushing defeat earlier that year at Nesbit Moor, where their countrymen had been butchered to the last. He had dismissed our proposals with a sneer and sent us back to the English lines, his laughter haunting long after.

The battle that followed had been a slaughter. The Scots were victorious, and we – those left alive – were hauled into captivity.

Lord Douglas laid the blood-soaked axe he'd used to dismember my friends to one side, bowing his head. A portion of his skull was missing, exposing the dark matter beneath. It didn't seem to trouble him. I hesitated, understanding the moment – my one chance. I glanced at the Scots guarding me. Fury – they wanted me dead. As the final prisoner's hair caught fire and his belly split, spilling his boiled entrails, I complied with Douglas's wishes.

It saved my life.

Before granting me leave to return, Archibald Douglas gave me one parting gift.

*

And now I sit beside Ailred Norman's still body in silent reflection, already feeling his absence. I fix his smile in my mind, determined to remember him that way – a man who found humour even when most would have yielded to darkness. I know that temptation only too well.

I scribed his early years what feels like a

lifetime ago, before his tale was fully told. Back then, I could walk. The pleasure Archibald Douglas and his men took in shattering my legs with hammers still haunts me – his parting gift. He graciously left my arms intact, so they couldn't have been all bad. And he kept his word – he let me live. A small mercy, perhaps, but enough that I can drag myself around on a trolley and write this.

That day is a faded memory now, its images refusing to die.

Ailred found me a year later under care of the nuns at St. Mary's. By then he was a frail old man, though his mind was as sharp as any blade. At that reunion, his eyes held a warmth that bridged our lost years. I asked if he would allow me to scribe the rest of his story. He went to speak, but his eyes filled instead, and I held up a hand.

'Let those tears flow as you recount your life, Ailred.'

And so he did. He laid bare every detail and shadow he had cast. He was never more alive than in those final hours, as he stitched together a life of war, love, and loss. We held onto every word.

Now, those words are yours.

*

The knocking escalated into a thumping, dragging me from sleep. I stumbled to the door. A dog barked in the distance as a flickering lantern cast its glow onto a lone figure. Cloaked in a filthy monk's habit, the cowl shadowed its face.

I blinked and rubbed my eyes. No matter how many times I blinked and rubbed, the vision remained.

The last thing I remembered was eating boiled pork with carrots and onions before slipping into bed beside Philippa. Her broth-scented voice had murmured that I'd be out of luck tonight – she was tired. Again. She was always tired these days.

The figure drew back its cowl.

'What the fuck?' It's my standard response to surprises. I ought to learn to express myself better.

It smiled. 'Hello, brother.'

'Paul?'

'Glad to see you haven't lost your grasp of the obvious, Ailred. Aren't you going to invite me in?'

I stepped aside in disbelief as he entered the dim room.

'Hope I didn't wake you?'

'Well, seeing as it's the middle of the night…' I halted. 'What the fuck…?'

He laughed – a sound I'd known since childhood.

'You look like you've seen a ghost!' He dropped into a padded chair, propping his feet on the polished table. He gestured around. 'Looks like you made good use of my money.'

And there it was. I'd thought this day of reckoning would never come.

A monk now, living out his days in Tintern Abbey, Paul had become a servant of God – the only way to leave that place was in a box. I was the beneficiary of a robbery he'd instigated years ago, but now a respected pillar of the community. Yet here he was, in my living room.

I shoved his feet off the table and wiped away the mud. The house was sparsely furnished to maximise space, but thanks to Philippa, the furniture we did own was of the highest quality.

'What are you doing here, Paul?'

He cocked an eye, hands clasped behind his shaved head. His eyes were darker than I remembered, his calm exterior a far cry from his upbringing.

'You don't seem pleased to see me, Ailred. Or should I call you Sire? Lord, perhaps?'

I sat opposite him, sliding the candle to the middle of the table.

'Of course, I'm pleased. Just... surprised. Last I saw you, you were...' His boots thumped onto the table again. I pushed them off. '...a monk devoted to the Almighty.'

He nodded, touching the small gold cross that hung around his thick neck. 'Still am.' He glanced around as if confirming we were alone. 'And besides – fuck that.'

I frowned. 'You've been living monastically for five years, Paul. You can't just say "fuck that" and walk out.'

He stretched, resting his boots on the table

again. 'You'd be surprised what I can do.' He smiled. 'Tintern's an abbey, not a dungeon, Ailred. We're free to come and go. Or did you imagine us chained to a wall, archdeacons shoving their pastoral staff up our...'

'Enough, Paul.' My voice was cold. 'You're under my roof. Show some respect.'

His words struck a nerve. He knew what Archdeacon Gruffudd ap Rhys had done to me in that dungeon years ago. He was dredging up what I'd spent years trying to bury.

I took a breath, pushing his feet from the table with deliberate calm. He wanted a reaction. I wouldn't give him the satisfaction.

'Ale?' I asked.

'I thought you'd never ask.' His feet found their way back onto the table.

With a sigh, I rose, filled two mugs, and shoved his feet off again as I set his drink down.

'You have a lot of explaining to do,' I said.

He smirked, raised his mug, and propped his feet back up. I glared, shrugged, and put my own feet up. I wasn't going to win.

He took a long swig, then smiled. He began.

Our visit to Tintern had changed everything. Philippa, the twins – Timothy and Frederick – our daughter Kimberly, and I had gone to the abbey at Bishop Rhosier's urging. I'd been asked to fill in the dark patches of Paul's past. His mind had locked away years of violence, fractures from wars and fights that he couldn't piece together.

It was a miracle he was still alive. Paul getting to understand his own story, they thought, might be the key to his recovery.

So I'd told him everything I could recall.

He'd listened intently, especially when I described how Philippa had posed as a nun in France – the ruse that got us home. Without that stolen nun's habit, we would've made it. He'd been appalled by some of my confessions. Who wouldn't be? When we left the abbey, he'd looked hollow, almost broken, a tear in his eye.

I was sure I'd never see him again.

How wrong I was. Very, it would seem.

'So… did my recounting restore your memory?' I asked.

He shrugged. 'No. Not a damned thing came back.' He looked down, fingers tracing the rim of his mug. 'But it reminded me who I am. And what I am.'

'And who are you? What are you?'

Philippa's voice drifted down the stairs.

Paul straightened as if called to attention. His expression softened as he watched her descend, a crinkled shawl clutched around her shoulders, hair tangled, eyes watchful.

Paul nodded slowly. 'Who and what am I? Good question, Philippa.'

She paused, pulling her hair back from her face. 'You… you know my name?' She frowned. 'In all these years, you never once called me by it.'

He touched the cross at his neck. 'You

mentioned it during your visit to Wales. Your loving family was the highlight of my novitiate. A catalyst for my recovery.' He looked skyward. 'Thanks to you, I found clarity.'

Philippa looked stunned.

I cut in, unable to hold back. 'Clarity? You were always fixated on yourself – on taking what you wanted and destroying what you couldn't have.'

She nodded, her gaze still fixed on Paul.

He looked regretful.

'I've changed,' he said. 'I have self-control now. Patience. The Church has given me strength.' He sipped his ale. 'I am a new man. Praise be to God.'

Philippa turned to me. 'He's more dangerous now than he's ever been.'

With one last, long look at Paul, she shook her head and climbed the stairs.

Paul waited until her door shut.

Then, a slow smile crept across his face.

He eased back into the chair and propped his feet on the table.

A low, cold laugh rolled from his throat, filling the room with an eerie chill.

*

That night, I let him sleep in our barn. It was standard practice back then. The children had slept through our night-time family reunion, and I saw no reason to disrupt the household. Kimberly had reached that impossible age where everything was an argument, the younger twins were at the first impossible age, and Philippa had invented a new one for herself. The last thing I needed was another person under our roof – even if he was my brother and had supplied the money to buy it.

By now, we lived in relative comfort. We owned the Chequers Inn and had recently taken on the Royal Oak Tavern. Philippa's parents, Tom and Emma, had returned to help run the inn, bringing years of experience with them. Tom's ready laugh and good nature made him a favourite among the regulars, while Emma's knowing eye ensured the local villains stayed away. Together, they worked hard and reaped the rewards.

Philippa had hired Mark Peterson, the Royal Oak's original owner, to manage that. He knew the clientele and everything about the place and had proved reliable. Overseeing both inns was no small task, but Philippa thrived on it.

On top of that, she ran a textile business, dyeing and producing linen and wool, with five workers keeping it all moving. Between her ventures and her parents' help, our corner of town bustled. We weren't just getting by – we were booming.

Me? I did whatever Philippa told me to do. Some things never changed. She had a knack for finding profit in the smallest venture, and I had a knack for staying out of the way. My habit of dodging responsibilities hadn't improved with age, and while it grated on Philippa, I was pretty sure she still loved me – or at least tolerated me. She had her ambitions, and I had mine. They didn't align. Not that I could have stopped her if I tried.

And now, here was Paul. Back in our lives. A quiet worry I couldn't shake. He was out of sight in the barn for now, but he wouldn't stay there forever.

*

'So, what are your intentions, Paul?' I asked, watching him closely as he slouched opposite me in the Chequers the morning after his grand return. He looked no better than a stray dog – flecks of hay clinging to his filthy habit, skin smudged with dirt from what I assumed was a night spent turning over dark thoughts. He hadn't washed, either. Seeing him now was like looking at a ghost of my own past – back when all I had was ambition and empty pockets. But now I had money. His money. Which was other people's money.

'Intentions?' He stroked his beard, flicking away straw with absent-minded satisfaction. 'I'm a monk, Al. I have no aim other than to serve the Lord.' He clasped his hands together, bowing his head as if absolving himself of some long-forgotten sin.

I sighed, realising I'd be sighing a great deal while Paul stuck around.

'Let's start from the beginning, shall we?' I said, filling two mugs of ale from the black barrel.

I slid one across, bracing myself. If I were to survive his visit, I'd need a sturdy drink – and the patience of a saint. Paul did nothing the easy way.

He opened his mouth to speak, hesitated, then leaned back, planting his boots squarely on the table. Leaning forward, I shoved them off.

'Must you keep putting those on my table?'

'Sorry, my Lord!' he muttered. He shrugged and settled deeper into his chair. 'You want the truth, Al? I lost my religion after you came to see me.'

I rolled my eyes. 'Lost it? You spent years in that monastery. Are you telling me you tossed it aside after our one visit? That isn't the image you gave Philippa last night.'

He took a long swig of ale and smirked. 'This is good, little bro. Let me guess – the wife sources the drinks as well?'

'Philippa, yes. But don't dodge the question.'

'And I'll wager she's running the other businesses too, no? Keeping it all afloat while you... drift.'

'Forget about Philippa.' He had a knack for peeling away at me, layer by layer. 'Why are you here, Paul?'

He shot me a knowing look, swirling the dregs of his ale. 'You're riding on her successes, aren't you? Enjoying the comfortable life.' He drained his mug and slid it across the table. My blood simmered, but I forced myself to breathe, counting the beats in my chest.

'Go back to the monastery, Paul. You were content there,' I said, scanning the familiar room. '*We* were content.'

He leaned forward, rattling the empty mug against the table, a mocking glint in his eyes. 'That's never going to happen. As I said last night – I'm a new man.'

I downed the last of my drink, snatched up his mug, refilled both, and settled back, allowing his words to sink in. A charged silence stretched between us.

'How much?' I asked.

He grimaced, clutching his chest in mock insult. 'You wound me. I'm here for a fresh start, Al. I don't care about money.' He leaned back, throwing his feet up once more with maddening casualness. 'I'm pleased you've made good use of what I earned. I'd like to think you could spare a little kindness for a poor soul, lost as I am.'

And so it went on. I pleaded with him to return to Tintern Abbey, but he twisted every word, turning my arguments into pangs of guilt. By the time he'd finished, he had me feeling unworthy to even breathe the same air as Philippa, let alone be her husband.

Ah, yes, I've not mentioned that, have I? Philippa and I wed not long after the twins were born. The ceremony took place in the same priory in Tonebricge that Paul had robbed years earlier. Sir Thomas de Clare attended and had the annoying habit of winking at me whenever I glanced his way. Remind me never to admit being party to stealing gold from a church to anyone, especially if their name is prefixed with "Lord". He even offered to stand as godparent to Timothy and Frederick, taking an unexpected shine to them. After his wife died giving birth to Nathaniel, he swore never to sire children again, so I believe he saw the twins as substitutes. He was forever joking that with looks so angelic, they couldn't possibly be related to me.

Paul finished dismantling what little pride I had and now sat, arms crossed, waiting for my verdict.

I stroked my beard, tapping the table with my free hand.

He chuckled. 'Using both hands to think? My, this must be serious. What's the ruling, oh wise one?'

I sighed and leaned forward. 'Fine. But there are house rules. No violence. If I hear of you intimidating so much as a dog, you're out. There are no second chances, no excuses. You've abused my hospitality before. Never again.'

I thumped the table for emphasis – and promptly knocked over my ale, soaking my lap. Paul handed me a rag from his pocket, still damp from whatever foul purpose it had served before. He tried but failed to hold back a grin as I dabbed my groin dry.

'On my honour, Al. No violence, no

intimidation,' he promised, clasping his hands in an exaggerated pose of saintly grace.

'Yeah, yeah. Spare me the act,' I muttered, handing back the rag. 'Just don't make a fool of me, Paul. Philippa will never forgive me if you do.'

He nodded, hands still folded in prayer.

'Right, then. Now all I have to do is break the news to Philippa.'

As expected, Philippa took it with all the warmth of a midwinter frost, and I spent the next few nights on the floor downstairs. All things considered, I got off lightly.

*

So, Paul moved from our barn to a room in the Chequers, courtesy of my generosity – or stupidity, as Philippa put it. To his credit, he kept himself in line – at least on the surface. I gave him routine tasks around the inn, and to my surprise, he charmed the locals. Even Sir Thomas, who had been deeply sceptical about his return, began to see him as almost human.

A few villagers still remembered him, of course – the Paul they'd once expected to see hanging from a rope. But over the weeks and months, "Father Paul", as he now styled himself, slowly regained their confidence. He became something of a fixture in town, and even I found myself beginning to trust him. His punctuality and reliability seemed almost too good to be true – yet I let myself believe.

In those months, Paul was the picture of change, a man finding redemption and restoring the faith he'd shredded to tatters all those years ago.

CHAPTER 2

You are late, Brother Michael. I know you have no legs, but raging over the men who shattered them will do you no good. God will have His own plans – if He hasn't enacted them already. From now on, pull yourself along on that trolley faster; the shins of bystanders are a small price for our work here. Heartless, you say? Perhaps. But, unlike you, my days on earth dwindle to their close. Time is no friend of mine.

I see you have already picked up that quill and started writing. Good. We have a long way to go.

*

'When's he leaving?'

We sat in the cramped back room of our home, where Philippa transformed cluttered accounts into order. She shifted parchments methodically, moving one aside only to replace it, her focus unwavering. She had once tried to teach me the meanings behind the squiggly symbols of written language, but that ended when I dared her to drink the ink.

Her question caught me off guard. 'I haven't asked him about his plans. He's no problem living here, is he?'

Philippa paused, her silence more revealing than any words. Then she let go.

'He's no problem living here, is he!' Her voice was

high-pitched and mocking.

I frowned. The tension between us had been simmering for weeks, but Paul's return had taken things to a new level. She refused to believe he'd changed, deaf to my reassurances. Years of experience had taught me to let her barbed remarks slide, to refrain from rising to the bait – so I did what I always did. I bit.

'He's my brother, for God's sake. I can't just tell him to leave.'

Philippa picked up her quill again, resuming her battle with the squiggly nonsense. Silence fell between us. I tapped my teeth, shifting in my seat, desperate to fill the void.

'What's that supposed to mean?' I snarled. I could never let a pause go unchallenged.

She finished a line, adding a dot for emphasis. Looking up, she opened her mouth to speak but stopped, a flicker of something crossing her face. I stared at her, and she looked away.

'And what's that look supposed to mean?' I pressed.

That's when I saw it – a shadow in her eyes. She nodded slowly. I opened my mouth for a scathing retort, but the seriousness of the moment struck me like a punch to the face. Pushing the parchments aside, she leaned back, her gaze steady yet pained.

I smirked. To this day, I don't know why.

'I can't do this anymore.'

In that instant, I understood what she was

saying but chose to ignore the red flag. I would have preferred a kick in the balls; it would have hurt less.

'You can't do what – spend more of my money?'

I have many moments in my life I wish I could erase – this was one.

It was the moment we broke.

So that's my long-winded way of explaining our separation. Being a man, I like to believe it was mutual – and in many ways, it was. We both agreed I was a fool. I won't bore you with the daily bitterness that followed; it belittles us both, and I have tried to bury those memories. Suffice it to say, I ended up sleeping in a barn. You've got to admire the versatility of those places. I could have petitioned Sir Thomas de Clare to remove her from our home and properties – all mine by marriage law – but that would have left my children on the street. I couldn't do that.

And there was another reason: I still loved her. I didn't show it, but deep down, I did. And sometimes, when she wasn't berating me or cursing my existence, I caught a glimmer in her eyes that gave me hope. It was enough.

And so it was, that the Right Reverend Paul Christian and I set out in search of new lodgings.

Finding a place was not difficult, as I still possessed a limited degree of wealth, allowing me to rent a modest three-roomed house to the north of town. Though a cheap wattle-and-daub structure, it served its purpose. I say limited wealth, but it was a comfortable sum compared to my impoverished upbringing. Since my separation from Philippa, I had lost track of her financial status as she continued to manage the inn, the tavern, and her textile enterprise. It was none of my damned business, as she often reminded me. An alderman appointed by Sir Thomas had deemed it reasonable that I receive a percentage of her combined income, and though she resented it, she was in no position to refuse. The Lord was satisfied as long as he continued to receive his taxation.

*

The landlord of our newly rented building, a sullen, God-fearing man of Norman descent named Cerdic Hauteyn, had taken to rummaging through our possessions whenever we left the house. It was infuriating. I held off complaining for about a week, hoping he might desist, but if anything, his behaviour worsened. So, I decided it was time to confront him.

'I'll handle it,' Paul insisted when I shared my intentions. 'I think he'll listen to me.'

I frowned at him. 'Well, I'm not sure I can...'

'Trust me?' he interjected with a calm smile. 'Let's stop in on him before our meeting with Sir Thomas – his home's on the way. We can't keep Sir Thomas waiting, so we'll nip in to see Hauteyn en route. It'll only take a few minutes.'

That much was true, Sir Thomas wasn't a patient man. One of his household servants had summoned us to a meeting at once. That was no mere request.

I hesitated, then nodded. 'Alright, but I'll do the talking,' I said as we locked the front door and set off. 'You just watch and learn how to interact with other businessmen.'

He raised an eyebrow. 'You're delusional at times, Al.'

It didn't take long to reach Cerdic Hauteyn's house. As I knocked on the door, I said, 'Watch and learn, Paul, watch and learn.'

'Reverend Paul,' he corrected, but before I could reply, the door swung open.

'What do you want?' Cerdic Hauteyn's face twisted in contempt. 'How dare you come to my home uninvited? I have a good mind to...'

'Apologies, Sir,' I interjected. 'We won't take much of your time.'

He noticed Paul standing a little way back, and his expression softened. 'Ahh, Reverend, I did not see you there. Good day to you, Sir.'

Paul nodded and clasped the wooden cross that hung from his waist.

Cerdic Hauteyn glared at me again. 'Well, what do you want?'

'I'd like to speak to you about your habit of entering our home...'

'My home, damn you. I own it.'

'...of entering the house we've rented from you without permission or prior warning.' I struggled to maintain my composure, feeling my confidence wane. I realised the separation from Philippa had sapped more than just strength from me.

'What are you saying, man? Are you accusing me of theft? Who says I enter that building when you're not there? I assure you, that is not the case.' I opened my mouth to respond, but he continued, his face reddening. 'Besides, how the hell would you know if I entered that house if you weren't there to see me? Now go away and don't darken my sight again!'

He slammed the door in my face.

'Well, that showed him, Al. Well done,' Paul remarked.

I looked around, but Paul stepped forward and knocked again – hard.

'For God's sake, Paul, no! We can't afford to get into trouble. I'll bring it up with Sir Thomas – he'll speak up for us.'

He regarded me with cold resolve. 'I vowed no violence or physical intimidation. I stand by that.'

But before I could reply, the door flew open again, and Cerdic Hauteyn stood there, furious.

'Did I not make myself clear…?'

Paul bowed. 'Apologies, good Sir, but would it be possible to enter and discuss this? It is a rather delicate matter not suited for public attention.' He gestured toward a family across the street who had stopped to listen.

Cerdic Hauteyn looked taken aback as he

stared at Paul. 'I'm sorry, Father, but I have said all there is to say. Good day to you.'

But Paul was insistent. He wedged his foot in the door. 'You are a good Christian, are you not, Sir?' Cerdic Hauteyn nodded, wary. Paul smiled. 'Then would you turn away God's arbiter? He would take offence at such action. As you know, I am entrusted with great powers by Him to shepherd and care for His flock on earth.' He crossed himself and gazed skyward. 'I have the power of absolution and limitless indulgence.' His expression hardened as he looked into Cerdic Hauteyn's eyes. 'Conversely, I hold the leverage to condemn any soul to eternal damnation.' His stare remained unwavering. 'Now – may we enter your home, My Son?'

Cerdic Hauteyn swallowed hard. 'Well, I suppose I can spare five minutes when you put it like that.'

He stepped back, allowing us to enter the cold, dark house. The smell of mildew and urine was overpowering.

I glanced at Cerdic Hauteyn; his assertiveness stripped bare. The corners of Paul's mouth twitched, hinting at a smile. Silence filled the room as we waited.

Paul began to growl. At first, it was almost inaudible, but then it grew louder. Cerdic Hauteyn looked confused but said nothing. Paul stared down, but slowly his head straightened, his eyes ablaze with inner fire. As the growl reached a crescendo, he straightened his back as though he had been paralysed, grasped Cerdic Hauteyn's head, and brought his face within an inch of his own.

His head turned sideways, and the ear-piercing howl from Paul abruptly ceased. He yanked his habit over his head in a frenzy and hurled it to the ground. His mouth gaped open, pupils wide with an unsettling intensity. A lattice of deep red scars crisscrossed his back and chest. Panting, he stepped back and pointed a trembling finger at Cerdic Hauteyn.

'This is my punishment for aiding sinners,' he rasped, his fingers clawing at his wounds as blood seeped from the deepest gashes, smearing across his torso. 'I fight on behalf of the cursed and condemned. I stand for you. God demands penance from the ungodly – but I speak on your behalf!' His voice rose to a higher pitch, saliva dripping from the corners of his mouth as he stared wide-eyed at Hauteyn. 'You are damned for eternity!'

As Paul's body shook, he clenched his fists and began to beat his head rhythmically. Then he fell silent, frozen as if an unseen entity had invaded the room, suffocating us, the air pulled from our lungs.

Cerdic Hauteyn dropped to his knees, struggling to speak but finding only silence.

Paul looked to the floor, clasping his hands together in prayer.

'What must I do?' Hauteyn begged. 'How can I lift God's curse?'

Paul remained silent, his eyes closed.

Tears brimmed in Hauteyn's eyes. 'Please, for the love of...'

'SILENCE!' Paul screamed, 'I am bargaining with the Almighty for your soul, you wretched sinner.'

Stillness enveloped the room once more. Then Paul smiled, a look of enlightenment washing over him.

'Yes, Lord – I hear you, thy will be done,' he declared, picking up the habit from the ground and slipping it back over his head.

Cerdic Hauteyn looked utterly broken. 'What, Father, what must I do?'

Paul fastened the braided cord around his waist and straightened the wooden cross. He looked skyward and nodded.

'Your will, Lord.'

Cerdic Hauteyn burst into tears and collapsed. '*What* is His will – tell me, for the love of Christ?'

'He says to cut our rent and cease rummaging through our belongings.'

Cerdic Hauteyn clasped his hands in prayer and looked to the heavens. 'It will be done, my Lord – thank you.'

We left, the air still heavy with God's presence.

As we walked away, Paul muttered under his breath, 'No violence, no physical intimidation. Watch and learn, little brother – watch and learn.'

*

We were met at the gatehouse by a guard clad in full livery, his expression betraying nothing but boredom.

'You're late, Master Ailred. Last I saw, his lordship was in the Great Hall. I warn you – he's not in a good mood.'

I shrugged. 'When is he?'

The man smiled. It was customary for outsiders to be escorted, but as a regular attendee, he waved us through.

'How did you get those scars, Paul?' I asked once we were out of earshot.

'Have you ever been forced to live in a monastery, Ailred?' Before I could respond, he halted beside a small chapel off the passageway. 'You left me behind – like a madman.' I opened my mouth to interject, but he silenced me with a raised hand. 'Call it what you like, brother, but you discarded me.' His jaw clenched, a flicker of despair in his eyes. 'At some point, I received these flagellation scars.' He shuddered. 'I don't remember them being administered; my early months are dark passages of time – but I must have needed punishment.' He nodded grimly. 'Be under no illusions – this is the cost I paid for your abandonment.'

Guilt crashed over me, heavier than any I had felt.

Footsteps approached, snapping me from my

reverie. I shook my head to clear it and walked straight into Sir Thomas de Clare and his daughter, Lady Maud, who were coming the other way.

'Ahh, there you are, Norman. Nice of you to finally show up.'

I looked at Lady Maud and smiled. I had seen little of her since my return to Tonebricge, and I'd heard her husband, Sir Louis, had been killed in France – a good friend and a fearsome warrior. She returned my smile, but her eyes were dull, lifeless.

'Apologies for our delay, my Lord. We were...'

'We? Who's this "we", Norman?' He peered behind me, his eyes widening. 'Aren't you going to introduce me to your invisible friend?'

I turned. Paul was gone.

Sir Thomas feigned excitement, clasping Lady Maud's hand. 'Oh goodie, we can play hide-and-seek with Ailred's imaginary friend! Does he have a name? May I suggest Pook...?'

Lady Maud laughed before he could finish. Sir Thomas smiled to himself; the strains of his daughter's unhappiness momentarily eased.

'One moment, my Lord,' I said, frowning and retracing my steps up the passageway. I glanced into the chapel. There was Paul, kneeling before the altar, head bowed, hands clasped in prayer.

Sir Thomas and Lady Maud joined me.

Sir Thomas sighed. 'No time for prayer, Christian. We have to find your brother's imaginary friend...'

Paul finished his blessing and rose. Bowing to the statue of the Virgin Mary, he kissed the medallion around his neck. Then, turning, he nearly jumped out of his skin.

'Sir Thomas!' He placed a hand over his heart. 'I didn't hear you approach! The Lord God Almighty was speaking to me.' He licked his finger and traced the sign of the cross on his forehead. 'But He has released me now. I am yours to command, Sire.' He turned to me, smiling. 'Lead on, my child.'

*

We sat in a brightly lit administration chamber on the castle's upper floor. Sunlight streamed through an arched window above a large, ornate chair where Sir Thomas sat behind a polished oak desk.

'Take a seat, gentlemen,' he said, not looking up.

Paul and I exchanged glances.

I scanned the room. 'There are no other chairs, my Lord.'

He shrugged and got straight to the point. 'You like fighting and killing people, don't you?' He bit into an apple.

I waited for him to finish chewing, but his next words didn't come. He seemed to expect a response, so I obliged.

'Is that a question or a statement, my Lord?' I asked. 'And are you referring to the reverend or me?'

He turned the apple and bit into the opposite side. 'Both of you.'

Paul crossed himself. 'I fight for the Almighty when the occasion arises, but only in the spiritual sense. God works through me and demands my total obedience…'

An apple core struck him between the eyes. He frowned but didn't react, wiping the juice from the bridge of his nose. 'Not the answer you desired, Lord?'

Sir Thomas shook his head. 'For whatever reason, you two are respected citizens of this parish.' He exhaled sharply. 'God help us, but you are.' Paul turned to me, raising his eyebrows a couple of times.

'Bearing that in mind,' Sir Thomas continued, 'I need you to help me recruit men for the king's forthcoming ventures into France.'

He leaned back, propping his feet on the table. I glanced at Paul, relieved we weren't seated – he'd have done the same. He must have read my mind and grinned.

Paul and I spoke in unison. 'Us, Lord?'

Sir Thomas slicked back his hair and leaned forward, noticing a speck of mud on his immaculate boots. He sighed, licked his finger, wiped it away, and then polished the leather with his sleeve.

'Yes, us,' he said, looking at me. 'You, me, and Father Crazy-Man here. Us.'

CHAPTER 3

It was an offer we couldn't refuse.

Paul and I had been attached to a predominantly Welsh division of archers and men-at-arms under Sir Hugh le Despenser a few years earlier. We'd fought across France and Flanders, but the tension between the Welsh and English had convinced Sir Thomas that local enlistment was best this time. Paul liked the idea; I wasn't convinced.

Paul might have been eager, but I needed more. I consulted the little voice in the back of my mind that never missed a chance to goad me into trouble.

'Alright, you little demon – make your case, and try not to steer me wrong again.'

The voice wasted no time. You need this. Think of it as a chance to prove yourself. Imagine what Philippa would think if you built the greatest fighting company King Edward's ever seen. They'd sing songs about you. It paused, then added that she'd have to take you back, wouldn't she?

'Oh, come off it,' I muttered, but the little voice wasn't done.

The King would knight you. Hell, Lady Maud might even attempt to seduce you now that Sir Louis is out of the picture. Face it, Philippa would be yours to lose.

I snorted. 'Thanks for that,' I said.

The voice was pleased with itself.

The voice and I are still close to this day.

Paul broke into my thoughts as we headed down the hill toward our house. 'You know, if we pull off this recruitment thing, we could have our pick of women. They love men of power.'

I shot him a look. 'Some holy man you are. I'm trying to win Philippa back, you idiot. Not that you'd understand the subtleties of love – they'd have to kick you between the legs for you to notice.'

Paul grimaced. 'Why do all your fancy words always end with a boot in my balls?'

When we reached the house, I unlocked the door and noticed it looked almost respectable – the pathway was cleaned, and the grime and excrement were scrubbed away. Cerdic Hauteyn had been busy. The Right Reverend Paul Christian could inspire repentance in others, if not himself.

Inside, I went to the fireplace and gathered anything that would burn. It was a far cry from when Philippa stocked us with logs and kindling. Even the best of men can fall without a good woman's hand to keep him upright.

Paul threw himself into the one unbroken chair, which groaned under his weight. He shifted, releasing an unholy stench that sent me reeling.

'Still dreaming of wooing the ex-wife, eh, Al?' he asked, his face a picture of innocence, though he knew exactly where my mind had wandered. 'No doubt you're spinning some grand, poetic reunion.'

'Her name's Philippa, as you well know,' I muttered, blowing into the embers as smoke curled back into my face. 'And tomorrow, we start gathering the finest company under Sir Thomas's banner.'

'Lance fournie,' he corrected.

I scowled. 'Lance, what?'

He shrugged. 'It's what we called a division of soldiers when I was squire to Sir Hugh.' Then he chuckled to himself. 'I love the smell of my own farts.'

I scowled. 'We're done with those Norman ways, Paul. We're Anglo-Saxons again now. Call them what you like, but tomorrow we're recruiting under our own banner.'

He grinned, leaning back with satisfaction. 'Oh, I'm sure it'll be that simple, Ailred.'

*

'It's your inn by right, Al – no one can stop you from walking in.'

We stood a hundred yards from the Chequers. It was a balmy August evening, and the noise from the bar carried through the warm air. It must have been packed, ripe for recruitment.

'I haven't spoken to Tom or Emma in months,' I replied. 'This could get ugly. They're bound to side with their daughter.'

We had spent weeks in discussions with Sir Thomas and his advisors, negotiating the limits on what we could offer men to join the new regiment. I'd assumed we'd just wander the parish and nearby boroughs, recruiting willing men before moving on to the next place. But when I mentioned this to Sir Thomas, he'd reminded me I was "so dumb" – a phrase I suspected he'd stolen from Philippa. Then he explained what he truly wanted: trained fighters, if possible, though he'd accept anyone willing. He'd drill them – or rather, we would. I would handle the archers, while Paul, having served under elite Normans as Sir Hugh's squire, would oversee the men-at-arms. Paul's campaigns in France had made him one of England's most brutal soldiers until he was forced into the monks' robes and sent back to Tintern Abbey. He never let me forget my part in that "treacherous action", as he called it.

'You're the father of what's-her-name's children,' Paul said, 'and from what I know, you've been good to them over the years. Have some faith, Ailred.' He straightened his monk's habit, pushed past me, and strode toward the inn. 'Come on, let's go – they'll be falling over themselves to join us and kill Frenchmen.' He smiled to himself. 'Everyone loves killing the French.'

I let out a deep breath and ran to catch up.

Paul waited for me at the main door, adjusting his habit. I watched a calm wash over his face, contrasting with the mess of scars crisscrossing his shaven head. It was remarkable how he could slip into the role with such ease.

He nodded, and we entered.

Inside, it was packed, the stench of sweat heavy in the stale air. No one paid us any mind as we elbowed our way through. Craning my neck, I scanned the crowd toward the bar, where Tom and Emma Brewer were hard at work. Tom was serving a flushed-faced lad, pouring ale while trading banter, their laughter lost in the tavern's din. Then he noticed me. His face dropped. I held his eye briefly before offering a smile. Then he noticed Paul's presence beside me, and his expression softened. He murmured something to Emma, who stepped forward and took his place at the bar, and then he glanced back at us and nodded toward the rear entrance.

We pushed through the crowd to the back door and stepped outside.

Tom waited for us near the stables – the same stables where I had once lived, where I'd first met Philippa. The same stables where her brother Richard had once tried to kill me, thinking I'd made her pregnant. He had abused her as a child, the filthy coward, and ran off when she'd threatened to kill him. No one had seen or heard from him since. Her parents never knew the truth, still lighting candles, hoping he might return. I pushed the memory away, but nostalgia hit hard, bringing a fresh longing for Philippa. It hurt.

I shook Tom's hand, and he stepped back, folding his arms.

Silence.

I broke the tension. 'It's good to see you, Tom.'

He hesitated but nodded. 'Are you here to recruit?'

That took me by surprise. I had no idea he knew. We were sworn to secrecy by Sir Thomas, only ourselves and his inner circle being party to the information. I looked at Paul and frowned; he shrugged and fingered his crucifix. I beckoned Tom closer and checked no one was listening. He leaned in and raised his eyebrows.

'You know about it?' I asked. He nodded and looked around, following my covert lead. 'Are you part of his trusted circle – one of *us*, Tom?'

He straightened, pulled out a parchment sheet from his pocket, and flattened it out so I could read it. I didn't understand the squiggly nonsense, so looked to Paul. He took it from Tom and read it out loud.

'NOTICE TO ALL RESIDENTS OF TONEBRICGE AND SURROUNDING AREA: I, SIR THOMAS DE CLARE, HEREBY GIVE NOTICE OF INTENT TO RECRUIT A NEW REGIMENT TO SERVE HIS MAJESTY KING EDWARD AND MYSELF ON OUR FORTHCOMING RETURN TO FRANCE TO MAKE CLAIM OF THE KING'S RIGHTFUL REALM.' Paul smiled to himself and continued to read the small squiggly nonsense written below. 'PLEASE CONSULT THE IDIOT, COMMONLY KNOWN AS AILRED NORMAN, OR THE RIGHT REVEREND PAUL CHRISTIAN, FOR MORE INFORMATION.'

I went to speak, but words failed me.

'These declarations are pinned up all over the town,' Tom said. He looked at my face and laughed. 'You thought you were Sir Thomas's close adviser...?' He shook his head. 'Philippa's right – you're so dumb, Ailred.'

He led us back into the tavern, pushing a path through the crush of people, and cleared a table of its clientele. Helping Paul and me to clamber up, he picked up two empty tankards and clapped them together to attract attention. This took some time as the majority were drunk, and the noise was deafening, but eventually, we managed to establish a level of silence.

'I'm sure you all know Ailred and Father Paul, here...' He gestured to us as a mug was thrown from the shadows and bounced off my skull, followed by cheers and laughter. He looked at me and realised I had not taken offence, smiled and quietened the crowd again. 'They have something to tell you, so if you rabble can manage to stay silent for more than a few moments, they have important news.' He leaned forward, nodded in my direction and said in a low voice, 'They're all yours. You'd better make a quick impression – this lot have the attention span of a housefly.'

I looked around at the expectant faces. Someone coughed. I cleared my throat and realised I had no idea what I was going to say. It had not occurred to me to plan a speech. I caught sight of Lee the Smithy towards the back as he downed the dregs of his ale and looked ready to throw the empty tankard in my direction.

'Okay,' I said, with as much confidence as I could muster. Could you all please listen to me? I have something important to discuss and would very much like you to...'

But it was too late. I'd lost them. A rain of tankards and mugs arced through the air, followed by general laughter and derision. A child's soiled swaddling-cloth struck me full in the face. To this day, I wonder why someone would have brought that into a tavern. I made a futile effort to regain their attention, but it fell on deaf ears. Humiliated, Paul and I clambered down from the table, retreating to the bar where Tom joined us, laughing.

'You had your chance – and made a pig's ear of it,' he chuckled, signalling to Emma for drinks.

We stayed, enduring good-natured ribbing from Tonebricge locals as Tom kept the free ale flowing.

So we drank. Then I started to drink wine. I'd had a bad experience years earlier drinking too much wine, but in my present melancholic state chose to ignore the warnings. Paul remained sober, never letting his monastic aura slip.

The night began to blur as I felt my grand plans falling apart. The possibility of regaining Philippa's love disappeared, and all ambitious intent turned to dust – not to mention the wrath Sir Thomas would unload. So I drank more.

As I drank, so did others. Small fights broke out, and with each, men crowded around, egging on the combatants. Either that or they joined in.

'They seem more interested in that,' I slurred to Paul as another circle opened and two men squared up.

And then it happened. I was in that period between knowing you had drunk too much and realising you didn't care, when I had my moment of clarity.

I grabbed Paul, pushed my way back to the table, and clambered up again, pulling him with me. I was going to speak to this rabble. It was important.

'It's important,' I slurred in answer to Paul's look of bemusement. 'And they're all fuckin' meatheads.'

He shrugged and smiled as if he had not a care in the world. The room was beginning to spin, and I held onto Paul to steady myself.

'RIGHT, YOU BASTARDS, LISTEN TO ME, OR I'LL KILL YOU.' That got their attention. Another tankard flew over, and I lunged forward and headed it back into the crowd. I received a round of applause, so I bowed, wiped a trickle of blood from the cut on my forehead and smeared it across my face. More cheers. A group of drunken men in front of us started heckling me, so I ran across the table and dived on top of them. The rest of the onlookers pushed forward and hoisted me arm over arm back onto the table, not before I was punched mercilessly and had my tunic ripped from my body. I felt my nose. It was broken. Blood poured down my face, and I smeared that over my torso. I kicked a man in the teeth as he tried to clamber up to join us, while the tavern's clientele cheered and laughed. In my crazed state, I glanced at Paul. He stood beside me, head bowed, exuding serenity as he blessed the baying mob, smearing small crosses on their foreheads with my blood as they lurched to get up. It was me against the world, and I wasn't going to lose. The more they attacked our table the more frenzied my defence became, every assault repelled by cold-blooded obstinance. I looked as if I had been through the battle of Slurs a second time. There were cuts and bruises all over, and I had a manic stare. I was happy.

In a brief lull in the chaos, as people took breath from laughing and trying to clamber up, I took the opportunity to deliver my speech. It was unscripted and the words of a drunken madman, but they came to me with total clarity.

'You all know me...' I waited for the cheers of agreement to subside, then continued. '... and you all know how I achieved my wealth through fighting for King Edward in France…' More cheers. '… and you've all heard the stories how Father Paul Christian here single-handedly killed every Frenchman in France…' Great laughter and merriment. My voice took a gentler tone to calm them. 'Look at me…' I held my arms wide and displayed the blood and bruises splattered across my torso. 'This is the body of a true Englishman…'

Before I could say anything more, Paul, in a stroke of unforeseen genius, took that moment to enter the fray. He stepped closer to me and rested his hand on my head. His eyes were closed. He was breathing deeply and mumbling to himself. A deathly hush spread through the crowd. Paul looked skyward and started talking in a tongue I did not understand before turning to the audience and speaking his first words of the night.

'My children – look upon this mortal as our saviour, Jesus Christ, incarnate.'

I looked towards him in wonder. His voice was as if giving a sermon in the grandest cathedral in the land. He seemed possessed by God's presence. I stood as if nailed to a cross, arms fixed wide and blood dripping, while Paul delivered his message. 'Listen to this sacred man, sinners, as he appears to you at the behest of God himself. Whatever he says, heed – he preaches on behalf of the Almighty. You are all wrongdoers – but take this chance for redemption.' He fell to his knees, looking towards the filthy tavern ceiling, and screamed, 'God, witness this day and proclaim thyself through Ailred Norman, your divine conduit on earth.' He glanced at me and winked.

I did the rest.

I pitched Sir Thomas de Clare's new company.

I told of Sluys, of Saint-Omer, of all the battles Paul and I had lived through. I told of the glory, the wealth, the carnage. You could have heard a pin drop. No tankards were thrown. Tom would mingle and distribute ale to patrons, myself included. I felt my heart beat faster as each arrow, each chaotic charge was narrated in stark detail. As men fell to our swords, as the screams of the dying and the exhilaration of bloodlust registered in the glazed eyes of my audience, I knew I had them. I left nothing out. They needed everything, good and bad.

The scars of war are buried deep within. All who bear witness understand, and each survivor is affected differently. I am no exception. That night, repressed spirits burst forth and demanded acknowledgement. That night, my inner conscience sought to express itself. Who was I to argue? Come forth and be heard, my friend.

By the time I finished, every man in that tavern was standing on a table, arms linked, cheering me, God, and Saint George. Many were on their knees praying, pledging their lives to the Almighty and England. It was a humbling experience.

As the sky to the east showed hints of light, Tom and a broom-wielding Emma threw us out, but by then, we had achieved our goal. Half the assembled gathering begged to join us. Projectile vomiting became a collaborative activity outside the tavern, but the signatures were secured. Our work was complete.

I remember Tom's parting words as he kicked me up the arse to send me home. 'You're not all there, Ailred – but you're a good lad. I'll remind Philippa she could do a lot worse.'

Our first attempt to recruit had been a success.

CHAPTER 4

The following day, bleary-eyed and unsteady, I scrubbed sick stains from my tunic. Who would believe the scent of rancid ale could be so hard to shift? After admitting defeat, I dragged myself to the castle to update Sir Thomas on our recruitment efforts, stepping over puddles of vomit as I walked. It can't have been just me who felt rough that morning. He barely looked up from his ledger when I entered, his expression one of mild annoyance.

'Why are you wasting my time?' he grumbled, eyes fixed on the parchment before him. 'Unless you've brought me a thousand signatures from that one night, you'd best get back out there.'

And so that became our routine – night after night. We crisscrossed the countryside, moving between bustling towns and quiet villages, selling Sir Thomas's grand vision. Word of our eccentric performances as the Preacher and the Idiot spread like wildfire, drawing large crowds eager for the spectacle. Many establishments had no choice but to turn hopeful onlookers away. More than once, the lively atmosphere soured – rowdy laughter turning to aggression, teetering on violence. If I'm honest, those were my favourite nights.

Over the weeks, I honed my storytelling,

learning to read the room, to sense the pulse of an audience, to know just when to speak and when to let the Preacher weave his ever-expanding sermon into our tale. Together, we created something that drew people in. Each night was different. With every tale I told, they drew closer, their hopes and dreams tangled with ours.

Even now, as I tell this to you, Brother Michael, I see that same look in your eyes – the same wonder I saw in the men all those years ago. I take pride in that connection – but I digress.

The recruits would travel to Sir Thomas de Clare's castle in Tonebricge, introducing themselves as the Preacher and the Idiot's men. Sir Thomas welcomed them, assigned positions in his refurbished barracks, and set about preparing them for training. Most were either ex-soldiers or desperate souls with no kin to turn to, many being criminals looking to escape justice. Sir Thomas was a fair master. He understood the value of loyalty, investing time and coin in his men, never asking too many questions. In one of his less antagonistic moments, he confided that he sought the most loyal, well-equipped, and brutal fighting unit King Edward had seen. I was honoured to be part of that vision.

As summer turned to autumn, we gathered nearly a thousand men housed in and around the castle. Many more had promised to come, but I soon learned that drunken pledges made under the spell of our showmanship did not always translate to bodies in training.

Sir Thomas, however, was satisfied with my contribution. A rare state, and one he never admitted to – but I could tell.

I told him we had one last date booked in Staplehurst the next day, just a few hours' ride away. He stopped what he was doing, eyebrows rising.

'Staplehurst, you say?' He glanced at his household banneret standing nearby, who grimaced.

I frowned. 'Is there something I should know about this Staplehurst place?'

The look they exchanged unsettled me.

Sir Thomas shrugged, turning back to his ledger. 'Oh, it's nothing, my good fellow. Just be careful down there. Try to keep that performing monkey you call a brother on a short leash.'

That was his final word on the subject.

Still, the event had been well advertised, and despite Sir Thomas's reaction, we felt obliged to attend.

We set off at first light. It was a cold, overcast October morning, and Paul was in a foul mood. He hated rising early, and travel made him twice as tetchy. Since parting from Philippa and the children, every morning followed the same routine – I would wake, reach for her beside me, and realise all over again that she was gone. And every morning, my heart broke.

Yes, I know that sounds dramatic, and I should man up – but some scars cut deep. I still missed her and the kids. Have a heart!

The journey to Staplehurst was uneventful, save for two rough-looking men travelling in the opposite direction who stopped to ask directions to Tonebricge. One had an eye that wandered like a flock of sheep without a shepherd, the other a jagged scar across his face. They looked like trouble, but after meeting the gaze of a bad-tempered preacher with a patchwork of disfigurement across his shaved head, they thought better of it and moved on.

Staplehurst lay deep within the Low Weald, a small village carved from dense forest stretching between Kent and Sussex. Originally a hamlet along an old straight road laid by long-gone invaders, it had grown into an insular community after the construction of a church. As we rode through the narrow, poorly maintained street, we drew nervous glances from the townsfolk.

I nodded at them. 'Good morning.'

Polite acknowledgements followed, but little more.

By the time we reached the King's Head tavern, where we were scheduled to recruit that evening, a small group of villagers had begun following us at a distance. They looked as if they wanted to speak but held back.

'I'm not sure why they're so nervous,' I

muttered. I laughed. 'Maybe we're so famous we intimidate them.'

Paul shrugged. 'They look like they need permission to approach us or something.' He swung off his horse, stroking its dusty muzzle. 'Or maybe it's that famous thing you just said. Either way, let's hope they turn up tonight – I'd hate to go through all this travelling shit for nothing.'

I climbed down and joined him, leading our mounts toward the stables at the back of the tavern.

'I'm glad this is our final recruitment,' Paul said. 'I'm a priest, not a fuckin' performing monkey.'

I laughed. 'That's exactly how Sir Thomas refers to you. He sees straight through your reverend facade.'

Paul feigned offence, then smirked. 'As lords go, he's one of the better ones. He could've had us hung, drawn, and quartered for that robbery we did.'

I gave him a pointed look. 'The robbery *we* did…?'

He shrugged. 'Alright, I did. But you were a party to it.'

'You can't remember half of what you've done. And trust me, you're better off not knowing.'

He put his hands on his hips. 'If I don't know, why should I feel guilt?'

I hesitated, then said, 'You know what? Every

day, you sound more like the Paul of old.'

'Thanks,' he said, leading his horse inside.

'That's not a compliment. And you're right – we owe Sir Thomas. Let's hope he never has cause to call in the debt.'

'You worry too much.' He grinned. 'I'll go find the owner, you wait here and…'

'You's two be the Preacher and the Idiot?'

I stiffened. The name had followed us since Sir Thomas first advertised us. I had never seen the humour in it. I was alone in that.

'That be us,' Paul laughed. 'And I'm the Preacher.' He gestured at me. 'So this be the... other one.'

The stable master, who also owned the tavern, a shifty-looking man with no teeth, pointed. 'Last stall on the left, Preacher. There are oats and grain scattered about, trough's over there, by the anvil.' He turned to me with a pained expression. 'Would you like me to help with your gee-gee, fella?' He patted me on the head.

Before I could answer, Paul said, 'Ah, my child, you have a heart of gold. He finds most things difficult.' He grinned at me. 'And he can't speak save a few grunts and snuffles. I think God is punishing him for a past life.' He crossed himself solemnly.

I sighed.

After settling into the tavern, we headed downstairs to look around the village before nightfall.

The owner called over from behind the bar. 'You's off out?'

Paul straightened his cassock, the picture of piety. 'Yes, my child, we hoped to visit your church and pray.'

The man grinned, his gums raw and blistered. 'Aye, well, don't stray too far.'

Paul frowned. 'And why's that?'

The man hesitated. 'Have you heard of the Curley family?'

We both shook our heads.

'Good,' he muttered. 'Keep it that way.' He looked as if he might add something but thought better of it.

Paul broke the silence. 'Why would that be my child? Are the Curleys the lords of this parish?'

'You might think that, but…' The tavern owner stopped himself.

'But what?'

The man exhaled heavily. 'The Lord of this borough is John de Cobham.'

'Ahh,' Paul said. 'Does he live locally?'

The man gathered a few tools and waved dismissively. 'I can't stand about gossiping – I've work to do.' He walked away, muttering under his breath.

I glanced at Paul, who shrugged.

We left.

As usual, we ignored the warning and wandered the village, bidding good morning to the locals but receiving little in return. It didn't take long to find the church. Paul never missed an opportunity to strengthen his guise as a man of the cloth, offering thanks for various bounties. He loved a good bounty. But over the weeks, I had noticed something beneath his act. Yes, the church gave him power, the threat of damnation bending common folk to his will, but sometimes I glimpsed something else. Moments of quiet. Of ease. A struggle played out behind his eyes – his natural brutality warring with pastoral teachings. Maybe that was his intent all along, to confuse even himself.

We entered the churchyard through the crumbling lychgate just as a young man was straightening the wooden cross above its arch. He wore a rough linen tunic, his feet caked in filth.

As we passed beneath his ladder, he called down, 'Would one of you pass me a nail?'

Paul stooped, picked up a couple, and handed them up.

'Many thanks, Sir.' The young man noticed Paul's clerical garments and hesitated. 'Apologies, Father, I didn't realise…'

Paul cut him short. 'No apology owed, my child. Go about your work. Do not let a couple of laymen delay you from God's business.'

The young man eased and resumed securing the cross.

'Here,' Paul said, stepping forward, 'let me hold the ladder. No sense in you breaking your neck.'

Paul steadied the rickety steps until the job was done. The young man climbed down and bowed low.

'Most gracious of you, Father.'

Paul nodded. 'I am no stranger to toil. I was worked half to death by an abusive taskmaster before my calling.' He cast me a look.

I sighed.

The young man slung his tools into a canvas bag. He had short-cropped blonde hair with a hint of ginger and a sun-weathered face.

'Oswald,' he said as a way of introduction, bowing again to Paul before shaking my hand. His grip was firm, calloused. 'I'm the curate here.' He nodded to the church entrance. 'I assume you've come to see our priest?'

Paul nodded.

'He'll be in the vestibule. Forgive me for not showing you the way, but I seem to have a splinter that needs seeing to.' He frowned at his thumb, picking at a bloody patch.

'Go, go,' Paul said with a smile. 'I'm sure we'll manage. And besides, I have my faithful hound here. He's got a keen nose for direction.'

Oswald gave a deep belly laugh and walked off.

We entered the dim church, walking up the nave. An old woman in black sat in silent reflection. As we reached the chancel, a calm voice called from behind.

'Father Paul Christian, is it not?'

We turned.

Paul smiled. 'You know my name, Father Le Strange. You're well informed.'

'As are you.' He glanced at me. 'I'd heard our small town was to be visited by the Preacher and the...' He hesitated. 'May I assume this is the...'

'This is Ailred Norman – my brother.'

Father Le Strange was tall and balding, his cassock belted with a knotted cord and a leather-bound Bible in hand.

'You are most welcome,' he said. 'We get few journeymen here, especially fellow ministers.'

He led us to the vestibule, leaving the old woman to her prayers.

As Paul and Father Le Strange spoke, I noted how alike they were. Paul subtly mimicked his gestures, letting the older priest direct the conversation – until he didn't. Whenever Father Le Strange shifted away from the subject, Paul steered it back toward the Curleys, the town's unspoken blight.

Sensing reluctance, Paul turned to me. 'Ailred, would you mind meeting me outside? The Father and I have church matters to discuss.'

A dismissal.

I stepped away, only to find Oswald loitering near the door.

'That means you too, Oswald,' Father Le Strange called.

We left together, but before I could speak, a well-dressed man approached, flanked by two labourers. He wore a chequered silk surcoat, a fine bycocket hat and carried a riding crop. He had a broad Irish accent and looked to be in his late fifties – clean-shaven, with greying sideburns and an air of self-assurance.

'Oswald,' he said, removing his hat and tapping it rhythmically against his thigh. 'Shouldn't you be mucking out my barn?'

The labourers closed in – one with a scythe, the other with a blacksmith's hammer.

Oswald looked sheepish. 'Sorry, Mr Curley. Father Le Strange asked me to mend the cross.'

So this was the infamous Mr Curley, I thought. Let's see what the fuss was about.

Mr Curley stepped forward and struck him across his cheek with the crop, raising a red welt.

'I'll have no backchat from you.'

Oswald staggered back, clutching his face.

Mr Curley turned to me. 'And who the fuck are you looking at, fool?'

'I've no idea yet – I've not had the pleasure of an introduction.' I smiled. 'From first impressions – I count myself lucky.'

Mr Curley stared at me in silence as his men edged closer.

Then Paul emerged from the church, Father Le Strange following.

The priest froze. He opened his mouth, but no words came.

Mr Curley turned from me to Father Le Strange. 'Did you set this simpleton to fixing your cross, knowing he owes me his labour?'

'I… I didn't realise…'

'You're not paid to think, you bumbling half-wit.' Mr Curley turned to Oswald, grabbed him and kicked him toward the barn. 'And it better be done properly, or you'll get the same as your father.'

Oswald ran.

Mr Curley turned to Paul. 'So… the infamous Reverend Paul Christian.'

Paul smiled. 'Not sure about the infamous part, but yes, I am he. And you are?'

'Terence Curley. Hand to Lord John de Cobham. These are my sons, Fergus and Niall.' He replaced his hat. 'Which means I am the law here.' He flicked a glance at Father Le Strange. 'I trust you've informed our guests how things are run?'

I'd had enough. 'I'll have you know my name is…'

Terence Curley butted in.

'You're Ailred Norman. Husband to Philippa.' That stopped me short. He waved a hand dismissively. 'I know more about you and Philippa than you might think.' His eyes were cold as he added, 'We may have cause to speak again before you go home to your wife and children.'

He stared at me for a heartbeat before they turned and left.

Father Le Strange spoke quietly once they were out of earshot. 'It would be wise for you to leave.' He hesitated, glancing between us. 'Whatever you're planning tonight – forget it.' He seized Paul's arms, his voice low, urgent. 'A dark shadow shrouds this place. It shades us from the Lord's light. The devil hides in plain sight.' His body trembled, but his gaze held firm. 'Leave while you can.'

Paul bowed his head, then turned away.

I went to speak, but he ushered me onward. 'He told me everything I need to know,' he murmured under his breath.

As we walked back to the tavern, Paul relayed what he had learned. Terence Curley ruled Staplehurst with an iron grip. Nothing happened without his say-so. Every transaction was taxed – most profits passed to Lord Cobham, but the Curleys kept their share.

'And those who oppose them?' Paul said. 'They vanish. Strung up and left to rot as a warning to others.'

I eyed him. 'Should we heed Father Le Strange's advice and leave?'

Paul laughed.

*

We threw ourselves into our final performance. I would miss this – I loved the attention. Over the past few months, we had recruited in many taverns like this, but tonight, something was different. The air smouldered with tension, thick and provoked. The rumours about the locals were well-founded. I'd sensed it the moment we arrived.

Until now, these nights had been celebrations – a chance for the townsfolk to drink, cheer, and revel in our madness. But tonight, the mood was off. I noticed clusters of faceless men scattered across the floor, watching, plotting. Still, we kicked into our routine. We were ever the consummate professionals.

After the usual brawl to claim a table and defend it from all challengers, I recounted bloody battles while the Preacher promised eternal life to any man who joined up. Normally, this was when the crowd peppered me with questions – about warfare, about army life, but mostly about money.

Tonight? Silence.

Paul leaned in. 'What's going on?'

I shook my head.

Then I saw them. A group of four, pressing forward as rough-looking men cleared a path before them. The leader was blonde, clad in a brown cape, his head tilted as he fixed his gaze on me. Following close behind were Terence Curley and his two sons.

Recognition flickered across the blonde man's face, and a slow, knowing smile took shape.

I smiled back, waiting for my brain to make the connection.

Then it did.

'Fuck,' I muttered, glancing at Paul.

He looked confused.

'Ailred, good to see you,' the blonde man said as

Terence Curley handed him a tankard. He raised it to his lips and downed the ale in one pull. I stared, stony-faced.

'And I hear you're looking for men to join your little army and fight for Sir Thomas?' His tone dripped with mockery. He already knew the answer.

I didn't reply.

Laughter swept the room.

'Who the fuck's this bastard?' Paul growled, his clerical mask slipping for a moment.

'Answer the Preacher, Ailred,' Terence Curley said, enjoying my discomfort.

Paul's eyes narrowed, sensing the hostility toward me. 'Well, who is this jester...?' His fingers twitched as if he might leap from the table and strike the man down, but he held his temper.

I forced composure into my voice. 'This is Richard.'

Paul looked at me, uncomprehending.

'Philippa's brother,' I added.

It still meant nothing to him. He didn't know what Richard had done to her when they were growing up. I'd never told him.

Terence Curley smirked. 'This is my adopted son. Forgot to mention him at our last meeting. He's family now. You know how it is with children – they do *everything* together.'

Richard snorted, then mimed a crude sexual act to the room's amusement.

'How's your hand?' he asked.

I glanced at the scar where he'd driven a pitchfork through my palm years ago. It still ached in the cold.

He chuckled at my discomfort.

Then came the question I was expecting.

'And how's that beautiful sister of mine? I hear you took over where I left off.'

I held his eyes, unwavering. His smirk faltered. He looked away.

Shaking his head, he added, 'Oh, and I forgot to ask – how are your children?'

A chill ran through me.

His eyes locked onto mine again, wide and unblinking.

'You shouldn't leave them alone while you travel, Ailred. Especially when you make your movements so well known.' His face didn't change. 'Anything could happen while you're away.'

The words took a second to register. Then hit like a hammer.

I grabbed Paul by the cassock, hauled him from the table, and ran for the tavern stables where our horses were boarded. He stumbled behind me, bewildered, as jeering filled the air.

'What the hell was that all about?' he shouted.

Behind us, Richard's voice rang out, taunting. 'Run, my little pigs, run – time is short.'

CHAPTER 5

As we rode back towards Tonebricge, Paul asked so many questions, few of which I could answer. All I knew was that my family was in danger. I prayed Richard's threat was empty, but I was clutching at straws.

The dim light of a new day crept across the land as we entered town, our horses exhausted and near collapse. Paul, sensing the severity of the situation, fell silent as we approached Philippa and the children's home. I still had a key but saw the door ajar as I bounded up the small wooden front steps.

'Wait here,' I mumbled as dawn broke, and stepped inside.

The first thing that struck me was the smell. This house had once been filled with the scents of children, food, drying clothes – of life – but most of all, of Philippa. Now, that was gone, those smells smothered beneath something darker, something that reeked of the Devil.

Terror seized me. I closed my eyes and begged for God's help. Please, let this be a dream. I could not open them, fearing the new day's light would confirm my dread. But I did.

And it did.

Those first rays of sunshine destroyed my life.

Timothy and Frederick lay in the middle of

the room, hacked apart in a frenzied attack. Their bodies had been dismembered, their limbs interchanged, twisted into grotesque puppets by some mad executioner. They had tried to escape. Blood smeared the floor where they had been dragged back and slaughtered.

I tried to move towards them, but my body failed me. I was numb, useless. Nothing I could do would change what I saw. At that moment, I knew life would never be the same.

A noise behind me – muffled screams, the creak of stairs – then nothing. My legs buckled, and the world went dark.

I must have been unconscious only briefly because I woke to Paul slapping me violently across the face.

'Can you hear me?' Slap. 'Can you hear me, Al?'

A weight like I had never known pressed upon me, crushing my will to live. I stared up at Paul but felt nothing. Then, my last memory struck me.

'Philippa and Kimberly.' The words barely formed. 'I heard them scream.' I gestured toward the stairs, tried to stand, and collapsed onto my face. 'Look upstairs, Paul. Please, Lord, please show mercy.'

Paul ran past me, taking the stairs two at a time.

I held my breath.

His cries confirmed my worst fears.

I cursed God in a way that shames me now.

'They're still alive – both of them!' Paul's voice rang out.

Again, I tried to move but found myself paralysed. A beam of light struck my face, blinding me. A figure appeared, caped and faceless. I knew it was time to leave this world.

'Ailred, are you alright?' The voice was familiar.

A terrible noise filled my head, and my breath shortened. 'Are you here to take me, my Lord God? Please take me.'

'No, I'm here to help.'

I heard Paul call down, 'Oswald! Is that you?'

As I drifted in and out of consciousness, I remember Paul saying something about fetching Tom and Emma from the Chequers as I slipped into darkness.

*

I died. Or so I am told.

I missed Timothy and Frederick's funeral, lost to two weeks of oblivion. When I woke, I was in my old bed, in my old house, and for a moment, I thought it had all been a nightmare. People often wake from long darknesses with no memory. I was not so lucky.

It pains me beyond anything imaginable to relive that night, but I promised you, Brother Michael, that I would disclose my life without exception. I am holding to that. But after this testimony, I will never speak of it again. That is my promise to God.

Over the coming days, people came and went from my bedside, filling in the missing moments.

Oswald had followed us on our hurried return to Tonebricge. He had overheard Richard's threats from where he stood at the back of the tavern and decided to accept Sir Thomas's recruitment, using it to escape the Curley family's shadow.

Philippa and Kimberly had suffered unspeakable brutality. Had we arrived just minutes later, they would have died. Their ordeal had stretched the limits of faith to breaking.

When Oswald returned with Tom and Emma, Paul had rushed downstairs. He had been so focused on Philippa and Kimberly that he hadn't noticed I was unconscious. Emma checked my pulse, then declared I had passed into God's care.

Paul exploded with grief, screaming his love for me before beating my still body and accusing me of deserting him in his hour of need. If Oswald hadn't pulled him away, he might have hammered his fists straight through my ribs. The Devil had dictated events that night, but Paul's pleas forced God's riposte – my heart resumed beating, granting me a stay of grace.

Paul later apologised for the bruises on my chest. They were nothing compared to my head – Lee the smithy couldn't have battered it into a stranger shape. The assailants had used a blunt object and fled through the back door.

I will not speak of what was done to the twins beyond what I have already told. No... I must never call them "the twins". Timothy and Frederick had names, and I must remember them that way. That is important.

Sir Thomas was shocked by the murders and ordered the shire-reeve to investigate. That evening, Tom and Emma recalled serving two strangers at the Chequers – one with a wandering eye and the other with a scar. They had been asking about the Preacher and The Idiot, digging into family connections.

It was not difficult to work out who was responsible.

For weeks, I was incapable of rational thought.

Father Jobe, the priest from St Mary's Priory who had tended my wounds long ago, visited and concluded I would die. But the body is stubborn. With God's help, it healed.

The mind, however, takes longer.

Timothy and Frederick's murder, Philippa and Kimberly's ordeal – it destroyed me.

*

As rain lashed the bedroom shutters one evening, Sir Thomas bounded up the stairs. He wore light mail under a family-crested tunic, his finest sword strapped at his side. Dispensing with formalities, he spoke without the sympathetic tone I had grown accustomed to.

'Right, Norman. Time to stop feeling sorry for

yourself.'

I looked toward the doorway as Philippa entered, Kimberly lingering just behind her at the threshold. Sir Thomas turned to Philippa and smiled. 'I'm sure, after all those nights tending to you, she wants to start breathing fresh air again – you stink.' He turned back to me and frowned. 'And I've no doubt she'll be glad to sleep in her own bed again.' His words struck me with a pang of guilt. The truth hurts. 'We've had more recruits than I thought possible,' he continued, 'and that's down to you and the Preacher. I've even started turning the bastards away – no room for them.' He laughed. 'Some of the men are real crazies, so you'll fit right in.' He removed his chaperone, shook the rainwater over me, and tossed it onto the bed. 'Speaking crazy bastards, that brother of yours has been working his nuts off training the...' He hesitated, glancing at Philippa and Kimberly. 'I'll rephrase since we have such beautiful women present.'

Both women laughed – the first time since their terrible ordeal.

Sir Thomas smiled. 'Paul's drilled the men night and day with a passion, and you have the makings of an outstanding division. He's a natural leader.' He winked. 'But if you tell him I said that, I'll put you back in this bed.'

Then, his face darkened.

'I loved my godchildren.' His voice cracked. 'Timothy and Frederick didn't deserve that. As

God is my witness – the people who did this won't be forgiven or forgotten.'

The mask returned. He picked up his hat, shook the remaining drops over me, and hurried down the stairs.

Silence.

Philippa and Kimberly held out their hands. I sighed, took them, and pulled myself up.

I rejoined the living.

And I locked the dark memories in a safe place, praying they would never break free.

CHAPTER 6

But I must have a drink, Brother Michael, so I insist on taking a break. What I told you in that last passage is enough to drive the most sober of men to ruin – and I give no apologies for my tears.

What's that you say? Don’t be ridiculous – if I tell you this story's ending now, it defeats the purpose.

'But what if I die before finishing the tale?'

Is that a jibe at my age? That's beneath you, Brother. Would I be so crass as to ask, 'What if you run off with the manuscript before we conclude' – mocking your lack of legs? I think not.

Now, straighten up – we continue.

*

Paul greeted me as if I didn't exist.

He stood in the castle’s outer bailey, clad in his monk’s habit, demonstrating the use of a war hammer before a group of recruits.

‘So remember, legs, feet, elbows – anywhere your opponent leaves exposed.’ He glanced at me, then back to his audience. ‘Always think one step ahead. No one is immune to a shattered kneecap.’ He nodded at Oswald. ‘Come up here and be an enemy.’

Oswald, now part of Sir Thomas’s fledgling army, stepped forward. Paul plucked a shield from the grass and tossed it to him.

'Be a one-man shield wall.'

Oswald took a defensive stance, feet square and steady. Paul moved like lightning. He feinted one direction, sending the recruit stumbling. The shield lifted just enough – Paul's hammer shot low, stopping inches from Oswald's shin.

'Bam. Leg's shattered,' Paul said, calm as ever. His gaze locked onto each man in turn, making sure none looked away. 'He's not dead, but after my next blow – he is.'

Hooking the hammer's claw around Oswald's leg, he yanked him down into the dirt, then surged forward, driving the spike towards his face, stopping just short.

The men laughed, but admiration flickered in their eyes. Paul held out a hand to Oswald. 'You're dead, Os.'

He turned to a broad-shouldered man watching from the sidelines, dressed in Sir Thomas's colours. 'Bonehead, take over. I need a word with the Idiot here.'

I rolled my eyes.

Bonehead took the hammer with a bow. 'You heard the Preacher, lads. With me!'

Paul sauntered over as the men set to hacking at hay-filled targets, pulling his hood low against the wind.

'You've got a good rapport with them,' I said.

'They're a fine bunch, Ailred.'

'I see you're still the Preacher. Doesn't the robe

work against you?'

He looked puzzled. 'How so?'

'Surely you lose authority over fighting men dressed like that?'

Paul chuckled. 'At first, yeah. Then I told them I'd quit if their hardest man could knock me out. After that, no one had much to say.' He nodded towards Bonehead. 'That one tried. I call him Bonehead for good reason. Wouldn't stop till he was unconscious.' He laughed. 'We're alike, really – like the brother I never had.'

'So does that make me the brother you wish was Bonehead?'

He grinned. 'Let's be triplets, then.'

We walked toward the chapel, and he filled me in. I had missed so much. The division had split into two – men-at-arms and archers. Sir Thomas wanted balance and had around twelve hundred men, most with prior experience. Paul had put the archers under a seasoned bowman from the battlefields of France and Flanders while he sharpened the men-at-arms. Sir Thomas, skeptical at first, was now more than satisfied.

'Once he realised I could function without the Idiot, he gave me free rein.' Paul laughed at my expression. 'Oh, stop sulking. Besides, Godric assures me some superb archers are among the ranks.'

'Godric? Not the same one from Cornualha?' A bowman of that name had served under King Edward at the siege of Tournai. I remembered standing sentry with him – his skill and humour had set him apart.

Paul shrugged. 'Could be. He's got a ridiculous accent, so maybe.' He nodded. 'But the lad can shoot. I'll introduce you to him and the rest of the idiots tomorrow.'

Inside the chapel, he led me to a small chamber at the rear. A narrow bed filled one corner, a personal garderobe tucked into a nook. Parchments and quills littered a sturdy wooden table – a world apart from the rough quarters the men endured.

Paul caught my look. 'Perks of being a priest and chief instructor,' he said, pulling up a stool. I sat.

'We're ready to move as soon as Sir Thomas gets the call.'

I felt deflated. The men had trained together and forged bonds. They'd be ready to fight and die for one another.

Paul saw it. 'You'll get there, Al. You're alive – you've beaten the hardest part.'

I said nothing, old memories pressing in. A dark mist clouded my thoughts, and before I could stop myself, I muttered, 'Sometimes I wish I had died that day.'

Paul's face dimmed. 'Don't talk like that, Al. You've got so much to live for. You have Philippa back, and there's Kimberly...'

But his words faded. Timothy and Frederick surfaced, as they did every night, dragging me into that dark, suffocating place. Anger simmered beneath the surface. I clenched my fists, trying to push it back down.

*

'I thought it must be you – how have you been? The last time I saw you, you were sharing food with a Frenchman at Tournai.' I shook Godric's hand, and he grinned.

It was true. Godric had shared his rations with a French crossbowman – a man who had terrorised us archers with his accuracy. We hated him but respected his skill. Every morning, he would salute us from the walls and we would wave back. During the day we would try to kill one another, before waving goodbye at sunset. It became a game. When the French began to starve under our blockade, Godric put food into a basket lowered down the wall, earning himself a whipping for his act of mercy.

'You have a good memory, Idiot, I mean, Ailred!' Godric laughed, his accent thick with the unmistakable cadence of the West Country. It wasn't far from how the Welsh sounded when they spoke English, a lilt I had grown accustomed to over the years.

'I warned you that you wouldn't understand a word he says,' Paul interjected before I could respond.

I ignored him. 'Yeah, we had some good times back then, didn't we?'

Godric frowned. 'Did we? I must have missed

them.'

*

At first light the following day, Paul gathered the archers in the castle's central bailey and I stood among them, awaiting my introductions. I had turned down the offer to bunk with the men, preferring the quiet of home and to return early.

Paul climbed onto a half-barrel and raised his arms. 'Settle down, boys.' He waited for the chatter to die. 'I think you all remember my brother, Ailred.' There were murmurs of recognition. 'He's a little late to the party, but I know you'll make him feel welcome.' His expression hardened. 'I want you idiots to treat him with the same respect you show me.' A ripple of acknowledgement swept the field. 'Godric, you'll continue to run training, but you answer to Ailred. Is that clear?'

Godric bowed and touched his heart. 'Yes, Preacher.'

Paul nodded. 'You can't be the Idiot Archers without the Idiot in command, can you?' He looked at me and smiled as the men burst into laughter. 'What can I say? The name stuck, and the men embraced it.'

I shook my head. 'This is what happens when the adults go missing.'

The men knew what I had been through, and their banter was a way of lightening the moment. I appreciated it. Paul hopped down, making room for me to take his place, but before

I could, Sir Thomas jogged across the bailey, his presence silencing the group.

'Right, idiots, I've got news,' Sir Thomas said, stepping up with authority. 'I know you're all itching to kill Frenchmen, and I don't blame you – the French are put on this earth to be killed, and it looks like that day is coming. I've had word from King Edward – he's requested our attendance in his campaign to liberate France from the French.'

A roar of approval erupted, fists pumping the air. My heart quickened, the familiar rush of impending battle surging through my veins. It had been years, but the feeling never dulled.

Sir Thomas looked towards Paul and me and said, 'Finish up here and then come and see me – I'll fill you in.'

He jumped down and headed back towards the castle's great hall.

Paul beamed. 'Well, there you have it, gentlemen – the wait is almost over.' He gave me a hearty slap on the shoulder before throwing an arm around me and giving a firm squeeze. 'Come on, Al, let's clean up and see what the old buzzard has to say.'

*

'Right, take a seat. There's much to tell.'

We stood in the administration room on the upper floor of the castle, the same place Sir Thomas had first pitched his recruitment idea to us. He was munching on a pear while squinting at a letter, holding it at arm's length. I looked around but saw no other chairs except the one he sat on. No surprise there.

'We'll stand if that's acceptable with you, Sire?' I said.

He shrugged. 'Suit yourselves,' he muttered and bit into the pear.

He flung the letter onto the polished table and cursed under his breath.

'Fucking eyes.' He lobbed the pear core at me and missed. 'See? Can't even hit an idiot from five paces.' He leaned back, propping his feet on the table, and stared at us. 'Preach, read this letter to your brother. I know what's in it but can't be bothered.'

Paul stepped forward, picked up the letter and began to read aloud. 'I have cause to instruct you, Sir Thomas de Clare, to...' but Sir Thomas leaned forward and thumped his head onto the table.

'Just read the damned thing and translate it into idiot language.' He lifted his head and glanced at me. 'Oh, it just so happens we have one here for reference – you're in luck.'

Paul read silently as Sir Thomas pulled another pear from a small bag by his feet and bit into it. Paul nodded, familiarising himself with its content, then placed it back on the table.

'We are to travel to...' but again Sir Thomas stopped him.

'Not now, tell him when you're back in your hovel, his very presence is making me nauseous.'

Paul bowed. 'As you wish, my Lord.'

I gave a respectful nod, and we turned to leave.

'Oh, one other thing before you allow fresh air to return to the room.' We stopped and turned back. 'I will not be coming with you on this expedition. I won't explain why – too much effort – but you will take my son, Nathaniel.' His expression softened a little. 'And I expect him returned in one piece, understood?'

'We will protect him as if he were kin, Lord,' I said, hand over my heart.

'That would make me related to you, Norman, which would make me some kind of swine. No, just make sure he stays alive.' I nodded in agreement. 'Oh, and before you go, and this is directed at both of you.' His voice lowered, taking on a more serious note. 'I've spoken to Lord John de Cobham...' He paused, letting the name sink in. I stiffened. John de Cobham was the lord of the borough where Staplehurst lay, and his name carried weight. 'I assured him that no harm will come to any family employed by him.' I started to respond, but his cold, unwavering stare made me think better of it. 'So, I suggest you toddle off and prepare to leave for Gascony in a couple of days.' He bit into the pear, his tone casual. 'That gives you time to settle what needs to be done. I imagine you'll want to say your farewells to a couple of individuals not too far from here... and I wouldn't interfere with that.' He looked straight into my eyes. 'I expect some of your men aren't ready for what's ahead, Idiot. Killing doesn't come naturally to everyone. Nathaniel, for one, has never taken a life. Some need to learn, maybe get first-hand experience of the act – there's no turning back once they face the enemy and the fighting kicks off.'

'I understand, my Lord,' Paul said. 'We do have a few unblooded men.' He glanced at me, a quiet signal passing between us. I wasn't sure what it was, but it seemed important. 'If I'm not mistaken, Oswald falls into that category, right, Ailred?'

I nodded. 'Yes. He's a big lad, but he's... sensitive. I'm not sure how he'll react when we're knee-deep in blood.'

I had my doubts – some men aren't made for killing, and I wasn't sure about Oswald – or Nathaniel, for that matter.

Sir Thomas placed the remains of his pear on the table and wiped his hands on his tunic, a clear sign the conversation was ending.

'Well, that's settled then – it's Nate and this Oswald fellow. The rest can learn the hard way.'

Paul seemed satisfied with the arrangement, a faint smile on his lips.

I wasn't sure what we had just agreed to – but nodded, all the same. It wasn't until we reached the door that the full weight of his words hit me. I swung round, just in time for the pear core to smack me square in the face.

Sir Thomas laughed. 'Bravo, me! It seems my

eyes aren't as bad as I thought.'

We left without another word.

I couldn't hold back as we descended the spiral staircase. 'Did he just give us the go-ahead to kill the two bastards that murdered Timothy and Frederick?'

Paul grinned. 'And take Nathaniel and Oswald with us.'

Anger surged, quickening my breath.

Paul glanced at me. 'Calm, Ailred. Revenge is for cool heads and cold hearts.'

I took a deep breath. 'And did he say we're going to Gascony, not France?'

Paul nodded. 'Yeah, we're going to meet Earl Derby there. I'll run you through the letter when we get back to my place.'

Gascony. That was where Izelda came from. I had saved her from our rampaging troops in Arques during our first sortie into Flanders – she was one of the only survivors of that day's massacre. She stayed by my side until the day she left to join a band of renegade French peasants bent on revenge for the plundering of their lands. Despite my love for Philippa, not a day passed that I didn't think of her.

CHAPTER 7

In the room behind the chapel, we schemed. It felt wrong to plot such deeds in a place of worship, but Paul's assurance that God favoured our cause eased my conscience. You can justify anything when it serves your purpose.

And my purpose? Retribution.

'I know this seems cold-blooded, Al,' Paul said, his voice hushed, 'but remember what they did to the twins.'

'Timothy and Frederick,' I corrected. 'And you don't need to convince me, Paul. I want those bastards dead more than anyone.'

I'd have taken my vengeance long before, but Philippa and Kimberly had already lost too much. I couldn't risk becoming another name among their dead.

A knock at the door interrupted us. I opened it to find Nathaniel standing there, his expression inquisitive. It had been years since I last saw him, and in that time, he had grown into a tall, striking man, much like his father.

'Sir Thomas sent me,' Nathaniel said as I stepped aside to let him enter. 'He said a matter needed my attention, though he wouldn't give details.' He glanced between us. 'I assume you know I'll be riding with you and the men when we join Earl Derby, in Gascony?'

He was well-informed – being the Lord's son had its perks. The letter stated the King had named Earl Derby his Lieutenant, a mark of trust in his command. It ended with reassurance that the Gascons' intelligence network in France was good and worth a thousand men in the Earl's view.

Paul passed Nathaniel the letter, and I poured him a mug of ale as he read through it before removing his helmet and sitting at the table. He wore light mail over his tunic, a finely crafted sword at his side, and a dagger strapped to his belt. Despite his air of casualness, I sensed he knew more about our plans than he let on.

'You are welcome here, my Lord,' I said, passing him the drink.

He accepted it with a nod. 'Call me Nathaniel,' he replied. 'No need for titles among equals.'

It took a few seconds to register the compliment before Paul broke the moment. Still dressed in his robe, he sat across from him and tapped the table with his fingers.

'Have you ever killed a man?' he asked.

Nathaniel blinked. 'Wasn't expecting that,' he said, taking a long drink before considering. 'I've seen many men die, but I've never delivered the fatal blow.' He smiled. 'My father always teases me about still being a virgin in that regard.' He shifted in his seat. 'But why ask that?'

Before I could respond, Paul leaned forward with a wicked grin. 'Well, tonight, my friend, we're getting you laid.'

Nathaniel laughed, spluttering ale across the table. 'You're not a typical priest, are you!'

Another knock came at the door. It was Oswald. I bade him welcome, introduced him to Nathaniel, and sat him down.

'Right,' Nathaniel said, his impatience growing. 'I'm sure you didn't bring us here just to drink ale – and the fact my father insisted on sending me…?'

We laid out our purpose, offering them both the chance to walk away. The consequences would be far-reaching, and they had to understand the full gravity of our intent.

'It will be a bloody affair, make no mistake,' I finished.

I awaited their responses. They were quick.

Oswald paced the room like an eager child, full of fire. 'You've every right to seek revenge,' he declared, breathless with excitement. 'The two men you're after are Curley's cousins. Horrible bastards. Trust me, they're lower than a snake's belly.'

Nathaniel was more measured, weighing his words. 'If we fail, there'll be no help from Sir Thomas – he knows nothing of this.' He gave a knowing smile. 'I know because he told me as much before sending me to you. This is strictly unsanctioned.'

He paused, studying my face. 'But something tells me there's no turning back – you have the look of a man ready to kill.'

*

The plan was simple – travel to Staplehurst overnight, find the men who murdered Timothy and Frederick and kill them. It wasn't complicated. Even I could manage that. We had thought about devising something more discreet, but in the end, simplicity won out.

Oswald had an addition of his own. 'We should kill the Curley family, too,' but Nathaniel had baulked at the suggestion, reminding us that his father had given his word to Lord John de Cobham that no harm would come to them.

'He's looking the other way, but don't think for a second he'll let you stray beyond the two murderers. He'll stomach a couple of the cousins going missing, but the Curley family is off-limits.' He grinned. 'Besides – he doesn't know what's going on.'

So it was settled.

We waited a couple of hours, reviewing the finer details, before setting out. We sailed from Southampton in two days. That meant we had to be back by sunrise. We needed to appear as if we had never left, and Paul had ensured it. The night's guards would look the other way – such was his hold over the castle watch. He ruled them with a blend of fear and piety, a potent mix that kept men loyal and silent.

It was a still, misty night, and we had a few hours before the sky began to lighten in the east

– plenty of time to make the journey unseen. We led the horses out through the unguarded gatehouse, their hooves bound to muffle any sound, and watched as unseen hands closed the vast, solid doors behind us.

The further we travelled from the castle, the more my mood darkened. I could not shake the memory of Timothy and Frederick – what was left of them – mutilated and scattered across the room that night.

The trail to Staplehurst was well-worn, and we neared the town in good time. My companions rode in silence, each lost in their thoughts. Paul had tried to talk, expecting me to share his eagerness for vengeance.

'What could ever make up for my children, Paul?' I asked when he grew impatient with my responses. 'This won't bring them back. This isn't a fucking game.'

He looked surprised for a second before shrugging.

And then it hit me – he was enjoying this. My grief was just a footnote in his game.

'I still don't understand you, Al. We have a chance to test Oswald's loyalty, and Sir Thomas wants Nate to be blooded.' He raised his eyebrows. 'And you get to kill the murderers of your kids.'

'Their names were Timothy and Frederick,' I said, my voice hard.

'Yeah, whatever – I'm sure you'll want to

make them pay. They need to understand what they're being punished for...' His excitement was growing, a nervous twitch flicking in one eye. 'Christ, I've missed this.' He reached behind and pulled out a mace tucked behind the saddle, its head studded with spikes. 'I love the feel of this,' he panted, caressing the smooth ribbed handle. He threw back his cassock's hood, eyes lifting to the sky as dawn bled through the mist. I thought he might howl at the sky for a moment, but he just breathed deep and steadied himself. In an instant, he was calm once more.

'Thank you, Lord, for your loving gift of a new day,' he said, turning to Nathaniel and Oswald, silently trailing us. 'Let us give thanks to the Almighty, entrust your souls unto His mercy,' he said solemnly.

They looked unsettled by Paul's character change but obeyed him as he led them through the Pater Noster prayer.

I began to realise – again – that I was just another piece on Paul's board.

*

We knew where the murderers lived, as Oswald had grown up here; he knew everyone. I never asked their names. They weren't men to me. They were Terence Curly's cousins – vile men tasked with the dirtiest work. The Curlys' brutal reputation drew the worst of society to the ward, all eager to earn their keep through violence. Easy money – just as it had been for my father before he drank himself to ruin.

We secured our horses a little way outside the town, and I cursed myself for not bringing a pageboy to watch them.

'This way,' Oswald whispered as we crossed the town's perimeter, slipping into the shadows as we followed the main thoroughfare.

After a few minutes, he halted near a grand house, its grounds well-tended. 'That's Bly Court,' he muttered, spitting onto the floor. 'The Curlys live there – the sons too, with a handful of servants. Those bastards made my life hell.' He glanced at Nathaniel. 'You sure we can't include them tonight?'

'It's not his call, boy,' Paul snapped, as he thrust his mace inches from Oswald's face. 'We're here for the fuckin' cousins – stick to the plan.'

Oswald recoiled, his hand drawing his dagger, the sudden threat sparking a defensive response.

Paul's eyes widened, and a dead-pan glaze set in. I had seen this look since we were born – it always heralded violence.

Nathaniel backed up, bewildered. 'What... what are you doing? Are you crazy – we can't fight each other, for Christ's sake.'

I jumped forward and hung onto Paul as he moved towards Oswald, dragging me with him.

Oswald stepped back, his anger short-lived, and Nathaniel moved to help me restrain Paul. He was stronger than both of us, but we slowed him just enough for my voice to cut through the haze.

'Stop, Paul, stop.' I repeated over and over until his eyes cleared enough to understand. 'Move away, Os, go down the street and stay there,' I ordered. Oswald hesitated, resheathing his dagger, his gaze flicking back at us as he backed off.

Nathaniel stared at Paul like he was seeing him for the first time. 'I'll talk to Oswald,' he said.

He shook his head before walking after him.

A dog barked somewhere within Bly Court.

I grabbed Paul's head, forced his attention and put my face inches from his.

'Breathe,' I said, my voice steady and calm, hoping to ground him.

The madness drained from his eyes.

'Jesus, your breath stinks,' he said, grinning.

'What the hell are you doing, Paul – you can't do this. He's a good man, a friend. You need to remember why we're here. You can't just...'

Paul cut me short, putting his arm around my neck and squeezing. 'Relax, Al. I wasn't gonna hurt him.' He ruffled my hair. 'Come on – we have to show some murderers what it feels like to be murdered.' He walked off in the direction of Oswald and Nathaniel, joined them, and shook Oswald's hand, looking back at me as a dog might look at its owner after performing a trick.

We moved on.

'There.' Oswald pointed to a rundown building within the compound of a disused pigsty. A sagging thatch, a missing gate – the place was rotting in its own filth. 'That's where my father used to keep our pigs.' He drew his dagger, gripping it tight, the whites of his knuckles showing in the growing light. 'I was brought up in that house until that bastard, Terence Curley, had my father flogged when Lord John de Cobham wanted us evicted.' He shook his head at the memory, his deep resentment showing. 'Now look at it – ruined. They'll be in there – living in shit like the pigs they replaced. My mother took so much pride in...'

Paul cut in. 'Oswald, I hate to interrupt your trip down memory lane, but could we get to the killing part? I don't want to seem rude.'

I sighed at Paul's sarcasm and scanned the street. Apart from a barking dog somewhere behind us, all was quiet.

'Al,' Paul continued, 'take Nate with you around back and make sure they don't escape into the woods, and me and Os will...' He stopped. 'You don't mind me calling you Os, do you? We *are* friends now, are we not?' He waited. Confusion crept across Oswald's face as he worked out whether Paul was serious, then nodded. 'Good man,' Paul continued.' 'As I was saying, Oswald and I will make our grand entrance at the front.'

This was all a game to Paul, and I questioned my decision to involve him.

As he started to move, I stopped him. 'One last

thing. They need to know why this is happening. And *nothing* happens to them until I'm there.' My sons' faces flickered through my mind. 'We need them to understand. It's important.'

He gave a curt nod. 'I understand.' Then he and Oswald moved.

Nathaniel and I crept around to the back, moving through a small yard bordered by the town's dark woods. We reached the rear door, its wood rotting, the smell of mildew everywhere. I tried the handle – locked.

'That'll kick in easy,' I whispered to Nathaniel, 'but we'll wait for Paul's signal.'

'What's the signal?' he asked, fidgeting.

I paused. 'We didn't decide on one! Probably screaming.'

We waited.

I pulled the dagger from my belt, and Nathaniel unsheathed his sword.

We waited.

Nathaniel stared at the door, unable to stand still. 'What's taking them so long?'

'Paul will be calming Os and preparing him,' I said. 'He's never killed before.'

'Me too,' Nathaniel muttered, glancing at me. 'I thought I'd be more nervous.'He held up his hand, steady as stone.

We waited, the silence stretching. Then, faint movement inside. My heart pounded, and I glanced at Nathaniel, who was already poised to kick the door in. His father's concerns seemed unfounded – he was born for this.

And then the door was unlocked from the inside and creaked open. Paul's face appeared streaked with blood.

'You'd best come in,' he said. 'It didn't quite go to plan.'

CHAPTER 8

Paul led us inside. A table and a couple of chairs sat at its centre, with two beds pushed hard against the opposite wall. Both beds were occupied – each man with his throat slit, blood still pooling beneath them. Draped across the table lay Oswald, his skull caved in, half his brains smeared across the wood.

I stared at Paul. His mace dangled at his side, its spikes dripping with ribbons of flesh and splintered bone. I tried to speak, but couldn't find the right words.

Nathaniel found his voice first. 'What in God's name...?'

Paul shrugged. 'It's not what you think. This little shitbag,' he pointed at what remained of Oswald, 'slipped in before me, slit their throats, then turned on me when I tried to stop him.' He kicked a bloodied dagger out from beneath the table. 'See? Lunatic.' He wiped the blade on Oswald's tunic. 'Some *friend* he turned out to be.'

Nathaniel looked at me, shaking his head.

'Why would he do that?' I asked as Paul unbuckled Oswald's scabbard, tied it to his belt, and sheathed the dagger.

'You'd best ask him.' Paul smirked. 'Oh. Maybe not.'

Nathaniel exhaled sharply. 'We need to get out

of here – like they won't know who did this?'

Paul shook his head. 'No, Nate. That's where you're wrong.' He hauled one of the bodies from the bed, dropping it beside Oswald's corpse. Then, with a dispassionate smile, he took his mace and placed it in the dead man's hand, stepping back like a child waiting for praise.

'What the fuck?' My standard response when confusion got the better of me.

Paul gestured to the bodies. 'It's obvious – Oswald did it. Slit their throats. They fought back and caved in his skull with that mace before bleeding out. Everyone knows Oswald had a huge grudge. It's perfect.'

Nathaniel stared, stunned. 'And you think they'll believe that?' He turned to me. 'And *we're* supposed to believe that, too?'

Paul ushered us out the back door. 'Hell, yeah – it's the truth.'

As we stepped outside, I cast one last glance at the carnage. 'Well, at least we learned the truth about Oswald before sailing. And they've got their culprit.'

Paul remained stony-faced. 'Aye. Lucky that, isn't it?'

*

'Sir Thomas wants Nate blooded.'

We were passing the well-kept lawn fronting Bly Court on our way back to the horses. I looked at Paul in disbelief. 'You can't be serious.'

He clapped a hand on my shoulder. 'My lunatic

friend Os can do so much damage in one night. Cousins, Curley family, anyone in this town.' His smirk widened at my blank expression. 'We'll never have a better chance.'

Nathaniel caught on, his face hardening. 'I want no part in this. Besides, my father said the Curleys are off-limits – we must respect his wishes.' He glared at me, voice low. 'This man's a monster. God turned His back on him long ago.' He crossed himself.

Paul laughed. 'Sir Thomas will be disappointed to know his son's a coward.'

Nathaniel's sword was halfway drawn when a massive dog charged across the lawn, dragging Philippa's brother, Richard, behind. Paul cursed and reached for his mace – then remembered it was gone.

Richard's face twisted with hatred when he saw me. He unsheathed his sword and let the snarling beast loose.

Paul barely had time to draw his dagger before the beast crashed into him, its slavering jaws lunging for his throat. He threw up his arm just in time, the dog's fangs punching deep into flesh, tearing through sleeve and skin. It wrenched its head side to side, trying to rip the limb off. Paul's dagger clattered to the ground as he staggered under the weight, blood spraying across the grass.

Nathaniel sprang forward, his sword flashing in the dim light. He cleaved the dog's belly open, nearly splitting it in two. Its entrails spilled across the grass.

'Norman!' Richard screamed. He was on me in seconds, slamming me to the ground. My head struck hard, stars bursting behind my eyes. He wrestled his sword free from beneath me, panting, snarling.

'Bastard – I'm gonna kill you,' he growled, spit flying. He clawed at my face, his fingers gouging for my eyes.

I lashed out, grasping for his head – only to find it gone, severed by Nathaniel's blade. The body held upright a moment before toppling forward. The head rolled to a stop near the dog.

Paul, nursing his wound, wandered over and nudged the corpse with his boot.

'I think he's dead,' he muttered.

Nathaniel yanked me to my feet.

Paul tore a strip from Richard's tunic to bind his arm. 'You're my new best friend now, Nate.'

I wiped blood from my face. 'Our work here is done.'

I grabbed them both and shoved them toward the horses.

*

'But he didn't see us, Father,' Nathaniel pleaded.

That evening, the three of us stood before Sir Thomas in the grand hall.

'He sees all, my son,' Paul said, making the sign of the cross and looking towards the rafters.

'I was talking to Sir Thomas, you fool,'

Nathaniel shouted at Paul.

'My humble apologies, Sire,' Paul muttered.

'You don't know that for certain,' Sir Thomas cut in, ignoring Paul. 'It only takes one person to tell that damned Curley fellow, and he'll report it to Sir John. Then I'll have a diplomatic disaster on my hands.'

'But how do *you* know what happened?' Nathaniel asked. 'We didn't tell you.'

Sir Thomas slumped back in his high-backed chair in despair.

'Have you been taking idiot lessons from the king of the idiots over there?' He pointed at me. 'Three men get killed in Staplehurst, one of them Terence fuckin' Curley's adopted son, and one of my recruits is found near the bodies – and you ask how I found out?' He buried his face in his hands. 'A rider arrived first thing this morning. The whole fuckin' town knows.'

Realising Sir Thomas needed to know the truth, I started to explain how Oswald had killed the men and then attacked Paul, but he wasn't interested.

Without lifting his head, he muttered, 'What was I thinking, trusting my son to the likes of you?'

'In what respect?'I asked.

He looked up and glared wide-eyed at me but said nothing.

Turning to Nathaniel, he said, 'You ship out at first light. It's too late to change plans, so you fools are on your own. Now – get out.' He cast a look at me and Paul. 'And God help Earl Derby when he inherits you in Gascony.'

*

It had been a stressful day, so I had conflicting emotions when I walked home after being dismissed by Sir Thomas. On the one hand, we had cleansed the world of two murdering bastards – and the filth that was Philippa's molesting brother. On the other hand, we had earned Sir Thomas's fury, and if this spiralled further, it would only be the beginning. 'Maybe I'll get lucky and be killed by the French,' I suggested to Paul, and he offered to cut out the middleman and do it himself. He was a thoughtful brother.

Now that Paul was settled in the castle and I was back living with Philippa and Kimberly, we had moved out of our temporary home, owing Cerdic Hauteyn, the landlord, a large sum of money. He was not happy. We had not paid him a coin while renting the place, slipping out under the cover of night, so that might have had something to do with his anger. In the eyes of the law, this meant that we were debtors, ripe for flogging, jailing, or working off the debt at the landlord's whim. It was another problem bound to end up at Sir Thomas's doorstep.

By the time I stepped into our house, I had everything planned. I wouldn't tell Philippa or Kimberly about avenging the deaths of Timothy and Frederick, as I had promised not to. I would leave that until we were old, sitting by a fire one night, and then gently break the news. She would be a little upset that I had kept a secret for years, but proud of me for...

'You fucking went back and killed Richard and the cousins after swearing you wouldn't! You useless piece of shit – I should never have taken you back!'

'I... I had to,' I replied. 'I couldn't let them get away with it.'

'BUT YOU PROMISED...'

'Yeah, I know, but...'

'There are no buts – you lied to me. And you know what? You'll go after that bastard, Terence Curley, when you get back from France or Gascony or wherever it is you're going, I know you will – and you'll hang for it.'

I couldn't deny that.

Halfway through taking my cloak off, Philippa ran across the threshold and dropkicked me in the chest.

I hit the floor hard and lay there as Kimberly came in from the backroom.

'MOTHER!' she cried, 'don't do that to him.'

As she held Philippa back, I got to my feet, regaining my breath. 'Thank you, Kimberly, at least one of you...'

'Do it like this, Mother.' She ran forward and kicked me in the balls.

*

The following day, we made ready to depart. It was a bright May morning, the air crisp, and I joined the men gathering on the castle's lawn. Family and friends crowded around, offering their farewells. I was still stiff from my night's fitful sleep in the stable where I had been banished, but was in good spirits.

I smiled as Philippa and Kimberly approached me. 'At least you've come to say goodbye,' I said, pulling them both into an embrace.

'We've not forgiven you,' Philippa replied, her voice soft, 'but we still want you back, safe.'

Before I could answer, a parade of horseback riders clattered through the main gate, hooves striking sparks from the cobblestones. They wore a livery I didn't recognise.

Sir Thomas, who had been drifting between groups of men-at-arms with his son Nathaniel and another nobleman, halted and watched as the riders dismounted before the grand hall.

'That's Lord John de Cobham,' Paul said, coming up beside me with his two lieutenants, Godric and Bonehead.

'This doesn't bode well,' I muttered, glancing towards Sir Thomas, who beckoned us over.

'Sir Walter Paveley, I present to you the Preacher and the Idiot. These men will serve as your eyes and ears among the fighting men.'

Paul removed his hood, and I offered a respectful bow. But before I could speak, Sir Thomas pressed on.

'Get to know one another on the road, Sir Walter. I've explained why you've been called to lead this campaign, and here is the cause.' He gestured towards John de Cobham's angry expression. 'And may I suggest you leave immediately?' He looked at Paul and me. 'And I'll attempt to clear up another of your damned messes.'

He tipped his hat and strode off towards the grand hall.

There was a moment's silence before Sir Walter spoke. 'You heard Sir Thomas. Let's be off – we must meet the Earl of Derby in Southampton. We have the whole journey to get acquainted.'

'Yes, Sire,' we answered in unison before hurrying to rally the men.

Our weapons, supplies, and everything required for a long campaign were stowed on pack horses and waggons, the organisation overseen by men of proven experience.

Bonehead marshalled the men-at-arms and infantry while Godric gathered the archers and support crew. These were now hardened soldiers – weeks of training, disciplined, and ready for war.

As I gave Philippa and Kimberly one last embrace, we left Tonebricge Castle behind, bound for Southampton and His Majesty's waiting fleet.

Next stop, Gascony.

CHAPTER 9

But believe me, Brother Michael, there is little of interest to recount on our journey to Southampton, save for Paul ingratiating himself as Sir Walter's personal priest and confidant. If there was, I assure you, you would have heard already. We met with the Earl of Derby, who turned out to be a studious fellow with a passion for anything anti-French. I liked him immediately. And can I just say, you've grown sour of late – I much preferred the old Brother Michael, the one with all his limbs attached. See, and now you're sulking – you know I would gladly give up my legs for you if the Lord willed it so.

*

Battles and wars are won and lost on the strength of discipline. I have been in the fray long enough to know this truth. I've faced Scots and Frenchmen, crazed and outnumbering, yet we triumphed – because our men held fast to their commands, enacting orders under the greatest pressure. That's what sets the English army apart. So when we embarked into the great fleet of ships waiting at the quayside in Southampton, good order and humour prevailed.

One day later, chaos descended.

The fleet had set sail as planned, but the weather turned foul the moment we cleared the quayside walls. I was stationed on the lead ship alongside Paul, Sir Walter, Nathaniel, and Earl Derby, and soon the swells began to lift and drop the massive hulls like they were no more than kindling.

'Holy God, Father Paul,' Sir Walter spluttered between bouts of vomiting over the quarterdeck rail, 'speak to your master and ask Him to grant us smoother seas.'

'He's a hard taskmaster, my Lord,' Paul replied, his face calm despite the storm. 'I sometimes think He tests us more than any others, due to our superiority.'

Sir Walter, ever the devout man, wiped his mouth with his sleeve, a trace of vomit still clinging to his beard, but Paul's words brought a glimmer of hope to his eyes.

'God was wise to choose you, Father Paul,' he muttered, spitting a small piece of carrot onto the deck. 'He will see us safely to our destination.'

Paul looked at me and grinned. 'I am here to serve, Lord. My life is yours.' He put a steadying hand onto Sir Walter's shoulder. 'I hear voices, my Lord – the Almighty is speaking to me right now.'

Sir Walter blinked, his sickly hue unchanged, yet he managed to show interest beyond heaving his lunch. 'What does He say?'

Paul closed his eyes for a dramatic pause. 'He

says He will send you instructions... through a third party.'

Sir Walter frowned, trying to stay upright and not slip on the pool of vomit I had just added to. 'What does that mean?'

Paul gave a solemn shake of his head. 'I'm afraid I cannot answer that, my Lord. I am unworthy of such knowledge. The manner in which God chooses to communicate will be revealed in the fullness of time.'

Just then, the ship's admiral, Sir Robert de Herle, called from the bow. 'Sir Walter!'

Sir Walter stiffened and straightened as much as his condition allowed. 'I am here, Admiral.'

He approached and doffed his grand hat. 'Lord, I have grave news.'

Sir Walter, now looking very much as though he expected this, glanced at Paul before answering. 'Go ahead, Sir Robert. I was expecting a third party intervention.'

Sir Robert looked a little confused at that but continued. 'We're putting into port at Falmouth, my Lord. This storm will be the death of us if we continue. We must wait it out and resume our task when the Lord sees fit. Have your men ready to disembark within the hour.'

'By all means, Sir Robert, I'll see to it personally.' He glanced at Paul. 'This is all part of His plan.'

The two of them left to prepare for the landing, leaving Paul and me behind.

I looked at Paul in amazement. 'I sometimes think you really do have the ear of God.'

Paul smirked, drawing me closer. 'I overheard the admiral telling Earl Derby earlier.' He winked. 'Sir Walter thinks the Almighty and I are this close.' He crossed his fingers to show me.

I raised an eyebrow. 'And which one is you – the one on top?'

It took him a second to catch on, but when he did, he burst into laughter and walked off, still chuckling to himself.

*

Don't get me wrong, Falmouth is a fine town, but after weeks of waiting for the weather to clear, even the best places lose their charm. We were stuck until July, the storms refusing to break. In that time, our men turned from frustrated tenants to marauding chancers – robbing, raping, and butchering one another in drunken savagery. Even I killed a man who cheated at dice. He struck first, but I was quick enough to dodge his blade and stamp on his head until he stopped twitching. I was cleared of wrongdoing, but it's not a memory I cared to carry as we set sail again.

Paul convinced Sir Walter and Earl Derby that it was all part of God's plan for an English victory in France, that He was hardening the men for the brutality ahead.

'Earl Derby says we'll rendezvous with local Gascon recruits and a brigade of Welsh archers in Bordeaux,' Sir Walter said as we hit the open sea once more, a stiff breeze filling the sails. He was in high spirits now that we'd been released from our enforced stay. 'I don't trust anyone Welsh, and God forbid we give them weapons.' He looked at me. 'Paul tells me you speak fluent Welsh and have a great rapport with our brothers from the west?'

'Did he now?' I shot Paul a look, but he only flashed that saintly smile. 'I've had dealings with the Welsh, yes, and believe me, they're every bit as skilled with the bow as we are.'

Sir Walter grimaced. 'So I've heard. My good friend Henry de Shaldeforde was murdered by the bastards during the uprising in Gwynedd – shot down like a dog while collecting taxes.' His jaw tightened. 'And now we pay them English coin to fight for us. I don't understand the thinking behind it.'

Before I could answer, Paul cut in smoothly. 'Ailred will explain, my Lord. He's well-versed in Welsh affairs.'

I sighed. I'd served with a Welsh battalion in France and Flanders and knew the uneasy truce well. 'Truth be told, they still hate us, Lord, but plenty will fight for whoever pays them. Some might say it's a mess of our own making.'

Sir Walter shrugged. 'Maybe, maybe not. But after the past few weeks, I've realised I'm leading a pack of volatile lunatics.' He shot me a grin. 'They don't call you lot "the Idiot Archers" for nothing!' He laughed at my expression. 'Take it as a compliment, man. I've seen enough companies to know you've got a solid fighting force, even if they're a bit mad.'

I nodded thanks, but his tone turned serious. 'Just make sure they're killing the right people. Welshmen are off limits.'

*

We entered Gascony, sailing into the Gironde estuary before following the river Garonne toward Bordeaux. As I leaned over the side, watching the lush green fields and tended vineyards slip past, my thoughts turned to Izelda. She must have gazed out over this same countryside, perhaps playing as a child in the pastures and sparkling streams along the riverbanks. She had often spoken of Gascony's fierce independence from France, how its ties to England had only deepened since Eleanor of Aquitaine's marriage to the Duke of Anjou in 1152 – soon to be Henry II. The French king, Louis VII, had raged at the loss of his sovereignty, and the region had simmered in conflict ever since.

At the time, I hadn't cared much for her history lessons – but she made me listen. And now, gliding along the glistening waters of the Garonne, I was glad she had.

As we bumped up to the Bordeaux quayside and the boarding planks were set down, I stepped off that ship, swearing never again. Long sea journeys and I were not made for each other. Paul had asked if I planned to walk back to England instead, to which I'd replied – again – that I could only hope to be killed before enduring such a voyage twice.

Earl Derby was already on the dock, Nathaniel alongside him, when we led our men onto Gascon soil. The earl had taken a shine to Nate, and we'd seen less of him as time went by. The perks of being highborn, I suppose. It was a scorching afternoon in early August, and the waiting Welsh and Gascon servicemen greeted us with a mixture of enthusiasm and, on the Welsh part, suspicion.

I was standing close to Nathaniel and Earl Derby as they organised the vast shipment of provisions being unloaded by local workers when a tall balding man stepped forward and confronted Earl Derby.

'I see you finally bothered to turn up – do we get paid now?'

The man spoke with a thick Welsh accent, his tone dismissive.

Earl Derby stopped what he was doing and looked the man up and down.

'I beg your pardon, boy, I hope that ridiculous accent clouded those words.' He stared the man in the eyes. 'Idiot, get over here and make that sound respectful.' He never once lowered his gaze as the Welshman looked towards me. 'And when he speaks again, I expect you to interpret something deferent, or, if God is my witness, someone will hang.'

I stepped forward, meeting the Welshman's gaze. There was a flicker of recognition on his face.

'Would you please thank Earl Derby for coming so promptly to take charge of this campaign, considering the awful weather. We Welsh are at his disposal to be used in any form he feels fit.' He swallowed hard. 'But could I respectfully remind him that we were promised payment upon his arrival for previous services rendered?' He bowed to the Earl, then said, 'If you would kindly relay my message of welcome, Ailred Norman.'

I was surprised he knew my name and stared at him. He smiled.

Before I could speak, Derby's expression softened. 'Ah, good,' he said. 'It seems I understand the Welsh tongue now. What's your name, my good fellow?'

'Wyn, Sire and I represent the Welsh archers here...'

'Yes, yes, I've worked that out.' Derby waved him off. 'I'll send for you once we're done unloading.' He glanced at me. 'I take it you know this man – one of your old friends?'

I looked hard at Wyn. He was still smiling. Then it dawned on me. He was one of the Welshmen who was part of the division of archers I had joined on our first campaign into France and Flanders.

'Yes, Earl,' Wyn said, not breaking his gaze. 'He and his brother met us on the way back to Sluys after months of besieging Tournai.' His smile widened. 'They were with a band of locals who, how should I put this...?' I swallowed hard. '... gave us a warm farewell in the traditional manner. Quite the experience.'

Earl Derby turned to Nathaniel. 'Good,' he said. 'It's nice to hear we're all on the same side now,' before walking away to continue supervising the disembarkment.

Wyn waited until the Earl was out of earshot before speaking again. 'I remember that day well, Ailred.' His voice was low, the smile dropped. 'I lost my brother and cousin.' He glanced over at the other Welshmen, armed with bows and swords. 'Many of us *sheepshaggers* remember, all too well.'

He walked over to join his countrymen, looking back every few steps with genuine hatred.

Paul sauntered over, 'I swear I know that man.'

'You should do,' I replied, 'you killed his brother and cousin.'

'Did I?' He scratched his head.

'Yeah, although, to be fair, that doesn't narrow it down for you.'

He laughed, noticed Sir Walter walking over, and straightened his cassock.

'My child,' he said, grasping his crucifix, 'God has delivered us safely, as I promised He would.'

'That he did, Father Paul, and I thank you.' He turned to me. 'Gather as many of Paul's men-at-arms as you can and help these useless Bordeaux longshoremen unload our things – I swear to Christ, they've never seen a horse before, let alone offloaded one from a ship.' I looked at Paul. It was about time he involved himself in manual labour. 'Oh, not Father Paul,' Sir Walter added, catching my thought. 'He has more important matters to attend.' Paul smirked. 'Come with me if you would, Father,' Sir Walter said, clapping Paul on the shoulder, 'I'd like God's opinion on...'

I did not hear the end as he ushered him away, Paul hanging on his every word like a faithful hound.

By the end of the day, I was stripped to the waist in the scorching sun, my hands raw with rope burns. We all were. As the final bundle of arrows was hauled onto a waiting wagon, we collapsed, exhausted, while local Gascon children brought warm ale. I had never tasted anything so good.

'Are we finished here, Master Idiot?'

I looked up to see the shape of Sir Walter silhouetted against the sinking sun as it set in a cloudless sky. Paul, standing close by as always, smiled.

'That we are, my Lord,' I replied. 'And may I say we couldn't have done it without Paul's invaluable input.' I glared at his smug face.

Sir Walter turned to Paul. 'My thanks, Father,

we are indeed indebted to you.'

Paul bowed. 'It is all in the service of the Lord, be it the Divine Protector or thy good self, Sire.'

Sir Walter nodded and pointed towards the town. 'Off with you, Idiot. You may have trouble finding lodging at this late hour – I imagine the best quarters have been snapped up by those lazy wretches who slunk off as soon as we arrived.'

Paul couldn't help himself, adding, 'At least you know who to rely on when hard graft is needed, Lord.' He smiled at my scowl. 'And Master Idiot here is a first-class leader.'

I could see Sir Walter take a mental note before the two strolled away. 'If you need anything, Idiot, we'll be residing in the local tavern,' Sir Walter said without turning round.

CHAPTER 10

'You just can't help yourself, Paul.' I glared at the beam on his face. 'I'm not fuckin' joking. You pulled this same stunt in France and Flanders – get a taste of authority, and it goes straight to your head.'

Paul had found me outside the barn where I'd slept the night, covered in mosquito bites. Godric and a group of the grafters from the previous day had stumbled on the place late that night. It was the best of a bad lot, our preferred lodgings packed with snarling occupants determined to protect their territory.

Paul ignored my annoyance and called the men from the barn. None looked pleased to see their leader. He had shed the monk's habit for standard army fatigues, his tunic unlaced to the waist in the rising heat.

'Gather round, gentlemen, and open those things on the side of your heads.'

We moved closer.

'I want you all on the quayside in an hour.'

'More heavy lifting to be done?' someone shouted from the back.

Paul stiffened. 'Who said that?'

A nervous silence fell as he pushed through the men, seeking the voice's source. He stopped before Ross – a hulking Highlander who'd come south as a child when his mother had been taken as collateral for a debt owed to an English lord. Ross was the most menacing man among us.

'It wasn't me, Paul,' he said.

'Who was it then?'

Paul's face had changed. I knew what came next. He moved in, his face inches from Ross's.

Ross refused to blink, his hand feeling for his dagger.

'Someone here wants to make me look a fool. Is it you, Jock?'

Again, Ross went to deny it, but the words did not leave his lips. Paul reared back and head-butted him in the teeth. He staggered, and I hoped he might fall and end this, but he was a proud man – Paul had chosen him well. He was sending a message.

Ross drew his knife, more through instinct than purpose, as his legs trembled. Paul saw the blade, and Ross's fate was sealed.

As the surrounding men stepped back, Paul launched himself at Ross, taking him off his feet and driving him to the ground, forcing the air from his lungs.

Paul sprang up, then leapt, both feet, down onto Ross's exposed face, sending shards of teeth into his throat as Ross struggled for breath.

'YOU THINK A KNIFE WILL SAVE YOU?' Paul bellowed, leaning in close, spitting the words into Ross's bloody face.

He seized Ross by the hair, yanking his head

up, and bit deep into his cheek, tearing away a chunk of flesh before tossing him back down like a rag doll.

Father Paul became Paul the Soldier.

A group of Gascon soldiers attached to our command had been watching. As Ross was carried away to be tended by the barber-surgeon, one of them leaned in and whispered to me, 'If that's what you English do to each other, what will you do to the French?'

I did not answer.

*

As expected, Paul stood beside Nathaniel and Earl Derby at ease. I could never fathom how he left such ruin in his wake without a trace of guilt. It was as though his years of ecclesiastical study had never happened – hadn't instilled any deeper reflection or burden of conscience. I had long since stopped trying to understand.

The three stood at the stern of a small ship, the Earl readying himself to address us as we gathered on the quayside. Most of the Gascons understood English well enough – years of trade had made them bilingual, especially after King John's tax exemptions strengthened the ties between our lands. The Welsh, on the other hand, were different. Although attached by a land border, many still refused to acknowledge the English tongue.

Earl Derby stepped forward and spread his arms across the ship's railings, waiting for silence.

'Right, here's what I know.'

I stood toward the back with Godric, but the Earl's voice carried. Nearby, a couple of Welshmen muttered, 'I bet he doesn't know when we get paid.'

It was a common contention among them, simmering wherever Welshmen mustered. Their loyalty was hard-earned, but coin was the only true currency. Without it, murmurs of discontent were never far from breaking into open defiance.

'Our Gascon allies expected us by June,' he said. 'We expected us by June, for that matter.' He glanced at Paul. 'I'm assured it's all part of God's plan, so all is well.' A few men chuckled. 'But in our absence, seeing the French in their usual disarray, the Gascon army took affairs into their own hands.'

Godric leaned in. 'That's a first – they usually need us to hold their hands.'

The Earl continued. 'They've captured the castles of Montravel and Monbreton down by the Dordogne and hold them securely.' A few Gascons cheered, though most of us had no clue where those places were. 'The point is, the Truce of Malestroit is well and truly over.'

That got the cheer he was after. We all knew what that meant – full-out war.

The truce, signed between King Edward III and Philip VI of France at the Chapelle de la Madeleine in Malestroit, had only ever been an uneasy pause in hostilities. None of us had believed it would last, and I'm sure the signatories knew as much. Now, with the Gascons attacking French castles in our name, there could be only one outcome.

'Listen,' he bellowed as factions began murmuring, 'I'm buried in administrative issues that will take weeks to sort, so I suggest you all ingratiate yourselves with the local community.' Smutty catcalls and raucous laughter erupted, but his tone hardened. 'I expect… no, I *demand*, on pain of death, that no civilians are assaulted or inconvenienced in any way.' He turned to Paul. 'I'm placing full responsibility for this order in your capable hands. You have my full backing to take whatever action you deem fit.'

Even at a distance, I saw Paul's satisfaction.

*

The next few days passed in a blur. Sir Walter had our barn brigade, as we'd been nicknamed, hard at work sorting the armoury, tending the horses, and preparing everything needed to move a couple of thousand men-at-arms, foot soldiers, and archers at a moment's notice. Most of the work was done by the end of the first week. Godric and Bonehead, veterans of these tasks, organised everything with practised ease.

I saw little of Paul during that first week, but as the hard work wound down, he made his presence known.

I was resting, chatting with Godric at an ale-stained wooden table outside a tavern on the outskirts of town – the English side of town. As expected, the Welsh kept to themselves, settling in a small area by the quay. They called it Gwynedd, after the land where Henry de Shaldeforde, Sir Walter's friend, had been brutally butchered. They were playing a dangerous game. With each passing day, they grew more antagonistic toward the English.

Godric and I had grown close, discovering we had much in common. Armies are held together by camaraderie – small pockets of like-minded men banding together, the common cause binding those pockets into fighting units. It was a sense of belonging like no other.

'What're you up to, Idiot?'

Paul sat down hard, knocking my drink over.

'Not you, too? I'm trying to earn these men's respect, and half of them call me the Idiot.' Paul laughed. 'It's not fuckin' funny, Paul,' I hissed. 'You need to set an example.'

'They call me the Preacher. We get given nicknames – that's what we do!' He thumbed toward Bonehead, who sat at a separate table. 'I doubt he loves his name.'

I shook my head. 'You gave him that name.' I got up and took Paul aside. 'Look, and I tell you this as your brother – you're spiralling again.'

He grinned and twisted around and around on the spot. 'So I am.'

'This is serious, Paul. How much of France and Flanders do you remember?'

He sighed. 'You know I don't remember anything. I get the odd flashback, but only what you've told me.'

I grabbed him by both arms to stop him spinning.

Paul's smile faltered, his eyes searching mine. For a moment, the bravado slipped, and something vulnerable flashed beneath the surface. I released my grip.

'Don't lose yourself – not now. We'll need each other to get through this.'

He gave a slight nod, his swagger subdued, at least for the moment. As he turned back toward the others, I knew this was only a reprieve. But for now, it would have to be enough.

We sat back down with Godric.

'Tell me about yourself, Godric,' Paul asked.

Godric looked taken aback. 'What do you want to know?'

Paul's leg trembled as he looked skyward, trying to control the tremor. Then he jumped up.

'I don't have time for this,' he said dismissively. 'While you idiots were lounging about drinking ale, I spent the morning trying to control those crazy Welsh bastards.' He glanced at the next table. 'Bonehead, I want you and the men on the parade ground in an hour – full armour. You lot have forgotten why we're here.' He turned to me. 'And get those archers on the range – they need to be sharp. I'm surprised I need to remind you.'

He turned and left.

Bonehead downed his ale, rallied the other men, and headed off, grumbling between themselves.

Godric slapped me on the back. 'Looks like I prodded the bear too hard.' He shrugged. 'At least he got distracted, and I didn't have to tell him my life's story. Not that there's much to tell. I was born, joined the army, killed a lot of Frenchmen, and now I'm here waiting to kill more or die.' He looked content. 'It's been bloody good so far when I put it like that.'

'Godric, you're an idiot,' I laughed. 'Come on, let's gather the others and shoot some arrows.'

*

That night, all hell broke loose. Earl Derby confirmed what we all feared – there was no money to pay the Welsh – or anyone else, for that matter. We had just wrapped up archery practice while the men-at-arms finished whatever it was they did. To me, it looked like a bunch of brutes battering the life out of each other, though they assured me there was method in their thuggery. Despite our exhaustion, we knew it was what we needed. Periods of rest weaken fighting men.

'Paul's wiser than you give him credit for, Al,' Godric said, leaning back in the same rickety chair outside the tavern, the sun dipping low into our eyeline. 'I feel that old battle spirit rush through my veins with every practice arrow.' He tapped his mug. 'And where's that drink you owe me?'

'Fair play, Godric – you can shoot.' I waved to a serving girl, who signalled she would be over in a second.

'Whatever happened to that woman you had a thing with after we raised Arques to the ground?' Godric mused. 'Pretty little thing – far too good for you. I remember seeing you two around camp.' He hesitated, looking embarrassed. 'We were all jealous. Many a night I... well, I used to visualise her and enjoy some alone time...' He trailed off, noticing my expression. 'Too much information?'

The serving girl attended, carrying two mugs of ale.

'Yeah, slightly too much, Godric.' A picture of her face flashed in my mind, and I sighed. 'Izelda was a fine woman – born here in Bordeaux.' The girl placed the drinks down but didn't move away. 'She would tell me how beautiful this place was and how much she missed it.' I looked around at the rolling hills and vineyards that stretched as far as the eye could see. 'And she was right.'

'Excuse me, Sire,' the serving girl interrupted, eyes wide, 'did you say you knew a girl called Izelda from this town?' She became self-conscious and stepped back. 'I'm... sorry, I shouldn't eavesdrop.'

She went to leave.

'No, yes, stay... please.' I could not contain my excitement.

She hesitated, but before I could say more, Godric stood. 'This is something you two need time for.' He clapped his hands together, drawing the attention of everyone outside the tavern. 'I'll be serving you idiots in this lovely lady's place for the next few minutes. If it ain't ale, you ain't getting it.'

He winked at me before wandering off to mingle with the others, leaving the girl and me alone.

She sat next to me and adjusted her dress.

'Did you know her?' My voice shook. I was married to Philippa, with children, and my time with Izelda had been brief – but in all the years since, she had never left me.

'I did,' she mumbled. 'I... I still do.'

A cold shudder ran through me.

And then the Welsh struck.

CHAPTER 11

I heard them before I saw them – thank God.

Fifty men swarmed the tavern, pouring in from the vegetable garden out back, their hollow drone of a war cry giving them away. Maces and war hammers gleamed in the dusk, and archers loosed their arrows from behind. We had a taste of what it must feel like to be French.

I dove under the table as arrows hissed overhead, the cries of those less lucky chilling.

'To arms!' Godric's scream cut through the disarray, but from where I lay, all I saw were legs darting in every direction in blind panic.

'Get down!' I shouted, dragging the girl out of harm's way.

Raising my head just enough, I saw a handful of our men, swords flashing, locked in a desperate fight for survival. Godric ran towards me, his blade dripping red.

'We're surrounded, Al – they're everywhere.'

I shot a look at the tavern door. 'Quick, through there.'

I grabbed the girl's hand and moved to cross the few feet, but felt dead weight pulling me back.

'Forget her – she's dead. Let's go.' Godric was already halfway there.

I hadn't noticed. An arrow had pierced her

neck, killing her without a sound. I hesitated, then dashed for the door.

Godric was there, sword in one hand, a stiletto in the other. As I reached him, he lunged. I barely dodged, ducking right as a whoosh sailed over my head. A cry rang out inches behind me – Godric's blade had buried itself deep in Wyn the Welshman's chest. Wyn clawed at me, his mace slipping from his grasp as Godric wrenched his sword free. The Welshman spasmed, vomiting blood as he collapsed.

I snatched up his weapon, nodding at Godric in thanks before we rushed inside. An arrow thudded into the doorframe as I slammed it shut – just in time to see the last Englishman fall, his skull shattered by a war hammer.

Two of our men had already taken refuge inside while three tavern maids cowered in the kitchen.

'Bar and bolt that door!' I shouted to Godric, struggling to be heard over the maids' hysterical screams.

'You two – secure the back!'

They dashed off. We swept through the rooms once the doors were locked, checking the window shutters. All were bolted tight. Then, the pounding began.

Axes bit into the oak, carving deep grooves until slivers of dusty light pierced the gloom.

'Are they coming through the back?' I shouted. 'No? Right, one of you stay there – the other, get here!'

I dashed into the kitchen, spotting a large cauldron of bubbling pottage on the range.

'Godric, help me with this – quick!'

He joined me, and we wrapped our hands in towelling, hoisting the cauldron between us. Staggering up the narrow staircase, we reached the small window above the front door.

'Send one of the girls up!' I called down.

Moments later, a trembling maid appeared.

'Open that shutter,' I ordered, my grip slipping.

She leaned over and pushed it open.

We heaved the cauldron onto the sill.

'NOW!' I shouted, just as my hands gave out.

We tipped the scalding contents over the edge – then came the screams. I risked a glance, arrows already whistling toward me, but not before I saw three Welshmen clutching their blistered faces, skin seared by the boiling liquid.

From my heightened position, I saw Paul at the head of a large group of archers and men-at-arms, charging in, fanned out and snarling.

My heart leapt.

I ducked back inside, raced downstairs and grabbed the mace.

'Weapons, boys! We're going out.'

The man from the back entrance rejoined us as Godric unbolted the door. No one questioned my call, trusting my command. I met each of their eyes and smiled.

He wrenched the door open, and we unleashed

retribution.

They had not yet realised our fellow Englishmen were behind them. We surged out, catching them unaware as they busied themselves with the scalded – shock took their eyes.

As did I.

The only man still wielding an axe didn't move swiftly enough. My mace caught him square on the forehead, its spikes bursting through his eyeballs, driving them deep into the shattered sockets. He dropped the axe, clutching his face, but my next blow split the back of his skull, spikes dragging grey matter to the floor.

By then, Paul and the others were upon them, cleaving and hacking. They saw their comrades lying dead and spared no mercy.

Some of the Welshmen fought their way toward the tavern to escape. The four of us tried to drive them back into the killing zone, but a few slipped by and bolted the door behind them.

That left the rest. There would be no escaping for them.

The hardened campaigners fought like demons, Welsh pride doubling their strength – but pride cannot stop cold steel.

I saw Nathaniel beside Paul, locked in his first true fight for survival, frantic swings, the weight of his blade barely under control. Paul was brutal as ever, shattering bone and steel alike, cleaving through flesh with sickening force.

One enemy staggered, blood spurting from his mouth – Nathaniel drove his sword into the man's belly, tearing through muscle and organs. The man choked on his last breath, slumping in a heap. Paul pulled Nathaniel forward, shielding him from another attack, then sent a man's skull caving in with a single blow, the wet crack echoing.

The Welsh were in disarray.

Within minutes, the fight was all but won, our sheer numbers making the outcome inevitable – yet they refused to yield. Paul faced their leading warrior and drove him to his knees. Nathaniel lunged, his blade sinking deep into the man's thigh, blood spraying violently. The man roared in pain, but before he could steady himself, Nathaniel recovered the blade and hacked into his neck with a savage stroke. The flesh split, head lolling to one side, held on by tendons stretched to their limit, veins pumping blood.

His death broke their spirit.

The remaining Welsh dropped their weapons, eyes still spitting hatred as their leader's body slumped to the ground, twitching in a pool of red.

We all breathed deeply.

Paul moved to the tavern's door and picked up a discarded axe.

'If you bastards aren't out within the count of five, I'll be in there within the next three – and believe me, you won't be invited to stand with the sheep penned over there.' He gestured to their already captured countrymen, surrounded by our men.

'One... two...'

They were out at three.

As Paul's men stripped the prisoners of their weapons, I knelt beside the lifeless body of the girl I had spoken to. Her blank eyes stared at nothing – answers stolen by a single arrow.

I had lost my link to Izelda.

What had she been about to tell me? Was Izelda back in Bordeaux – maybe just steps from where I stood? If so, why? Had the brutal uncertainty of life, never knowing if this day might be your last, brought her home? She had always longed for a quiet life, far from war and bloodshed.

The questions clawed at me, but the answers lay silent and cold.

In desperation, I questioned the three remaining maids, hoping they might know something, but terror had scattered their thoughts.

I was left with nothing.

*

Paul and I were summoned to Sir Walter and Earl Derby's headquarters, a commandeered wharf near the quayside. They stood behind a large desk cluttered with maps of France and Gascony. Nathaniel was in the corner, busying himself with placing books on shelves alphabetically. At our entry, he glanced at the Earl and left.

It was an ominous sign.

The Earl spoke first. 'Tell me, gentlemen, do you recall when we first arrived and I was accosted by a rather irate Welshman named Wyn?' His gaze settled on me. 'Shall I take that as a yes?' I nodded. 'Good. Now, during that brief exchange, did it ever occur to you to mention that you and Father Paul had slaughtered half his family? Perhaps a simple, "By the way, we killed half his kin" would have sufficed.'

I opened my mouth to speak, but he raised a hand to silence me. 'No need. Sir Thomas's son, Nathaniel, has already filled me in and vouched for you, so we'll leave it at that. Besides, once they named their living quarters Gwynedd – after my dear friend Henry de Shaldeforde's murder, they were owed no respect.'

'That's most gracious of you, Sire,' I said, 'though I think there's more to the Welshmen's actions tonight than...'

'Yes, that is why you're not swinging with them.' He turned to Paul, who had donned his monk's habit and was silently mouthing prayers. 'Father Paul, I commend your quick action in quelling the rabble. Without your intervention, things might have taken a darker turn.'

Paul bowed. 'God guides my hand as well as my soul, my Lord. Nathaniel is a fine young man and...'

'Yes, *Father*, I see many things guide you.' The

Earl's eyes flicked to Sir Walter. 'And I hope *everyone* sees you for who you are.' Sir Walter reddened.

'Anyway...' The Earl sat back, his warning delivered. 'You weren't the main target, as it turned out. After discovering I didn't have coin, that rabble broke into the ale store and then tried to stir the rest into defecting to the French. Most refused, but after speaking of rebellion openly, they couldn't linger for me to catch wind of it, so they broke camp.' He eyed me. 'I suspect you were a drunken afterthought. If they hadn't stalled for Wyn's personal vendetta, I fear the French might be fifty bowmen better off.' He sighed. 'You never know who you're fighting when the French field an army these days. Scots, French, Welsh... it could be anyone.' He glanced about the room. 'Is it not grand to be hated by everyone?'

'No one likes us,' Sir Walter said proudly. 'And we don't care.'

'Precisely.' The Earl rose. 'Now, let's go hang some Welshmen.'

*

It had been a long, gruelling day, ending with the deaths of the Welsh renegades. I took no pleasure in it and averted my gaze. Many had been swept up in drunken fury after months of risking their lives for a king they owed no allegiance to, only to be denied their pay. They were good archers. Most had remained loyal, but those swinging at the rope's end had been fine soldiers.

No matter his nation, every man was forced to watch, all understanding the significance.

Before we dispersed, Earl Derby announced, 'Tomorrow, we march for Langon. In two days, we'll rendezvous with the Earl of Stafford, our forces will double, and we'll find some Frenchmen to kill.'

If he expected a rousing hurrah, he was sorely mistaken.

CHAPTER 12

The next day, we marched. I lost count of how many times I turned, hoping Izelda might come running. With every backward glance, part of me died. I knew she'd had some recent connection to Bordeaux; the tavern's maid had said as much, and I just wanted to see her. Was she watching me now? But I couldn't afford distractions. None of us could. Earl Derby's orders were clear: we were not to jeopardise England's fragile alliance with the Gascons. Without their support, King Edward's pursuit of the French crown would falter.

As we left Bordeaux, Derby made his intentions clear. 'We are here to keep Gascony independent, not bleed it dry,' he declared to his senior commanders. Then, with a pointed glance at Paul, added, 'Anyone caught flouting my orders will pay.'

'That's going to hit the Welsh pockets,' Paul said, loud enough for everyone to hear, drawing laughter from the English and Gascon contingents.

Before leaving, Paul presented me with a chestnut-brown mare to ride. Sir Walter had given him authority to assign horses to senior personnel, his trusted men-at-arms being the recipients. I was honoured. In all my years under arms, I had never known the luxury of a mount, always marching through dust and mud. I could get used to this. I don't think I'd ever seen Paul walk; his links to the Almighty and favoured status with those in charge meant he lacked for nothing.

'She's all yours, Al,' Paul said, tossing the reins with a grin. 'And don't say I never take care of you.'

By the end of the first day, I was saddle sore. The years of easy living under Philippa's shadow had softened my backside. We had made camp near Podensac, a small but vital town tied to Bordeaux's vast wine trade. As I dismounted, I reached out to stroke the horse's muzzle – she bit me.

Laughter erupted behind me. Turning, I saw Paul and Bonehead beside their mounts, stroking their muzzles with exaggerated affection. Those two had grown increasingly close, reminding me of Paul's old bond with his mentor, Sir Hugh le Despenser – only now, Paul was the influencer. That was worse.

From that moment on, unless I was sitting on her, the mare tried to bite me at every opportunity. I conjured a fitting name for her: Bastard.

Our army sprawled across the land, pitching tents wherever the ground was flat enough to hammer in pegs. I shared mine with Godric and soon regretted it; the moment his head hit the makeshift pillow, he farted and snored in unison. How could a man sound like a steerhorn from both ends at once?

It took hours for the camp to settle. Men lay in the dark, talking of how they wished they were tucked up with their wives – before trading stories of infidelity and what they'd like to do to their best friend's wife.

Midnight came, but sleep did not. Godric was still bellowing, so I crawled from the tent and lay on the damp grass, staring skyward. The warm night was thick with stars, clustered like shimmering clouds against the blackness. God was on form tonight, and a rare sense of peace drifted me toward sleep.

It didn't last.

Footsteps. A muffled curse. Then, someone tripped over a tent line.

I sat up, still groggy. In the pale light of the new moon, I glimpsed Paul helping Bonehead to his feet. Bonehead was dishevelled and looked shocked to be seen by me. Paul drew his dagger, then, recognising me, exhaled and raised a finger to his lips. His face was cold and deadpan. Bonehead looked worried, but he moved onwards without a word.

Paul lowered his finger, held my gaze a second longer, then slunk after him.

I stood, scanning the way they'd gone, but saw only a sea of canvas. Then I turned in the direction they'd come. Podensac. The town we'd been forbidden from.

Bastard, tethered to a tree nearby, tossed her head at the sight of me. I stepped closer, reaching out – then she bit me again.

'Bastard,' I muttered before crawling back inside the tent to spend the rest of the night kicking Godric whenever he snored.

Hours later, all hell broke loose.

*

'Get out of your beds, you lazy, flea-bitten swine!' Paul's voice shattered the dawn silence.

It felt as though I'd only just fallen asleep.

'What now?' Godric groaned, sitting up and expelling more wind.

'Surely there's a limit to your bodily gases?' I muttered, kicking off the sheet and fumbling for my boots.

'You'd think so,' was all he managed before Paul's voice turned angrier.

'If you dung-eating louts aren't out in ten seconds, Bonehead will drag you out by the balls.'

You'd be amazed how quickly men can scramble from a tent with the right motivation.

Blinking against the low morning sun, we stood rubbing our eyes. Thousands of men stretched across the fields, those at the edges hearing the orders secondhand. But I knew they were meant for us – the closest to Paul. He stood in his monk's habit, flanked by Sir Walter and Bonehead, waiting for our full attention. Once satisfied, he stepped aside, letting Sir Walter take the lead.

'Right, men, this is serious – I want the truth. I understand loyalty, covering for each other, but this goes beyond that.'

'This is gonna be bad,' Godric muttered.

'Someone – or some men – left camp last night and went into Podensac.'

Tension drained away. A few groaned while others muttered their annoyance.

'What's he getting so worked up about?' Godric grumbled. 'Hope they had a good time.'

I wasn't so sure. Paul's eyes hadn't left me.

Sir Walter's voice hardened. 'Let me finish. Whoever it was murdered seven whores, their madam, and two minders at the brothel.'

Silence.

Bonehead was sweating.

'Now, I need to know – did anyone see anything? The pickets report nothing, but someone here knows something.'

I glanced at Paul again. He hadn't moved. His face was empty.

Then he spoke. 'Be under no illusions, my brothers – we will find these cowardly bastar...' He shot a glance at Sir Walter. '...these godless men, and we will punish them.'

His arm rose, finger sweeping over the gathered men, slow, deliberate. It landed on me.

'This is the work of the devil, and the devil must be driven out before he infects every man here.' His arm dropped, but his stare held. 'Men will hang for this – and I will tie the knot myself.'

He stepped back.

'As Father Paul says,' Sir Walter continued, voice strained, 'this has shattered the trust of our Gascon allies. We must show them we take this seriously.' A pause. His jaw clenched. 'I've been told the man – or men – forced themselves on the women before killing them…' His voice cracked. 'I think you understand.' He swallowed, fury returning. 'These are our allies, for Christ's sake – the people we need to…' He trailed off, shaking his head. 'Just give me the bastards who did this.'

He stormed off, Paul and Bonehead falling in step behind him.

Godric whispered, 'Who in their right mind would do such a thing?'

'Damned if I know,' I muttered. 'Someone without a soul.'

*

The rest of the day was spent preparing to leave. Men wandered about, speculating.

I was helping Godric take down our tent when a voice startled me.

'Any ideas, Al?'

I spun to find Paul standing there, flanked by his most trusted men-at-arms.

'About the murders?'

'No, about the chance of rain this afternoon.'

His men chuckled.

'I… I'm…'

He frowned. 'You look guilty, brother. If I

didn't know better, I'd put you at the top of my list.'

I turned my back on him, refusing to be intimidated.

'Got a list, then?' I asked, hefting the half-packed canvas toward Bastard.

'I might have.'

As I tied the bundle to her rear, she swung her head back and bit my ear. I flinched, feeling for blood.

'Who's on it?'

Paul's voice dropped. 'You know full well. The same ones you saw creeping back last night.'

I froze. 'What?'

'The ones you came and told me about after Sir Walter's speech.' I stared at him, my blood running cold. He glanced at his men. 'Don't worry. They won't think less of you. Your information is invaluable. We've questioned most leaders, and you're the only one who saw anyone returning.'

I couldn't speak.

'You never said anything to me.' Godric stepped closer, frowning. 'Who did you see?'

I looked between Paul and Bonehead.

Paul raised his chin. 'Well, tell him, Ailred.'

'I... I saw...'

'Feeling guilty now, are you? You shouldn't.' Paul's voice was smooth, coaxing. 'Everyone knows Cuthbert and Elgar are drunken crazies capable of anything.' His expression went blank.

'You've said yourself they weren't trustworthy. Now we know.' Cuthbert and Elgar were archers, good men who drank too much. But not cold-blooded murderers. 'Don't worry, Ailred,' Paul continued, clapping my shoulder. 'They're under guard. They won't be coming after you for squealing.' He laughed. 'And they'll be squealing soon enough once we hoist them from that tree.'

He pointed, grinning. His men laughed as they strolled off, leaving me dumbfounded.

*

Paul gagged them. I never knew if it was out of guilt for their cries of innocence, or simply because their pleas annoyed him.

We were made to watch as he led them to the tree, his newly cleaned habit fluttering in the freshening breeze. Bonehead's face was a mask of despair as he threw the ropes over the branch.

Paul stepped forward, tightening the nooses. They struggled, but once secured, the fight left them, their bodies slack with resignation. Anger ate at me. Paul knew I wouldn't have told the truth, and those in the camp who doubted the pair's guilt – as many did – eyed me with revulsion.

Anyone hoping for final words was disappointed. Paul refused to remove their blindfolds or gags. The Devil needed silencing.

With the ropes tied to saddles, Bonehead led the horses on. God, in all His glory, vanquished Satan's minions. They kicked and spun, bodies slowly surrendering their will to remain on earth.

Paul made the sign of the cross, leading the gathered men in the Apostles' Creed before pulling his hood over his head and walking away, leaving the lifeless bodies to sway in the breeze.

It was time to march to Langon.

CHAPTER 13

By the time we reached Langon, Bastard had mastered the art of twisting her neck backwards and biting chunks out of me whilst moving. It was a new talent – and I swear she grinned every time. Our relationship sank to new depths.

The town rivalled Bordeaux in beauty, though the crowds of English, Welsh, and Gascon troops dulled its sheen.

I rode behind Earl Derby and Sir Walter as we led our men into the centre, guided under the watchful eyes of pickets who met us on the outskirts. Lord Stafford had the town on high alert. The lord greeted us as we approached the Église Saint-Gervais de Langon, a beautiful church by the Garonne River that served as the base for Stafford's high command.

'Gentlemen, it is good to see you,' he said, shaking hands with Earl Derby and Sir Walter as they dismounted. 'Come, join me. We have much to discuss.'

Both lords dusted themselves off while a couple of young Gascon pages scurried around, distributing water.

Paul and Bonehead cantered to a halt beside us. The Earl had ordered them to bring up the rear, ensuring none of the men got waylaid. He sensed a tension between Paul and me after the hanging, and the Earl, a shrewd judge of character, kept us apart.

'Paul and Ailred, with us,' Earl Derby barked, tossing his cup to the nearest page. He glanced at Nathaniel, who was behind me. 'You too, Nate.' We followed Lord Stafford into the church.

Inside was immaculate. The English command had treated the church with the respect its grand design deserved. The high beams straddling the roof took my breath away. Their stunning blue and gold arches created an impression of a skyward link to God, His only son hanging helplessly on a wooden cross above the altar.

'Sit, my good fellows.' Lord Stafford gestured as chairs were brought to his table at the north transept.

We sat.

'Did you have any problems en route, Earl Derby?' Stafford said, waiting for the Earl to sit before taking his seat.

Derby rolled his neck, grimacing. 'It's been a long and gruelling march, my Lord, but no, nothing to speak of.' He looked concerned. 'Did you expect we might?'

'I had it on good authority our French friends were arranging an ambush.'

'Did you receive this information from your *source*?' Derby asked, choosing his words with care.'

'Yes, Earl, he was quite certain they intended to

catch you on the hop, so to speak.'

The earl cast a glance at Paul before responding. 'That would make me a rabbit.' He smiled. 'We also received his warning, so we changed our route.'

Stafford nodded. 'Our friend's been busy.'

'Seems he's using his initiative,' Derby agreed. 'Thank God.'

I had noticed we'd taken a less direct path after leaving Podensac. I frowned at Paul, sensing I was missing a piece of the puzzle.

Paul stared through me.

Before I could dwell, Earl Derby pressed on. 'Right, Lord Stafford, let us talk strategy.'

Stafford's smile was knowing. 'I thought we might.'

'As I'm sure you're aware, the King has tasked me with overseeing this region. I don't know how you feel about that, but I can convey his thanks for your work thus far, and it's no slight on your handling.' Stafford smiled but said nothing. 'So, I'll be blunt. Until now, you've led a cautious approach of small sieges and hit-and-run tactics.' Lord Stafford went to speak, but Derby pressed on. 'Yes, the King and I understand you lacked the manpower for more, but now you have it – well, I have it.'

Resignation spread across Stafford's flushed face. 'I am at your disposal, Earl. Use us as you will.'

Derby smiled. 'You've built a fine force here in

Gascony, Lord – seasoned fighters and valuable intelligence. Both will help us strike fear into King Philip.' He pulled a large map towards him, smoothing it out before pointing. 'Here.' His finger rested on Rennes, Brittany. 'This is where the Earl of Northampton is stationed.' He glanced at Stafford, then pointed north to Flanders. 'And the King is here, in Sluys.' He turned to Paul and me. 'A place you boys know well.' Paul raised an eyebrow at me – his first acknowledgement of my existence since the hanging. 'The King was delayed by the same beastly weather we faced, but he's there now.' Derby tapped the map. 'And that leaves us here.'

'A three-pronged assault,' Stafford said, nodding. 'That'll split their forces.'

'Precisely.' Derby smiled. 'The time has come to strike hard and direct.'

'The timing is perfect, Earl,' Stafford said. 'Our man confirms their armies are scattered, trying to second-guess the King. He's been feeding them all sorts of rumours.' His voice dropped. 'And I have it on good authority that a significant part of their intelligence network – operating in a whorehouse under our noses – was wiped out in one night recently. We have them at a powerful disadvantage.'

Derby grinned, his eyes flicking to Paul. 'In that case, it's time to let slip our dogs of havoc.'

*

Over the next few days, we settled into our new

surroundings. Once again, we were ordered to stay on good terms with the locals, and for once, there were no reports of reckless behaviour. Even Paul and Bonehead seemed at ease.

Our days were spent preparing for the next stage. The Earl was a stickler for preparation. Everything had to meet his exacting standards, and the endless drilling and double-checking was beyond tedious.

'He's working to peak us.'

I was grumbling to Godric about confirming whether a hundred thousand arrows were stored in the baggage train when Paul's voice cut in.

I spun around. 'Oh, you're talking to me again, then?'

Paul shrugged. 'The Earl just wants us ready when it's time to fight.'

I understood his logic. It was how he'd won every battle he'd fought, but the process was mind-numbing.

Paul, dressed as a soldier, his face stern, continued. 'The French are gathering at Bergerac, guarding the bridge over the Dordogne – we're hitting them there. The Earl wants the town. It's strategically vital, giving us access to the river and a clear road to Bordeaux.'

'And how do *you* know all this, Paul? I thought we were equal on this chevauchée.' His tone rubbed me the wrong way.

He sniffed. 'You are, little brother, but the Earl's got intel coming in daily. I just happen to be with him when it arrives.' He gestured at the bundles of arrows. 'You archer boys need to know when to throw your blankets of death over the dozing Frenchmen.'

'So, who's feeding us this information?'

'I've not met him – he could be anyone.' He shrugged. 'We get letters, but whoever it is, he's a God-send.' Paul turned to leave. 'Let the Earl know the exact number by day's end – we leave tomorrow.'

'Thank Christ for that,' Godric said, slapping me on the back. 'I'd rather face ten thousand crazed Frenchmen than spend another day counting arrows.'

He wasn't wrong there.

*

The final exchange between Earl Derby and Lord Stafford was held in private, seeing us leave without him. I saw no satisfaction on the Earl's face as we left. Stafford didn't see us off, keeping back the bare minimum of troops to guard the town.

I felt sorry for him. I liked him and thought he deserved better, but war leaves no room for sentiment.

It would take a few days of hard marching to reach Bergerac, but we could only move as fast as our baggage train.

'Ailred, a word.'

We were crossing a shallow stream, and Bastard had stopped to drink. Sir Walter drew level, Bastard raising her head as he stroked her muzzle.

'Yes, my Lord?'

'What do you know of Bergerac?'

'Only what Paul told me,' I replied.

'And what's that?'

I gave him the rundown Paul had shared the day before.

'I see.' His voice sounded confused.

'You didn't know?'

He shrugged. 'First I've heard of it.'

Godric cantered over. 'Are they expecting us, Lord? Can we expect a warm welcome?' He laughed.

Sir Walter looked taken aback. 'Even you know? No point asking me – Derby tells Nathaniel more than he tells me these days.'

It was true. Earl Derby had taken Nate under his wing and was mentoring him. The Earl and Sir Thomas had known each other for years, and I suspected he'd asked Derby to keep a watchful eye on his son.

I could tell Sir Walter was getting annoyed, so changed the subject. 'At least he has a good source of information – that's...'

He yanked the reins before I could finish, his horse stepping back. 'Agreed, Ailred. Intelligence saves lives.' His eyes hardened. 'But I've been given none – you're better informed than me.' With a sharp tug, he turned his horse away. 'I'll see you in Bergerac.'

I watched him gallop off through the stream, my grip tightening on the reins, ready to move on.

'You've had enough to drink, Bastard,' I muttered, giving her a tap. She ducked sharply, flipping me over her head and into the water.

Godric rode up and offered a hand, helping me to my feet. 'That's a fine nag you've got there, my friend.'

I stood, squeezing water from my tunic, as Paul approached and stroked Bastard's head.

'We'll be striking blind,' he said, excitement creeping in.

I frowned, then caught on. 'The French have no idea we're coming?'

Paul grinned. 'Exactly. We strike at dawn, so ride through the night.' He looked at the archers marching past, some sniggering at my fall. 'Get your boys ready. We're invisible now. I'll let Bonehead and the men-at-arms know.'

He rode off.

'Invisible?' Godric asked, raising an eyebrow.

I nodded, Paul's inference needing no explanation. 'No sound, no light. We move in silence now. Seems our spy's done his work.'

'Finally, we see some action,' Godric said before hurrying to spread the word.

*

We moved like ghosts towards the outskirts of Bergerac, each man sure-footed and silent, knowing one wrong step would mean disaster.

We left the baggage and horses behind; a frustrated Nathaniel ordered to supervise and remain behind with a select few as we covered the last miles on foot. No one had slept since the day before, but we were tireless.

Earl Derby led the men-at-arms and used us archers as infantrymen, each carrying a deadly tool of destruction. The bulk of the French army was camped between us and the town, with only a sparse picket stationed. Their long-held position gave them a false sense of security. All Gascon resistance in the area had been crushed, save for the castle at Montcuq, which was still under siege. The French believed they were untouchable.

It was our job to disprove that.

The Earl split the men-at-arms and infantry into two forces, leading one himself and Sir Walter commanding the other. I stayed with the Earl and Bonehead while Paul and Godric followed Sir Walter. Their orders were to circle behind the French camp and strike from the rear.

'Do not attack until you hear my steerhorn – do you understand?' Earl Derby addressed Sir Walter and Paul before our two groups parted ways.

'Understood, Lord,' both answered.

'Good, now go. We must crush this French army before turning our sights on the town. Bergerac will be hostile. Once we smash these bastards, we'll break their spirit.' He paused, eyes sweeping over us. 'There will be no mercy for those who resist. Clear the camp.'

Paul gave me a final nod before he and Sir Walter led their men into the night.

The waiting began. Only a seasoned warrior knows the tension in those moments leading to an assault. War may have changed over the years, but the surge of adrenaline before the killing erupts – that feeling is timeless.

'Take the archers left, Ailred, and cover the area over there.' Earl Derby pointed to a gated opening in the hedge encircling most of the camp. I could see thousands of tents in the dim light, far more than expected. We were outnumbered at least two to one.

But we had everything – intelligence and surprise – thanks to one man moving among them like a ghost.

Before I moved off, the Earl grabbed my arm. 'Those tents over there are barber-surgeons and camp followers – they're no threat,' he said, gesturing to a separate cluster of tents, cold fires with hanging pots above waiting for breakfast.

I nodded.

The Earl had sent out small bands of Gascons familiar with the terrain to silence the sentries, each returning with the same report: all dead, their throats cut to the larynx.

'Off you go, boys,' he said, looking between Bonehead and me 'Let's make our introductions.'

Bonehead led his men-at-arms to the right-hand side whilst I skirted around the hedging to the left until we reached the gap, then fanned out, encircling the silent tents. Earl Derby remained central, watching and controlling.

'Spark them,' I whispered.

Half of my men carried unlit torches alongside their weapons. On my order, they brought out tinderboxes. The sound of flint scraping metal set my teeth on edge.

Once lit, the men snaked between the tents, Bonehead's men opposite doing similar.

We waited. I glanced towards Earl Derby. As the flames caught each torch, men's eyes shone, unable to contain their primitive desires to kill. He raised an arm, then dropped it.

'GO,' I screamed as hundreds of tents burst into flames.

For a heartbeat, nothing moved. Then all hell erupted.

We swept across like a black tide, weapons flashing in the firelight. I waited at the exits of burning tents, my mace in hand, crushing skulls as they stumbled out, blocking their comrades' escape. Flames leapt, engulfing the camp, the screams of men, their hair and clothes alight, filling the air. Their agony was brief – we pounded them into oblivion.

On the other side, Bonehead's men advanced, driving survivors into a funnel. Naked and half-armoured, they scrambled to form a defence, but it was futile. I swung the mace, shattering faces, limbs, flesh, and bone caked the iron head, the spikes tearing through bodies without pause. No hesitation. No mercy.

As their ranks thinned, fresh waves surged from the tents beyond – those untouched by the firestorm. Armoured men clawed for survival, but we met them with bloodlust, smashing into them again and again. Bone snapped, flesh tore, but still they came. For every man we sent to hell, two more replaced him, their shields battered but their resolve fierce.

Just as I thought the tide might overwhelm us, the long, cold blast of the steerhorn split the air. Earl Derby had held off just long enough, letting them gather, confident they had the upper hand. Now, Paul and Sir Walter fell on them from behind.

The men facing me, snarling in their certainty of victory, turned in panic. The joy of watching that confidence drain from their eyes was pure, a savage delight. They turned to defend themselves, but we surged forward, hammering them into the dirt without hesitation, without remorse. Each blow a satisfaction as blood splattered across the battlefield.

And then we knew – that pivotal moment in every battle. Many had slipped away, but those who remained cast down their weapons and fell to their knees, pleading for mercy.

I looked towards the Earl for guidance, knowing the answer. He wanted to deliver a stark and intractable message. This was it.

With a stern shake of his head, we moved in and finished the slaughter.

*

The small cluster of tents Derby had ordered us to spare remained intact, untouched by the flames. Women and children huddled together, their faces blank with shock. A wounded man limped through the wreckage, looking for salvation but disappearing as soon as he caught sight of us.

I glanced down at my hand, noticing for the first time a gash seeping blood. I had no memory of receiving it; the pain only then starting to make itself known.

Walking towards the tents, I spotted Paul rushing, ushering someone away.

By the time I reached him, he was alone.

'Who was that?' I asked, gripping the wound to stem the bleeding.

'Just a barber-surgeon,' he said, avoiding my eyes. 'Gascon. Thought we could use him.'

'And you didn't think to have him tend me?' I held my hand up.

Paul hesitated. 'Yeah, right, it's all about you! Meanwhile, those French bastards are getting away while you're after sympathy. Get patched up and move – we're in pursuit.'

He dashed off, joining Bonehead and the others as they chased the fleeing French who had slipped our net.

Seconds later, Earl Derby, now mounted, rode past.

'I don't pay you to stand around and whinge about a scratch, Idiot, get moving. It's three miles to the town – plenty of time to hunt them down. I want to be dining on the finest French cuisine by day's end.'

*

The outcome was inevitable with so many of our men-at-arms now on horseback and most French without footwear. Even Bastard took a break from living up to her name, letting me mount her and join the hunt. You'd be surprised how little you feel when you know God is on your side as you bury steel into a man's skull. The injured and lame cowered, our foot soldiers dragging them from their hiding places like foxes from dens while we, on horseback, persuaded the hares.

Those still fleeing made for the St Madeleine suburb of Bergerac, heading toward the bridge that led to the town. As I neared the barbican, the fortified structure guarding it, I was met by total disarray. Hundreds of French surged across, cramming onto the narrow span, fighting one another to get across the bridge and through the gates. Our men pressed in from behind, cutting down those trapped at the rear.

I dismounted, ready to charge down the hill, when I noticed the town's main gates creak open on the far side of the bridge. For a moment, I thought they would let their survivors in.

But instead, French men-at-arms poured out, many on horseback, eager to face us. It was madness. They couldn't push more than a few yards onto the bridge before their own panicked men forced them back.

By then, thousands of our archers had swapped swords for bows.

'Godric, take half the Idiots to the right. I'll take the left.'

He grinned, already understanding my plan.

As our men-at-arms shoved the remaining French into a tight knot on the bridge, we archers formed a crossfire on both sides. It was no more than target practice. In the growing light of morning, arrows tore into their panicked ranks, and the dead stood propped upright by the crush of bodies.

A small chapel stood in the centre of the bridge, men clambering inside, desperate to shield themselves from the unrelenting onslaught, but it only choked the flow. Arrows thudded into walls, flesh, and bone, pinning them where they stood. Screams rose from inside the chapel as those trapped were crushed underfoot, doors splintering under the weight of bodies.

The bridge's dead piled high, their corpses forming a grisly barricade. French men-at-arms realised their attempt to reach us was futile and so turned, stumbling over bodies to retreat to the town's safety. In panic, the guards dropped the portcullis, its deadly weight slamming into their own. The spiked grill impaled a mounted man, splitting him in two and pinning his horse to the ground, blood pouring from puncture wounds as the beast thrashed.

That was the moment all was lost. Frenzied, they hacked at the body and horse trapped beneath the grill, desperate to free the portcullis as our firepower intensified. Arrows poured down like hail, driving deep, forcing the defenders to scatter. Moments later, our men surged across the bridge – trampling the dead and dying, hurling bodies into the moat. They slipped under the half-raised gate and spilled into Bergerac, bringing slaughter with them.

We ran out of Frenchmen to kill. Bows unstrung, we took up hand weapons again, plunging steel into the few left cowering behind carts and walls. The portcullis creaked upward, lifted from within. Our men surged forward, ushering in blood and ruin. The streets filled with dead and dying as our men set to work destroying and looting the once beautiful town.

CHAPTER 14

Tell me, Brother Michael, before we continue, with all this talk of war, do you regret following in my footsteps? You once said the men who shattered your legs couldn't have been all bad. Were you serious? Really? You're more forgiving than I, Brother.

Yes, I know you're meant to be narrating my life, but there's time enough for that. You sit there, nodding like a monk at prayer, never a word out of place. Do you ever have an opinion, or are you saving them all for Judgment Day? If you relay them now, I'll give the Almighty prior warning, as I'll be seeing him before you. I'll put in a good word – though with my backstory, I doubt he'll listen.

No? Nothing? Just more of that quiet, knowing look?

Very well, I'll continue – but one day, Brother, I'll get you to open up.

*

The aftermath of battle can break even hardened men. When the bloodlust fades, I've seen the cruellest of soldiers kneel amid the carnage, weeping for their souls. But not today. Today, there were coffers to fill.

I spotted Bonehead for the first time since we took the town. He was picking through the dead, stripping them of anything of worth.

'Have you seen Paul?' I shouted above the sounds of destruction. 'Do you know where he is?'

He turned over the battered, half-naked body of a young girl, terror still etched on her face. He sighed. 'This reeks of him – I doubt he's far.'

I have fought in enough battles to feel nothing for fallen enemies, believing it was us or them. We all knew what we signed up for. But civilians were different. I remembered the French town of Arques on my first sortie to Flanders and France; civilians, especially women and girls, were targeted without remorse. It was no different here. While the Earl had given his blessing to plunder, a depraved faction sought something darker. As we wandered the frenzied streets, I lost count of how many times I pulled men from young women, threatening death when they resisted. Godric, of a similar mindset, backed me, and all but one relented. We put him down like a rabid dog.

And then we stumbled upon Paul.

He was dragging a girl by the hair across the street toward an empty tannery, its contents long since looted. She couldn't have been more than fourteen, younger than my daughter. It wasn't just her screams for mercy that repulsed me but the sickening smile across his blood-soaked face. He carried a human hand, severed at the wrist, each finger adorned with gold rings, trophies of his savagery.

He slung her like a rag doll against the wall outside the tannery before picking her up by the ankle and dragging her inside.

'Paul, what the hell are you doing?' He turned to me, his face blank, struggling to grasp my words. 'It's me, Ailred – are you alright?'

The girl stirred inside the shop and tried to stand, only to fall again. Paul's eyes sharpened, surprise crossing his features. He moved toward her as if she were a broken toy to mend.

She froze, paralysed by fear, as he stopped inches from her. His eyes widened.

Neither moved. Neither breathed.

I approached slowly, urging her outside. She flinched at my touch but allowed me to guide her, her gaze unfocused. Once outside, I turned her around, and she stumbled away, drifting like a dried leaf in the wind. I could only pray she found sanctuary amid the destruction.

I returned to Paul.

'I found gold rings,' he said, holding the severed hand out.' I couldn't get them off the fingers.' His voice was childlike.

'Would you like Godric and me to look after them for you?' I asked gently.

He twisted his head, a wicked grin rising like the devil was shedding its skin. 'No, my brother, I'll store them with my other limbs.' He paused. ' And when I remove the rings, I'll make soup.'

He walked off, biting the fingernails.

*

Godric and I sat by a fire that night under a cloudless sky. We had avoided the drunken excesses that followed every battle, choosing to find a corner of Bergerac left unscathed. It had not been easy.

'Derby could've chosen to siege this out,' Godric said. 'At least most of the town would still be standing.'

I chewed a length of straw, watching a shooting star arc across the heavens. I made a wish.

'He promised us wealth to make us hunt down the French,' I said without looking at him. 'A siege would've deprived us of that – he'd have had a mutiny on his hands.'

'Yeah, true.' He fumbled in his bag. 'All that bloodshed and I only found a few coins – and this...' He pulled out a long, crusty loaf and a string of onions.

I laughed. 'I'll see that bread and raise you a lump of this.' I pulled out a slab of cheese that dripped between my fingers.

Godric brightened. 'Oh, I like it runny.'

I looked at it, trying to scoop it off the floor. 'It's a bit runnier than you'd like it, Godric.'

'No matter, fetch it here – we can have a fair meal between the two of us.'

We ate in silence before Godric lay back, looking skywards.

'I don't know why they didn't just surrender,'

he said, twisting sideways and expelling wind. 'It would've saved them a whole heap of heartache. Most of their army was dead or captured – they must've known it was only a matter of time.'

I nodded. 'I've seen it before. They feel safe behind their walls, but that resolve soon crumbles.' I shrugged. 'Not that we gave them much chance to surrender, did we?'

'Aye, true enough. We never took Tournai, did we? Sieges don't always work.'

'That was different. They had a decent army to defend it – this lot didn't. It wouldn't have taken long.'

Godric expelled more wind. 'It's all irrelevant anyway – we didn't give them the chance.' He pondered for a moment. 'I met a wanderer from the Far East years ago – a strange little fella. He spun tales of his homeland, a different world entirely. Their leader, Genghis or something, used a system of coloured tents when he besieged fortresses. Each day, he'd ask those inside to surrender. First, he'd raise a white tent, then a red one, and finally, black.'

'What did the black tent mean?' I asked, curiosity piqued.

'If they hadn't surrendered by then, he'd take the fortress by force, killing everyone – men, women, children, even animals.' He shook his head. 'That's one ruthless bastard.' He leaned back, adding, 'The wanderer also spoke of a great plague ravaging his lands. That's why he was here – to escape.'

'What's a plague?' I asked.

He wrung his hands together and shivered. 'From what he said, let's hope we never find out.'

I shrugged. It didn't seem important. 'I wonder where we can get a black tent – the way Derby's conducting this war, it might come in handy.'

*

The next day, Earl Derby summoned me.

With August heat already putrefying the bodies in the streets, I had a fair idea of what he wanted me for.

'Ah, my good fellow, the Idiot.' I knew I was in trouble when he used my nickname. After the previous day's sacking, he sat in the church, the least affected building. I knelt before him. 'I hope I find you well?'

I stood. 'Yes, my Lord, very well.'

'Good, that's what I like to hear.' He glanced around, then raised his head and sniffed the air. My heart sank. 'Do you smell something, Ailred?'

I sighed. 'Yes, Lord.'

'Tell me, Ailred. What is it?'

I sniffed the air to humour him. 'Mmm… if I'm not mistaken, it's rotting corpses and shit, my Lord?'

He gave a great belly laugh. 'Well, yes – there *is* that, but there's something else too.'

I gave him my well-used, vacant look. 'There is?'

'It's the smell of victory, my good man, victory.'

I nodded. 'I learn something new each day under your leadership, my Lord.'

He grinned. 'But now that you mention the unpleasant stench, I need a workforce to burn it.'

I resigned myself to the inevitable. 'Certainly, Sire, can I commandeer a working party from...'

He raised his hand. 'No, Idiot, you misunderstand me.'

'I do?'

He stood and grasped my shoulder, his face serious. 'You showed good leadership traits yesterday – you took command of the archers and set up that firestorm across the bridge. It was masterful – you saved God knows how many lives.' I nearly fainted! 'You show great promise, Idiot.' He smiled. 'Your brother may be a monster on the battlefield, but a man with insight and a connection to the men's souls is invaluable.' He nodded. 'That's something your brother sadly lacks. I will be calling on you more often, Ailred.'

It was clear my audience with him had ended, and he pointed the way out. 'Oh, and can you send your brother in – I have a rather unpleasant job for him.'

Paul waited outside in his monk's habit, his face a mask of serenity, as if the night before had never happened.

'What did he want, my child?'

I looked at him and, for the first time in years, didn't feel intimidated.

'I think my life just changed, Paul.' His fixed

smile dropped. 'Go on in – he has a little job for you.'

I walked away.

*

Earl Derby weighed the risk of delaying before striking the castles and Bastides of southern Périgord but thought better of it. If our intelligence was good, the French's likely was too. Their reinforcements could already be on the move. He made his decision and ordered us to prepare.

That evening in Bergerac, I sensed a weariness among the men. The bloodlust had burned out, leaving only reflection.

The following day, I approached the Earl as he left the church.

'Sire, forgive my candour, but the men aren't fit for another immediate campaign.'

He sniffed. 'That wasn't my first battle, Idiot!' He smiled, softening the sting of the nickname. 'But yes, they could use more rest – a luxury we can't afford.'

I started to speak, then thought better of it, stepping aside.

'But thank you, Ailred,' he added, nodding. 'I meant what I said the other day. I'll think on your words.'

'You honour me, Lord.' I walked away, feeling ten feet tall.

An hour later, he gathered the men. He stood atop a wagon stacked with arrows and addressed us.

'I know you're tired – you've not slept in days, and that small exertion recently took its toll.' A few laughs broke out, though the men sensed where this was going. 'But…' A loud groan rippled through the crowd. He paused, letting the anticipation build. 'But the smaller Bastides hold vast wealth.' He pointed towards the open countryside beyond Bergerac. 'As we speak, that fortune is being hidden or shipped out while their runners fetch reinforcements. If we do not act now...' He let the silence hang, heavy with implication.

When the mumbling quieted, he turned to me, revealing his compromise. 'Until now, other than here in Bergerac, I've demanded restraint from you men. We needed to keep the Gascons as allies. But from here on... they are *French*.' Excitement surged around me. 'We owe them nothing.' He drew his sword and raised it high. 'The towns are yours, my friends – and everything in them!'

A great roar erupted. Earl Derby knew how to motivate exhausted, greedy men.

*

We stood before the Bastide d'Eymet, a day's march from Bergerac. Its walls were formidable, but the defence was stretched thin. Even from here, I could smell their fear. Two days of wasted arrows and failed assaults passed before Earl Derby gathered his commanders in his tent.

The tent was an oven, hotter inside than out. I sat with Sir Walter, Paul, and the other men of influence.

'Right, gentlemen, we have a dilemma.' Derby sat beside a water barrel, dabbing his red face every few minutes. 'I have word that those French who escaped us in Bergerac have rallied around John, Count of Armagnac, and have retreated north to Périgueux.' He looked at us and awaited our response.

'Eh, forgive my ignorance, Earl, but where's that?' I asked as a ripple of relief passed through the tent – the idiot had asked for them all.

'At least one of you was listening. Good man, Ailred. It's a day's march north.'

Once I'd broken the silence, the others leapt in.

'Are we going to leave here and attack them?'

'Will you split the army and go north?'

I raised my hand.

'Yes, Ailred?'

'We need another tactic to breach these walls, Sire, or they'll regroup and...'

'Precisely, we've already spent too much time here.' The others glared at me, and Paul kicked me in the shin. 'As you know, I've been negotiating with their commander behind the walls, Jean d'Armagnac, through written correspondence. I'll give him credit – he's a wily old fox.' Derby looked around at our eager faces. 'I've agreed to let them surrender and take their valuables.'

Disappointment swept the tent.

Sir Walter spoke for us all. 'So we get nothing, my Lord?'

Derby grinned. 'I never said I'd honour it, Walter – only that I agreed to it.' Smiles crept back onto our faces. He turned to Nathaniel. 'I want you to go speak to d'Armagnac. He's granted safe passage for one, likely expecting me, but I won't give him that satisfaction.' He dunked his head in the water barrel, re-emerging with droplets streaming from his thinning hair. 'Do your father proud, lad. Use your boyish charms and get those gates open.'

Nathaniel grinned. 'I'll play the babe in swaddling if it gets me inside!'

Laughter followed him out.

An hour later, Nathaniel strode toward the gates, head held high. We stood well back to ensure the French didn't think we'd rush at the last moment.

'Don't worry, they trust me implicitly,' said the Earl. 'Those fools in there are only too eager to escape with their lives.'

Sir Walter nodded beside him. 'Sending Nate was wise, Sire. He's a fine orator, and his father will thank you on our return.'

'I'll admit, Walter, you were right. Sir Thomas asked me to protect him, but this could be his making.'

I squirmed. Sir Thomas had asked Paul and me first, but I doubted he still trusted us after the

Curley family incident.

As the drawbridge lowered and the portcullis lifted, Nathaniel entered. Earl Derby smiled. 'Simple fools,' he muttered.

Only I heard him.

CHAPTER 15

Nathaniel's body skipped across the dry grassland, tumbling to a halt near Earl Derby's tent. Launched from the Bastide's trebuchet, his skin was riddled with shards of bone, jutting out like splinters from a shattered mast. Blood soaked the torn flesh; his limbs twisted as if he'd been broken on a wheel before being hurled over the walls.

As I approached, my chest tightened. Earl Derby stood over the mangled body, staring in disbelief.

'Why?' was all he could manage.

I couldn't answer. Nathaniel – Sir Thomas's son – reduced to this twisted wreck. I dropped to my knees beside him, trying to control my trembling hands. His face, what was left of it, was barely recognisable. My throat was raw, words hard to form.

'They expected you, Sire,' I murmured.

Derby blinked as the shock set in. 'Me?'

'They meant for you to be lying here,' I whispered, 'this was always their plan.'

I wiped away a tear before it fell. Sir Thomas had trusted us to keep his son safe, but we had failed him.

Derby straightened, unable to hide his disbelief. 'And I called *him* a simple fool – I underestimated Black Bull of Gascony.'

Sir Walter arrived, glancing at the body, his face ashen.

Derby's expression hardened, cold rage setting in. He straightened, took a deep breath, then turned and strode toward the walls. We watched, frozen, as he planted his feet in the dirt and drew his sword. Pointing it toward the watching French on the battlements, he raised his voice, deep with anger.

'We go in – we spare *no one*.'

Godric joined me, staring at Nathaniel's distorted body. 'What the hell happened?'

'The Earl just pitched our black tent,' I said as dark thoughts consumed me.

*

We buried Nathaniel the next day. Paul led the service, his feelings buried beneath a mask of clerical detachment. Either that, or he didn't care.

As Earl Derby walked away from the graveside, his composure returned. Yesterday had shaken him, but now his resolve was set. He had sent Nathaniel into the Bastide and would live with that decision. Now was the time for retribution.

'Sir Walter, rally the men – we'll hit them from three sides. When I finish with these bastards, they'll wish they'd never been born.' His eyes showed cold calculation.

We readied ourselves. The Earl had drilled us for every possibility, and this plan required precision. We'd focus our forces on three sides, leaving the fourth unthreatened.

'I'll draw their forces away from the rear wall,' the Earl said during his final briefing, ensuring we understood our roles. 'd'Armagnac isn't stupid – he'll know what I'm doing but will have no choice. He's short on regulars – most men there are peasants and serfs. I underestimated the Bull yesterday, but you only need to be gored once to learn your lesson.'

The Bastide's walls hadn't been built for a long siege, hastily thrown up in anticipation of our invasion with the Gascons. We were confident. About two hundred yards from the rear wall lay a tangled heath where the local gentry hunted, its dense growth and rolling hills making it the perfect black spot to hide a small, lethal force of the Earl's finest, ready to strike when called upon.

I was among the chosen five hundred, and I thanked God for the chance. With Bonehead at his side, Paul would lead three hundred of our fiercest men-at-arms while Godric and I commanded the remaining two hundred archers.

'We circled to the back, taking a wide detour to stay out of sight. Crawling through the bracken, I glanced up at the rear walls. A tall gatehouse loomed over a small, fortified entrance, accessible by a narrow bridge spanning a dry moat – the river not yet diverted to complete its natural defence.

On the Earl's order, hell was unleashed as he assaulted the three sides. I watched the wall clear within moments, all men rushing to support their comrades.

Paul crawled over, shock in his voice. ‘They’ve left a couple of men in the tower, but that’s all.’

‘What the devil is d’Armagnac playing at? Why so few?’ I asked.

'Maybe the Bull’s gone mad,' Paul replied, signalling for Godric to approach. 'Can you nail those two in the tower?'

I glanced at Godric, who smiled.

I pointed. ‘If we reach that wagon unseen, we’ll drop them without a sound.’

‘Bring the ladders and keep quiet,’ Paul whispered, passing the order back to where a dozen were held out of sight. He watched the men in the tower craning their necks toward the battles on the other walls. ‘Go.’

We moved. Seconds later, we lay beneath the disused wagon, bows and quivers at the ready.

'I can’t believe d’Armagnac's allowed this wagon to be left here and this place unmanned...' I whispered, gesturing to the unguarded walls.

Godric shrugged and pulled out an arrow. I nodded and followed suit, looking to Paul for the signal.

The guards were still looking the other way when Paul pointed towards them and made a cutthroat gesture. We crawled out and knelt.

‘I’ll take the one on the right,’ I hissed.

I accounted for the stiff breeze from the south and drew a deep breath, my chest expanding as my back and shoulders strained to pull the bow to its full range. This shot demanded power and precision – there would be no second chance. The guard's head bobbed as he scanned the walls, unaware. I held steady. As the string whistled, I released.

Godric's arrow flew in perfect unison with my own, both arcing upward before finding their marks. Mine struck the base of his neck, dropping him like a marionette with its strings cut. Godric's arrow pierced the upper back, spinning the man around as the arrowhead burst through his ribs, silencing him instantly.

I glanced at Paul, who spoke with one of the page boys. The lad nodded and darted off to update Earl Derby.

Godric and I rushed the final stretch to the bridge, reaching the reinforced oak doors without being spotted. The sounds of battle grew louder as word of our successful breach reached the Earl, who committed everything to keep the defenders occupied.

Moments later, ladders were propped against the walls, and men led by Paul and Bonehead began scaling the battlements.

'To me,' I shouted to the milling archers and redundant men-at-arms, 'they'll open the gates.'

We gathered, desperate to rush inside.

'Godric, take fifty left once we're inside. I'll

take the same right. That should be enough to seize the gatehouse and get it open.'

He nodded, and we assembled our men.

A brief clash of steel echoed from the other side of the gates, heralding creaking sounds as they swung open, their movement hindered by the bodies of fallen French guards.

We surged through.

Godric and I split left and right, racing to locate the main gates while our archers and men-at-arms unleashed death upon the stunned French within. Arrows flew, picking off defenders from the walls, their bodies falling from the gantries like leaves in autumn.

Paul led from the front, bounding up the stone steps, smashing into the waiting French as he targeted the wall's platforms. Wielding his sword with both hands, he ducked their panicked defences, precisely targeting their legs. He shattered kneecaps and stripped muscle from bone, crippling the front rank time and again before pressing forward, leaving their mangled bodies to be ripped apart by those that followed.

A cloister encircled the perimeter of the Bastide, the area within a labyrinth of small shops and alleyways, making our route to the front gates easier than expected. As we ran, we encountered few souls, most opting to hide as we drew near.

Godric was already at the gatehouse's stairwell when I arrived. 'There are no regular soldiers here,' he gasped, breathless from exertion.

He was right. I hadn't seen any soldiers, and the men defending the battlements wore no livery. My heart sank as reality settled in. 'He's gone.'

'Who's gone?' Godric asked, his expression confused.

'D'Armagnac, that's who.'

Godric sighed and nodded. 'That explains their lack of defensive strategy.'

Then it struck me. 'The bastard caused this and slipped away last night with his men.'

Fighting and dying echoed around us as we spoke, but now felt hollow. The cries of torment pierced the air, transforming background noise into a haunting lament. These weren't men of violence, men who chose this path; they were townsfolk, victims of a cruel game played by men far removed from their suffering.

I glanced up the spiral staircase. 'Let's get these gates open and finish this.'

The two men guarding the main gates were still in their bakers' aprons. As soon as we stepped into the upstairs room, they dropped their weapons and begged for mercy.

'Godric, get these gates open,' I ordered, shoving the guards into a corner. 'Où est Jean d'Armagnac?'

They looked at me with terror in their eyes. I kicked one to persuade him to speak.

'Il est parti. Il est parti hier soir avec ses

hommes – s'il te plaît, ne nous fais pas de mal,' he stammered.

While Godric and the others cranked the wheel to raise the portcullis, he asked, 'What did he say?'

I'd picked up enough French over the years to understand. 'That Jean d'Armagnac left with his men last night.'

Godric stamped his foot. 'Bastard! Just as we thought – he's left these...' He gestured at the bakers. '... left these civilians to pay for his crimes. He's a bloody monster.'

I peeked out from a gatehouse slit, narrowly avoiding an arrow loosed by one of our own.

The main gates stood open, with only the final barrier left for Godric to lift. Beyond, the horde had gathered – a pack of wild dogs growling, their thirst for blood making the hairs on my neck bristle.

Then the dam broke. Godric jammed a wedge into the flywheel, and the portcullis jammed open. Thousands of men bent on destruction surged through the narrow entrance, hungry for wealth and slaughter.

By the time I reached the bottom of the spiral stairs, unarmed Frenchmen lay scattered across the floor, hacked to pieces by wide-eyed Englishmen. Wherever I turned, men and women cowered as the invaders exacted their revenge. Most had never met Nathaniel, yet his spirit fed their cruelty. The defenders deserved this fate. Skulls were split, bodies disembowelled without a shred of mercy. Each victim was savoured as if the violence itself had become a source of joy. This was pent-up frustration unleashed upon an opponent without pity.

I looked to find Earl Derby. He needed to know that the Bull had bolted. He would never allow this level of cruelty to be inflicted on civilians. I waded through a sea of suffering – blood soaked the ground, spattered the walls, and crazed men revelled in the agony they wrought. I saw hell.

I stumbled through the carnage, my faith in humankind eroding with every depraved act I witnessed. An archer, clutching a cross and weeping, pointed me toward the Temple d'Eymet, the Bastide's only church. Failing to find the earl above, I descended into the crypt.

In the flickering candlelight beneath the church, I found Earl Derby – centre stage among a circle of masked and cloaked men, their voices a low, rhythmic drone. He wore a white gown, his face partly hidden behind a ceramic mask, kneeling over a bound and gagged nun.

I went to speak, but words failed me.

Earl Derby looked sideways. 'Speak, Idiot, or get out.'

'D'Armagnac isn't here,' I said, my voice stuttering.

He laughed. 'Of course he isn't here.'

My legs nearly gave way. 'You knew?'

'Of course I knew.' He stared down at the

petrified nun. 'As soon as your runner told me the rear walls had cleared, I knew he had gone.'

I looked around at the demonic scene. 'Then why are we doing all this…?'

The Earl shook his head as if disappointed in my stupidity. 'If you think wars are won by firing a few arrows against men who enjoy it, you're more of a fool than I give you credit for. Grow up, Ailred. This is our message to Jean d'Armagnac and every Bastide and town in Périgord.'

'So that's what this is – cold calculation. You're using purgatory as a weapon?' I turned to leave, my faith in tatters.

'Join us, Ailred.'

My blood ran cold as a man stepped forward, pulling off his mask.

'If we break this one, we have others.'

It was Paul.

*

A dog barked as a naked woman clutching a child stumbled through the body-strewn street.

'Next time you fire an Englishman from a catapult, you might think twice.'

A group of men toasted the jibe as the morning sun glinted off the blood-soaked walkway.

I hadn't slept.

'Alright, you rabble – fun's over.' Earl Derby's voice exuded promise as he, Paul, and Sir Walter rode through the Bastide, a gleaming gold chain and newly claimed crucifix hanging around his neck.

I was sitting against the still-warm wall of a fired home. Most of the thatched roof was gone, its contents charred and unrecognisable.

'It's a beautiful day, and God favours our cause.' He looked towards an ever-eager Paul riding beside him. 'Is that not so, Reverend?'

Paul stopped his steed and breathed deep, closing his eyes. He looked towards the heavens. 'I had a premonition last night, Earl Derby. An angel appeared and spoke to me. The Lord said, "As the sun rises, I will give you a sign that the Almighty favours the cleansing of French abomination."'

As Paul spoke, a cockerel crowed long and loud somewhere nearby. He breathed out and glanced towards the Earl, satisfaction etched on his weary face. 'Hark, that rooster is the promised sign. Lo, the Lord is generous in His blessings, but He is not one for idle chatter. He will allow but one signal –the cockerel will not make another sound.' He held his arms wide. 'And this, my children, is God's revelation to you.'

The rooster crowed again.

He frowned. 'The devil's minion sounds a second wicked cry…' His gaze darkened as the cockerel echoed a third time. 'The beast walks amongst us – bring forth that foul creature of Beelzebub. Fill the demon with garlic, roast it, so I may consume the sins of man in your stead.'

Men around me, bleary-eyed and sick from the night before, crossed themselves and murmured thanks.

As usual, Paul would eat well.

*

We left Bastide d'Eymet and marched north toward Mussidan, where our Anglo-Gascon forces had held an isolated garrison for three years. I rode Bastard at the rear, not by choice but through her refusal to obey. As I bent forward, muttering threats into her ear, the Earl drew beside me.

'Talking to your horse, Ailred? They say it's the first sign of madness.' He laughed.

I glanced up. 'Maybe you could have a word, my Lord. She might listen to you.'

He raised a brow. 'So you think I'm mad?'

Before I could reply, he beamed. 'I'm joking, Ailred. But it brings me to why I sought you out.'

I wasn't sure what to expect, but I braced myself for whatever was coming.

'Who you saw in the crypt back there wasn't me.'

I frowned. 'He wasn't? He certainly looked familiar.'

His eyes blazed. 'I'll remind you who you're speaking to, Idiot. There's no disputing that your Lord is seated before you.'

Realising I had overstepped, I bowed my head. 'Please accept my apologies, Earl Derby. I spoke out of turn.' I lowered my gaze. 'I'm honoured to be worthy of an explanation.'

He relaxed a little and sat back on his horse.

'Apology accepted, Ailred. I'll remind you that my sunny disposition has clouds occasionally.' He paused, glancing at the horizon. 'What I did in that crypt... some might call justice. Others, madness.' I wasn't sure how to answer, so waited. The Earl filled the silence. 'Everything I do, Ailred, has a purpose.'

'Yes, Sire, I understand,' I replied, though I didn't.

'That nun was left unharmed.'

'That's good to hear, my Lord,' I said, second-guessing what I thought he wanted to hear.

'Do you know why?'I tightened my jaw, searching for a response. Luckily, he went on. 'I need that nun and every soul in that church to spread word of my evil.' I wouldn't have guessed that if given a million years. 'This is war, Ailred. We fight body and soul. I must conquer both, or none of us leave here alive.' His eyes bore into me. 'The next town will tremble at our approach. They'll know true fear – and that, my friend, will be our strongest weapon.'

The penny dropped. The suffering of their innocent was essential – their blood used for our advancement. 'They'll be too afraid to deny us, my Lord, and open their gates, throwing themselves on your mercy.'

He nodded, smiling. 'Precisely. As long as I give them the opportunity to surrender, they'll jump at it. We might need to rethink your nickname, Ailred.'

'Thank you, Lord. May I ask something?'

He considered, then shrugged. 'By all means.'

'And Paul? Was he part of this grand plan?'

At that, he broke into hysterical laughter. He wiped his tears, shaking his head. 'Don't be naive, Ailred – Paul does it because he enjoys it. There's method to my madness. Him – he's a bloody fool. You should recruit him into the Idiot Archers.'

I chuckled. 'With respect, that's a terrible idea.'

His eyes narrowed, mock offence creeping in.

I quickly added, 'I said "*with respect*", Lord. It absolves me of any wrongdoing.'

He laughed again. 'Well played, Ailred. I'll have to remember to say that next time I call the King a stupid...'

Sir Walter pulled up beside us, cutting him short.

'My Lord, we approach Prigonrieux. Do we bypass or stop for supplies?'

'Is it fortified?' the Earl asked.

'It is, my Lord, but no real threat.'

The Earl removed his cap, slicked back his hair, and checked his water container with satisfaction. He glanced at me. 'We're well stocked from d'Eymet, but let's see their reaction, shall we, Ailred – see if word has spread?'

I grinned. 'Could be interesting, my Lord.'

I tried to follow, but Bastard veered left.

'Going somewhere, Ailred?' he called, laughing.

*

The gates stood open as we arrived.

A select few of us accompanied the Earl and Sir Walter through the unmanned gatehouse. In the market square, a group of finely dressed elders waited, holding ceramic jugs of wine. They offered one to the Earl, who drank deeply before nodding for us to do the same. Fear rippled through the townsfolk, who peered out of windows to watch the English Devil accept their hospitality.

The Earl tossed the jug back to an elderly nun, her face a mix of fear and defiance. He stared into her eyes until she looked away.

'Finish up, boys,' he said. 'I have my answer.'

We left for Mussidan.

CHAPTER 16

The people of Mussidan welcomed us with unbridled enthusiasm. Their town, allied to us, had withstood every French assault, reinforced only when King Edward or Gaston Fébus, Count of Foix, could spare a few men. Seeing an army of our size stirred excitement, and they swarmed around us as though we were royalty.

Their joy soon faded.

I sat at a long table in Commander Bidal d'Auos's study as his kitchen staff served boiled pork with baby eels.

Since Nathaniel's death and witnessing Derby's ruthless display of power, I had been included in most of the Earl's meetings. Nathaniel's death was my gain. With it came the weight of command. I began to see Earl Derby in a new light. Everything he did had meaning and was considered, and I could see why King Edward held him in such high regard. Paul sat at the far end of the table, his sullen glare a reminder of how far we'd drifted. He saw my rise as a threat. He'd belittle me whenever I tried to speak, and my indifference only fed his anger. I was beginning to enjoy the control I had over him.

'So, in short, Lord Bidal, I cannot leave you any of my men.' Earl Derby's tone left no room for debate as he watched the Gascon commander grasp the hard truth. 'I'll be leaving my sick and wounded with your chirurgeon, too.

'But, Earl Derby, we scarcely have enough food. More mouths will hamper...'

'I'm under strict orders from King Edward. I tell you this as a courtesy, nothing more. Once we've rested, we head east towards Périgueux.'

Lord Bidal looked crestfallen, but Derby found a way of softening the blow.

'We've ample supplies, my Lord,' Derby added, his voice firm but reassuring. 'I'll leave most of it with you. It should see you through until this phase of the campaign concludes. We'll find enough towns and Bastides to keep us fed.' He turned to me. 'Isn't that right, Ailred?'

I met Paul's gaze before answering. 'It seems so, my Lord. The townsfolk won't soon forget us.'

*

Over the next few days, we rested. The wounded from the attack on d'Eymet took beds in the Hôtel-Dieu, displacing the less critical already housed there. Commander Bidal d'Auos wasn't pleased but had resigned himself to the inconvenience. The men found accommodation wherever they could, with the Earl and Sir Walter given priority. I had hoped I might be favoured too, being at the side of the Earl most of the time, but I soon found special treatment only stretched so far.

'I have a barn.' Paul's voice pulled me around.

He sat alone on a low wall outside the church, his silhouette stark against the fading light.

I folded my arms. 'Good for you.'

He snorted and spat on a scavenging dog. 'Want to bunk in with me?'

I hesitated, catching something lost in his eyes.

'Where's Bonehead?'

His expression hardened. 'Haven't seen him since d'Eymet.'

'Not staying in the barn with you?

'No, it's just me.' He paused, softer now. 'There's plenty of room for us both.'

After Bergerac and d'Eymet, the men had distanced themselves from Paul. His brutality at both those towns had been too much even for them.

We locked eyes before he smiled and rubbed the dog's head, wiping his spit into its fur.

And so, I moved in with Paul. As a favour to me, he agreed to let Godric stay as well, but Godric wasn't having any of it.

'You're a good man, Al, but your brother's got you wrapped around his finger,' he said before wandering off to find his own sleeping quarters.

His words echoed something Philippa used to say, reminding me that perhaps I was too easy on Paul.

That night, as we lay in the dark, the sounds of restless cattle and pigs close by, we settled down. Paul grew reflective. 'What happened to Izelda?'

'Paul, I've been married to Philippa for years, and you never remember her name – now, out of the blue, you bring up a woman I had a brief fling with! What goes on in that brain of yours?'

He chuckled to himself. 'I remember her. She was smart.'

'Philippa's smart,' I said, irritated. 'If you'd bothered to get to know her, you would know.'

He went silent for a few seconds. 'How come you manage to attract intelligent women?'

I'd never considered this question and wasn't sure whether to take it as an insult or a compliment. Then I realised I had no answer.

'You'd have to ask them both.' I turned over and closed my eyes.

'I will,' he replied, and within seconds, the barn was filled with the sounds of resting animals and Paul's snoring.

'You'll ask *both*?'

No answer.

*

I awoke to a rough tongue licking my ear.

'What the fuck…?'

Paul laughed. 'Just 'cos you sleep till noon doesn't mean these beautiful creatures have to.'

He had released the pigs from their pens and was ushering them outside. One had stopped to sample my earwax.

I scooped slime out and flicked it in Paul's direction. 'What time is it?'

'I told you, it's noon.'

It patently wasn't, as the sun was just peeking through the barn's wide-open gates. Chickens were hurrying around, picking up food scattered on the floor outside.

'Should you be letting all these animals loose?' I asked, pulling on my boots and glancing around for a place to relieve myself. 'Very charitable of you to do the farmer's job for him, Paul.'

'That's me – Mr Charitable,' he grinned, leading me around the back. Behind a rusting anvil, he pulled out a wriggling sack. He loosened the cord, revealing half a dozen dead or dying chickens and a piglet with its legs bound.

'I'll fill it before we leave – we'll not go hungry.'

I sighed. 'You'll never change.'

He raised an eyebrow. 'A good woman might change me!'

I laughed. 'She'd have to be a bloody big one.'

He knotted the top again, replaced it, and we returned to the barn's entrance. As we arrived, Sir Walter approached.

'Get your men together, lads – we move out within the hour.'

'Your will, my Lord.' I grabbed my few belongings and went to find Godric and the rest of the Archers.

'I'll see you on the road, Paul,' I called back, but he was already darting about, cleaver in hand, cutting down anything that looked edible.

*

We rode towards Périgueux. We were in good

spirits, and every village we happened upon opened its gates to us, offering food and water.

By the afternoon of the second day, I rode at the head of the column with Earl Derby and Sir Walter as we neared Chancelade, a town an hour from Périgueux. Though we had full provisions, the Earl insisted on gathering intelligence, cautious, despite believing Périgueux lacked a French presence.

'The Abbey of Chancelade, here, is said to be stunning.' Those were his final words before we passed through the gates.

Like other towns, the people stayed hidden behind shutters, leaving the clerics to speak for them. The abbey was a disappointment – whitewashed and plain, nothing like the splendour Derby had hoped for.

His face betrayed a hint of frustration, but he rode ahead alone to meet the Abbot, who welcomed him with polite smiles and cautious gestures. They spoke out of earshot, the Abbot pointing toward Périgueux while the Earl listened, nodding.

Monks approached with water and practised smiles as we waited in the afternoon sun, welcoming us warmly. The place was calm, yet something beneath the surface put me on edge. Still, the Earl seemed satisfied when he returned.

'I was right. Few soldiers remain in Périgueux, and the defences are crumbling. The Abbot insists we camp here for the night.'

Sir Walter rallied Paul and me and ordered us to make camp. I was relieved – rest was welcome.

'Godric, get the Idiots to work,' I snapped, enjoying my newly gained authority.

Godric snarled and bowed. 'Your will, my Lord,' he replied.

Paul sent Bonehead to do the same with the men-at-arms.

We'd sleep in the shadows of the abbey and continue onto Périgueux in the morning.

*

'Get your men up. NOW.'

I was shaken awake by Sir Walter.

'What's going on?'

'The French are coming!'

Godric scrambled for his boots.

'Get them ready, Godric,' I shouted, 'I'll find the Earl.'

I ran to catch up with Sir Walter.

The Earl stood with his inner circle – Paul among them. As I arrived, I caught the tail end of their exchange.

'No, it's sound intelligence,' Derby said. 'Our spy delivered it personally.'

The men's expressions were dark with fury.

Paul saw my confused look. 'It's the Abbot, Al,' he said. 'He's set us up.'

Derby's voice cut through. 'Get the men ready to move. Leave anything we don't need. Thousands are coming – we can't fight them here – it's strategically untenable.'

I stared at Paul in disbelief.

'We run, my Lord?' I asked.

'Don't question my orders. Move.'

Godric and I scrambled together supplies, loading them onto horses. As we prepared to escape, the Earl and Paul approached. There was fire in Derby's eyes.

'I want you two to wait behind and burn this abbey to the ground. I can't allow the Abbot to double-cross me.'

Paul grinned. 'And if the monks resist?'

'I have no quarrel with them. Defend yourselves, nothing more. The same goes for the Abbot. Stay close and report how many French arrive – I need to know their strength.' He met my gaze. 'And don't get caught. I don't want another Nathaniel on my hands.'

He tossed me a flint and walked away.

'The Earl will dig in a mile east,' Paul said as we gathered kindling. 'The French won't give chase. They'll retreat back to Périgueux when they don't find us here.'

'Did you see the spy? What did he tell you?'

Paul laughed. 'Yes, I saw him.'

'What's so funny?'

'A fuckin' spy? We're about to torch this place, and that's what's on your mind?' He shook his head.

'I just want to know if it's solid intel. We're about to torch an abbey, for Christ's sake.'

Paul chuckled again. 'It's solid. And it's an

order. We'll talk about the spy after we've finished here and thousands of Frenchmen show up, if you want. By then, you'll realise he just saved our lives.'

We took the kindling to the church, finding the front doors locked.

'They don't lock abbeys at night,' I muttered, ramming my shoulder against the door. 'People come to pray at all hours.'

'Aye, and the Abbot likely wants to keep nasty folk out.' Paul smirked. 'He'll know the Earl's reputation. Come on – round the back.'

The door by the sacristy was locked too, but it didn't take long to knock it down. The room smelled of wax and incense, a reminder of Sundays with Philippa and the children at Mass. Dozens of candles were scattered throughout the abbey, their pale flames flickering, casting just enough light to guide our heretical actions.

'These wicks are fresh,' I said. 'Someone's been here recently.'

Paul stared at the windows, where Christ's suffering was painted in shards of coloured glass. 'There's no trust left anymore. When we were kids, churches and anything religious were sacrosanct.' He shook his head. 'What's happened to us, Ailred, when priests have no choice but to lock away God's earthly treasures? I despair sometimes.' He picked up a cassock and pulled it over his light armour. 'I want to look the part when we burn this place,' he said, his voice dripping with excitement.

'Don't you feel the slightest guilt, Paul? You spent years in an abbey, living this life.'

But it was pointless. He had already piled the kindling next to the altar, tossing choir boys' clothing and ruffs on top.

He halted, tilting his head back, his face bathed in the moonlight filtering through the stained glass. 'The altar, the beams – it's all timber,' he breathed.

'What are you doing, for God's sake?' The voice broke Paul's spell. In the dim shadows of the apse behind the altar, the Abbot knelt, hands clasped in fervent prayer. 'You must leave God's house, my children. He will forgive your blasphemous thoughts and deeds. Go now, before it is too late.'

His English was broken, his plea faltering through repressed sobs.

'Before what's too late?' Paul asked. He stepped past me, straightened his cassock, and pulled the hood up.

The Abbot's eyes flicked to him, his fear heightening. He struggled to his feet. 'The soldiers, they come for you – you must leave.'

Paul halted, his hood still drawn. 'How do you know?'

'I... I just know.'

'You swore to us safe refuge here.' Paul began to sway. 'You promised there were no soldiers in Périgueux. All lies.' He pulled down his hood and darted forward, his face stopping inches from the Abbot's. 'You're no better than Judas Iscariot.' He drew a coin from his pocket, twisting it between his fingers. 'Is this the cost of your loyalty, or do you need thirty pieces of silver?' The Abbot was silent, his eyes staring into Paul's. 'And how did Judas identify our lord in those final moments?'

I sank to my knees, bowed my head, and prayed silently. There was nothing I could do.

The Abbot lowered his eyes. 'He kissed Jesus on both cheeks.'

Paul lifted the Abbot's chin and kissed him, slow and deliberate. He placed the coin into the Abbot's gaping mouth before silently drawing his knife and plunging it deep into his heart.

He turned to me and smiled. 'Let's burn it.'

*

I lit the kindling in silence, Paul insisting I be the one to do it.

'No choice, Ailred – it's Derby's order.'

'But this is so wrong.'

Paul laughed, nodding at the dead Abbot sprawled across the altar. 'Time for reflection passed a while ago.'

As the flames caught, the scrape of a key echoed from the nave.

'Let's go,' I urged, shoving Paul toward the sacristy exit.

We fled outside.

From the east, hooves and marching boots pounded toward us.

'They're here,' I whispered. 'Quick.'

We sprinted for a low hill shrouded in thick woodland.

By the time we reached it, breathless, I glanced back. Smoke poured from the abbey, flames breaking through the roof tiles.

'Forgive me,' I whispered.

At the summit, sunlight spilt across the dry late-summer landscape. I shaded my eyes, watching thousands of French soldiers swarm the abbey, desperate to save the church.

'That's why he wanted us to fire it,' Paul said. I frowned. 'He knew they'd stay to put it out.'

It made sense – typical of the Earl's cunning.

'We have all the information we need,' I said, scanning for a path through the trees. 'They outnumber us two to one.'

Paul nodded. 'At least.'

*

We found the Earl and our army in a fortified position on a hill about a mile away and made our report.

'That's about the number I expected – enough to hold the city.' He sat at the summit in his tent, surrounded by counsellors, setting out our position. 'Despite their numbers, the French are in disarray. Those who escaped us at Bergerac split in two.' He pulled a map closer, and we leaned in. 'The ones who went south regrouped under Bertrand de L'Isle and are dug in here, at La Réole.' He tapped the parchment. 'It's their strongest Garonne fortress, so they likely feel safe.'

'We'll see about that,' someone muttered.

Laughter rippled through the men, but the Earl waited for it to die. Then his voice dropped. 'The rest rallied around our old friend Count Jean d'Armagnac, and we all know how that ended.'

Silence fell. A murmur of disgust swept the ranks. Every man here had sworn vengeance for Nathaniel, butchered at d'Armagnac's hands. His name alone was enough to set fire to their rage.

The Earl traced a line from Bergerac to Périgueux. 'And as we've just discovered, they've arrived here.' He circled the city with a piece of charcoal. 'So, this is what we face. They outnumber us, and they have the advantage of fortifications.' He tossed the charcoal into the fire. Sparks flared, and anger simmered. 'Thoughts, gentlemen?'

Sir Walter stood back. 'Your intel is impeccable, my Lord.'

The Earl nodded. 'We'd be dead without it, Walter. I am hopeful it continues, but the French aren't fools…'

'I beg to differ, Sire…' A few chuckles.

He let them pass. '…they're not fools, and they'll search for the source.'

'Is it someone within their ranks?' I asked before I could stop myself.

The Earl smiled. 'Ailred, *forget* the spy. That's my concern.'

Paul nudged me, whispering, 'Told you.'

We debated strategy, settling on a course of action.

'I need us on the same page. We harry and besiege, cutting off their supply lines. No heroics. We wait for the right time before launching a full assault.'

We pledged our cause, and the Earl dismissed us.

'Ailred, a word before you leave?' I stopped. Paul hesitated beside me. 'Alone,' Derby said.

Paul shot me a glare but left.

Once we were alone, the Earl leaned back, scratching his greying beard. 'How did Paul behave back there?'

The question caught me off guard. 'In what way, Sire?'

'I've lost trust in his mental state. Did he do anything beyond carrying out my orders?' I hesitated. 'I need the truth, Ailred. I've heard terrible stories…'

'He followed your orders to the letter, my Lord.' I felt my face warm.

'And the Abbot – Paul told me he attacked him. True?'

'As we reported, Sire, the Abbot had ample chance to flee, but his violence forced Paul's hand.'

The Earl studied me, waiting. I glanced away.

'Fair enough, Ailred,' he said at last. 'Trust is everything. I'll keep an eye on him. You may leave.'

Outside, Paul was waiting, his eyebrows raised.

'What did he say?'

I kept walking.

'WHAT DID HE SAY?'

He grabbed my shoulder, spinning me around. His eyes blazed before he forced himself to steady.

'I said we carried out the orders to the word.' I shrugged him off.

'Good.' Paul stepped back. 'As long as you told him the truth, we'll be fine.'

He turned and strode off, but something lingered – a tension beneath his words. His control was slipping. I watched him walk away.

I wondered, not for the first time, if Paul was losing his grip on reality. Tintern Abbey had been the only place to steady him, the only thing that had ever tamed his madness. But we were a long way from Wales. And if he unravelled here, there would be no way back – for either of us.

CHAPTER 17

'There are two strongholds defending the main routes into Périgueux,' Derby said as we gathered around his table the following day. 'Here, at Coulounieix-Chamiers… and there, to the south, at Boulazac.' He turned the map for all to see.

The heat lingered, another warm day after a long, dry summer. Our scouts had returned in the night, confirming the enemy's withdrawal to Périgueux.

'If we're to choke the city, we need them neutralised.'

Around the table, every face was intense with anticipation, hungry for the honour of leading the task.

'I'll take Coulounieix-Chamiers. Sir Walter, Boulazac is yours.'

'I am honoured, Lord Derby,' Sir Walter replied, bowing.

'Speak to the scouts about numbers and defences. Choose who you think best.' Derby turned to me. 'Ailred, pick two hundred of your finest Idiots.' His gaze flicked between Paul and Bonehead. 'And I'll need a couple hundred men-at-arms… Paul. Bring a company of Gascons, too.'

Paul beamed. 'As you command, Lord Derby.'

By the end of the briefing, everyone knew their place in the apparatus Derby was building.

'Well, that's reassuring.' Paul sidled up as the meeting broke. I was talking to Godric, who made a quick excuse and left to round up our archers.

'What's reassuring?' I asked.

Paul punched my arm. 'Derby picked me to lead the infantry. He needs men he can count on when the killing starts.' He grinned.

I shook my head. 'No, Paul. He wants to keep an eye on you.'

Paul stopped, eyes narrowing. 'Didn't know it was *this* bad...' He studied me. 'I knew you were jealous as a kid, but I figured you'd grown up.'

I stared, lost for words, then found two. 'Fuck off.'

Paul laughed. 'Truth stings, doesn't it?'

I moved to confront him, but Sir Walter and the Earl exited the tent.

'What are you two lingering for? Didn't I ask you to sort out the raiding party?' Derby frowned. 'Did I choose the wrong men?'

Paul shot me a look of contempt. 'Apologies, my Lord, Ailred was seeking my advice.' He turned, striding away, then tossed over his shoulder, 'Think for yourself, little brother – I can't wipe your nose forever.'

*

I threw myself into work, refusing to let Paul chip away at my confidence. Earl Derby knew my worth – he wouldn't let the ramblings of a man losing his grip sway him. Or would he? The two had been close at the start of this chevauchée, and I suspected Derby had even entrusted Paul with the spy's identity, though Paul denied it.

By afternoon, my archers were primed and ready. I'd been meticulous – thousands of arrows secured on dozens of wagons, with Godric grumbling about me wasting time as I added hundreds of maces and war hammers. Finally, satisfied we had everything, I took my place at the head of the convoy on Bastard.

Earl Derby approached. 'Nice of you to turn up, Idiot. If you hurry, you might catch up with your brother and the Gascons.'

I grimaced but held my tongue. Paul had left early on purpose, making me look slow – and worse, stretching our column thin. If enemies were lurking, he'd given them the perfect chance to ambush.

As we pushed forward, I vented to Godric. 'Paul's making a bloody spectacle – and putting us all at risk.'

Godric gave a half-smile. 'There's no French army outside Périgueux, Ailred. And I doubt any locals would dare attack.' He shrugged, knowing that wasn't the point. I needed to let off steam before Paul got under my skin.

We didn't catch up to the rear wagons until we neared Coulounieix-Chamiers. As I rode into camp, Paul's men-at-arms were already lounging, their tents set up.

Earl Derby rode in, his bodyguard close.

'No fire, no smoke. We are mice until tomorrow.'

He needed to say no more.

*

The next day, I woke to Paul's barked orders – unusual, since he never rose early by choice. As a child, he was a whirlwind all day, unable to sit still until he crashed. Mornings were a different story. Waking him was like rousing the dead.

'If the Idiots sleep in, they'll miss the spoils.'

I pulled on my clothing as the sounds of horses and clanking armour shattered the dawn's tranquillity.

By the time I emptied my bowels and grabbed a few slices of cold mutton and a hunk of bread, Paul and his men were leaving with the Earl.

'I'm not sure we need the girls, my Lord,' Paul laughed as I wrestled with Bastard, trying to get her to line up at the front of the procession.

The Earl chuckled. 'Now then, Paul, you won't feel that way when they're dropping all sorts on our heads, and their girls are peppering us with arrows.'

They likely exchanged more words, but Bastard chose that moment to wander off in the opposite direction.

An hour later, I arrived with a squire leading Bastard by the bridle. We gathered in the woods overlooking the stronghold guarding the bridge to Périgueux. Towering gatehouses flanked the river, their walls stretching into the distance.

At its centre, a drawbridge linked the stone structure to our side, its chains poised to retract. Wagons trundled in and out, each load scrutinised by ever-watchful guards.

'I want that bridge taken before they even think to raise it,' the Earl said as we weighed our options. 'No point charging in and finding the drawbridge is gone.' He gave Paul a pointed look. 'Are you hearing me?'

Paul said nothing, only nodding.

The Earl turned to me. 'Ailred, scout east. The river's too wide and fast to the west – no chance for rafts. Godric, go with him. We'll ferry men across and strike from behind. Stay unseen and report back the moment you find a suitable place to ford. We move the instant you return.' As Godric and I readied to leave, Derby added, 'Paul, get the men cutting wood and find a long length of rope.'

'Yes, Sire,' Paul replied, a hint of annoyance in his voice.

Godric and I left through the thick woodland, staying out of sight as we headed east. The trees pressed close to the river, and after a while, we were far enough from the gatehouse and bridge to avoid being seen.

'Men are patrolling those walls, Ailred,' Godric said as we stopped and crouched in a thicket a hundred yards from the river.

I'd already seen heads bobbing along the platform – only a few men, by my reckoning.

The wall was no more than fifteen feet high, built on raised earth banks with a muddy marsh between it and the river. We could use a grappling hook to scale it, but the operation required complete secrecy.

'What if Derby and the men-at-arms hit the main gate like at Bastide d'Eymet?' Godric whispered as another guard paced the battlements.

'Won't work. These are professionals – they won't budge. We need those lookouts gone.'

Godric sighed. 'Too far for arrows.'

I sat back, staring at the walls. 'We need someone inside to take care of those guards.' Then it came to me. 'Godric, I need to speak to the Earl.'

*

On our return, I pitched my idea, and Earl Derby turned to Jouan de Montfort, the leader of the small Gascon company accompanying us. 'So, Jouan, do you think it's possible?'

Jouan smiled, his eyes alive. 'I'm honoured to get the chance, Lord. I was a businessman before a soldier, Earl Derby, so, yes, I could convince those guards to grant four Gascon merchants entry. Any more than that would raise suspicion.' He looked around at our scattered belongings. 'But I would need something to sell.'

Derby looked at me and frowned. 'Would four be enough – we get one attempt at this?'

I nodded. 'If they could take them out without

raising the alarm, I could get enough over the wall to secure the gates, Sire.'

The Earl paused, then commanded, 'Jouan, search the camp for anything worth selling. Paul, help him load a couple of wagons with whatever you decide on. Stash their weapons beneath the wagons somehow – and have as many ropes with grappling hooks as you can find ready for Ailred.'

At once, everyone scattered to carry out his orders.

With ample provisions, Jouan decided to pose as a caterer, knowing Périgueux's dwindling supplies meant any food would be welcomed. Guards would take their share, but that was expected.

Half an hour later, everything was ready.

Paul pulled me aside. 'You think you're so clever, don't you?'

I was dumbfounded. 'What the hell are you talking about?'

'You've been planning to undermine me this whole trip; now I'm just someone to fetch and carry...'

I cut him off. 'Me? Everything you've done has aimed to make me look incompetent.'

He opened his mouth to retort, but the Earl interrupted. 'Ailred, take a hundred of your men and those ropes and get into position. I'll give you enough time before sending the Gascons in. No bows – this will be hand-to-hand.' He turned to Paul. 'Outfit your brother with maces and hammers.'

Paul's face reddened. 'We only have enough for our men-at-arms, my Lord. If I give them to Ailred...'

Derby's eyes widened. 'You didn't bring extra? If you'd not rushed about, you might've done your job properly.'

I jumped in. 'Don't you remember, Paul? You asked me to bring them with our arrows.'

Paul looked astonished, then reacted with scorn. 'Of course.' He raised his eyebrows at me. 'I told you we'd need them – luckily, you listened.'

The Earl shook his head. 'Just go and take that bridge.'

I glared at Paul and left.

A short while later, we crouched by the river, the crude raft we'd built hidden beside us. Godric, a strong swimmer, volunteered to cross with the rope as soon as Jouan and his men took out the sentries. Once inside, he'd secure the rope, allowing us to pull the raft back and forth across the water until everyone was safely across.

Just as I considered sending a runner back to Earl Derby to see if they'd been apprehended, the first guard was tossed over the battlements, landing in a heap below. Three others followed, their bodies crumpling on impact. Moments later, Jouan appeared, raising his arm and beckoning us forward.

We sprang into action. We all wore the

bare minimum – any heavier mail would have dragged us straight to the riverbed. Within seconds, Godric was in the water, rope tied around his waist. He slipped in, the current taking him downstream a few yards, but once across he came back up the bank opposite us. He hauled the raft, loaded with weapons and the non-swimmers. I managed the rope on our side, pulling the raft back for the next load and repeating the process until we all stood at the base of the wall. While this was underway, ropes with hooks were thrown up, secured by the Gascons above. Minutes later, we were in, lying silently on the upper walkway.

I led as we crept along the narrow rampart, staying as close to the wall as possible, out of sight of anyone below. About two hundred yards ahead, I could see the gate towers.

'Hang back with half the men, Godric,' I whispered. 'We'll capture both towers at once. I'll take the furthest one. As soon as you see me kill the guards on that tower, you strike the nearest.

He nodded, and I signalled for the men to split into two groups.

We reached the steps at the rampart's end and descended single file.

A watchman's cry cut the silence.

'*PRENDRE LES ARMES*!'

It was only a matter of time and expected, and as the French guards ran to arm themselves, we fanned out, cutting them down. Within seconds, rooms built into the walls were emptied, and dozens of armed men were piling out. The guards retreating took heart and joined the attack. We met them head-on, the sound of metal meeting bone echoing. Only the duty guards were fully armoured, and the rest were as vulnerable as we were.

I was first into the fray, my mace ripping the face from the first man as he took his eyes off me. Instantly, I was forced into a desperate defensive parry as a pike was thrust towards my belly. Once I'd dodged the jagged spike, the man was within my range, his hands gripping the shaft. I crushed his kneecap, bending it until he fell forward; the man next to me caved the back of his skull and put him down. Again, I had to defend, and neither side gave an inch. My next opponent swung a curved sword, howling like a banshee. He was young and terrified. I allowed him to swing at my head, stepped back, and as the sword whistled past my face, he left himself open. I headbutted him square in the face, stunning him. He held his hands up in panic, eyes closed, inexperience his downfall. He never saw the spikes as I buried them into his forehead. I glanced towards the gatehouse door, but there were so many Frenchmen in between. They started to push us back, my men fighting like wildcats. If we didn't take the towers and keep the gates open, we were all dead. Cries of pain became overwhelming; most were my companions. I realised we were losing. The men facing us could sense it, too, their eyes alive and murderous. This is when training and belief win or lose battles and lives. My instinct was to flee, but I knew that would mean death. So I fought on. Every man I killed was a bonus. I resigned to my fate and killed until I would meet my own. Four crazed Frenchmen drove me back. I took the first in the ear, spikes ripping half his face away – but it left me defenceless.

Then came the crash of steel behind them. Godric and his men had disobeyed my orders and flanked them. They steamed into the rear and smashed them, their explosive violence crippling the French resolve. Heads turned, and I could hear Godric screaming challenges. With every head that swivelled, I broke another body. Blood, brains and shit spilt as the battle turned.

I have never felt so happy to see Paul. He and his men charged across the bridge to join the fray. He took on three weary French soldiers as one and destroyed them, his face the devil reincarnated as he swept all to hell. He was growling and laughing as the enemy broke.

I slumped to the ground as the fresh legs of the new men chased and finished the slaughter.

*

Too many good men died that day.

Seeing our trouble, Godric had split his men – sending a small group to secure his tower while diverting the Gascons to the other. Thank

God he did. They overpowered the drawbridge controllers and held it down. Once Paul and his men crossed, the French defenders' fate was sealed.

We secured the area, buried our dead, and put the wounded and captured French to the sword. Their bodies were tossed into the river, the current carrying them to Périgueux as a warning.

Later, Earl Derby rode up, smiling. 'I am reliably informed that Sir Walter had a similar result to us, so we now control the thoroughfares into Périgueux.'

We mustered a halfhearted cheer, but too many friends lay dead for it to mean much.

'Will we attack the city, Lord?' I asked as Godric bandaged a minor wound to my arm.

He drew in a breath through his teeth. 'I haven't decided yet, Ailred. I'm still waiting on the numbers inside. We'll likely have to play a waiting game with their defences and the forces I suspect they have.' He gestured toward a wagon of food. 'But they'll be a lot hungrier than us. When you boys are ready, get fed. You've earned it.'

He turned his horse and trotted back to his command post.

I glanced toward the city, which was about a mile away, with its encircling curtain wall.

'Without siege engines and another twenty thousand men, we'll never get in,' I muttered as the bandage tightened.

'Aye,' Godric said, nodding, 'but they won't risk attacking and leaving themselves exposed either.'

I nodded. 'Stalemate.'

*

For weeks, nothing went in or out of Périgueux – or so we thought. We sent out scouts, searching for signs of starvation. We found none – far from it. In mockery, they waved live chickens at us, so we picked off a few guards from the battlements in return. It became a game of sorts. But one thing was clear – they had the numbers.

So we braced for a long siege. But it wasn't to be.

One morning, Derby summoned his advisors. We found ourselves before a stern-faced Earl.

I leaned toward Godric. 'Bet he starts with, "I have it on good…"' But Derby beat me to it.

'I have it on good authority that King Philip has appointed his son, John, the Duke of Normandy, as senior military leader in Périgord.'

'Philip's son?' I cut in. 'I thought the Duke of Bourbon held that post.'

'Sharp as ever, Idiot. But he's been replaced.' Derby seemed to relish using that name again, enjoying my irritation. His praise after our last fight had steadied me, so I'd spoken up. 'So, you know what that means?' Derby asked, his eyes sweeping the room.

'I'm sure Ailred will enlighten us,' Paul

quipped, drawing chuckles and a few rolled eyes.

The Earl's stare locked onto him, silencing the room. 'You tell us, Paul. I'd like to hear your thoughts.'

Paul flushed, shifting in his seat.

'Go on,' Derby pressed. 'You seem to have all the answers – what's the significance?'

I opened my mouth to speak, but Derby raised his hand to stop me.

A tense moment passed. I half-expected Paul to snap – attack Derby or storm out. Instead, he stood, walked to the map fixed behind the Earl, and studied it.

'He'll be baying for our blood, my Lord,' Paul began, his voice steady. 'And if the Duke of Normandy plans to face us on the field, he'll have his father's full backing. That means he'll come with twenty thousand men at least – veterans, all of them.' His eyes flicked to me. Then he pointed to a spot on the map, distant from our two strongholds. 'He'll want to join Jean d'Armagnac's men, so they'll follow the river down, entering Périgueux here.' He tapped the map with precision. 'Well fortified. We can't stop them with our numbers.'

He turned back to Derby, his face impassive. 'Have I missed anything, my Lord?'

The Earl leaned back, a hint of a smile on his lips. 'Paul Christian, you astonish me. Demons drive you to madness, yet in moments like these, you show flashes of brilliance.' He looked around the room, reading the astonishment on our faces. 'And he's spot-on.'

Paul sat back down. I gave him a nod of approval for handling the moment so well, to which he leaned sideways and farted.

Back to square one.

The rest of the meeting was spent convincing the Earl to let us stand and fight, but he was dead-set on playing the long game.

'We'll get our moment in the sun, boys,' he said, gathering his things together. 'But until then, have faith – we're leaving.'

And that was that. We were turning tail and running.

CHAPTER 18

We made our way toward the small town of Boulazac Isle Manoire and set up camp. It felt like defeat, though not a single arrow had been fired. Sir Walter arrived shortly after, bound by the Earl's command, his face set in the same grim frustration. His losses had been heavy; each inch of ground gained drenched in blood, only to be handed back by retreat. As the sun dipped below the horizon, casting long shadows over the camp, a grave silence fell over the assembled men. Our combined forces gathered, weary and disheartened.

Sir Walter put on a brave face as he shook the Earl's hand. 'Greeting, Lord Derby. It would seem we find ourselves at a disadvantage.'

The Earl nodded but smiled. 'A disadvantage is an opportunity, my friend. It leads to overconfidence in our foe. We will exploit such oversights.' He slapped Sit Walter on his shoulder. 'Rest and take sustenance – we will reconvene later. We have much to discuss.'

The Earl turned and glanced over the camp. I sensed he was always two steps ahead, seeing further than any of us.

I was halfway through an ale with Godric at the time. 'You have to give it to Derby,' I said, 'I've never met a more optimistic man in my life.'

Godric grinned. 'He could sunbathe in a snowstorm.'

*

'We have twelve hundred men.'

A heavy silence settled over Earl Derby's tent after his bleak summary.

Sir Walter sighed. 'We're lambs caught in a wolf's den, my Lord.'

Derby chuckled, shaking his head. 'Lambs? I see lions, Sir Walter, ready to roar. Don't underestimate our strengths. We have twelve hundred of the finest warriors I've fought beside.' He glanced around at our doubtful faces and laughed. 'You think I'm feeding you nonsense?' He leaned in, as if revealing a secret. 'These men are our lifeblood, the foundation of victory.' We sat up straighter, drawn in by his certainty. 'Respect them – they are our path to greatness.' A bolt of energy shot through us, a collective surge of invincibility. Derby pointed to a spot on the map in front of him. 'Louis of Poitier is besieging the castle of Auberoche, and I intend to go to their aid. Frank van Hallen is holed up there.' Derby glanced in my direction. 'I should prefix my next sentence with "I have it on good authority" for Ailred's benefit.' He smiled knowingly at me. 'I have it on good authority... that Louis has at least seven thousand men in the field.'

I couldn't help laughing out loud. Even my hushed words behind his back didn't escape the

Earl's attention.

'True, we're outnumbered, and that's a reality I couldn't change, but we're in the privileged position to be free provocateurs.' He looked at our confused expressions and laughed. 'We can cause as much havoc as we like – no one knows where we are.' He glanced at Sir Walter. 'A disadvantage is an opportunity.'

I leaned back in my chair, swept up in his confidence. If he saw a way forward, I'd gladly follow.

The rest of the meeting dealt with camp chores – sentry duties, latrine setup, the usual. As we were about to break, Derby said, 'Oh, almost forgot – we might have reinforcements coming.'

Sir Walter laughed. 'And you nearly forgot such a trivial matter, my Lord?'

Derby grinned. 'Slipped my mind. It's not definite, but Laurence de Hastings might meet up with us – if he can find us.'

'The Earl of Pembroke?' Sir Walter's excitement was barely hidden.

'The very same.'

'I served with him on the Welsh borders a few years ago. A fine man. We'll wait for him before relieving the castle?'

Derby nodded. 'That's the plan, Walter. I'd be crazy not to.'

*

Three days later, one of the Earl's outriding scouts returned with damning news. John, the

Duke of Normandy, commanding an army of ten thousand men, was closing in fast, searching for us. It was exactly what we'd dreaded.

'We move – now.' Earl Derby's voice cut through the tension. 'We can't wait any longer for Pembroke.'

As we rushed to break camp and load the wagons, I muttered to Godric, 'Looks like we're going solo. I just hope he knows what he's doing.'

We were set to leave late in the day. With October closing in, the days grew shorter, but Derby gave the order as night fell. He wanted to put as much distance between us and the French army as possible and vanish into the night.

The cold bit deep, the air crisp beneath the pale light of a full moon. Derby had us covering our tracks at every step, even wading through shallow rivers to throw off any pursuit. To say our legs and feet were cold would be an understatement.

But it paid off. By dawn, half-frozen and dead on our feet, we reached a wooded hill and stopped.

I stood with the Earl and Sir Walter, looking out over the low countryside to the east.

Paul wandered over. We hadn't spoken much in the past week, and I'd feared he was giving me the cold shoulder. Truth be told, despite everything, I'd missed him.

The Earl pointed. 'That, gentlemen, is our target.'

As the sun cast its first rays over the dew-drenched fields, Auberoche castle came into view, perched on a rocky peninsula overlooking the Auvézère River.

'No wonder it's still holding out against such odds,' Paul said. 'Are we to join them, my Lord?'

Derby laughed. 'I think you're overlooking something, Paul.'

Paul frowned.

And then I saw it. 'There.' I pointed to the flat land at the bottom of the shallow valley between us and the castle.

Paul chuckled, catching on. 'Ah, I didn't account for the thousands of Frenchmen between us and the castle!'

Earl Derby murmured quiet orders, rallying the men before shifting us deeper into the woods.

'They've no idea we're here,' he said. 'Let's keep it that way.'

A now familiar order spread: no fires, no sound. We sat in the makeshift camp, trying to keep warm. A weak sun clawed at the night's lingering chill, our brief excitement fading into exhaustion.

As many dozed, the Earl made his rounds, speaking to groups of men, each feeling valued.

'Sleep, young Ailred. Make the most of this downtime,' he said to me as he passed, Sir Walter at his side.

'Will we attack, Sire?' I asked.

He paused. 'I'm not sure yet. I was hoping Pembroke might make an appearance before we do. We have the advantage of surprise, but we're vastly outnumbered.' He removed a boot, rubbing his blistered foot. 'I have one trick left up my sleeve, but I'll hold that as a last resort.'

I could tell he had no intention of elaborating, so didn't push. He moved on.

Paul appeared, swathed in a blanket, another draped over his arm. 'You look cold, Al. Here...' he tossed me the woollen fleece. I wrapped it around myself, its warm folds pressing the chill from my bones.

'Thanks.'

He slumped down beside me in silence, and my eyes grew heavy.

'I think we have a big day ahead.'

I opened my eyes. 'You think? The Earl told me we're waiting for Pembroke before moving.'

'I know him well,' Paul replied before falling silent momentarily. 'I should say, I *did* know him well. He's cold towards me now.'

I looked over, expecting a tirade, but he lay back, looking at the sky.

'It's not my fault you've...' I began, but he cut me short.

'I know, Al. But sometimes... I can't stop myself. The voices, the sounds – they've been getting louder.'

I sat up, knowing where this might lead. 'For how long?'

Without moving, he stared into the blue sky. 'They never went away. I've learned to live with them. Sometimes they overwhelm me; other times they're a nagging I can suppress.'

'Why didn't you tell me?'

He sat up, glancing around. 'Because of this. This is all I'm good for. You've Philippa and Kimberly; I have this. If I'd told you, you'd never have let me come.' He lay back down, closing his eyes. '*This*... is the only thing that reminds me I'm alive.'

Dread gnawed at me. He was telling me something I'd known deep down, something I had chosen to ignore. All the signs were there; I just hadn't wanted to see them.

'Why tell me now?' I asked, lying beside him on the damp grass.

He sighed. 'You're my brother, and I love you.' We lay in silence before he added, 'There's a good chance one or both of us won't live through whatever's to come. I needed to say it.'

I swallowed hard, brushing a tear before it rolled.

'Don't be daft, Paul. Derby's got something up his sleeve. He'll get us through this.'

'Maybe. But if Pembroke doesn't turn up, we'll go in alone.'

My eyes closed, and Philippa and Kimberly came running to me.

*

I was woken by Godric.

'Ailred, your watch.' Godric shook me, just as I was about to bed Philippa.

'Thanks, Godric,' I grumbled, stretching and throwing the cover off. Paul was gone, and the sun was setting.

'And you say I snore!' Godric chuckled. 'Surprised you didn't wake the entire French army.'

The Earl had trebled the guard, taking no chances. The sun had gone down within the hour, and a substantial picket encircled the camp. I stationed myself at the eastern edge, keeping within the treeline. A steep slope ran down to the valley below, levelling out into pastureland where the French had based themselves. Beyond that, to the east, loomed the castle of Auberoche. By day, the French kept a steady bombardment, trebuchets hammering away as their siege towers stood idle, useless against the castle's position on the headland.

I settled in for a long, dull night.

'Ailred?'

I spun, shrugging my cloak to the ground, my grip steeling around the mace.

'Who goes there?' I demanded.

A muffled chuckle answered. 'I know your name, so it's safe to say I'm not the enemy. But good – you're alert.'

Earl Derby stepped into view, dressed in simple peasant clothing like a local farmer.

'My Lord – I didn't realise…' I started.

He waved it off. 'No need to apologise, Ailred. On the contrary – if you hadn't challenged me, you'd have cause to worry.'

I relaxed, eyeing his attire. 'Fine threads, Sire,' I said with a grin.

'And that brings me to why I'm here.' He glanced around. 'I am not here.'

I stared, caught off guard by the man telling me he wasn't standing before me. But I nodded, catching his meaning. 'Aye, my Lord was never here – and never will be,' I replied.

'Good. And I am not going in that direction.' He gestured toward the French camp. 'And when I return, I never came back from that way. Understood?'

My head spun, but I managed to keep up. 'Understood, Sire. If anyone asks, I know nothing.'

He smiled. 'Clever lad, Ailred. You'll go far.'

And then he was gone, slipping into the dark and down the slope toward the French lines.

I scratched my head, then slapped myself to make sure I wasn't dreaming.

An hour later, he returned. He slipped past me. 'I have what I need, Ailred. Carry on.'

*

'No more waiting,' the Earl declared.

It was the following day, and his advisors and commanders gathered around. Paul stood beside me, dressed in light mail.

'Told you,' he whispered.

'Pembroke's delay puts our advantage at risk. Sooner or later, some French hunter will stumble onto us. Lucky for us, they've been lax with their pickets.'

Excitement flared. Rested and restless, the men were ripe for action, and he was tossing red meat to hungry wolves.

'We go mid-afternoon. The French are celebrating Fête des Vendanges early this year,' he said. 'Someone I trust is handling their midday feast – a grand affair, I'm told. Reliable words tell me they take this day seriously – and by sundown, they'll all be half asleep.' He eyed our blank faces. 'It's a religious festival – they honour their dead. It's been their custom for centuries. We'll strike hard once they've let their guard down.' He grinned. 'Fitting, wouldn't you say, gentlemen?'

We laughed.

I had to ask. 'This "reliable word" – the same one who's kept us alive?'

'That it is, Ailred.'

I nodded. 'Good enough for me, Sire.'

'And if you need more reason, Jean d'Armagnac's in the camp.'

Silence fell. We all remembered Nathaniel's murder – and his cowardly flight from d'Eymet.

He took each commander aside and briefed them. I remained with Godric to command the eight hundred archers while Sir Walter, Paul, and Bonehead led the four hundred mounted men-at-arms. The Earl kept himself free to move where he deemed fit, adopting a roving role.

'Go now, my beauties – prepare yourselves. When we return, I want this valley awash with French blood.'

CHAPTER 19

You grow quieter by the day, Brother Michael. What happened to the cocky young priest who chronicled my early years – the one forever questioning me? Now you sit there, locked away, searching for your voice, as if the light behind your eyes has dimmed. But the words are there. I'll extract them one day.

*

From our vantage on the hill, we could shift the skies. It was a bright October morning, but we'd make it rain arrows. Below us sprawled the French camp – seven thousand men spread across the flat pasture, tents pitched in neat lines, fires roaring beneath iron cooking pots.

We had watched their routine for days, hidden in the trees. They pounded Auberoche's walls every morning, broke at midday, then resumed the assault after a leisurely meal. No rush, no urgency. But it was the evenings that caught our attention.

To the south, a section of tents was hived off from the rest. Scantily clad women strolled between the pavilions, their laughter drifting over the camp. Senior commanders followed them like pups on a leash, disappearing into the shadows for hours. Most of our men grumbled with envy, some joking about donning French uniforms to taste the delights.

Another thousand men lay entrenched to the north, cutting off any hope of reinforcements or supplies for Commander Frank van Hallen and the desperate souls trapped inside the castle.

Today was different. Camp followers bustled, setting up long tables and hanging garlands of grapes and coloured pennants across the grounds.

'As I said, they take this fête des vendanges seriously,' the Earl muttered, stepping beside me. 'They'll feast through the afternoon. I'm surprised they didn't take the whole day off – it's Sunday, after all. What sort of heathens are they?'

'It's Sunday?' I asked. I'd lost track.

Derby laughed and clapped me on the shoulder. 'That's what makes me the commander and you the Idiot!' Then his voice turned sober. 'We need to send a blanket of arrows, Ailred, a storm the likes they've never seen. I need every one of those Frenchmen to believe they're outnumbered and break any spirit they have.' He nodded towards Paul and the men-at-arms, all fully armoured, checking straps, preparing their horses. 'If we don't… well, these men are riding into…'

His voice tapered off.

'We have enough arrows to shoot until next year's fête des vendanges, Sire, and these men are the best in the business.'

He gave a brief nod. ‘I know. I wouldn’t make this call if I didn’t have total faith.’

A silence settled over us as we watched the French camp being readied.

‘A lot of those camp followers are Gascons,’ he said finally.

I raised an eyebrow. ‘You have it on good authority, Lord?’

He nodded. ‘A spy is down there right now.’

'He's Gascon?'

The Earl didn’t answer, just watched the camp with the same quiet conviction.

I scanned the sea of tents and bustling figures, catching glimpses of women darting between tables. ‘Do these followers know what’s coming?’

‘Some,’ he replied, catching my eye. ‘When you loose, Ailred, I expect no hesitation. If you let sentiment creep in, your brother and the rest of us die. I need you to remember that.’

‘Will our contact give a signal when to attack?’

The Earl said nothing, his eyes fixed on the French warriors trailing back from the besieged castle. Then he turned to me. ‘Get everyone ready. I want all in position the moment I give the word.’

He strode off toward the men-at-arms for their final instructions. I caught Paul’s eye and held my bow high in silent acknowledgement; he returned a grin.

The following hours were a waiting game. The French had shed their armour and were feasting.

I watched as one soldier tried to grope a woman and received a swift slap across the face. I chuckled. She reminded me of Philippa.

I moved about, rousing the men and ensuring everyone knew their part.

'And no one kills Jean d'Armagnac but me,' I told each group.

'Fuck off,' came the familiar response.

*

When the horn sounded, I was stretching my calves, trying to ease a cramp.

This was it – time to kill. Moving through instinct, I snatched up my bow and quiver and darted forward. I didn't check if my archers did likewise – I knew.

The sun dipped low as we broke cover, stepping from the forest's shadows. We drew and loosed. Our Devil's harp sang, the hum of hundreds of arrows darkening the sky. Before the first struck, the second and third were airborne.

Our men were positioned so that every inch of the camp's west side was exposed. There was no shelter. The still air carried the screams of men skewered and falling. We did not let up. By my tenth shot, I let my eyes wander. Those within range lay motionless or writhing in agony while the luckier ones scrambled back, beyond reach. We pressed forward, squires at our heels, replenishing our arrows as the iron-tipped storm continued. A few of their bravest formed ranks, shields locked, and tried to advance. But sheer numbers pinned them – arrows striking feet, legs, arms, each desperate shift to shield one limb, leaving another helpless. Again, we moved closer, and again, men fell. I heard French shouts through the mayhem – the commanders rallying, finally trying to steady their terrified troops. They could see our numbers were few and took heart – their war cries now drowning the screams of the wounded.

Then came the thunder of hooves. His livery stretched taut across his breastplate, Paul led our men-at-arms in a tight formation from the woods onto the open pasture. They rode shoulder to shoulder, inches between the heaving flanks, the front ranks gripping massive lances lowered to chest height. The coloured banners snapped in the wind, half-lost in the churned-up dust of the charge.

The French realised their doom too late and scattered between tents, scrambling in all directions, struggling to pull on armour and find order. But it was hopeless. Our mounted knights crashed into them, sweeping aside all in their path. Men were impaled, two or three at once, until the sheer weight of bodies wrenched the lances from the riders' grips.

Still, we advanced, our aim precise, picking off stragglers. I spotted one man tugging a great helm over his head, the eye slits misaligned, and sent a bodkin straight into his throat. He dropped, choking, before my next shaft buried itself in the stomach of a bare-chested man, snake tattoos curling along his arms.

We had slain or maimed hundreds, but still they gathered, a tide of thousands surging with renewed fury. Our knights had broken ranks in the initial rush and now found themselves isolated, their horses tiring. Though we laid cover upon cover of arrows, it wasn't enough. The Frenchmen advanced in grim formation, dragging riders from their saddles and hacking them apart. Horses screamed as war hammers smashed their legs, those still mounted fighting to turn back, only to be cut down before reaching safety.

The battle swung. My fingers were raw, blood seeping over the bowstring, yet no matter how many we struck, more filled their places. Earl Derby stepped up beside me, his gaze fixed on the lines now tightening as the French formed their defences.

'Archers, spread wide,' he commanded. 'I want their ranks covered.'

We filed across, our line facing the five deep divisions of French soldiers, as we unleashed a steady stream of arrows.

The French troops, shields interlocked, advanced. I noticed them pushing hard on our left and right.

'Lord, they're trying to flank us!' I yelled over the din.

'I know, man, I'm not blind.'

It was the first time I had seen Derby flustered.

More Frenchmen splintered off, drawing our sparse flanks to follow. These were well-drilled soldiers, nothing like the easy targets we had been dropping at will.

And then I spotted him – Jean d'Armagnac, commanding from the centre.

As I rallied my stretched archers, directing them to hold against the French flanking manoeuvre, Earl Derby's shout cut through the disarray: 'Concentrate to the right!' He waved his arms urgently.

I looked both ways, in panic. The French were edging left, closer to the woods, trying to get behind us. I threw Derby a desperate look, but he kept signalling right. Swallowing my doubts, I nodded and ordered our remaining reserves to the right, praying he knew what he was doing.

Then the dam broke. The French surged behind us, only feet from the cover of the woods.

D'Armagnac's men were seasoned campaigners, tearing into our ranks with a hatred for archers that drove them to merciless slaughter.

I spun and loosed, dropping two sword-wielding men quickly – only for them to be replaced. As our line turned to face the threat behind, the enemy at the front closed in. We were surrounded.

Just when it felt all was lost, a crazed cry of defiance rang out.

Jouan de Montfort and his Gascon warriors burst from the treeline like men possessed. They circled behind the French and plunged into their ranks, their fresh ferocity splitting the formation apart, ripping flesh and breaking bone. The French turned to defend against this new threat, and we seized the moment.

Dropping our bows, we drew side arms and struck, our fury unleashed on those who, moments before, had taunted us with promises of death. They did not give up without a fight; each man knew we'd take no prisoners. But as we fought, as their bodies broke beneath us, I felt no pity as the last man fell lifeless at my feet.

The battle raged on. Paul and his men-at-arms charged again and again, their mounts lathered with sweat, flanks bleeding from relentless spurring.

I staggered to the Earl's side, gasping for breath. He stood as calm as I had ever seen him, blood-soaked and smiling.

'About bloody time, van Hallen,' he muttered, eyes fixed on the distance.

I followed his gaze.

From the direction of Auberoche castle, a new force thundered forth – fresh, determined, and eager for vengeance. Frank van Hallen and his men-at-arms covered the short distance to the battlefield in moments, crashing into the rear of the frantic French forces. Horses became weapons, their iron-shod hooves kicking and stamping while the riders bent low, slashing and thrusting, dispensing death. Disoriented men reeled, some falling back only to be trampled underfoot, others ripped open by flashing steel.

Paul's men regrouped, turning to seal off the escape routes. The enemy was now hemmed in, crushed between us and van Hallen's mounted killers – trapped in a slaughterhouse with no exits.

'Time to avenge Nathaniel!' Earl Derby shouted, and we surged forward into the fray.

The ground turned slick as we hacked through the press of bodies, shoulder to shoulder, each strike tearing flesh, each step crushing the fallen underfoot. A Frenchman lunged at me with a dagger, his face twisted with fear and fury. I turned, ramming my sword beneath his ribs and wrenching it free, feeling the jolt of bone on blade. He slumped, but there was no pause – another soldier crashed into me, swinging a mace wildly. I ducked, feeling the air shift above my head, and slammed my fist into his throat before stabbing deep and slicing down hard, my blade severing his arm as he staggered back, screaming.

To my left, one of my archers wrestled with a Frenchman, both men grappling for a knife that glinted between them. I tore my sword free and rammed it into the enemy's exposed back, feeling him jerk before going limp in the archer's grip. The archer nodded thanks, wiping blood from his face before plunging into the next fray.

Paul leapt from his horse mid-gallop, landing with a laugh – brutal, unhinged. His blade drove deep into an opponent's neck, yanking free with a savage twist that sprayed red across the battlefield. Godric was a blur beside him, his axe crunching into another man's face, the force splitting the soldier's face in two.

The French began to falter, their formation splintering as we tore through them. Some raised their hands, pleading, eyes wide with desperation. But there was no appetite for mercy here. Bloodlust had taken us all. We had no patience for prisoners. Only the wealthier gentry were spared – their lives worth a ransom that would help fund our next campaign. The rest met their end where they stood as the blood-soaked ground drank deep.

*

We picked over the dead – the reason we risk our lives for this work. I snagged a few coins, and there was plenty of food left from the disturbed banquet – not that anyone was hungry. Well, that's not strictly true.

I found Paul at a long table, covered in blood, his feet propped on the body of a dead horse as he munched on a chicken leg.

'Well, that was fun!' He tossed the stripped bone over his shoulder and tore another from the carcass. 'Did you kill d'Armagnac?'

'Nah. Derby's got him and the other valuables

safely tucked away.'

Paul shrugged. 'You should've nailed the bastard during the battle.'

'Or you could have,' I shot back. 'You wanted him dead as much as I did after what he did to Nate.'

Paul used his stiletto to pick at his rotting teeth. 'I couldn't give a toss – I barely knew the kid.' He laughed. 'He flew better than this chicken did when it was alive.'

I opened my mouth but thought better of it. No point. I turned to walk away.

'Oh, and Derby wants to speak to you,' Paul added.

I found Earl Derby and Sir Walter in a tent they'd requisitioned from the French. A barber-surgeon was treating a deep cut along Walter's arm while Derby sat speaking to a flamboyantly dressed knight. His armour was draped in startling blue and yellow livery depicting back-to-back eagles. His helmet rested under one arm, and his hair was flat with sweat.

He noticed me enter and raised a silent finger for me to wait while he addressed the newcomer. Leaning back, he smiled.

'Cousin Pembroke, you are most welcome. Just in time to sprinkle holy water on the dead.'

Lord Pembroke bristled. 'You begged my urgent rally and then dismissed my sword like I were a common errand boy.'

Derby thumped his boots onto the table inches

from Pembroke's nose.

'If you hadn't stopped at every whorehouse between here and Bergerac, you might've heeded my call in time.' He thumbed backwards in an exaggerated gesture. 'You'd have a claim to the spoils back there.'

Lord Pembroke's face darkened. He spun on his heel. 'You haven't heard the last of this,' he said, unable to contain his fury. He crashed into me on his way out.

'Out of my way, fool,' he bellowed, shoving me aside.

Derby grinned. 'Always nice to catch up with family.' He beckoned me forward. 'Good work today, Ailred. You might've shed your nickname.'

'Thank you, my Lord. Your strategies won the day.'

He smiled. 'I can only work with the men at my disposal, and I've inherited the best.'

I hesitated. 'Did you know van Hallen was coming? That's what turned the tide.'

Derby glanced at Sir Walter, who nodded and left, the barber-surgeon mumbling at him to stay still.

'Yes, Ailred. Our connection sent a runner to alert them.'

I nodded. 'He's been a busy spy today, thank God, Sire. Did he survive the battle? Without his work, I dread to think where we'd be.'

'Yes, they're alive.' Derby held my gaze but said no more.

The silence stretched, making me wonder if I'd overstayed my welcome.

'Thank you, my Lord. If there's nothing more, I'll take my leave.'

'Actually, there is.' Derby gave me a long, considering look, his voice calm as if what he was about to say were routine. 'You've done your work well, Ailred, but there are pieces in play here you haven't seen. They've kept us alive.' I waited, feeling the unspoken tension. 'We've... allies, you might say, in places we can't reach. Some bring us what we need to know and do so without fuss.'

I nodded, though I wasn't much for riddles at the best of times.

Derby gave a faint smile. 'There's been one in particular. She's been more than useful.'

'She?'

'Her name is Izelda.'

CHAPTER 20

I stood in a daze.

'Izelda? My Izelda?'

He laughed. 'I'm not sure you own her, Ailred, but you know her.'

Footsteps sounded behind me.

'Hello, Ailred.'

The voice – that soft Gascon accent, woven with memories I'd never buried. I didn't look at her, my gaze still fixed on Derby, who watched me with a faint smile.

'I'll leave you two alone,' he said quietly, stepping past. Then, as he drew level, he clasped me on the shoulder. 'Outside this tent, you do not know each other. And you do not speak each other's names – to anyone.'

I nodded, still staring at nothing, his words setting our boundaries. The flap fell shut behind him, and I stood, heart pounding and unable to move.

'You'll have to face me at some point.'

I took a deep breath and turned.

And there she was, more beautiful than I remembered, her olive skin and raven hair pulled back, highlighting her features.

'What the fuck!' I still needed to learn to express my emotions better.

She laughed. 'Same old Ailred – always so

eloquent.' Her smile melted my heart.

I stepped forward, pulling her close as she buried her face into my neck, her arms tightening around my waist. *God, I missed you.* We stood there in silence, my heart pounding in my ears, my hands trembling. 'What are you doing here?' I asked, my voice unsteady.

She pulled back, holding both my hands in hers.

'There's much I can't tell you…' I started to protest, but she held up a hand. 'I'll tell you what I can.' She led me to the table where Earl Derby had been sitting, and we sat opposite each other. I reached across, and she took my hand, her lips curling into a small, sad smile.

'I'm no one,' she said with a shrug. 'That's why I'm still alive. I travel between camps and…' She stopped and bit her bottom lip. 'I'm no one.'

'You are to me,' I said, my gaze locked on hers.

She let go, her face softening before hardening, her hand clenching into a fist as she leaned away and rapped it against the table.

'No, Ailred. The minute people notice me, I'm dead. You have to understand that.' She softened again slightly, reading the sadness on my face. 'I'm sorry, Ailred, but it starts now.'

I opened my mouth to argue, but the person before me felt like a stranger. Her face cleared of any warmth, her gaze sharp and unreadable.

'What happened to Henri?' I asked, breaking the silence.

Henri had led a band of French rebels hungry for vengeance against the English invaders. After we parted ways, Izelda had fallen in with him out of necessity, bartering her safety for loyalty.

'He was killed not long after you left.'

'I'm… sorry to hear that,' I said, feeling the emptiness of the words.

She laughed. 'Are you? He would have had you and your brother slain, given half a chance.'

I stared at her, stunned. 'He gave us leave that day – let us go and even encouraged us to seek his cousin, Guillaume, in Calais.'

She shook her head. 'You always see what you want to, Ailred, not the truth. I'm the one who gave you Guillaume's name and pushed you to go after we ambushed that Welsh company. Henri was furious when he found out you'd slipped away. It took everything I had – lies, pleas, every last ounce of persuasion – to keep him from hunting you down.'

'I had no idea,' I said.

'That doesn't surprise me.' She chuckled and then fell silent for a moment before speaking again. 'So, how did you get home to England after you escaped? And what are you doing here now?'

So I told her. If you've read Brother Michael's transcript of my early life, you'll know the story – and if you haven't, go read it.

When I finished, she smiled. 'So, you're still in love with your wife, Philippa?'

As I took in her beauty, the question felt

impossible to answer. I looked away. 'And you,' I said, deflecting, 'how did you end up here?'

I heard footsteps that stopped near the tent's entrance, but ignored them. Izelda looked up for an instant, then continued.

'After you escaped, Henri changed. I tried to persuade him to settle and return to farming since the English had left, but his bitterness grew. He swore he'd purge every last foreigner from France.'

'But there weren't any – we left after the Truce of Espléchin between Edward and Philip.'

'He turned his attention to Gascony.' She gave me a hard, unwavering look.

'But… that's where you were born and grew up, right?' I said.

'It is. My heart is Gascon, and when he began obsessing over our loyalty to England, he pledged himself to Jean d'Armagnac.' I could see a mix of sadness and anger in her eyes. 'That pig Armagnac gave him a hundred of his most ruthless men and free rein to spread fear and violence wherever it would hurt the English most.'

'And he died in the process?'

She fell silent, looking as though she might answer, but then changed the subject. 'I see that brother of yours is as vile as ever.'

'You've seen him?' I asked, caught off guard.

She shook her head as if recalling something terrible. 'Yes, I've had the misfortune…' She stared at me. 'He's sick, Ailred. You know that, don't you?'

I faltered. 'He's Paul, but he's...'

'You're doing it again, seeing what you want to see. He tried to...'

The tent flap opened abruptly, and Earl Derby strode in. 'I think that's long enough. I'm sorry, but you'll have to go now, young lady.'

She stood dutifully and nodded. 'Yes, my Lord.' She glanced at me with a look so carefully blank it hurt. 'It was good to catch up, Ailred.'

'I... Is that it?' I was crestfallen. 'I have so many questions.'

Her face softened as though she might say something more, but a look from Derby silenced her. 'I must go.'

'I'll try to answer any questions you have, Ailred,' the Earl said, steering her towards the entrance with a hand on her shoulder. She turned, meeting my gaze for a second, and in that brief moment, I knew it was goodbye. And then she was gone.

Sir Walter entered the tent, his arm bandaged. I stood.

'At ease, Ailred,' he said, gesturing for me to sit. He poured three mugs of ale. Derby returned, picking up two, and offered me one.

'She's a brave woman,' he remarked as I took a long pull.

'I wouldn't know,' I muttered, unable to hide my frustration, 'you took her away before I could...'

'Careful, Ailred,' Sir Walter growled, his eyes darkening. 'Remember who you're speaking to.'

I drew a steadying breath. 'Apologies, my Lords. I was only...'

'It's fine, Ailred,' Derby interrupted with a sidelong glance at Sir Walter. 'Your reaction is understandable. We know all about your time with her and this Henri fellow.' He raised an eyebrow. 'There's little we don't know about your history with our connection behind the enemy's lines.'

'Your connection is called Izelda,' I prompted.

Derby's posture stiffened. 'Forget that name. As of now, you have *never* spoken to her. I know you want answers, but there's little to tell. She only delivers what those behind the scenes want us to know. She's but a mule, carrying messages from... well, let's say less visible hands.' His smile was faint but knowing. 'A beautiful and effective mule, but a mere go-between, all the same.'

I went to speak again, but he downed his drink, stood, and said, 'If that is all, Ailred, I must attend to other business. You may leave.'

I stood and bowed, his dismissal leaving my imagination to fill the hollow space with unanswered questions.

I stepped outside, the cold air biting at my skin, the conversation still nagging. My thoughts were racing as I tried to piece together everything said or left unvoiced.

Paul stood by the tent's edge, leaning against a support beam, his eyes scanning the camp with his usual detached look.

He turned and caught my eye. 'Did she remember you?' he asked, suppressing a grin.

I clenched my fists. 'You knew,' I said, barely containing my anger. 'You knew about Izelda all along.'

His lips twitched into that same forced smile, the cold one that never reached his eyes. 'Did I?'

My stomach knotted. 'Don't play games, Paul. How long?'

He shrugged, pushing off from the beam and stepping closer, savouring every second. 'Depends how you define long.' He watched me like a wolf toying with prey. 'Fine-looking filly, isn't she?' He laughed at my expression. 'Bet she's less stubborn with you than she was with me!'

I snapped. I swung wildly, my fists landing wherever they could – his jaw, his ribs, anywhere that might break. If I'd had a weapon, I would have used it. He didn't flinch, just laughed as he caught my arms and drove me to the ground.

Within seconds, he had me pinned to the ground, my teeth gnashing, legs kicking uselessly.

'Whoa, little brother, lighten up,' he laughed, staring into my face. 'Or at least learn to fight better!'

In my helpless state, my anger eased a little. I swallowed hard. 'Why didn't you tell me?'

Paul's eyes flicked around the camp, then back to mine.

'Because it wasn't my place. You had your path, and Izelda had hers.' He paused, his voice quieter. 'Sometimes, the less you know, the better.' Sitting back, he added, 'If I let you go, are you gonna do something stupid? You'll be the first man I've ever given a second chance to. You won't get another.'

I nodded, knowing I was beaten.

He let go of my arms and stood, offering a hand to pull me up. I had a few bruises, but nothing serious. He, as always, was unscathed.

'Forget about her, Al. She's a nobody. Probably being ploughed by every smelly Frenchman...' He stopped himself, holding up his hands with a look of regret. 'Sorry, Ailred. That was out of line.'

I shook my head, done with it all, and walked away.

He called after me. 'What I meant to say was probably being ploughed by every smelly Gascon.'

His laughter echoed around the quiet camp.

CHAPTER 21

The months passed in a blur of conquest and plunder. After our crushing defeat of Jean d'Armagnac's forces at Auberoche, the French armies fell silent, leaving us free to roam as we pleased. We carved a path of destruction through their lands, growing rich from the spoils. Scattered bands of disorganised militia crossed our path, but Earl Derby's scouts always saw them coming. We quickly crushed them or sent them fleeing before they could dream of striking back.

In September, Earl Derby received word that his father, Henry, the 3rd Earl of Lancaster, had passed away. He was crushed, and I overheard him confide in Sir Walter his guilt over being unable to bid his father farewell. This loss marked his ascension to the title of Earl of Lancaster. I had no idea what the new title meant, but the noble class did, offering their congratulations despite the sombre circumstances. On many occasions, I earned a clip around the ear for continuing to call him Earl Derby, so I quickly learned the title's significance.

During this time, covert dispatches continued to reach us. In April 1346, we learned that Philip had proclaimed an arrière-ban across the

South of France – a call to arms for every able-bodied man of fighting age. Once more, Philip's son, John, the Duke of Normandy, was tasked with ending our exploits. We were honoured to warrant such high disdain, though the gravity of what lay ahead tempered our mirth.

The steady flow of intelligence left me scanning for Izelda whenever I had a moment, hoping for even the briefest glimpse or word from her. Now and then, I noticed a civilian – always male – slipping in and out of camp under cover of secrecy, but she was never among them. Anxiety crept in. What if she had been captured or killed? The thought haunted me, and a darker one followed: what if I was the cause? The weight of that possibility was one I knew I could never bear.

One night, in a moment of madness, I approached one of the men I assumed to be an informant as he slipped into camp. We were stationed close to Agen, fresh from looting the town after a lengthy siege. A young man dressed in the tattered garb of a Gascon peasant entered just as dusk fell. I was on picket duty and had cause to intercept him.

'Halt,' I commanded. 'State your business.'

The man froze, tugging off his soiled coif. His face was gaunt, his eyes darting. 'I am here to speak to Earl Derby,' he said in halting English, his accent similar to Izelda's.

'He is Earl Lancaster now,' I corrected. 'You're

Gascon?'

He hesitated, glancing away as though weighing the risk of answering. 'I would rather speak my piece to Earl Lancaster, please.'

His refusal to engage confirmed my suspicions, and I prepared to escort him to the Earl. But in a moment of petulant desperation, I lost my head and blurted out, 'Do you know Izelda?'

The words hung between us like a noose. I regretted them immediately.

His reaction was telling – his posture stiffened, fear flickering in his eyes. 'I... I do not know this person you speak of,' he stammered.

'Is she dead?' The words escaped before I could stop them.

He shifted, looking ready to bolt. 'Can you take me to the Earl, please?' His voice trembled. 'Or I must go...'

I cursed my stupidity, realising I'd overstepped. Motioning for him to follow, I kept my mouth shut. If he left before delivering his report, I'd be in serious trouble – if I wasn't already.

As we neared the Earl's tent, I halted and turned to him. 'Say nothing of our conversation to Lord Lancaster,' I warned, forcing conviction into my tone. 'He needn't be burdened by idle talk.'

He nodded, and I showed him in.

Lancaster was conversing with Sir Walter

when I entered, but his expression shifted to unease upon seeing the visitor and me together. 'Ah, thank you, Ailred. That will be all.'

I lingered a moment longer than I should have, then stepped outside. Curiosity gnawed at me, and I dawdled near the flap, moving closer to catch their words. The muffled voices stopped, so I pressed my ear against the fabric.

The next thing I remembered was lying on the ground, clutching my head, with Lancaster looming over me, holding a chair.

'I said, that will be all, Ailred. Did I not make myself clear?'

'Yes, my Lord,' I muttered, crawling back to my post, my pride as bruised as my skull.

Resuming my watch, I cursed my foolishness. 'Hopefully, the messenger will keep his mouth shut,' I muttered. 'As Philippa would say, "You really are dumb sometimes, Ailred".'

Half an hour later, I heard footsteps approaching. The messenger appeared, looking nervous at the sight of me.

'I must go now,' he said, his voice a whisper.

'Did you tell the Earl about our conversation?'

He shook his head. 'No, Sir – what we spoke about, I will take to the grave.'

I exhaled in relief and palmed him a handful of looted coins before sending him back into the shadows.

*

The repercussions were immediate.

'WHAT THE HELL WERE YOU THINKING?'

Earl Lancaster's fist struck me, snapping my crooked nose back into place as he loomed over me, two men-at-arms standing behind.

'I assume he told you then, Lord?'

He hauled me up and headbutted me. 'I ought to have you flogged, Idiot. You've endangered everything – put every man and woman in Gascony at risk.'

Through swollen eyes, I met his gaze. I had never seen him so enraged. I opened my mouth to defend myself, but the contempt in his eyes silenced me.

At that moment, I knew my relationship with the great man was finished. A year of loyalty and service had been erased by one moment of weakness. I cursed myself, realising this was the turning point – the moment a commander decides a man is no longer worth the risk.

As I was dragged from the tent, Lancaster's voice thundered behind me. 'I've had my fill of you and your brother – tomorrow, I'm clearing out the dross once and for all.'

The words hit harder than his fists.

*

He was true to his word. The next day, Paul, Bonehead, Godric, and anyone unlucky enough to be associated with me were rounded up, placed under the watch of Lancaster's highest-ranking scout, and given horses. We were sent packing to Aiguillon. Even Bastard suffered the indignity of being included. Behind us, the remaining army prepared to march to La Réole, ready to add to their spoils.

'Thanks, Ailred.'

The voice from behind could have been any man, but this time it was Godric. I had been dreading this moment.

'I'm sorry,' I offered, hollow and useless.

He didn't answer. Instead, he kicked his horse and cantered ahead. That stung. Not even anger – just indifference. That was all I was worth.

'You fuckin' idiot.' Paul's voice cut through my thoughts, sharp and familiar. He trotted up alongside me, his scowl dark as a storm cloud. 'Whatever you've done has damned us all.'

I didn't have the energy to argue. 'Paul, I've spent my life cleaning up after your stupidity. See what it's like to walk in my boots for once.'

'While Lancaster and the others get fat off the spoils, we get sent to Aiguillon,' he spat. His voice dropped, venomous. 'Do you even know what's waiting for us there?'

We were soon to find out.

CHAPTER 22

Aiguillon was a fortified town perched above the convergence of the Lot and Garonne, rivers vital to supplying the region around La Réole, where Earl Lancaster was to station the bulk of the Anglo-Gascon army. Already under English occupation, we had been sent to bolster its defences and rid Lancaster of our presence.

As we approached the gates, we were met by the Earl of Stafford.

'I heard you were coming,' he said, gesturing for the guards to allow us entry. 'If this is Lancaster's way of unloading his undesirables, I'm pleasantly surprised.'

The last time I had seen Stafford was before Earl Derby – now Lancaster – had taken command ahead of the assault on Bergerac. There had never been love lost between the two men, but I was glad to see a familiar face.

'I'm honoured you remember me, Sire,' I said, filing in behind the others.

Inside, Aiguillon revealed itself as a patchwork of fortification and vulnerability. The perimeter walls weren't as old as I expected but had gaps that'd been patched with wood and other makeshift materials. Two small forts stood within the town, both overlooking the Garonne. To the north, the Lot offered protection, and the

Garonne did the same to the west. The southern and eastern walls were far more exposed and would be the most likely targets of any attack.

Once we were settled in our new barracks, Lord Stafford introduced us to his senior advisors and commanders. They were desperate to hear about our chevauchées' exploits across the French countryside, though I sensed resentment over the wealth being amassed. Their orders were to hold and defend the town, given its strategic importance, which limited their ability to earn.

So we drifted into town life, a stark departure from the previous year spent in tents and digging latrines. Even Paul settled down, and after a few weeks, we, the rejects from Earl Lancaster, found a strange comfort.

Our comfort was short-lived.

*

'John, Duke of Normandy, is en route, my friends.'

We sat in the church hall Lord Stafford had commandeered and designated as his war room. It was late March 1346, and the first signs of new life began to show across the fields and orchards. Buds pushed through the newly thawed earth, and the air carried the faintest scent of spring. But inside those stone walls, talk of death and ruin already overshadowed the season's fragile promise.

‘Is this information solid?’ asked Bonehead,

sitting beside Paul, idly scratching at the scar along his jaw.

'Yes,' Stafford replied. 'Our contact hasn't been wrong yet. We can expect them in a week or so.' He gestured to the map pinned to a wooden board, its edges curling under the weight of damp air. 'They're here at the moment – in Agen.'

'That's where we came from,' Bonehead said, frowning. 'Didn't they come against Lancaster's army?'

'Earl Lancaster to you,' Stafford corrected with a sharp look, 'and, no. He's since retreated to La Réole.'

Bonehead placed a hand over his heart. 'Apologies, Sire. What sort of numbers are we talking about, my Lord?'

Stafford exhaled through his nose, nodding. 'Anything between fifteen and twenty thousand men.' He fell silent, letting the weight of the words settle on the room like a shroud.

'And we have…?'

'Three hundred men-at-arms and six hundred archers.'

Paul, leaning forward. 'And you're sure they'll come here next rather than go after Earl Lancaster?' His voice was measured, his eyes ablaze with expectation.

Stafford met his gaze. 'I am. The Duke's intent is clear – he wants this town and its rivers. Without them, he can't sustain an extended push into Gascony.'

A murmur rippled as the men exchanged uneasy glances. I sat back, the numbers repeating in my head like a drumbeat. Twenty thousand men. Against nine hundred.

Details consumed the rest of the meeting, each dissected with precision. Stafford ordered the breaches in the walls not just secured but doubly reinforced with timber, stone, and anything that could withstand an enemy's siege. He demanded every weapon inspected, sharpened, and accounted for. The stores of arrows were redistributed so that no archer would need to stray more than a few feet to replenish his quiver during the frenzy of battle. His voice carried a calm authority, each word weighted with experience and resolve.

As he spoke, the room seemed to shift. The men around me, many of whom had arrived sullen and uncertain, began to sit straighter, nodding along. It was impossible not to be swept up in the quiet conviction of his planning. I realised Stafford was as meticulous and exacting as Earl Lancaster, but his manner lacked the cold distance that Lancaster carried like a shield. Here was a man who could command respect without shouting, who made men believe in the plan simply by laying it bare before them. Confidence grew in that hall like a fire catching light, steady and warming but no less fierce.

'Are there any other questions before we break?' Stafford asked, his gaze sweeping the room.

I raised my hand.

'Yes, Ailred?'

'Was the person who brought you this information a woman?'

Looking back, I still cringe at my stupidity.

The slap to the back of my head came before I'd even finished the thought. Godric glared at me, his fist clenched like he was deciding whether one punch was enough. Then, a mug of ale smashed against my face.

'Do you ever learn, Idiot?' Paul growled.

He stormed past me without waiting for an answer, the others trailing behind with barely concealed smirks or rolling eyes. One by one, they filed out, leaving me standing alone – wet, humiliated, and painfully aware I'd shattered whatever trust Stafford might have had in my judgement. It was a marked contrast to only days ago when I was helping shape the war. Now, I was a rusty tool no one used.

The rest of the day was spent carrying out the Lord's orders, punctuated by pointed jabs and reminders of my embarrassment from anyone who'd been at the meeting. I became the dog everyone wanted to kick. By sundown, the weight of it all – humiliation and exhaustion alike – dragged me into an uneasy sleep.

*

The following day, Paul jolted me awake.

'Wake up, Idiot, and muster your archers –

we're going on a jolly.'

It was still dark, the chill of dawn bringing goosebumps to my skin. I sat up on my straw-filled palliasse, rubbing the sleep from my eyes.

'A jolly? Where to?'

Paul's grin gleamed in the dim light. 'Not my place to say. I'll let Stafford tell you en route. Just hurry – and bring as many arrows as you can carry.' He smiled. 'We'll have some fun over the next few days.'

His idea of fun differed from mine, so suspicion nagged.

The morning was overcast, and I grew more irritable with every repetition of the same question as I finished harnessing Bastard and loading the arrows.

'No, I've no idea where we're going or what we're doing,' I answered for what felt like the hundredth time.

Paul had assembled around a hundred men-at-arms, and I'd mustered two hundred archers.

By the time we'd loaded the wagons with supplies and inspected the weaponry, Lord Stafford was already waiting by the front gates, impatience etched across his face.

'A vanguard of French forces is camped five miles ahead,' Stafford said as we rode out. 'They're building a bridge over the River Garonne.'

I frowned, unsure of the significance.

'It means that if they finish it,' Stafford

continued, 'the rest of their army will follow – thousands of the bastards, straight for us. But without that bridge, they're trapped on the southern bank.'

'We're going to take it out, Lord?' I asked.

'That's the plan, Ailred. We're going to torch it.'

Paul's eyes gleamed. As a child, he'd been drawn to fire, with more than a few suspicious blazes left in his wake. This was right up his street.

I nodded toward a barrel one of Paul's men had hauled onto a small cart.

'Tar, Lord?'

'Keen perception, Ailred,' Stafford replied, his gaze lingering. 'Can you swim?'

'He swims like a fish, Lord,' Paul butted in, his need to be included overriding good sense.

Stafford gave him a weary glance. 'And you, Paul?'

Paul flushed and fumbled for a response. 'I… I never learned, Sire, but I can…'

Stafford cut him off with a curt wave. 'Then let's keep it that way. You'll be of more use on dry ground.'

Paul scowled but held his tongue as Stafford turned back to me. 'When we reach the bridge, you'll swim under with a team and ready the tar. Once it's set, we'll wait until they're back at work and send flaming arrows to light it up. With luck, they'll think their own carelessness caused the blaze.'

'Subtle,' I said. 'Though the retribution will be anything but subtle if the French catch us under their bridge.'

Stafford cracked a faint smile before spurring his horse forward.

The road was rough, and the overcast sky mirrored the grim mood of our small company as we trundled northward. Bonehead and Godric had been left behind to oversee the defences at Aiguillon, Stafford not willing to gamble the town's safety for this mission. Their absence left an odd hole in our ranks, and I missed Godric's wit and calm nature.

Paul, however, seemed unaffected as he rode at the head of the column, barking orders to keep the pace brisk. Behind him, the men-at-arms rode, and the archers marched with good humour. They talked of long-overdue rewards, though their eyes stayed wary, scanning the dense woodland flanking the road. Stafford had sent scouts ahead and fanned out for miles, which gave me confidence we wouldn't be ambushed.

Although it was only five miles away, it might as well have been fifty. The creak of the wagon's wheels and the steady thud of hooves were a constant reminder that stealth was impossible.

Word spread quickly about our task, and the men crackled with anticipation.

A voice piped up from the rear, loud enough to be heard over the noise. 'Best we can hope for is to roast a few steaks over the embers later.'

After another hour, Paul slowed his horse to fall in beside mine. He nodded toward the treeline ahead. 'Just over that ridge.'

I could just about make out the faint sounds of construction, the steady thump of hammers and the occasional shout of a worker. We slowed the wagons to a crawl, hoping to lessen the noise. The path curved ahead, and Stafford signalled for us to steer off to the right into a patch of thick forest that offered us cover as we neared the ridge.

We guided our horses through the trees, finding a small clearing where we could hide the wagons, wedging them between the trunks of the largest trees and allowing the horses to crop at the short grass. The air was cool and damp beneath the canopy, the ground soft underfoot. We dismounted, readying ourselves for the task ahead.

'Ailred, choose your best twenty archers and distribute this tar into those,' Stafford murmured, pointing to a pile of ceramic pots. His voice was a whisper, and he moved with purpose, cracking open the barrel before plunging his hands into the black pitch and pulling them out with a thick, dark coating. 'By the time you're finished, I want you all as black as a raven.'

I opened my mouth to laugh but stopped myself when I saw the look in his eyes. He was serious. Without further word, he smeared the tar across his face, neck, arms, and legs, his movements swift and methodical, leaving streaks of glistening darkness in the dim light of the forest.

We began distributing the sticky pitch between the pots. It clung to everything it touched – hands, tunics, and the air thickened with its choking scent that stung the back of the throat. By the time we were done, we resembled men who'd fought through a vat of the stuff, grimy and dark from head to toe.

We settled into the forest's encroaching darkness, blending with the shadows. In the silence, we took the chance to eat cold pottage. The remnants of tar crept into every mouthful, a grim reminder of the task ahead.

At twilight, Stafford gathered us and gave his orders. Paul, the men-at-arms, and most of the archers were to stay behind in reserve, guarding the horses and supplies. We, however, would press on into the night alone. We collected the tar pots, each man receiving a single knife strapped to his belt – anything more would be a hindrance.

'I don't want to hear another word from now on,' Stafford hissed, his voice low but firm as we left the forest shelter and crept toward the ridge. Work sounds had fallen silent, but faint voices still drifted on the wind, a reminder of how close we were to the enemy. The night was clear and cold, the new moon offering little light. Carrying the tar pots in near-darkness was challenging enough, each snap of a twig or rustle of underbrush making my nerves jump. One archer, burdened with carrying a fresh, watertight barrel, followed behind – its purpose a mystery that Stafford chose not to explain.

On reaching the crest of the ridge, we paused. Below, the dark waters of the Garonne slithered like a black serpent under the pale light. Stafford gestured towards the riverbank. 'We go in upstream. Quietly.'

I nodded, my hands already slick with tar, which would soon be our weapon. The night was still, save for the occasional splash of a waterbird and the soft rustle of trees. I glanced at the others, their faces grim beneath the tar, the whites of their eyes the only visible feature.

We crept to the edge of the ridge, and Stafford signalled for us to drop to our knees. The river was closer now, and we continued at a crawl.

Stafford stopped a couple of hundred yards from the half-built bridge and motioned for the barrel to be set down. 'Open it,' he whispered, his voice barely audible over the sound of flowing water. The designated archer pried off the lid, revealing the barrel's smooth, empty interior.

'Pack the pots inside,' Stafford ordered.

We crouched low, working by touch, our tar-sticky hands making the task messy and slow. Each pot was nestled together, the residue binding them like glue.

'Pack them tight,' Stafford commanded, his

eyes scanning the bridge for movement. 'We can't afford them to shift or break before they reach the supports.'

Ropes were secured around the barrel's middle, the ends coiled in the hands of two archers, Edgar and Harold, who would guide it downstream. They were massive men and had the best chance of controlling the barrel if the current took it.

'Into the water. No splashing. Keep low and stay focused,' Stafford instructed. 'Ailred, you lead. Cover the driest timber sections – get as much on there as possible. When it's fired, I want the whole thing up in flames as one.' He clapped me on the shoulder. 'I'll stay on this bank as close as possible to the bridge and watch. If you're caught, there's little I can do to save you – but I trust you'll get it done.'

I nodded. We all understood the stakes. Stafford couldn't afford to cross with us; if he were caught or killed, Aiguillon would be without its leader.

With that, we slipped toward the riverbank and removed our boots, the cold mud gripping our feet as we neared the edge. The water was ink-black, cold enough to bite through flesh. We stood a few hundred yards upstream, the bridge still out of sight where the river swept around a gentle bend. Dressed in nothing but black tunics and leggings, it was almost impossible to make out faces. It was a comfort – if I couldn't see my comrades five feet away, what chance did the French have at a hundred paces?

I waded to my waist, and the cold struck like a hammer. My balls retreated so far into my body that I thought I might bite into them. I opened my mouth to speak, but no sound came out.

Edgar's voice cut through the darkness, jolting my heart back into rhythm. 'Ailred, lead off – we've taken the strain. It's secure.'

I squinted toward the barrel bobbing just ahead, held steady in the current by the ropes.

'Will you and Harold manage, or do you need more hands?' I asked, keeping my voice low.

'Na, it's fine.'

'That's 'cos you're still standing,' I muttered. 'It'll be different when the water gets…'

Harold chuckled. 'Are you doubting us, Al?'

'This isn't the time for jokes,' I replied, though their confidence was reassuring. 'Hang back a few minutes. I'll take the rest forward, and we'll climb into the bridge structure, ready to haul the barrel up when you arrive.'

It sounded reasonable enough.

I pushed further downstream, past the stationary barrel, the water rising to my chest before the river bottom levelled out.

'Not as deep as we thought,' I whispered to the soft splashes of men following behind.

We rounded the bend, and the bridge came into view for the first time. A few torches burned on the newly built platform, casting faint light onto the walkway, but the underside remained pitch-black.

Perfect.

But then it wasn't.

My next step landed on nothing, the riverbed dropping away. I stumbled forward, my body plunging beneath the surface as the undercurrent sucked me down with frightening speed. I hadn't had time to take a breath, my lungs screaming for air as I was dragged along the riverbed.

I knew I was in deep water now, the biting cold cramping my muscles into spasms. My limbs felt useless, and every movement was a battle for survival. My head struck the bottom, the impact jarring me as I tumbled. My lungs gave out, my chest convulsing with the desperate need to breathe.

Instinct forced me to twist my body, using every ounce of strength I had left. My feet found solid ground, and I pushed hard, shooting forward like an arrow loosed from a bow.

The effort tore through me as the last of my air escaped in a violent hiss. A piercing pain ripped through my skull, and I opened my mouth, surrendering life.

But I breathed air. Cold and spray-filled, but air. It had never felt so good. I coughed and spluttered as the river flow smoothed again. Taking a moment to orient myself, I realised I was fast approaching the bridge. With just enough strength left, I guided myself towards one of the wooden struts supporting the platform and managed to grab it as I floated past.

I waited a few seconds to regain my strength and composure, then hauled myself onto one of the horizontal crossbeams spanning the struts. The beam was sturdy and wide enough to sit on, my legs dangling over the side. I was shaking.

And then it started. Men unable to reach the safety of the bridge began to drift past – some struggling to swim, others already drowned. Quickly, I lay on my stomach and leaned over, reaching down, trying to grasp anyone within reach. It was nearly impossible in the darkness, but I managed to grab the hand of one man alert enough to realise his chance. I held his wrist, but the tar on my hands made him slippery.

In all our terror and confusion, neither of us cried out. Our oath of silence overrode instinct. Just as he was about to slip from my grasp, he managed to grab the shaft and pull himself clear.

Within seconds, another man drifted past. As hard as I tried, I couldn't reach him, and I watched helplessly as his head disappeared into the night.

Just as the first man clambered beside me, ready to help, another soul drifted into view. He, too, managed to grasp my hand, but now there were two of us. We hauled him up, and he sat panting next to us.

'The barrel,' I whispered, trying not to cough.

'Harold and Edgar won't be able to...'

It was too late. At first, I thought it was another man, but then I realised it was the barrel bobbing towards us, the ropes attached but with no one on either end.

I shifted over to the shaft and slithered down, splashing helplessly as I made a desperate dive to grab it. But I was too late. It struck the wooden pole before I could reach it, halted briefly, then rolled around and drifted downstream.

I cursed silently just as one of the attached ropes passed by.

Lunging forward, I grabbed it but was too far from the structure now. The current pulled me away, dragging me downstream alongside the barrel.

Just as I was about to give up, the rope went taut, and I stopped dead in midflow. So did the barrel. I was confused before realising I had gone one side of the shaft while the barrel had gone the other. I clung on for dear life, wrapping the rope around my arm.

I could just about make out the other two men working hard to pull us back, and soon, I felt the reassuring sensation of slowly being dragged backwards, the barrel and I moving against the current.

*

By the time we had hauled the barrel up and secured it beneath the bridge, my body was numb, my lungs cored hollow. Harold arrived soon after, saving himself as I had, and clambered onto the structure. Without a word, we set to work.

Cracking open the barrel, we found the small pots intact, packed snug inside. Each of us took one and crawled through the wooden lattice, smearing tar onto the driest planks and pillars. It was slow, filthy work, the sticky substance clinging to everything it touched. When a pot was emptied, we tossed it into the river and grabbed another, moving like ants over a carcass.

Above, French guards patrolled the walkway, their boots thudding across timbers. Now and then, they paused to chat, their voices blending with the river's hum. At any moment, I expected them to spot us – a splash, a creak, anything – but cold, our greatest ally, drove their apathy.

By the time we emptied the barrel, my hands were blackened, my muscles screaming for rest. I scanned the south bank and spotted a small inlet downstream – a perfect escape. Though I couldn't see him, I knew Stafford was crouched in the rushes, his watchful gaze urging us on.

The guards above had settled into a rhythm. They left the warmth of their guardhouse, crossed to the bridge's midpoint, lingered in conversation, and then returned. We waited for their retreat.

At last, we slipped into the river's dark embrace, vanishing like black otters. Spent and trembling with cold, we let the current carry us towards the inlet and safety. Behind us, the bridge was primed – a silent promise of destruction.

CHAPTER 23

'Even you can't miss,' Paul muttered as we crouched in the river's margins, watching the French engineers swarm the bridge at dawn.

In daylight, the structure bustled with movement. Fresh planks gleamed under the sun while horses hauled more into place, stacking them high. With so many hands at work, they'd have it finished in hours – if left undisturbed.

We had other plans.

The two-hundred-yard gap was nothing from our vantage point. Archers stood ready, fire arrows nocked, waiting for Lord Stafford's signal. Paul and his men-at-arms lingered nearby, restless and brooding – this was an archer's work, and their inaction gnawed at them.

Of the men sent to tar the bridge, only a handful had made it back. Some were swept downstream and crawled ashore, but many were lost to the current. Cold and exhausted, we'd been given the choice to retreat and rest or see the job through. It wasn't a choice at all.

Stafford crawled beside me. 'You did the hard graft, Ailred – it's only fitting you take the first shot.'

Pride swelled. 'An honour, Sire.' I reached for my firebox, but he stayed my hand.

'The honour is mine.' He struck his own twice

against the tarred rag below the arrowhead, setting it alight.

With my eyes locked onto my target, I loosed. My arrow arched high, its flame trailing like a comet, and struck the tar-soaked pillar dead-on.

That was the signal.

A storm of fire followed. Hundreds of arrows poured into the bridge's undercroft. By my fifth shot, flames leapt from beam to plank, devouring the structure. Above, engineers and guards scattered in panic, their cries lost in the rising inferno.

Crossbowmen rushed to the far bank, loosing bolts that took down a few of our archers, but it was too late. The fire spread fast. Some men caught alight where they stood, staggering ablaze before crumpling into the river.

'Beautiful,' Stafford murmured, eyes fixed.

At the bankside end, flames cut off any retreat. Men and horses baulked, trapped between fire and the unrelenting hail of arrows. Many flung themselves into the river. We cut them down as they floundered, their blood turning the current frothy red. Those swept downstream found no salvation – a unit of Stafford's men waited, butchering any who crawled ashore before tossing their corpses back into the churning waters.

On the far side, fresh reinforcements surged forward, rallying crossbowmen – but the bridge was already lost.

Paul strode to the riverbank, lifted his sword, and laughed. 'Here I am, you bastards! Take a good look – when next you see me, I'll be standing over you!'

They couldn't hear him over the fire's roar and the screams of burning men and horses, but he seemed to be enjoying himself, jeering at the bolts that whistled past.

By the time the French withdrew, the riverbank lay strewn with their dead. The bridge's charred skeleton groaned and collapsed into the water.

Stafford exhaled, his face set with grim satisfaction. 'Ailred, gather the men who made it through last night. Get them to the forest – food and rest await. You've earned it.' I nodded, exhaustion creeping in. 'The French will regroup,' he continued. 'The Duke's army will push upstream, try to flank us. We'll make it costly. It'll be like holding back the tide, but we'll kill thousands before we fall back to Aiguillon.' He cast a glance at Paul, still taunting the distant enemy. 'Your brother will get his day in the sun. That much, I guarantee.'

*

The next few days followed a relentless pattern of feints and ambushes. We retreated into the forest, drawing the French into a false sense of security. They took the bait at first, hauling timber and supplies to resume construction on the bridge. Makeshift rafts ventured onto the river, attempting to secure a foothold, but each attempt ended the same. Arrows rained down as we emerged from the shadows, sending their crews scrambling or sinking into the current.

The French adapted. Thousands of crossbowmen crouched behind pavises and makeshift barricades, their disciplined volleys pinning us back. Our sallies grew fewer, with every clash taking a high toll. We turned their men back time and again, but the bridge inched its way ever closer to our bank. They were resolved, I'll give them that.

Night-time brought confusion, with the French testing our defences through cautious crossings. We held them back with sheer will, the relentless vigils wearing us down. And still, the bridge loomed larger with each passing day. We had no fire arrows left, and the unending volleys of crossbow bolts kept us pinned.

It seemed a stalemate – until their real plan revealed itself.

After a week of attrition, our scouts brought word. The Duke's army was closing, pouring over the horizon like a flood. Banners whipped in the wind, a tide of steel and spears stretching farther than they could see. It became clear – while the bridge was their focus, the Duke was sending the bulk of his forces upriver to ford and outflank us.

Ever the strategist, Lord Stafford had seen it coming. He wasted no time, ordering an immediate retreat.

We moved swiftly, but the French guarding the bridge reacted in kind. Spotting our withdrawal, they pounced, launching their rafts within minutes. Progress was slow, horses shrinking at the unstable crossings, buying us precious time.

As we trudged back toward Aiguillon, the Duke's vanguard forded upriver, reinforcing the troops already on our heels. The retreat descended into a game of cat and mouse as we fought for survival. Stafford stationed Paul and his men-at-arms at the rear. They had their moment at last. After weeks of frustration, they hurled themselves into the fray with savage determination. Time and again, the French attacked, pressing at our tail, but each assault was met with brutal ferocity. Paul and his men tore through their foes, blood soaking the trampled fields, bodies sprawled where they fell. Still, the French were relentless, their numbers swelling with reinforcements. Every step of our retreat became a running battle.

Hours passed, and the attacks never ceased. French crossbowmen, out of bolts, grabbed maces and axes, knowing it was kill or be killed. Paul and his mounted men-at-arms dashed from one point of attack to the next while we fought hand to hand, desperate to survive and return to Aiguillon's defences.

But we kept moving, leaving bodies in our wake, inching our way to safety.

Finally, the town's walls loomed ahead. Behind

us, the French knights closed in, preparing for one final assault. They formed ranks – mounted knights in the centre, foot soldiers fanned out on the flanks. Paul called his men to his side, facing the oncoming storm. We archers shadowed their flanks. This single battle would decide the day – our fate, the town's.

Our men-at-arms spread, horses snorting beneath them, visors snapping down. Paul turned in his saddle, scanning our lines before his gaze met mine. With a single nod, he lowered his own visor. We were outnumbered, battered, and running on nothing but the will to live. It was a powerful motivator.

The French charged, their fury a howl that shook the earth. Dust billowed as horses surged forward, the thunder of hooves deafening.

Paul raised his sword, spurring his steed, ready to meet their charge – when a voice bellowed behind us.

'SPLIT LEFT AND RIGHT – DO NOT CHARGE!'

It was Lord Stafford.

Paul yanked his reins, his horse rearing as he spun in the saddle. We obeyed without hesitation, peeling away to create a gaping void in our line. If Stafford had miscalculated, it would be our end.

The French charge thundered closer, the ground trembling. At a hundred yards, the sun caught the foam-lathered hides of their horses, their muscles straining as they poured forward.

Behind, foot soldiers pushed on, desperate for blood.

'LOOSE!' Stafford's voice rang out. A black cloud of arrows hissed through the air, striking mercilessly. The leading ranks jolted as if hit by an unseen battering ram. Horses reared, riders tumbling to the earth.

I glanced back. Hundreds of archers, reinforcements from Aiguillon, crouched behind us. They'd seen our approach and sprinted across the fields to join the fight, tipping the scales.

Another barrage struck the French, then another, the volleys shredding their momentum. Their charge faltered, hooves skidding to a halt. Confusion ripped through their lines.

'GO.'

Stafford's single word was all we needed. Archers dropped their bows, drawing swords, maces and axes, rushing to join the fray. It was time to kill. We crashed into the disarrayed French. Many had already turned to flee, but those who stood met their end beneath our fury. Each swing of an axe or thrust of a blade carried the venom of revenge. We killed without mercy.

The bodies of their elite warriors – the vanguard who had led the charge – littered the ground, broken and bloodied. Their loss was a knife to the French rank's heart. They collapsed into panic, faith turning to fear.

While Paul and his men clashed with the remaining mounted knights, we overwhelmed the defiant few still standing, breaking their will through sheer numbers.

They scattered, and we rushed to pursue, only to halt at the Earl's command. He stood among us, his polished sword now smeared with blood, flesh clinging to its handguard.

'Let them go. They've thousands behind them. If we push, we'll leave ourselves isolated.'

It was the wise call.

Knowing we needed the safety of Aiguillon's walls, we turned to the grim task at hand – finishing off the wounded and stripping the dead of anything valuable.

I stumbled upon a Frenchman pinned beneath his dead horse, arrows riddling its chest. His armour was lavish, a blue and yellow silk surcoat marking him as nobility. A gold-handled sword lay just out of reach.

He thrashed in desperation to free himself, freezing when he saw me. His hand darted to a knife on his belt.

'English pig-dog! I will kill you and rape your daughters when we...'

My mace crashed down on his helmet, the force denting in the metal. His words faltered into a grotesque stammer, blood bubbling from his lips as the crumpled steel pressed into his skull. Three more strikes silenced him.

'You shouldn't have done that, Ailred.'

I turned to see Lord Stafford approaching, wiping blood from his sword.

I raised an eyebrow. 'Unlike you to get sentimental, my Lord.'

He smiled. 'That was Enguerrand de Coucy.' He bent to retrieve the gilded sword, studying it before offering it to me. 'A high ransom lost, but the blade will fetch a fine price.' His gaze flicked to the horizon, hardening. 'Finish up. They're regrouping, and the Duke's main force is closing in. We need to get back to Aiguillon.'

I rifled through de Coucy's belongings, pocketing coins and unhooking a pendant from his neck. With effort, I freed his ornate belt and scabbard, tying them around my waist before sliding the sword home.

'Move!' Paul barked, galloping past toward the town. 'Or do you plan to fight the entire French army yourself?'

Mace in hand, I sprinted toward the gates with the others. As I reached safety, I turned just in time to see the Duke of Normandy's army cresting the horizon. Banners fluttered, and the earth trembled beneath twenty thousand men and horses.

The last of our men scrambled inside. The gates slammed shut. From beyond, the French roar of fury reached us, carried on the afternoon breeze.

We were safe – for now.

CHAPTER 24

Over the next few days, we watched from the gate towers as the Duke's army entrenched itself, encircling the town. Earthworks rose, the French leaving no tree standing in their quest to raise barricades, while a sea of tents grew into a city. A magnificent red-and-white marquee stood at its heart – unmistakably the Duke's command. Smoke spiralled from thousands of fires, filling the air with the acrid tang of charred wood and meat, as the rhythm of hammers and shouted orders became a constant drumbeat.

Lord Stafford surveyed the grim tableau below. 'They're here to stay, fellas – the Duke and his commanders have even brought their whores.'

Near the marquee, a cluster of elaborately decorated tents bustled with women, unlike the usual camp followers. They moved with an air of practised confidence, their silks and painted faces marking them as courtesans of the highest order.

Paul, leaning on the parapet, muttered, 'We'll share them between us, then toss the husks to the ranks to fight over when we're through.'

Stafford's head turned, his expression stiffening. 'I think we've much work to do before that, Paul.'

Paul blinked, as if only then realising he'd

spoken aloud. His dead-eyed stare lingered before he glanced back at the siege preparations.

I strolled the walls with my newly acquired status symbol – Enguerrand de Coucy's sword. I would draw it whenever Paul appeared and polish it, adjusting my hair in its reflection. It drew the required response every time.

'You French tart.'

I would smile and move off, checking the town's defences.

The French toiled like ants over the following days, clearing great swathes of land beyond the walls. Trees were felled and dragged away, bushes and brambles hacked back to bare earth. Seven shallow hollows took shape, spaced evenly along the southern wall where the Duke's forces gathered. Their purpose was obvious to anyone watching.

On the fifth morning, through the haze, they came: siege trebuchets, lumbering forward, drawn by straining oxen and creaking ropes. Their hulking frames loomed like monstrous sentinels, shadowing the land as they advanced.

'As I predicted, gentlemen, they're concentrating on our southern and eastern walls.' Stafford glanced around as we looked down in dread. 'Which leaves the north and east as our link to the outside world. They'll lock us down tighter there, but I think we'll still be able to keep a line of communication open with Earl Lancaster. I sent a runner to him days ago, so he'll be aware of our standing.' He stared at me. 'And with our spy network working so well, hopefully, he'll keep us informed.'

I shrugged, feigning indifference, though Stafford's watchful gaze lingered. My mind flickered briefly to Izelda – her secrets and loyalties – before I put the thought aside.

'Right, we know what to expect. Brief your men and double-check every detail of our defences. Water, food, arrows – everything.' Stafford's fist crashed against the parapet. 'If I see any man neglecting his duties, he'll be hanging from the city gates.' He called out after us as we scattered to carry out his orders. 'Any break in discipline will see our blood turn the rivers red.'

Within hours, it started – boulders the size of barrels raining down, sparks flying from granite-infused walls, thunderous strikes making the ground tremble. They targeted the town, too; boulders lobbed into the void, crumbling buildings on impact. It never let up, night and day, though the damage to the sturdy walls was minimal. A couple of times, the French inched their trebuchets forward, desperate to land heavier blows, but each attempt met with deadly volleys from our archers, forcing them back under a hail of arrows. For all their efforts, they gained nothing but broken men and shattered pride.

The Duke placed a minor guard division around the north and east walls, those closest to the Lot and Garonne rivers. His strategy was obvious – cut off access to the waterways, our lifeblood. The rivers lay within bowshot of the town's walls, making any Frenchman venturing too close an easy target. Every few days, they attempted a sortie, and we greeted them with arrows, scything them down like wheat until they retreated. Their efforts ensured we kept those walls manned at all times.

The Duke, however, used these skirmishes to bleed our resources and distract us from the south, where Stafford remained convinced the actual assault would come.

By early May, a month after the Duke of Normandy had encircled the town, the siege fell into a predictable routine. The French pounded us relentlessly, yet the walls stood firm. By day, the Duke and his commanders observed from their grand marquee, directing their futile operations. Each attack, half-hearted and poorly pressed, cost them dearly in blood. But the Duke appeared untroubled – he had thousands more lives to spend.

By night, we watched with envy as women moved between the French tents, their forms flickering in the darkness. No matter how hard we strained our eyes, we couldn't make out their faces – leaving the rest to our imagination and solitary nighttime pursuits. One woman in a crimson dress, in particular, glided with a grace and confidence that set her apart. We decided she must be the madam. While the others scurried, she moved purposefully, always ending her journey at the Duke's tent. She would pause now and then, staring towards our beleaguered town before slipping inside, vanishing from view.

Lucky bastard.

*

'We have news,' Stafford said, his voice cutting through our chatter.

It was late in the day, and we stood in his quarters, the cramped space now awash with anticipation. He had summoned his senior advisors and commanders, and we gathered in tense silence. Stafford sat on a simple three-legged stool, as unyielding as ever, while Jouan de Montfort, the Gascon, stood behind him.

The last time I'd seen Jouan, he had saved my life at Aiguillon, his Gascons striking just as the French threatened to flank us. Their timely charge had turned the tide of battle, and I would be forever grateful. Since then, he had remained with Earl Lancaster, far from the frontlines. Now, he was here – with urgent news.

Jouan caught my eye and winked, a familiar gesture that stirred a brief smile.

'Jouan de Montfort has just arrived,' Stafford said by way of introduction. 'He's come from Earl Lancaster. I'll let him report to you personally.'

Jouan stepped forward, his muddy boots thudding against the wooden floor. He cleared his throat.

'First and foremost, Earl Lancaster is aware of your plight and is doing everything in his power to support you.' A ripple of relief spread through the room. 'As you know, there's a massive army out there...'

A voice from the back interrupted him. 'Is there? I hadn't noticed!'

Laughter cut the tension, and Jouan let it run its course before resuming. 'Yes, well. As I was saying, we're hitting their supply lines hard. None of the Duke's men dare forage beyond their boundaries – we've made sure of that.'

He paused, eyeing our blank expressions, then added, 'In short, gentlemen, we're starving them out.'

A few muttered words of approval, but I needed more. 'May I speak, Jouan?' I asked, keeping my tone respectful.

He nodded. 'Of course, Ailred.'

'That's all well and good, but we're running low here, too. Unless we get some food...'

Jouan raised a hand, cutting me mid-flow. 'We know.' He hesitated, then glanced at Stafford, who gave a small nod. 'We intend to float a couple of barges down the Lot with supplies. We believe it's doable, with most of their forces concentrated on your southern walls.'

'Amen to that,' Paul muttered, clasping his hands together in prayer and looking skyward. The Father Paul act had lost its grip on those around him, but whether it had loosened its hold on him was another matter. I often caught him talking to God, seeking His thoughts – sometimes even berating *Him* for His choices. The room erupted into laughter, easing the strain.

Jouan waited for the noise to settle. 'There's one more thing before I take my leave. Our spies report that body flux is spreading through their ranks by the day – meaning they're eating at one end and firing it out the other with interest. Between that and their dwindling supplies, they're suffering as much as you.' He smiled and nodded. 'If not worse.'

Satisfaction swept through the group.

Stafford rose and shook Jouan's hand. 'Thank you. You've set minds at ease. We'll have a party ready to escort the supplies in when you're close to the walls – just let us know.'

Jouan nodded, then left, heading toward the marshy ground by the river – our lifeline and his safest route back to Lancaster.

*

I stood, gazing out over the town's walls, idly twisting the pendant I had looted from the neck of Enguerrand de Coucy. I thought it looked good on me alongside his sword at my waist, the pair adding to my ever-increasing grandeur. I had noticed men look at me and attempt to suppress their admiration. Well, I think that's what they were suppressing.

It was a hot, sunny day in June, the French summer dropping on us without warning. April and May had been cold and wet, but as June arrived, the clouds parted, and the sky never blemished. Hedgerows burst into life, honeybees plundered foxgloves, and Philippa and the children would've been out chasing blue butterflies. The pang struck the moment I let myself picture them. Frederick and Timothy, with their endless energy and mischief. Kimberly, with her mother's eyes and smile – those two forever a team, siding against anyone foolish enough to cross them. Too often, that fool had been me. If I made it through this, I swore I'd never leave Tonebricge again – not that it would ever be the same.

'Thinking of that Gascon tart, Al?' Paul had come up behind me without a sound. 'Some sentry you are,' he laughed, slapping me around the head, 'I should report you to Stafford for dereliction of duty. He'll hang you!'

'Fuck off, I knew you were there, I just couldn't be bothered to acknowledge your existence.'

He chuckled and wandered off, continuing his rounds.

It was true – I *had* neglected my picketing duties, too caught up in my own thoughts. If anything happened because of it, that was on me. The lives of the town relied on every man staying alert. I leaned on the battlements, looking out over the southern ramparts. The trebuchets had been silent for the last hour. Maybe the Duke fancied a nap.

'She's not a tart,' I muttered as my mind wandered, the sound of Paul balling out Godric a hundred yards further down the lookout platform drifting to nothingness.

But then it struck me. Our last meeting had left me questioning – was the entire relationship just a construct of my imagination? Sure, we'd shared something physical years ago, but so what – most of the English army had found solace in one form or another, and I didn't see them dewy-eyed and losing sleep.

I pictured Izelda's face, her naked body and my stirrings took me back to our time together. I had saved her from the marauding English and Welsh army after we attacked and sacked Arques in France, killing two Welsh archers in the process. She showed her gratitude in many ways and positions over the next few weeks, and I closed my eyes, allowing myself to relive those intimate moments. I could see her as she...

An arrow spoiled the moment, hissing past my face so close that the goose-feather fletching brushed my cheek. My head twisted towards the source as Godric nocked his next shot and drew the bow to its limit.

'TO ARMS!' he bellowed, his voice bringing me back to reality.

I whipped around in time to see French ladders cresting the walls, soldiers scrambling over, one collapsing with an arrow in his chest, blood already showing through his livery. The battlements were narrow, with barely space for two men to pass, and those who'd cleared the wall now charged, weapons drawn.

'DROP!' Godric yelled, his voice decisive, as more archers joined him from further down the wall.

I threw myself flat, the stone bruising my ribs, and scrambled forward on elbows and knees as arrows hissed overhead.

As I reached Godric, he grabbed my tunic and hauled me behind him, his eyes never wavering from the fight. The others loosed a relentless stream of arrows, pinning them back. My bow was still leaning against the wall where I'd dropped it, and I cursed myself. Without a word, Godric drew my sword from its scabbard and thrust it into my hand before snatching up his bow and turning back to the fray.

I glanced past him. French bodies lay strewn, blood streaking the stonework. More soldiers hauled themselves over the battlements, only to stumble on the dead or meet the same brutal end. Some lost their footing and tumbled from the platform, where our men-at-arms hacked them apart.

Paul and Bonehead appeared, striding up the spiral staircase with long-handled forks and shoved past me.

'Those ladders need to go,' Paul barked, and

they charged forward.

Gripping my sword like my last chance at salvation, I followed. This was my fault – now was the time to atone. As Paul and Bonehead shoved the ladders back outwards, sending screams and bodies crashing into the massed soldiers below, I struck with blind desperation. One man met me head-on, his eyes blazing, refusing to step back. He swung his mace toward my face so fast I barely managed to flinch away. The head of it caught the leather strap of my pendant, yanking me forward. I hit the ground at his feet, the cord still tangled around the weapon. He tried to rip it free for another swing, but in that split second, I drove my sword up into his groin, slicing into his bladder and spilling its contents all over me.

There was no time for reflection. I jumped up and attacked those still left. Bone shattered, and blood sprayed as I lashed out at anyone still living. As the final ladder was pushed away, I thrust my sword into the chest of the Frenchman at the top. Its bloodied blade buried deep but snagged between his ribs, ripping the weapon from my grip as the ladder crashed beyond the walls. I cursed and grabbed a discarded war-hammer, taking my frustration out on the handful of French soldiers stranded atop the ramparts.

I was in no mood for pity.

*

We secured the southern walls, the final Frenchmen being either killed or captured, and the Duke resumed his trebuchet assault before we'd had time to wash away the blood.

As we picked over the French bodies, I searched for the pendant but never did find it – probably squirrelled away by one of our men. It nearly got me killed, so I wasn't too disappointed.

I'd sought a barber-surgeon to tend to a minor injury, hoping to evade the inevitable enquiry into how the French gained such easy access, but even he seemed to know what awaited me.

'You're Ailred Norman, aren't you?' he asked as I sat on a low stool, staring at the floor while his curved needle stitched the gash in my arm. 'I've been treating some of your fellow watchmen.' He shook his head and looked me up and down with contempt. 'You're the lookout who didn't notice…'

His words trailed off as I looked up and glared at him. He hesitated, the needle hovering above my arm.

'Just do your job and shut up,' I snapped.

He nodded once, a faint smile concealed, and returned to his work.

One of Stafford's squires summoned me to his tent within the hour. Two guards flanked the entrance, refusing to respond to my questions. The camp around us was quiet, with muffled voices inside the tent, the only sound save for the destructive strikes from the trebuchets.

I stood under their watch for what seemed like a lifetime before being called inside.

Lord Stafford and his senior advisors sat in silence as I entered, their eyes fixed on me as I stood to attention before the long table. The air in the tent was stifling as the long, hot day drew to a close.

Still, silence.

Sweat ran down my back. I glanced around, but Paul, Bonehead, and Godric were nowhere to be seen. Their absence left me feeling exposed – alone, and friendless.

The Earl rose, his gaze cold.

'Nice of you to come, Ailred. Do you know why you're here?'

'Well,' I started, but my voice faltered, barely audible. I cleared my throat and tried again. 'I presume it's about the attack, my Lord.'

I couldn't meet his probing eyes.

He let the silence stretch, then spoke again, measured and deliberate. 'Correct. I've always said you were more than an idiot, Ailred – so, yes, that small matter of the French nearly taking the town and massacring us.' He gestured to the men seated on either side of him. 'We need to ensure this never happens again and determine if any man was in dereliction of his duties.' He sat back and thumped the table hard, making me flinch. 'And if so, I must make an example of any such man.' He shook his head slowly, his voice concerned. 'If I don't do that, Ailred, where does that leave us?'

I went to answer but realised it was a statement.

The tent seemed to close in on me, the sweat-laden air heavier. Lord Stafford leaned forward, eyes narrowing. 'As I said, you're no idiot. I think you know where I'm going with this.'

His words hit me like a blow. With icy clarity, I remembered what he'd said he would do to any man caught neglecting his duties.

He would hang them.

In the silence that followed, raised voices drifted in from outside the tent.

Stafford's eye shifted from me, his attention distracted as footsteps approached.

I turned my head just as one of the guards stepped in and bowed. 'There's a Godric Applewhite outside, my Lord,' he said apologetically. 'He claims to have information relating to this meeting. Says it can't wait, Lord.'

Stafford leaned back in his chair and exhaled before giving a curt nod. 'Let him in. Let's hear it.'

The guard ducked out, pulling the flaps wide as Godric strode inside, his boots stirring the dust on the tent floor. He halted beside me without so much as a glance in my direction.

'I hear good things about you, Godric,' Stafford began, his tone calming. 'Your quick thinking turned a disaster into an incident today, and I commend you.' Murmurs of agreement rippled through the aides and advisors. 'So, what can you bring to this *trial*?'

Stafford's voice hardened. It was the first time he'd used that word, and the stakes doubled.

Godric shifted beside me, a faint twitch betraying his unease. I had never seen him nervous, not even in the thick of battle.

'Thank you, Lord.' He glanced at me for the first time, then back to Stafford. 'I cannot allow Ailred to take all the blame for this afternoon's incursion.'

'Go on, Godric, who else is to blame?' Stafford's tone was blunt, his stare unrelenting.

Godric swallowed hard. 'The French gained access between Ailred and me, Sire. I agreed to cover a part of his section when he went to relieve himself, my Lord.' He turned to me, an eye twitching. I couldn't tell if he was winking or about to faint. 'Ain't that so, Ailred?'

'Did I?' His wink turned to a look of exasperation before I seized the lifeline. 'Erm, yeah, Lord Stafford, hadn't I mentioned that?' I hesitated, then added, 'It wasn't just a piss, Lord – I thought I had that body flux thing. I was desperate for a good...'

'That's enough,' Stafford cut in, his hand raised. 'We get the picture.'

'The French are riddled with it, Sire – I think it comes from that garlic stuff they eat all the time – I might've caught it from one of them while I was fighting,' I added, trying to sound earnest.

Stafford glared, his aides biting back grins. 'I could fetch the bucket to prove it if you like – unless the escaping French took it with them – they *do love* a bucket of...'

By then, even Stafford was shaking his head, a reluctant smile breaking through as the laughter spread.

'I see he hasn't changed much.'

The deep voice boomed from behind Stafford's aids as the tent finally hushed. It was a voice I recognised.

Stafford grinned. The men surrounding the Earl moved apart, giving me a clear view.

It was Sir Thomas de Clare, Lord of Tonebricge.

CHAPTER 25

'Wherever I go in this world, you seem to be there,' Sir Thomas said, carving a path through the men to stand at Stafford's shoulder.

'It's good to see you, Sire,' I replied. 'A surprise, but a pleasant one.'

He nodded. 'Just in time to watch you hang.'

I glanced at Stafford, who was looking between Godric and me. After a moment, he spoke. 'Indulge me, Sir Thomas. You've heard Ailred's defence and Godric's attempt to get himself hanged alongside him. What do you make of these two?'

Sir Thomas shrugged. 'Knowing Ailred as I do – and not a day goes by that I don't regret the fact – he does have redeeming qualities.' He scratched his chin. 'I'll think of one in a minute. Give me time.'

We waited.

'All right, hang him.'

The tent erupted with laughter before Sir Thomas raised his arms, smiling to silence them.

'Ailred is a pain in the arse, but he's our pain in the arse. It wouldn't have been his intention if he had anything to do with today's incursion. And if this Godric fellow risked his life to share the responsibility, it speaks volumes about his standing among the men.'

He turned to me, his expression softening. A flicker of sadness lingered in his eyes. 'I entrusted my son to his protection before they left our home town.' Stafford crossed himself. 'I've spoken to Earl Lancaster and know Ailred did everything he could to keep Nathaniel from harm. I'd trust him with my life.' He paused, then grinned. 'But he's still a fuckin' idiot.'

The tent broke into more laughter as the tension lifted.

He saved my life.

*

'How did you get past the French?'

I sat with Sir Thomas and Godric outside the only tavern still open. I'd planned to celebrate my lucky escape by buying them enough beer to make them vomit as a thank you, but the mood remained sombre.

He sipped his ale. 'Stafford's kept the arteries open through the rivers, and the Duke's hands are tied through Early Lancaster's constant harassment.'

Silence settled as we stared into our drinks.

'Why did you come out?' I asked.

He sighed. 'I got the news about Nathaniel and needed to understand the circumstances.'

'He was a credit to you, Sire. His bravery and...'

'Save it, Ailred. He's dead.' His voice wavered. 'I've been told the backstory. I just wanted to hear it for...' He stopped, shaking his head. 'In truth, I don't know what I wanted.'

A tear ran down his face. I'd never seen the lord so vulnerable. He sniffed and wiped it away. 'And if either of you mentions this moment again, I'll hang you myself.'

I chuckled. 'That seems fair, Sire. Who's looking after your affairs?'

'My daughter, Maud. She has a flair for…' He drifted off, lost in thought. 'She has it covered.'

'And when are you going back home?'

He sniffed and laughed. 'You sound like you're trying to get rid of me, Alired!'

'No, I was just wondering…'

'I'm here to kill Frenchmen, like you two. I have a debt to pay. I've grown soft, living safely in Tonebricge. It's time I remembered why the Lord put me on this earth.'

'To kill Frenchmen?' I asked.

'Precisely.'

We finished our drinks and ordered another round.

'What happened to that status symbol you called a sword and the pendant that made you look like the Duke's whore, Ailred?' Godric asked as he blew the froth off his ale. He grinned. 'Don't get me wrong, you look better without them, I just wondered.'

I shrugged. 'Lost them both during the battle.'

'Probably the Almighty's way of punishing you for your sins,' Sir Thomas grinned, 'of which there are many. The lord giveth, and the lord taketh away.' He looked me up and down. 'Mostly taketh away in your case – your brain being one such example.'

*

I awoke, a bucket of water tossed over my bed as I tried to finish the fantasy about Izelda and me. Every time we got naked, something ruined it – this time, she spoke with Philippa's voice before turning into a snake. The water jolted me back to reality.

I shook the water from my ears and looked up into Sir Thomas's face. 'I'm so pleased you're here, Sire. Have you brought me breakfast in bed?'

'Get up, Idiot; we have a long day ahead of us.'

I sat up. 'I'll take that as a no.'

He bent and grabbed the half-filled chamber pot by the side of my bed. 'Unless you're up and out in the next few seconds, this'll be the next bucket.' He stood above me, his eyes alight with mischief. 'The Duke's floating two barges down the Lot,' he said. 'You know what that means?'

'He has two barges he wants to float down the river?'

He went to throw the contents on me, but I held my hands up in defeat and jumped out of bed.

'It means the Duke's bringing food and supplies down to his troops, Ailred. They're starving.'

I jumped out of bed and joined the small group gathered in the near darkness. Godric was already there, his bow unstrung, ready to travel; the rest were some of our fiercest men – unsuited to subtlety but perfectly matched for what lay ahead.

'I know you're all wondering what this is all about and want to go back to bed,' Sir Thomas said, his voice carrying just enough edge to wake the men properly. 'But today, we have the chance to break the spirit of those bastards behind the trebuchets.' He gestured toward the river with a jerk of his chin. 'A spy tells us that two barges are coming upriver this morning. They're loaded with food, medicine – everything they need to keep this siege going.' That got their attention. Sir Thomas pressed on, his voice calculating. 'The enemy's starving – worse than we thought – and the flux has ravaged them. These barges are their lifeline. Cut them off, and their hope crumbles.'

The sleepy band of brothers stiffened as the task's importance sank in. Godric gave a quick nod, and the rest fell silent. We had a chance to strike where it hurt most.

We followed the river upstream, fifty of us eager to impress the new lord. I questioned his leadership; his mind wasn't entirely in the game. He seemed too consumed with avenging his son's death – but I kept such doubts to myself. If Stafford deemed him capable, that was good enough for me.

The march was slow, our path winding

through dense woodland that kept us out of sight. Scouts ranged ahead, ensuring we remained unseen, and just before dawn, one returned with word of an approaching convoy. Guided by the whispers of an unnamed informant, we took position. As mist hovered over the water, early morning dew clung to our clothes as we waited.

A massive Percheron emerged through the haze, then another, each horse pulling barges along either side of the river. We had split between the banks, Sir Thomas leading the men on the far side. Low foliage lined both edges, enough to keep us hidden as archers nocked arrows and men-at-arms drew weapons.

'This will be easy,' I muttered.

As usual, I was wrong. Within moments, both riverbanks were filled with escorting French soldiers.

Sir Thomas had given us orders before we left the town, so we knew our roles. As the barges approached, we sprang the trap.

Godric and I loosed arrows into the men leading the horses, their bodies crumpling before they could react. One of our squires on either bank rushed forward, seizing the reins and calming the startled beasts. Our second volley struck the helmsmen – both dropping, arrows through their necks.

Shouts in French echoed through the mist as soldiers scrambled to defend themselves. They had set no scouts, so were caught unprepared, their weapons remaining sheathed or lashed to their mounts. The rest of our archers turned their sights on the panicked troops, volley after volley cutting through them.

In the confusion, I broke cover and sprinted to the barge on our side of the river, leaping onto the stern. The helmsman lay slumped over the tiller, his dead weight pulling the barge toward the river's centre, dragging the struggling horse with it. Grabbing the lifeless man, I heaved him aside and seized the rudder. As the horse's hooves skidded at the edge, seconds from plunging into the water, I forced the vessel back towards the bank.

Across the water, Sir Thomas stood at the stern of his craft, the helmsman having tumbled backwards into the Lot from the force of Godric's flight. He caught my eye and nodded, exhilaration lighting his face. On the riverbank, the squires urged the massive Percherons into a steady trot, keen to put distance between us and the fray.

I glanced back. The battle on the riverbank teetered – our archers held the French down, but their numbers swelled. Groups of enemy men-at-arms, now armed and organised, broke off to flank us, but our own shifted to counter, mirroring every move. More Frenchmen emerged from the mist with every passing second. Then I saw him – Godric, isolated, surrounded by three men-at-arms. His bow was drawn, but he was hopelessly outnumbered.

My hands tightened on the rudder, torn between duty and the instinct to run to his aid. Without help, Godric was as good as dead.

'Don't even think about it, Ailred! Every man back there knows the risks. Get the barges to Aiguillon, or their sacrifice is for nothing!'

Sir Thomas's shout left no room for argument.

I didn't look back again. With crushing realisation, I focused on guiding the barge toward Aiguillon, letting the screams of battle fade behind me.

*

The Percherons pulling the barges were exhausted as we caught sight of the town's walls above the treeline. We had to round a bend, leaving us a short, straight run to safety. The dawn mist had burned away, leaving a stillness in the air, with the promise of a sunny day. We were too far from Godric and the rest to hear any sounds of battle, but Sir Thomas's furrowed brow showed unease. He strained his eyes, scanning the towpath.

'Looks like our men have broken and are retreating to Aiguillon, Ailred,' he shouted.

I followed his gaze as figures emerged from the haze. Moments later, the truth hit.

'It's the French, Lord. They must've got past our men.'

Thomas swore under his breath. His eyesight

had been poor at Tonebricge Castle – it seemed worse now.

The squires struck the flanks and urged the Percherons on, screaming commands to drive them harder, but the beasts refused to comply.

'Move them, damn your hides – we'll not make it!' Sir Thomas shouted, his head whipping back and forth as he judged the shrinking distance between the town's walls and our pursuers.

'If we can get round this bend, we'll be in sight of Aiguillon,' I called back, though I could see the squires' struggles. 'The men will see us and come to help!'

'They'll never get here in time,' he replied, his voice edged with resignation. 'Arm yourself, Ailred. Let's go out like men.'

I released the tiller, jamming my mace into a crevice to keep it steady. Grabbing my bow, I drew an arrow from the quiver at my side. The squires stuck to their task, refusing to flee despite the inevitable consequences. I flashed a look of thanks at my lad, and he returned a shaky smile before drawing a sword from its sheath, his knuckles white around the hilt.

As the French closed in, we reached the bend in the river, and a battle cry erupted. My heart pounded as I drew my bow to full draw, taking aim – but they were still too far. The cries grew louder, closing in like a storm. I took a final breath, steeling myself. It was always going to end this way.

I drew again, targeting the commanding Frenchman as he came within range. The screams became deafening, and they seemed to engulf me. Then, just in the corner of my eye, I saw the truth.

It wasn't the French who were screaming. The cries came from behind us. Our forces. Paul. Reinforcements.

Relief and fury stretched my emotions as I saw the glint of swords and the wave of arrows. The fight wasn't done. Not yet.

The squires skidded to a halt, and I shoved my mace free before leaping onto the towpath. Paul thundered past me, a wild look in his eyes, as he strived to be first into the enemy.

The first wave of arrows had torn through their ranks, felling horses and riders in a chaotic storm of screams and peppered bodies.

'With me, Al!' Paul shouted, his stride unbroken.

I plunged into the thrashing mass of bodies as both armies crashed together – steel slicing flesh, axes splintering skulls. Though the French had lost much of their cavalry, they still fought like wolves, but the chase down the towpath had sapped their strength.

I reached the melee just as Paul shattered their defensive line. He drove his sword into the chest of an officer and was trying to wrench it free, blood pumping and covering him. A Frenchman lunged at Paul with a pike, point aimed straight at his belly. Paul released his sword and spun around just in time, finding himself inside the weapon's killing distance. I hurled him my mace. He caught it and smashed the pike-wielding man's face in one single brutal motion. Paul's sword was still caught in the man's rib cage as he lay gurgling blood; without hesitation, I stamped on the man's face repeatedly as I tore the blade free.

By now, Bonehead and the rest of our men-at-arms had the French ranks in disarray, their discipline shattering like glass. I lost sight of Paul as I scanned the enemy, looking for another victim. Many of them crouched, bodies spent and broken.

I found a man kneeling, his lower legs shattered. He raised trembling hands in surrender. I saw Godric surrounded in my mind's eye, our dead strewn along the riverbank – and my sword took the man's head.

Those still standing fled but were too weak to escape. We hunted them down in frenzied rage and vengeance. We hacked limbs and spilt blood, avenging our fallen comrades in a merciless slaughter.

Nothing would bring back Godric – but he'd cost them hundreds as payment.

*

Sir Thomas and I stood before Lord Stafford in his command tent, still spattered with the blood of our enemies. Summoned to deliver our report the moment we returned, we barely had time to catch our breath while the barges were stripped of their cargo and hauled inside the town's walls. Aside from the two squires, we were the only survivors of the morning raid.

'Can we not send out a small party to retrieve the bodies – or at least check if any were captured?' I asked once we'd finished our recount.

'Don't be absurd, man,' Stafford snapped. 'We've lost enough good men today. The French will be smarting from their losses and will have doubled their guard on the river. I had my reservations about letting your brother and his men linger beyond the walls when you failed to return on time.' He pushed his papers aside with a sigh and leaned back in his chair. 'But he proved me wrong, so I can't complain. I only hope the sacrifice was worth it.'

The tent flap rustled, and Bonehead entered, bowing. 'I have the inventory from the seized barges, my Lord.'

He handed a scroll of parchment to Stafford, then stepped back while the Earl spread it across the desk. Stafford's eyes scanned the list, his lips curling into a satisfied smile.

'We have them,' he muttered, nodding to himself. His gaze lifted to meet ours. 'This will set them back massively. Everything on here is critical to their campaign. It'll take months to recover, and I trust Lancaster will do everything in his power to ensure they don't.'

He turned to one of his advisors, who had been scribbling notes. 'Get word to Earl Lancaster of the capture. Send a couple of Gascons – if one's caught, the other might still make it out under cover of darkness.'

The advisor bowed and left the tent without a word.

Stafford looked at us as if seeing us for the first time since returning.

'You look like you've been to hell. Go and clean yourselves up – take the rest of the day.' He offered a faint smile, his finger tracing down the parchment until it stopped midway. 'There are ten barrels of wine on the list. Break the seal on one – you've earned it.' His face darkened. 'And drink to the men who gave their lives so you could stand here now.'

We turned to leave just as a fresh barrage of boulders crashed against the town, shaking the ground beneath our feet.

*

The following day, I woke with a pounding headache. Instinctively, I turned to speak to Godric, half-expecting him in the bed beside mine – then yesterday's events crashed over me.

I lay there, trying to piece together why I had woken unprompted. It was unlike me, especially after the amount I'd drunk the night before.

Minutes passed in confusion before it struck me – silence. The bombardment had ceased.

I bolted upright, vomited into the chamber pot, then dressed and made my way to the gate towers.

Lord Stafford and Sir Thomas were already there, conferring with the guards and staring over the walls.

'Good morning, my Lords,' I said, joining them. 'The silence woke me. What's happening?'

The Earl gestured toward the French camp with a sweep of his arm. 'See for yourself, Ailred – they're packing up and leaving.'

I rubbed sleep from my eyes and squinted into the early light. The trebuchets were being hauled back, most tents already gone. Only the Duke's marquee and another larger tent, likely belonging to his madam, remained of the command tents. I could make out Duke John standing with her as his commanders darted about, overseeing the retreat.

'It seems the siege is over,' Stafford declared. He clapped Sir Thomas and me on the shoulders. 'You boys broke them.'

I looked towards the river where I'd last seen Godric and whispered a silent farewell.

CHAPTER 26

As I look over your shoulder and scan the squiggly nonsense you've scrawled, Brother Michael, I wonder what secrets lie within. You could be scripting anything – painting me as the villain of every scene. Perhaps I was. I've never considered the prospect. What I would give to have accepted Philippa's offer of tuition – but foresight was never my strength.

Yes, I suppose I *will* have to trust you.

Fine, I'll sit down and continue. Where were we? Ah, yes – of course.

*

The French retreat heralded the arrival of Earl Lancaster, bringing much-needed supplies. He also brought news of King Edward's campaign to claim the French throne.

In July, the King and his sixteen-year-old son, Edward, the Prince of Wales, had landed at Saint-Vaast-la-Hougue on the Cotentin Peninsula in Normandy. Their presence brought a storm of destruction. They swept through northern France with a ferocity that took King Philip by surprise, plundering towns and killing those who opposed them. The most notorious of their exploits was the storming of Caen. For five brutal days, the city was laid waste under Edward's hand: defenders slaughtered, streets turned into rivers of blood, and civilians perishing to fire and barbarism.

With their unbroken power, Edward and his son sought to link up with an allied Flemish force besieging Béthune. But that hope crumbled when the Flemish army disintegrated under poor discipline. Left exposed, Edward's forces pressed on, only to find themselves relentlessly harried by Philip's men. The French king had gathered a massive force that trailed Edward's every step, dispatching small bands of skirmishers to hunt down any foragers. Philip's men also ravaged the countryside, burning their own fields, looting villages, and severing supply lines to leave Edward's troops on the brink of starvation.

After weeks of pursuit, Edward and the Prince of Wales sought confrontation, setting up defensive positions close to Crécy-en-Ponthieu.

While Edward and his son braced for battle in the north, we in the south had our own part to play in the king's war.

*

'If we take our leave now, Earl Lancaster, we'll reach Edward's forces before Philip attacks. If your intelligence holds true and he remains firm near Crécy-en-Ponthieu, our arrival will provide the bolster needed against the imbalance of their numbers. He's ordered you to continue your chevauchée, but that command does not bind us.'

The atmosphere within the tent was suffocating as Stafford and Lancaster faced each other for the first time since Lancaster had assumed command of the Gascon campaign. Behind each stood their guard, silent and with menace, their readiness for violence profuse.

'And who, Lord Stafford, would assume command here at Aiguillon should you abandon the garrison to pursue this fantasy of yours?' His tone was calm, a smirk flickering.

Lord Stafford snorted, his contempt barely concealed. 'I said nothing about leaving this town defenceless, Earl. I will leave sufficient men to hold against another siege should you fail to secure the surrounding area.' He allowed the jibe to land before continuing. 'Sir Hugh Menil, who currently commands the town in my stead, will maintain defence.'

Lancaster's jaw tightened, his calm veneer threatening to crack. When he spoke, his tone was harsh, his words calculated.

'Let us not waste time on *pleasantries*, Stafford. The King charges us with responsibility and decisive action. I will consider your request to join Edward's forces and give you my answer by morning.'

He turned to leave, but Stafford's voice stopped him.

'You misunderstand me, Earl Derby... Lancaster... whatever, I am not seeking your permission. I am informing you of my decision.'

Stafford spun on his heels and strode out of the tent, his men falling into step behind him with a precision that underscored his authority.

Earl Lancaster's gaze swept the room, resting on me. I met his stare with a grin that I couldn't suppress – the men he had banished to Aiguillon months before were now following Stafford to Crécy-en-Ponthieu. The decision had been made, and there was nothing Lancaster could do to stop us. Orders would be given, supplies gathered – by dawn, we would be on the road.

We were leaving.

*

At first light, we rode out – none of us doubted the course ahead. We travelled light – three hundred archers and a hundred men-at-arms – driven by the need to reach Crécy-en-Ponthieu before King Philip attacked Edward. Even Bastard seemed to sense the urgency, at one point even doing as I commanded. We gambled on Philip delaying his assault until his son, Duke John, could join him with his army. Along the way, French homesteads and villages barred their doors to us, unwilling to rise in armed defiance but equally unwilling to welcome invaders. We simply broke down their gates and stripped them of what we required, leaving ruin in our wake as part of a brutal scorched-earth campaign.

Outstripping the Duke's army wasn't difficult, as the logistics of moving such vast numbers weighed them down. Like Philip's tactics against Edward's forces, we razed everything behind us, ensuring their already starving ranks would find nothing to scavenge. Reports from our spy network managed to keep stride with us, detailing their low morale. The Duke's mistress was even rumoured to be on the verge of abandoning him.

By the time we approached Crécy-en-Ponthieu, both men and horses were spent. The scorching August heat dictated our movement: we rested during the hottest part of the day and marched into the cooler nights.

*

We found King Edward's army encamped in the woods east of Crécy, its position well-chosen on a gentle slope overlooking the surrounding land, so set up our own camp about a mile away. Lord Stafford had chosen Bonehead, Paul, and me to accompany him and ride ahead to announce our arrival and avoid being mistaken for a French column. He would leave Sir Thomas in command.

It was another stifling day, and I searched for Paul as the others grew impatient, muttering threats of leaving without him if he didn't hurry. He had been uncharacteristically silent of late, withdrawing from his usual circle of friends in favour of Abbot Robert Copgrove of Fountains Abbey in Yorkshire. Earl Lancaster had assigned Abbot Copgrove to Stafford's company after the liberation of Aiguillon, filling the void left by Father Nicholas Ravenshurst, who had been killed near the siege's end.

Abbot Copgrove seemed to have taken a liking to Paul, speaking warmly of his childhood home in Ripon and the splendours of Yorkshire. In turn, Paul listened with an intensity I hadn't seen since his time as "Father Paul". There was a new light in his eyes – or perhaps an old one, rekindled – and he was beginning to speak more of scripture and salvation.

As I was about to give up, I walked past a tent with a squire stationed outside.

'Have you seen Master Paul Christian?' I asked.

The boy shifted uneasily, his eyes darting to the closed tent flaps before flicking back to me.

'No, Sire, I have no idea where he is,' the boy mumbled, his voice shaky. He looked petrified.

My heart sank. Over the years, Paul's reputation had weighed heaviest on the squires and pages. He treated them like tools for tasks he deemed beneath him, driving them to tears with brutal belittlement. Any defiance was met with the back of his hand – or worse. For Paul, cruelty wasn't just a means to an end; it "passed the time".

'You may go,' I said, waving my hand.

His eyes widened. 'But Sire, I've been told not to allow anyone...'

'Just go,' I cut in, raising my voice enough for Paul to hear inside the flimsy tent. 'I'll take full responsibility.'

The boy hesitated, then bowed his head. 'Your will, Master Ailred. As you order.' He scurried away.

I took a deep breath and pulled back the tent flaps, dreading what I might find.

The sweltering heat hit me first, then the stench – thick and rancid, like a hammer blow. Flies swarmed in a low, incessant hum above Paul's rambling voice. He knelt at the centre, naked, his bloody hands clutching a psalter as he chanted the first line of the Pater Noster over and over.

In front of him lay organs, skin, and bone scattered across the grassy floor.

He looked up, his eyes shining, his chant faltering into silence.

'You are most welcome, my child,' he said softly. 'Are you here to give confession?'

I said nothing, staring at the gore, unable to identify its source. A child? No – a pig. Relief flooded me as I realised the pile was a desecrated animal, not human remains.

Paul stood and spread his arms wide. 'Come, brother, embrace me. Do not be afraid.'

I stepped forward, wrapped my arms around him, and rested my head on his shoulder. He did not move.

'I have made a sacrifice to God,' he whispered, his breath warm on my ear. 'He will guide us now – we fight for Him.'

Tears welled in my eyes. 'Yes, Paul, but I think God will work in silence – no one else need know. This can be *our* secret.'

He broke the embrace and stood back, closing his eyes. 'You are right, Child. God labours tirelessly and without the need for earthly praise.'

We stood unmoving before the sounds of footsteps outside jolted me into action.

'We must dress you, Father,' I said, though I had no plan beyond that. A search of the tent revealed no clothing.

'Do you know where my cassock and surplice are?' he asked, 'I must have mislaid them.'

I gripped his shoulders and forced him to meet my gaze.

'You haven't worn them since the first weeks of this campaign,' I said, steadying my voice. 'You're a soldier now.'

A serene yet unnerving smile swept his face. 'I am a soldier of God. He will lead us to victory through me.'

I peeked outside. The footsteps had passed, and the camp was clear.

'Right. Wait here. Do not move – I'll find clothing.'

He nodded, his gaze dropping as he noticed his nakedness for the first time.

I darted out and spotted the squire I'd dismissed earlier. He stiffened as I approached, fear still present on his face.

'Where are his clothes?' I demanded.

He jumped up and disappeared into the shadows, returning moments later with a bundled tunic and tabard.

'Here, Sire. I think... I think perhaps he's unwell.'

'He is suffering from nothing. Do you understand me?' I snapped, my voice quiet.

He stared at the ground, shoulders hunched. 'Yes, of course, Sire.'

'Does anyone else know?'

The squire hesitated, his gaze darting before settling somewhere near my boots. 'Not that I'm aware of.'

I gripped his arm, and he flinched. 'And it will remain that way.' My fingers tightened until I saw him wince. 'If anyone finds out, I'll know where it came from.'

He nodded, his breath shallow, but said nothing.

I took the clothes and returned to the tent. Paul hadn't moved. As I stepped inside, Paul's eyes cast downward, and his hands came to rest on his hips.

'Naked, like Adam when the serpent tempted him,' he murmured, then raised his face to mine. 'But I am not so easily led astray. I walk in the light of His truth, unashamed.'

I held his gaze for a moment. He believed every word, and the realisation gave me a strange comfort.

'Put these on,' I said, dropping the bundle beside him. 'I'll inform the others that you're unwell and won't be joining us to herald our presence to the King.'

Paul took the garments in silence and began to dress, a calm assurance in his every movement.

*

Stafford, Bonehead and I cantered towards King Edward's camp.

It wasn't long before a group of men blocked our path, circling us with their horses.

'And who might you be?' the leader growled, his Welsh accent challenging to decipher, as he pushed his mount forward. 'French spies?'

Lord Stafford leaned back in his saddle, unbothered by the surrounding men. The leader grabbed his horse's bit, but Stafford laughed. 'Some spies we'd make – strolling up to the front door and announcing ourselves!' He gestured downhill, where our troops waited in formation. 'I am Lord Stafford, commander of His Majesty's forces from Aiguillon.'

The man glanced down at the ranks, his hand releasing the bit as he gave a slow nod. 'Aiguillon, you say? I heard it was under siege... though your Lordship's name lends some credence.' He raised his chin. 'And is the Earl Norfolk with you, the Lord who helped defend the town?'

Stafford's smile widened. 'I believe you mean Earl Lancaster, Sir. Though I suspect you already knew that.'

The man grinned and turned toward the main camp, gesturing for us to follow. 'Very well, Lord Stafford. Come with me – the King will be glad of your presence. We need every man we can muster.'

As we rode in, men looked up from sharpening blades, mending mail, or cooking. The camp seemed disciplined and harmonious, with shouts of welcome as men recognised Lord Stafford.

Stafford nodded to a passing soldier.

'There's plenty of Englishmen here, too,' the man quipped, grinning at our escort.

The King greeted Stafford as an old friend, clasping his hand with genuine warmth as he raised him from his kneeling position.

'My Lord Stafford, it is a rare pleasure to see a friendly face in a land riddled with vermin. Come, sit with me.'

Bonehead and I held our places until he gave a brief nod of permission. Only then did we step back and stand to attention.

'You honour me, My King,' Stafford said as he seated himself opposite. 'I trust I find you well?'

The King leaned back in his wicker chair and clicked his fingers toward a nearby squire. 'As well as can be expected, Earl.' The squire stepped forward with a jug and two glasses, pouring wine into both. The King handed one to Stafford, raising the other. 'Your health, gentlemen,' he said, downing its contents.

Stafford followed his lead, satisfaction sweeping his face as he lowered the vessel. Silence settled as both men savoured the moment, broken only when the King spoke.

'God must have listened, Earl, for He's answered my prayer.' His smile was genuine. 'I can't say I expected His answer to hail from Aiguillon, given what you endured there, but you are a welcome sight all the same. I heard of your triumph with Lancaster – breaking the siege, no less.' He stroked his long, greying beard. 'Have you two settled your differences amicably?' Stafford raised his eyebrows but said nothing. The king laughed. 'I commend you both, regardless.' He poured another measure of wine before glancing toward Bonehead and me. 'Ah, where are my manners? Leonard, fetch two more glasses.'

The squire disappeared before returning with two wooden mugs, filling each and passing them to us. I raised mine and sipped, before draining it. I couldn't help it – it was the best wine I'd ever tasted.

The King's eyes fixed on me, and he laughed. 'It's good wine, is it not?'

I blushed. 'Yes, my Lord, I mean King, I mean…'

'We've met before, haven't we?' he said.

I froze, caught off guard. 'Your memory is remarkable, My King,' I stammered. 'We met at…'

'Sluys and that confounded siege of Tournai,' he interrupted, nodding as he sipped his wine.

'I never forget a man who serves his king with distinction.' He hesitated as if grasping at something just beyond reach. 'Didn't you and your brother disappear after being accused of...?' He studied me, waiting for illumination.

I wasn't about to confess to slipping out of Tournai after being linked to the brutal murder of an archdeacon – or to my brief entanglement with a French company that slaughtered dozens of Welshmen. Can you blame me? So, I played dumb. You'd be surprised how easily that role came.

'You may be confusing me with someone else, Sire.'

He held my eye, searching, before a faint smile surfaced. 'Yes, I think that must be the case. A new campaign, a new beginning. You are most welcome here.'

Stafford and Bonehead turned to me, their faces a picture of surprise.

'That is news to me,' Stafford said, recovering fast, 'but not unexpected. Ailred is a modest man, yet loyal to the core.' He glanced at Bonehead. 'As are all your men.'

The king smiled and raised his glass. 'To loyalty, then.'

The tent flap opened as we drank, and a young man entered wearing a black tabard with a white cross over a full set of mail. He clutched a segmented helmet in one hand and an ornate sword in the other, its pommel carved into a small cross, which he sheathed. Sweeping back his sweat-soaked hair, he glanced around at us.

The King finished his wine and wiped his mouth with the back of his hand. 'Ahh, Edward, just the man I was hoping to see. I want you to meet Lord Stafford.'

The Prince of Wales nodded but said nothing. The King smiled. 'He is a man of limited vocabulary, but I hope this tour of France will teach him a few words.'

The Prince stepped forward and accepted the wine a squire offered him.

'I'm pleased to make your acquaintance, Lord – you are just in time. How many men do you bring to the field?'

Stafford bowed. 'Three hundred archers and a hundred men-at-arms, My Prince, all seasoned men.'

The Prince raised an eyebrow, swirling the wine in his cup. ‘If you made it here through hostile country and lived, you must be formidable – though we could use more men.’ He took a swig. ‘But beggars can’t be choosers.’

'Where's Beauchamp?' the King asked as his son sat beside him.

'I was teaching him the finer arts of swordplay, Father. I think he's sulking – I showed him to be the bumbling fool that he is.'

The King laughed deep and loud. 'Of course you did.' He looked at us. 'Thomas Beauchamp, Earl of Warwick, I'll introduce you to him later.'

'He is an old friend, Sire,' Stafford said, smiling at the Prince. 'And if you can teach that old dog anything, I'll gladly stand beside you in battle.'

The King leaned forward. 'Richard Fitzalan, Earl of Arundel, is here too, although out foraging now. Are you acquainted with him, also?'

Stafford shook his head. 'We have never met, My King, but his reputation precedes him.' He smiled. 'You have gathered a formidable body of men, Sire; we are at your command.'

The King's expression grew thoughtful as he gestured toward a nearby map strewn across the table. 'Reputation alone will not win the day, but a blend of experience and sharp minds might give us the edge we need.' He looked towards his son. 'We stand more than a fighting chance with Arundel, Warwick, and you at the Prince's side.' He straightened. 'Now, to business. Tell me everything, Earl. I want to hear of Aiguillon and your journey here – leave out no detail.'

For the next hour, Stafford recounted events. The King listened intently, his aides and advisors taking notes. He was meticulous, pausing often to ask for specifics on troop numbers or minor details. Though already well-informed through his spies, much of Stafford's report seemed new to him.

When Stafford concluded, the King sat back, nodding slowly.

'So we have a week before Duke John and his

men arrive. From what I hear, King Philip is furious that he ignored his call to abandon the siege weeks ago and believes he already has the troops to crush us. I suspect he will attack within the next day or so.'

Stafford inclined his head. 'That would suit King Philip's temperament, Sire – strike before his disloyal son can join the glory of our slaughter. That will be the Duke's crowning punishment.'

The King slammed his glass onto the table, shattering it. 'Bring him on – and may God judge the righteous.'

*

Paul's face did not flicker as I finished recounting the news of our meeting.

We were one army now. Sir Thomas, Paul and our men had joined us and dispersed into the King's camp, absorbed into the vast force under his command.

'So, besides the King, we have the Prince of Wales, Lord Beauchamp, Sir Richard Fitzalan, and the cream of English nobility to stand beside us – probably the greatest military minds assembled under one banner. They've chosen the perfect ground for battle. Now let's see if Philip dares meet us.'

I'd never felt so alive. These men exuded a confidence that only true leaders commanded.

It was dark, the oil lamp casting flickering shadows against the low tent's canvas. Paul lay on a sheepskin pelt, his head near the lamp, his gaze unfocused. His lips twitched as if answering someone unseen.

I waited for Paul's response, but he said nothing.

'Did you hear what I said, Paul?'

He blinked and looked at me, his eyes alive with a focused intensity. 'I heard you, but I knew already.'

I hesitated. 'You knew already?'

He nodded with the conviction of divine purpose.

'Yes. An angel appeared last night and delivered His holy proclamation. Praise be the Lord.' His smile was eerie in its serenity. 'I think my sacrifice lit a beacon to God.'

'And now He speaks directly to you?' I asked in amazement.

Paul pressed his crucifix to his lips. 'He does,' he said, voice soft and fervent, but something about how he spoke made the hairs on the back of my neck stand on end.

'Is this still a secret, Paul, just between the two of us?'

His smile remained unnervingly calm. 'Father Paul, and no, it's between the three of us, Ailred. God watches over you now – I've begged Him for that blessing.' His face grew solemn. 'You are immortal too.'

I stared at him, trying to find the right words, but none came. Paul turned onto his side and reached for the lamp. His fingers pinched the wick, and the flame snuffed out, plunging the tent into darkness.

As I backed out into the night, the moon slipped behind the clouds. A chill ran through me as the darkness closed in – I couldn't shake Paul's words.

CHAPTER 27

King Edward and the Prince of Wales led us across their defensive positions the next day. It was overcast, rain threatening from the west as it had been all week, and every member of Stafford's command was present, including Paul. He'd cast off the black shroud that had clung to his spirit of late, a new creature clawing its way from a familiar cocoon. It was a nerve-wracking sight, and I wondered what form it might take. As we walked and listened to Edward's vision, we pledged our undying allegiance, Paul at one point dropping to his knees, his sword drawn and offered up in a gesture that didn't escape the king's notice. I kept an eye on him as we neared the windmill – he was changed, but whether for better or worse remained to be seen. We halted at its base, where watchmen stood at the peak, using the vantage point to survey the surrounding terrain.

The king turned to Paul. 'I saw you speaking with our Abbot earlier today, Paul. Is it true you were a priest once?'

Paul smiled. 'Remembering my name is honour enough, Sire, but knowing my former calling is beyond imagination,' he replied. 'Yes, it is true. I find a kindred spirit in Abbot Copgrove, and we have grown close. If I should die this day,

Sire, he has vowed to assist my ascent to heaven with prayers and absolution.'

I noticed Stafford and Sir Thomas exchange glances before we moved on.

The king's eye for planning and detail was evident in every battlefield aspect. Thousands of men stood ready, their positions precisely calculated, though the French were nowhere to be seen. Edward had divided his forces into three battles: the Prince of Wales and Lord Beauchamp commanded the right flank, the Earl of Arundel secured the left, and Edward himself held back nine hundred men-at-arms and his royal guard in reserve.

A couple of cannons had been stationed between the left and right formations. I'd seen them in action firsthand during the siege of Tournai and thought them more trouble than they were worth. Still, the King, ever ahead of his time, recognised their potential to shape the future of warfare.

'They'll strike hardest here, our right flank,' he said, gesturing to the ridge. 'The slope's less steep, and I've fought Philip enough to know his mind.' He plucked a long blade of grass and began to chew it. 'The incline on our left is terraced from years of farming. Scaling it will be like assaulting fortress walls – but I'll leave nothing to chance. Arundel and his men will hold that flank.' He turned, and, with a sweeping arm gesture, said, 'And this forest behind hinders any attempt to encircle us.'

A quiet intensity in his voice made it clear he visualised every threat and covered every move.

'I would have you, Earl Stafford, and your men support the Prince and Lord Beauchamp if you would be so kind.'

Stafford bowed low. 'The honour is mine, Sire.'

'If our spy speaks true and Philip's army is as huge as claimed, we'll be vastly outnumbered.'

Stafford grinned. 'Perfect, Sire. It will lull them into overconfidence.'

The King nodded. 'Yes, my Lord Stafford. It will fall to us to turn that arrogance to our advantage.' He chuckled. 'Though calling an enemy's superiority in numbers a weakness is bold!'

With that, he dismissed us. 'Go and learn the lay of the land and acquaint yourselves with my captains and commanders,' he said and strode on alone, pausing now and again to speak to his men.

A firm hand gripped my shoulder, startling me. 'Ready to fight in God's name, my child?'

I turned to find Paul standing there, his expression distant. My eyes swept the area, ensuring we were alone.

'You don't need the priestly act with me, Paul,' I said, shaking my head. 'I know you too well for that. I thought you'd left that behind.'

His face clouded with hurt. 'Your words wound me, Ailred. Did you think I'd turned my back on God?' He held my gaze, letting the silence stretch before continuing. 'My apparent deviation from His callings has been the act, as you call it. I have been working to God's instructions this entire time.' I laughed, but his face remained solemn. He was serious. 'King Edward and the Prince are pious men, drawing strength from prayer and religious counsel. It is my duty to help guide them through the Lord's maze.'

The others had dispersed, retiring to follow the king's orders. I noticed the king looking across, frowning.

Paul followed my gaze, then grasped my shoulder and led me away. 'We must leave here, my child, and enact the king's wishes,' he said, as if instructing an infant.

As we wandered up the gentle slope toward Lord Stafford and the king's commanders, I said, 'You're forgetting Abbot Copgrove is the Royal Confessor. Edward relies on his counsel in all matters of faith. Besides, there are at least half a dozen other priests here, Paul – surely the king favours them over you?'

'That is true, but our Lord God and King Edward favour strength over subservience. I am a good judge of character, Ailred.' A hint of a smile dawned. 'There is room to manoeuvre.' Paul nodded as if speaking to himself. 'The Abbot has shared that his duties extend far beyond spiritual guidance. As his faithful servant, I'm honoured to assist him in whatever he requires. The King and his court are fortunate to have such a capable guardian. I only hope to be of greater importance if called upon.'

Earl Stafford and Lord Beauchamp stood in silence, awaiting our arrival. Dressed in mail with matching white tabards, both wore heavy swords at their sides.

The Earl greeted us with scorn. 'Take your time, fellas,' he mocked. 'We've got all day.' He glanced at Beauchamp. 'I must apologise for the brothers' idleness, my Lord.'

Lord Beauchamp glared at us and stepped forward. His broad chest and frame blocked our path. 'It would seem you mistake the king's candour for weakness,' he said. 'Do you think you can disregard his orders when it suits you?'

The look in his eyes made it clear – we were being reprimanded.

Lord Stafford opened his mouth to intervene, but Beauchamp turned on him, voice low and threatening. 'Say nothing, my Lord, or as God is my witness, I'll hold you responsible for these men's disrespect.'

Stafford fell silent, stepping back.

'I… I'm sorry, Lord Beauchamp,' I stammered. 'I meant no insolence. Paul and I were…'

Beauchamp raised a hand, silencing me, his gaze never leaving Paul's face. Paul, untroubled, met his stare, a faint smile on his lips.

Beauchamp spat in Paul's direction. 'You think

this is funny, boy?'

Paul's head tilted slightly. His smile broadened. 'It's been a while since I've been called *boy*, my Lord. But given your advanced years, I suppose it's a fitting title.'

The laughter that followed came solely from Beauchamp. No one else dared.

'I could have you hanged for that,' Beauchamp said, his false humour gone, 'but I'll save the hangman the trouble.' He removed his bascinet, tossed it to his squire, and drew his sword. 'Let me show you how old I am.'

The Prince of Wales pushed through the gathering crowd, his black tabard unbelted and hanging open, his long hair damp as if he'd come straight from bathing.

'Another young pup schooling you in swordplay, Beauchamp?' he called, his voice laced with amusement. 'Ought to at least offer the lad a sword.'

Paul stood unmoving, his eyes locked on Beauchamp's. The Prince took his own blade from his squire, unsheathed it, and stepped closer to Paul.

'Here,' he said, grinning. 'It would seem I'm the only gentleman on this field.'

Paul nodded. 'Thank you, My Prince. I'll ensure it's cleaned and polished before I return it.'

The Prince's laughter boomed. 'You hear that, Beauch? The pup cleans up after himself. That's more than can be said for you.'

Beauchamp's glare flicked to the Prince, his face hardening. 'Your timing is impeccable, Sire. After yesterday's playful exhibition, I'll show you what a real lesson in swordsmanship looks like.'

The Prince smirked and waved the crowd back. 'Do try to teach me something new this time, Beauch – yesterday's performance was a might lacking in substance.'

Clad only in a simple tunic, Paul glanced around, his expression calm yet searching.

'Looking for somewhere to run?' Beauchamp sneered, stepping forward and rolling his sword arm in loose arcs.

Paul tilted his head. 'Actually, I was hoping Abbot Copgrove was near.'

Beauchamp scoffed. 'God won't save you here, boy.'

'I was hoping he'd offer you the Commendation of the Dying,' Paul replied. 'It's the least I can do, my Lord.'

The Prince of Wales roared with laughter, slapping his thigh. 'God's teeth, you have to admire his spirit, Beauch. It's a damn pity you have to kill him. Squire!' He turned to the boy trailing him. 'Go fetch Abbot Copgrove. Tell him his services will soon be needed.'

He sank into a folding chair brought forward by an attendant, his grin unwavering. 'Proceed.'

I was about to intervene when Stafford moved to my side.

'Say nothing, Ailred, or you'll be next. There'll be no stopping this – and we've both seen Paul fight. He has more than a chance.'

It was true, though Beauchamp's reputation was legendary.

Beauchamp stepped forward, his blade raised, as Paul adjusted his grip on the borrowed sword, feeling its weight. His posture shifted to a defensive position, every movement considered.

The watching crowd fell silent; all bets quickly settled as Beauchamp's smirk melted into a grim mask. He began circling. Paul tracked his every move.

Without warning, Beauchamp lunged – his agility belying his size, the blade arcing towards Paul's head. Paul's reaction was just as quick, stepping aside as the sword whistled inches from his face.

Straightening, Paul nodded. This was real – unlike any opponent he'd faced. He settled again, moving toward Beauchamp, who had regained his balance. As Paul shuffled sideways, his foot caught on a bevel in the ground, and he stumbled.

Beauchamp's eyes remained unmoving as he darted forward. But Paul reacted with lightning speed – it was a feigned loss of balance, a trick I'd seen him use countless times. Yet, to my shock, Beauchamp had anticipated it. He shifted opposite to Paul's strike, dodging with ease. As Paul's sword swept empty air, Beauchamp struck his arm with the flat of his blade, then rammed his forehead into Paul's face. The impact was brutal, and Paul collapsed to the ground. Blood poured from his nose.

The Prince leaned back and laughed. I held my breath.

The fight was over in seconds. Beauchamp stepped forward, sword raised to kill.

'WAIT!'

The single word carried an authority that froze everyone in place. All eyes turned toward the voice.

King Edward was standing with the squire sent to find Abbot Copgrove.

'Do not kill that man.'

Beauchamp scowled but held his tongue, looking to the Prince of Wales instead.

'But, Father,' the Prince protested, 'this is a matter of honour. Your honour.'

The King's voice cut through the silence. 'Put your sword away, Lord Beauchamp. The abbot is dead – murdered – and this man will serve as his successor. From this day forward, he belongs to God and the crown.'

*

I nursed Paul's face as he sat slumped on a stool. We'd retreated to his tent, the King's intervention sparing Paul from Beauchamp's wrath.

'He just got lucky,' I said. 'Caught you off balance.'

Paul brushed my hand away, standing with a grimace and spitting blood. 'No, he didn't, Al.' He met my gaze, shaking his head. 'I should be dead. He knew my every move before I did. He's the best swordsman I've ever faced.'

Just then, Lord Stafford entered, grasping Paul's chin and turning his face to examine the injury.

'You'll live,' he muttered, nodding. 'You owe the abbot's killer thanks.'

Paul's face darkened. 'I'd gladly have given my life for that not to have been the cause of my salvation. I won't rest until I discover who murdered God's representative.'

Stafford raised an eyebrow. 'You're not alone in that. The King's finest minds are on it.' He stroked his beard. 'Lucky you asked for the abbot to be present at the duel… it would've ended with your death had they not searched for him.'

Paul remained stoic. 'Such butchery reeks of the Devil. I'd not be surprised if the French were behind it.'

Stafford's expression darkened. 'You know he was mutilated, aye? Gutted like a beast – ripped open, entrails laid bare. Whoever did it wanted him to suffer, wanted to send a message.'

Paul sat motionless, his expression blank. Then, with a slow nod – more measured than mournful – he exhaled. 'I feared as much. Only a disciple of the antichrist would commit such an atrocity.'

Stafford studied him for a long moment before nodding. ‘Yes, it’s a foul business. Strange how it worked out – his death spared your life and placed you in a seat of power.' Paul started to speak, but Stafford cut him off. 'That’s why I’m here. The King wants words with you – he’s a new role in mind and wishes to settle the details. As for me, I’m to see to the abbot’s burial and ensure his soul finds its way.'

I thought I saw a flicker of a grin cross Paul’s face, but it was just a reflex from the pain of his injury.

'Very well, Lord Stafford,' Paul said, 'I'll follow shortly. In the meantime, find a place for him. Somewhere fitting, near the chapel, perhaps? He deserves dignity, even if his killer does not.'

Stafford stiffened, glaring at him. 'Killer, not killers? You think it was just one?'

'Only the Almighty knows, my Lord.' He glanced toward the back of the tent. 'Ailred, be a good man and fetch my cassock.' He turned back to Stafford. 'Anything else, Lord? I’m on the King’s business now, and time is of the essence.'

CHAPTER 28

'I have to ask you this, Paul. Did you kill Abbot Robert Copgrove?'

He was fresh back from meeting the King and had finished telling me about his new royal position.

Paul exhaled, rubbing his temple, wearied by the accusation. 'After all these years, you still question me?' He met my pained expression. 'To kill an abbot is sacrilege. You know that. An affront to God. Why would I risk my soul?'

I shook my head. 'You've just listed a dozen reasons why. You're no longer bound to any lord but the King. You've free rein to come and go, and when the French attack, you'll position yourself anywhere within earshot of Edward. Add to that your seat at the royal table alongside the King and the Prince, and I'd say that's motive enough to kill an abbot – or anyone, for that matter.' I eyed him with suspicion.

Paul laughed. 'Or maybe someone who suspects me of wrongdoing? Don't worry, you're safe! As always, you take life too seriously.' He leaned in, lowering his voice. 'And here's something we wouldn't know if the abbot hadn't been so accommodating.'

He peered outside the tent, checking for eavesdroppers. Satisfied, he stepped back. 'While

I was with the king, a woman came with news.'

'A woman? *My woman*?'

He saw my excitement and sighed. 'Yes and no – it doesn't matter who. She said the French are massing south of us and will arrive tomorrow – likely late afternoon.'

I shrugged, disappointment gnawing at me. 'The king probably knows already through his outriders. That's why he's positioned the men and organised…'

Paul cut me off. 'You didn't let me finish. She gave him a list as long as your arm – names of the nobility in attendance.' He shook his head, his expression grim. 'They're all coming for us, Al.'

'All of them? Like who?' I asked with scepticism. The French lacked discipline, and a coherent strategy seemed beyond them.

'Well,' he said, holding up his fingers as he counted. 'King Philip. His brother, Charles of Alençon. King John of Bohemia. Rudolph, Duke of Lorraine…' By the time he finished, he'd run out of digits.

I stared wide-eyed. 'That's just about every lord and duke in their kingdom. How many men can they field?'

'She reckoned about thirty thousand – that includes crossbowmen from Genoa.'

I swallowed hard. 'Jesus, they've even brought in mercenaries!'

Paul smirked. 'Yes, my child, we'll need all the help we can muster.' He looked skyward. 'And now I am of great worth here; Jesus's help is assured.' He turned to leave but paused at the entrance. 'You didn't hear this from me. Keep it to yourself.'

I left soon after to help with the defensive preparations. The King had us digging pits before our lines and embedding thousands of sharpened stakes deep in the soft ground. A charging horse would be impaled on a stake if it didn't shatter its legs in a pit. Add the arrow storm we archers would unleash, and I almost pitied the horses.

The sky hung grey, a constant drizzle soaking through everything. Pennants and banners of the king's loyal lords drooped lifelessly, awaiting the inevitable battle. Like the other archers, I had my bow wrapped in waxed leather and my bowstrings carefully stored.

As we toiled over the small details that might keep us alive, I joined the banter born of impending death. Thousands of men from every corner of the kingdom laughed and ribbed one another, forging a bond only soldiers could understand. Welshmen, raised to despise the English, swallowed their pride to stand shoulder to shoulder with former foes, discovering their lives no different, their gallows humour the same.

Just as fatigue set in and the jokes faded to silence, King Edward and the Prince of Wales rode past. The King caught my eye, and he reigned in his mount. I saw him lean towards the Prince and exchange words before they dismounted.

As they approached, I stood straight, unsure whether to continue working or step forward to greet him.

'Let me see your hands,' the King said, beckoning me forward.

On seeing the raw blistering, he cast off his stately garments and joined us. Without a word, the Prince did likewise.

I stared in astonishment.

The King picked up a shovel and rolled up his sleeves. 'A king's strength is his men, and our honour is to stand among them. Let none here think themselves too grand for toil.'

That single gesture, simple as it was, struck deeper than any speech or sermon. For those lucky enough to witness it, the lift it gave was worth more than a thousand lashes of a whip. At that moment, we would have died for these royal men without a second thought.

*

The next day began as most others. I woke expecting to trade pointless banter with Godric, only to be struck again by his absence. It isn't until someone close to you is gone that you truly appreciate them. It also serves as a grim reminder of why keeping some distance, even from your closest friends in war, is necessary.

'Get up, you lazy bastard – plenty of time to

lounge about once Philip's boys have hacked us to pieces later,' Paul barked. Subtlety was never his strong suit.

'You think it'll happen today, then?' I asked, pulling my tunic over my head before reaching for my mail.

'If the girl was right, they'll be here this afternoon.'

'Which means they'll wait until tomorrow,' I countered. 'They'll want a full day's work out of it. No sense starting late and losing the light.'

Paul sniffed. 'Maybe. It's in God's hands now.'

I tugged on my boots, tied back my hair, and slipped on my tabard, bracing for whatever the day had to offer.

'God's hands are always juggling, Paul. One of these days, he's gonna drop something.'

Paul laughed. 'I'm holding several services today. Many of my flock mightn't be here tomorrow, so I must ensure they're prepared.'

I sighed. 'We've only been here a few days; most of your *flock* don't know who you are and...' My words drifted to silence. What was the point?

Paul wrapped his robes about himself. 'Be at the one o'clock service, Ailred. Even you aren't immortal.'

*

Paul was using the church in the town of Wadicourt, a smaller settlement east of where we camped. The King and the Prince of Wales had taken up lodgings in a local tavern in

Crécy, flitting between the town and the chosen battle site. I made it to the one o'clock service and was surprised to find Lord Beauchamp in attendance. His usual disdain for Paul – the man-at-arms – seemed temporarily shelved when Paul donned his priestly robes and played the part of God's servant. During Holy Communion, Paul, his head now shaven to a tonsure, served bread and wine to the lords and gentry with solemn grace – until he reached Beauchamp. There, he hesitated, forcing the man to open and close his mouth like a beached fish. Beauchamp's jaw chewed at nothing before he snatched the bread from Paul's grasp, his face reddening. The display earned raucous laughter from those watching and hammered another nail into the coffin of their strained relationship.

On leaving, I was intercepted by Sir Thomas.

'Ah, Ailred, just the man I hoped to find.'

I smiled. 'The feeling is mutual, my Lord.'

'I'm sure it is,' he replied, his tone dismissive. 'Anyway, Earl Stafford and our division from Aiguillon are assigned to the Prince of Wales on the right flank. He'll be commanding our men-at-arms.'

I nodded. 'Yes, I am aware, Lord. And you? Will you be shadowing the Prince as one of his bodyguards – or perhaps the King himself?' It seemed a fitting role for His Lordship.

Sir Thomas sighed. 'This is where the bad news comes in. Normally, delivering it would bring me immense satisfaction, but since working alongside you, I've developed a grudging respect.' He glanced away as if reluctant to continue. 'Think of it as my way of saying I now rank you above pond-slime.'

I gasped. 'You honour me, my Lord. Words I'll treasure until my final breath.'

He grinned, though it seemed forced. 'I'm to take command of the archers.'

That shook me. 'You, Lord? Surely, I am to command the...'

He hesitated, weighing his words before delivering the stark truth. 'Blame your brother. I just spoke with Lord Beauchamp, who handed me the order directly. Because of Paul, his hatred now extends to you.'

Disappointment crossed my face before I could hide it. 'But you're not an archer, Lord.'

Sir Thomas shrugged, irritation creeping into his tone. 'I know warfare better than most, Ailred. I can guide archers as well as any man.'

'My apologies, Sire. I did not mean to imply you were incapable of the task.' I lowered my eyes, swallowing my frustration. 'I am honoured to serve under your command.'

He turned to leave, pausing at the doorway. 'I know you will, Ailred. I'll be counting on you for secondary supervision.' He laughed. 'See? I've already elevated you to worm status.'

*

By the time we trudged back to the ridge, it

was mid-afternoon. Rain had come and gone all morning, leaving the air damp and the ground sodden. As I passed below the windmill, the drizzle eased, clouds thinning just enough for a shaft of sunlight to break through, warming my soaked clothing.

Then came the shrill blast of a buisine from above.

I looked up.

'TO ARMS.'

It was the signal we had awaited since arriving.

Scanning the incline, I saw no sign of the enemy; only the windmill's height could reveal what lay beyond. Every man sprang into action, each knowing their purpose, drummed in over the previous days. I sprinted to my tent, grabbed my bow and a quiver of arrows, and took my place on the right flank with the other archers. Around me, palpable energy surged – men spoke in hurried bursts, their words overlapping as no one stopped to listen. All prepared themselves, knowing full well this day might be their last.

Then, Sir Thomas de Clare's voice cut through our chatter, silencing our band of brothers from Aiguillon.

'Listen to me, gentlemen. You've heard me bawl often enough to know my voice – now let it be the only sound that matters. Shut out the clamour, the cries, the thunder of hooves. When I give an order, you obey without a second's thought, without taking your eyes off the enemy. When this day is done, when the field is ours, I will return home to Tonebricge. But before that, you will do your king proud. You will do me proud. More than that – you will stand as one, your spirits bound together, an unbreakable wall of steel. Let history remember you not just as men, but as the iron that forged victory at Crécy!'

I turned to see him standing behind our ranks, his presence commanding. We stood at the front line, mere feet from the stakes and pits, with our men-at-arms arrayed behind us.

Sir Thomas nodded toward me. 'If I fall, you listen for Ailred's voice. You all know it – it sounds like a woman's, but heed it regardless.'

Laughter broke through the tension, softening the what lay ahead.

As we strung our bows, page boys delivered more arrows, which we dug into the ground before us, ready for quick retrieval. By my side, a grey-haired veteran from Wales ran through his pre-battle routine, speaking constantly to a young lad of about fourteen next to him. Though they spoke in Welsh, it was clear the lad was his son, the older man preparing him for what was to come.

'Your son's first action?' I asked in a break in their conversation.

'Aye, he's been running arrows and the like till now. I think he's ready.' He clapped the lad on his shoulder. 'And he's been desperate to step up, ain't that right, Emyr?'

The boy nodded. 'Ie, yn wir,' he said, unable to hide his anxiety.

The older Welshman laughed. 'Show some respect and answer in English, Emyr. You'll be fighting at his side soon – you might need his help amid the carnage.'

Emyr glared at his father but relented. 'Yes, sir, I am ready for whatever the enemy throws at us.' He looked down the slope, awaiting the first sign of the French ranks. 'I was born for this.'

I couldn't help noticing his hands shaking, though said nothing. I exchanged glances with his father and wished each good luck before retreating to my own ritual.

I thought of Izelda and prayed she was all right, wherever she was. But then, a terrible feeling of guilt washed over me as my second thought was for Philippa and Kimberly. I cursed myself. What if my final thoughts before dying were towards Izelda?

The King's voice jolted me from my self-loathing.

'Men of England, today we stand not as lords and commoners but as brothers bound by purpose. The enemy marches, thinking us weak, outnumbered, and afraid. Outnumbered, yes, but they do not know us. They do not know the iron in our hearts or the strength in our love of nation. Fight not just for crown and country – but for the man beside you, your homes, and the future we forge today. Hold fast, hold true, and let the courage of England shine so bright it blinds them. Now, to your places – let us show them who we are!'

A great cheer rose, and the King moved off to inspire each section of his army.

We waited.

'They'll not attack today, Emyr.' The Welsh accent rolled thick from my left, barely intelligible. 'It's too late in the day.'

He sat back and fished a small brass flute from his tunic, the scratched surface catching the day's faltering light as the sun broke through the parting clouds again. The damp clung to us, steam rising from our clothing like mist from a morning field.

'Relax, son,' he said, easing the bow from the white-knuckled grip his boy had on its shaft. 'Save that strength for the morning. They won't come until then.'

Emyr twitched, glancing at his trembling hands before noticing me watching. A hollow laugh escaped him, more show than amusement.

And then I saw them – rank upon rank, surging into position at the foot of the slope, their eagerness palpable even from afar. Men and horses jostled for space as each division manoeuvred into place, vying for the chance to lead the killing.

'Jesus Christ, there are thousands of them,' Emyr muttered, his eyes wide.

I nodded. 'And thousands more to come,' I said as columns of men poured in from every direction.

A tuneful melody from a small brass flute played, then halted. 'They'll not attack today – I know these things.'

The next few hours passed in a tense rhythm. We watched in awe as the enemy gathered, a sea of French military might bent on our destruction, while pageboys scurried back and forth, bringing us food and ale.

Again, my thoughts drifted to Izelda. What might she be doing at that moment? Had she vanished into obscurity, leaving King Edward's spy network behind to live her own life? I wanted that for her, but I never got to tell her. Hopefully, she was back in Gascony, free from the constant fear of capture.

'CROSSBOWMEN!'

Sir Thomas's voice shattered my thoughts and silenced the low murmur of idle chatter around me.

The image of Izelda faded as my eyes focused on the enemy. Thousands of Genoese soldiers moved into formation before the thick ranks of French mounted men-at-arms.

Again, the brass flute fell silent. 'They'll not attack today,' the confident Welsh accent muttered.

'I'm not so sure, Taffy, ' I said, standing to get a better look. 'Why would they bring crossbowmen into position for nothing?'

He shook the spit from his flute and tucked it away. 'True enough, but they've no pavises to shield them, and why the hell would Philip start so late in the day? Makes no sense.'

I nodded and grinned. 'I think I know the answer to that, Taff.'

He cocked an eyebrow, waiting. 'Enlighten me, English boy, why do something that dumb?'

'They're French.'

He grinned back. 'Fair point – which makes them slightly cleverer than you English.'

I laughed. 'And you told your son to show respect! You're wrong on this, Taff – they're coming. This is it.'

CHAPTER 29

I scanned King Edward's reserves. If a soldier ever needed a reason to stand firm with resolve, it was the sight of those grizzled veterans at his back – hard-faced, battle-scarred, and unshakable as the earth beneath their feet. With these men ready to bolster any weakness, I would challenge the Devil himself to attack.

And then I saw him. Paul. He was looking towards me, still robed in priestly attire, with his hood over his head. He was close enough to the King that if he fell, Paul could administer the Commendation of the Dying. He caught my eye and raised his arm. He was smiling. As he moved between the reserves, speaking words of comfort and prayer, I noticed beneath his robes he wore mail and was armed. I smiled and shook my head. He had no intention of staying out of harm's way to pamper the King's pastoral obligations. This was Paul at peace with himself – never more alive than at moments before impending death – when the impulse to flee was at its height in others.

I raised my bow and nodded, but a voice cut through my thoughts.

'You'll not see the enemy back there, Ailred Norman.'

Sir Thomas's commanding tone snapped my

head forward.

Nearby, Lord Beauchamp and the Prince of Wales moved through our ranks on foot, their words steadying the men with quiet assurance. Across the field, on our left flank, I spotted the Earl of Arundel doing much the same. His soldiers were arrayed in a disciplined formation to match ours.

'All right, they'll attack today.' The Welsh voice was low, meant only for his son and me.

I smirked.

'Here they come, boys!' Sir Thomas called from behind, his tone laced with amusement. 'Genoese crossbowmen without pavises – it would seem King Philip is feeling charitable today!'

I turned to the enemy's slow advance – five ranks deep, slogging through churned mud at the base of the slope. Behind them, French noblemen sat rigid on their destriers, polished armour glinting under the fading sun.

A sea of flags rippled in the breeze – except one. At the centre, it hung lifeless, damp fabric clinging to the pole until a gust unfurled it, red and gold blazing against the sky.

'The oriflamme,' I murmured, unaware I'd spoken aloud.

Emyr turned to his father, his brow furrowed. 'The what?'

'It means no prisoner, no mercy,' his father said, pointing to the flag being swung with theatrical flourish. 'It's kill or be killed today.'

Emyr swallowed hard but said nothing, turning back to the scene below.

'Wait, boys... wait...' Sir Thomas's voice was steadier now, almost a growl of anticipation.

A few enemy crossbow bolts fell short, thudding uselessly into the mud.

In the distance, a muffled thud was followed by a plume of smoke. One of the English cannons had been fired. The ball sailed over the enemy's heads, landing in the woods without apparent impact.

'What's the bloody use of that?' Sir Thomas barked, frustration rippling through the ranks as we watched the gunners scramble to reload. The French crossbowmen marched on, unfazed by our new toys.

I picked my first arrow and kissed its tip, a ritual I hadn't bothered with in years but felt compelled to honour now. Nocking it to my string, I drew back, the tension biting into my fingers as I aimed, allowing for the incline.

'L-O-O-S-E!' Sir Thomas called, stretching the word, savouring the moment.

Relief surged as I released the string, sending the arrow skyward. In the instant before I reached for the next, the air filled with a thousand shafts, a sound like the sudden rush of wind through a forest.

And then, the screams began. There is no describing the serene sound of iron biting flesh, the shouts of men turning to wails of agony as arrows found their mark. Unless you are there, you cannot comprehend the satisfaction.

'Don't let up, my beauties.'

Sir Thomas was the only voice I could hear. No one deviated, no one paused.

By my tenth arrow, my arms burned, but I allowed myself a moment to focus. Below, the field was carnage. Thousands of shafts had rained down, leaving the Genoese crossbowmen broken and scattered, their ranks dissolving as survivors turned to flee. Why they had been ordered to advance without pavises – those vital shields for cover – was beyond reason. Not a single one was in sight.

'HOLD!'

Sir Thomas's calming command halted us. I followed his gaze.

The crossbowmen were in full retreat, stumbling through the mud, broken. But behind them, the French knights surged forward. Their destriers reared, hooves striking the air, swords flashing as riders bellowed.

And then it began.

The knights charged, sweeping over the retreating Genoese in a tide of pounding hooves, trampling them without hesitation. Screams of the dying crossbowmen mingled with the thunder of advancing cavalry.

'What the hell... they're killing their own?' The Welshman beside me growled.

I laughed, shaking my head. 'Looks like we might not be needed today, Taffy!'

Our mirth was short-lived.

'Look alive, archers. Here they come.'

The field was strewn with broken Genoese, but now the ground trembled beneath the French charge.

'Horses, gentlemen. Bring them to their knees,' Sir Thomas bellowed, steady and unwavering.

While the French knights wasted precious moments cutting down their own, our pageboys worked fast, replenishing our quivers. Then we let fly.

The destriers fought against the sucking mud, riders urging them forward even as they fell. Arrows peppered the beasts, piercing necks and flanks. Screams of agony tore through the field as animals collapsed, thrashing and dragging their riders down with them.

Those still standing fell – legs shattered in pits, impaled on spikes, or their skulls crushed by hammers and poleaxes. Their shrieks were hideous – panicked, prolonged, inhuman. Some reared and toppled backwards, crushing their riders beneath them. Others crashed forward, flinging men from their saddles like broken dolls.

The charge faltered, the way to our line choked with dying beasts and flailing men. But still, they came – stumbling, surging, unrelenting – like the tide crashing against jagged rocks.

A hand yanked me aside.

'You girls have had enough fun plaiting hair – it's the boys' turn now.'

Earl Stafford shoved past as the men-at-arms stormed forward, eager for their first kill.

Moments later, the remnants of the charge slammed into our line. The last of the horses, spent and staggering, were put down without hesitation. The knights barely hit the mud before our men were upon them, knives flashing, axes hewing. Some were hacked apart where they lay; others dragged down and drowned, weighted by their armour. Men sat on their heads, roaring with laughter as they shoved them face-first into the mud – a grotesque theatre of violence, each act more depraved than the last.

But the carnival of blood didn't last.

The next wave was already halfway up the slope – a disordered mass, no sign of coordination. We had time to realign after the first assault, archers retaking position, their quivers replenished by the tireless relay of pageboys.

'LOOSE!' Sir Thomas's command rang out, and our deadly flock wheeled high before plunging to feast.

Another wave of French knights and their mounts collapsed in a flurry of iron and blood, littering the hillside with bodies.

The pattern was relentless. Each brigade surged forward under its own banner, leaders desperate for glory, each determined to be the first to break the hated English lines. And every time, they fell like skittles at a fairground – anguished cries the only prizes.

A short lull. We drank weak ale and stripped chicken from the bone while watching the field. King Philip rode up and down his ranks, gesturing, his voice carrying even at this distance. His men straightened under his command, rallying.

He stopped, surrounded by his lords and advisors. A heated discussion followed – then, a curious sight. A nobleman was being tied to his horse, reins secured to other riders' saddles.

'That's John of Bohemia,' a voice said behind me. The Prince of Wales stood nearby, watching with interest. His lips quirked in amusement. 'The man's blind.' He chuckled. 'Should I feel insulted or honoured that a blind man might lead an attack upon us?'

'Are we to resist striking him down if he does, Your Grace?' I asked, bowing my head. 'He'll be worth a great deal in bounty.'

The Prince didn't look away. 'No, Ailred. Anyone coming up that field today is fair game. They have the numbers – we don't have the luxury of picking and choosing.' He turned to me. 'If the King of Bohemia leads the charge, he'll be surrounded by their best warriors. Blind or not, what he brings will be unlike anything we've seen yet.'

'Then we have our answer, Sire,' I said,

gesturing down the slope.

The Prince stayed by my side as I reached for another arrow.

Below, John of Bohemia led the next charge, flanked by thousands in perfect formation. No disorganised rabble – this was a wall of steel and flesh, moving as one.

'No more glory-hunters now, men,' the Prince called. 'This is where the battle's won and lost – take out everyone.'

During the lull, Earl Stafford had ordered his men-at-arms to roll corpses – man and horse – down the slope, forming makeshift barriers to slow the French advance.

'D-R-A-W!' Sir Thomas's voice silenced our murmurs.

Raw fingers took the strain. Thousands of archers breathed deep, bows groaning.

'LOOSE.'

They began to drop, but many now carried shields held low against the horses' flanks, creating a fragile barrier.

As they closed, John of Bohemia's guards pressed around him, willing to die for their blind king.

Horses fell in droves – broken in pits, legs tangled with the dead, impaled on spikes, or pierced by arrows – but still, they came.

And then, they struck.

We archers had no choice but to step aside as our men-at-arms shoved past us to absorb the impact. They needed no orders, pride driving them to shield our position.

These attackers were no ordinary soldiers. Their brutality marked them as elite warriors. John of Bohemia's mount still stood, its hind legs riddled with arrows, while he thrashed instinctively with his massive sword, guided by the shouted directions of those around him.

'À gauche... et maintenant la droite...' He flailed left and right, knocking men from their feet and growling like a wild, baited bear. I think his blindness helped – his fear swallowed by darkness, his recklessness striking its own terror.

As he and his guard carved a foothold, more Frenchmen surged forward, many dismounted and abandoning their broken lances for the raw savagery of axes, maces, swords, and anything capable of tearing flesh or cracking armour. Time and again, as we followed Sir Thomas's orders to stay focused and move to the flanks, we loosed arrow after arrow, striking from an angle. The rising body count left the French less room to manoeuvre; they stumbled, tripped, and fell over their own dead.

'Stay on those still coming, archers!' Sir Thomas's voice rang out over the cries of pain and the roar of battle, forced calm masking desperation. 'Isolate those bastards at the front!'

Still, they came – wave after wave, howls of elation driving them on as they slammed into our ranks. Bludgeoning, jabbing, shields used as battering rams, they thought they had us retreating. But the Prince of Wales, Earl Stafford, and their men-at-arms held firm, planting their heels and shoving them back with fierce resolve.

'Low... low!' Stafford bellowed, and the front ranks dropped to their knees, scything beneath the French shield wall. Tendons were severed, ankles shattered, and groins ripped as our second rank leaned over them, driving their blades into any exposed flesh. It was a tactic honed and rehearsed, something only men with utter faith in their comrades could dare attempt.

Though they fought like rats in a sack, the French began to falter. The long climb up the slope, the weight of the mud clinging to their legs, and the sheer ferocity of our resistance slowed their once-potent charge. Behind, new, fresher troops joined, pushing forward, desperate to be part of the slaughter. As they slipped in the blood-sodden mud, we dropped them, their bodies mounting into walls.

'THE PRINCE IS DOWN...'

It was the first time I'd heard Lord Beauchamp's voice in the battle. He'd been standing firm with the men-at-arms away to our left, his towering presence holding them together like a solid, immovable wall. No man would consider a backwards step while he stood beside them.

I scanned the area he was pointing towards

and saw the Prince on his knees as those behind fought to encircle and protect him. His distress spurred on the French attackers, led by Charles of Alençon, their fervent desire to claim the ultimate prize driving them to frenzy. They swarmed like rabid dogs, shoving and striking one another in their scramble to be first.

I leaned past Emyr's father and seized the boy by his tunic. His fingers were raw and bleeding, the skin torn and blistered from the unrelenting draw of his bow. His flushed face glistened with sweat, his breaths short and panicked.

'Take a message to the King,' I said, shaking him to bring his focus on me. 'Tell him his son is in trouble and needs reinforcements.'

He stared at me wide-eyed, then glanced at his father, uncertain.

'You heard the man,' the Welshman said, his voice strained. He caught the boy's arm, halting him for a heartbeat. I could tell he was desperate to protect his son, yet knowing this might keep him away long enough to save his life.

'Go quickly, lad,' his father said, letting his arm go and watching him disappear into the ranks behind.

When I looked back, I saw Beauchamp carving his way through the throng. Others stood over the Prince, shields raised – a desperate barrier. Clambering over dead horses and broken stakes, Beauchamp forced his way through just in time, stepping in as another layer of protection. His arrival couldn't have come sooner. Still mounted and guided by his escort, John of Bohemia stormed into the melee, his sword dripping red as he hacked his way closer.

Grabbing a bodkin-tipped arrow and kissing it before nocking, I drew and released without thinking. 'God's speed,' I whispered.

The arrow struck the pig-snouted helmet in the right eye, bending the steel just enough to let the arrowhead drive deep into the narrow slot. I heard his scream of pain and frustration even from where I knelt, already repeating the action. This time, the arrow glanced off the steel at an angle.

'Stupid blind goat didn't need his eye anyway,' Taffy said in a deadpan Welsh accent. 'But a fine shot... for an Englishman.'

Charles of Alençon wasn't so obliging. On foot and wielding a double-handed sword, he fought tooth and nail among our men, determined to capture the Prince. I had no clear line of sight on him – or any other Frenchman. At that moment, I had no time to think. I dropped my bow, seized my mace, and charged to the Prince's aid.

By the time I reached him, his eyes had cleared, and he seemed aware of his surroundings. He knelt, taking great gulps of air and adjusting his dented helmet while those around him fought to keep the enemy at bay. Occasionally, a Frenchman darted through the defensive ring, attempting a solo attack, only to be struck down and slain.

But as the enemy's numbers grew, the men shielding the Prince thinned, overwhelmed by the relentless surge.

As they fought to hold the line, the Prince, still dazed, was guided away to safety by the last of his protectors. Lances, spears, axes, and swords – each wielded by crazed soldiers desperate for the fortune a royal ransom would bring, tore into the fray, leaving men bloodied and broken in their wake.

As I forced my way toward the killing ground, I saw one man holding the line – Lord Beauchamp. He fought three men at once, his massive sword sweeping one moment, stabbing the next, while his shield smashed foes into unconsciousness. He was fighting to cover the retreat of the Prince.

Stepping over and around the fallen – men and horses alike – I managed to reach his side as all seemed lost. There were simply too many. Grabbing an abandoned shield, I stood shoulder-to-shoulder with him as another wave attacked.

I hadn't survived until now without understanding the ways of battle. The enemy would fight with restraint, searching for a weakness. But once they believed they had dominance, an unspoken belief would spread, and they'd drive into us with everything they had. That's where the real killing happens. If you trust the men beside you and hold your nerve, anything is possible – even against overwhelming numbers.

The impact drove me back a step. The Frenchman at the front, shoved forward by the press of bodies from behind, smashed into my shield. His arm swung wildly over the top, aiming for my head. I ducked low, instinctively crouching as I dropped my mace and snatched his wrist. He roared, pulling back with frantic strength. The tug of war was animalistic – pure rage and desperation as I bit deep into his hand, forcing him to drop his sword. Blood from the bite slicked my grip, but I held fast, twisting his arm to wrench him off balance.

Lord Beauchamp ended the struggle. His sword descended with incredible force, cleaving through the man's shoulder. The shield's edge trapped the limb like a butcher's block, slicing flesh and disjointing bone. Blood sprayed, drenching my face and body. The Frenchman screamed a guttural sound before collapsing, leaving me with his severed arm.

I glanced up and swore Beauchamp was grinning before returning to the slaughter.

The enemy hesitated, but only for a heartbeat. I hurled the severed arm into the next wave and snatched up my mace. The first man charging at me wore no helmet – a mistake he never lived to rue. The mace arced close, its spiked crown raking his face. Flesh peeled away in shreds, his features torn apart in an instant. One eye burst like overripe fruit, his jawbone dangling through the ribbons of cheek. He staggered, a wet, rattling gasp escaping his ruined mouth before he crumpled, his hollowed skull grinning up at the sky.

A pike swiped past my head, close enough to tug at my ear. Pain flared as a section was sliced away.

As the man to my right crumpled, breathing blood from the lance buried in his chest, only Beauchamp and I remained. The French, sensing victory, began to close in, their smiles predatory, knowing we were alone.

Though we fought on, it was clear – absent a miracle – that we were doomed. Back to back, Beauchamp and I hacked and parried, each French soldier seeking the opening that would spell our end.

Then, a deafening roar rang out. I thought it came from the enemy. But it wasn't the French, the words lifting our spirits.

'FOR THE KING AND SAINT GEORGE!'

The enemy's smiles faltered, replaced by concern, then fear. I turned and saw the revitalised Prince of Wales charging back into the fray. On one side of him, Sir Thomas de Clare; on the other, a wild-eyed priest swinging a sword like a man possessed.

The sight of the Prince – alive, defiant, leading the charge – fired our men's resolve. The French were thrown into disarray, retreating in panic, many stumbling over the dead or tumbling into pits. With momentum shifting, we descended on those still standing, cutting through them brutally. No man – noble or otherwise – was spared.

I heard the blare of a great horn behind us, high up in the windmill. The signal was clear – our final order from King Edward.

'NO PRISONERS!' The Prince of Wales roared, his voice laced with triumph and exhaustion.

The French fled. All evening, they had charged in their thousands, each assault shattered by arrow storms or men of steel who gave no ground. Now, battered and broken, their resolve crumbled.

King Edward, wary of feigned retreats but wise enough to sense the truth, seized the moment. This was no ruse. This was their collapse. With so many dukes and counts present, he understood the stakes. This was more than a victory. We were dismantling the French nobility.

I looked to my left and saw the Earl of Arundel and his battle sweeping down the slope. They'd been bystanders until now, most of the French having assaulted our flank. This was their moment. Their discipline had held, but now they surged forward, aiming to outflank the fleeing enemy.

As the cannon fire ceased, our men struck, smashing the exhausted French as they stumbled toward safety. We leapt over bodies and skirted wrecked horses, and with each stride, another Frenchman fell. Blades rose and fell, adding red to the blood-soaked mud. It was slaughter on a grand scale.

But then, amidst the carnage, our instinct for coin surfaced. Among these desperate men, wealth was scattered. Noblemen cowered in bloodied armour, their lives worth more than the price of victory. They were prizes to be claimed, their ransom the reward for our labour. We refined our butchery, now selective, death reserved for the worthless, as we searched out those of fortune.

As I approached one such knight, he dropped to his knees, his grand armour battered and caked with mud. His sword gleamed in the dying light, an offering. He bowed his head in surrender, and I stepped forward to claim him, accepting his weapon and life as my prize. His hands trembled as he removed his helmet, sinking to the ground, his strength spent, his pride broken.

Paul appeared beside me, dragging another captive by his arm and throwing him to the earth.

'Damn, that was good,' Paul wheezed, bending double, his hands braced on his knees as he caught his breath.

I smiled, signalling the knights to stay put. 'Are robed monks even allowed to spill blood on a battleground?'

Paul straightened and shrugged. 'I heard it's frowned upon. But I consider it my holy duty to rid the world of these vermin.' He kicked his captive's face, forcing him to cry out in pain. 'You'll fetch me a fortune if you're who I think you are.' He drew his sword, its edge stained red. 'Unless I decide to carve you up first, you dirty...'

A deep voice interrupted. 'You know who these men are, don't you? They'll be worth a pretty penny.'

Paul fell silent, and we turned to see Lord Beauchamp striding towards us. The Prince of Wales and King Edward walked at his side, their retinue close behind. Banners hung limp in the smoky air, barely visible through the haze left by the cannons.

Paul sheathed his sword and folded his hands, the picture of saintly innocence. 'I've no interest in worldly gain or wealth. My only reward is to serve God and you, my Lord.'

Lord Beauchamp snorted. 'I wasn't talking to you, imbecile. You're of no importance.'

Paul gave a theatrical bow. 'That may be so, though my statement stands.'

The Prince of Wales clapped Beauchamp on the shoulder, grinning. 'This priest fought as fiercely as any man today. In truth, I owe him a debt of gratitude – as do you.' He turned to the king, who watched the exchange with a wry smile. 'After my Father commanded I win my spurs rather than send aid, I've gained a deep respect for every man who stood with me in that endeavour.' His gaze lingered on Paul. He nodded. 'Especially if they happen to be monks who fight like demons.'

I glimpsed anger across Lord Beauchamp's face before his head overruled his heart.

'We all fight for the same king and country, my friend,' he said, extending a hand in reconciliation. 'Let past misunderstandings be forgotten.'

For a moment, I thought Paul might refuse. But then he stepped forward, clasping Beauchamp's hand, his gaze never wavering.

'You are most gracious, my Lord,' Paul said, their hands still locked, neither willing to release first. 'As a show of gratitude, I would love to offer you this man – The Count of Artois, nephew of King Philip – to ransom as you will.' Beauchamp's eyes lit up at the magnitude of the prize, but Paul wasn't finished. '...but, alas, I cannot, as he has already been claimed by Ailred Norman here.' He gestured to our other captive. 'And this one's mine, whose ransom I have pledged to the church, so I'm afraid...'

King Edward, who had been listening in silence, stepped forward, ending the charade.

'Gentlemen, there will be time enough for disputes. For now, go and finish this day's work. Thousands of Frenchmen are still at large, and the light is fading.' He gestured toward the windmill. 'I have ordered a token of celebration to mark this auspicious occasion.'

Beauchamp reluctantly released Paul's hand and turned toward the rout. As he departed, the mill behind erupted into flames. The fire climbed quickly, its glow illuminating the mounds of dead strewn across the battlefield.

'Did you mean it, Paul?' I asked once we were out of earshot. 'You're donating your ransom to the church?'

Paul laughed. 'You're so dumb sometimes, Ailred. Come on, let's get these bastards secured.'

Forcing our captives ahead, we moved across the field, weaving between the bodies. The burning windmill cast long shadows over the twisted remains of men and horses. The stench rose – smoke, blood, and released bowels – a reminder of victory's cost.

'Half of these aren't even dead, and they're stripping the bodies,' I muttered, nodding toward a group of soldiers rifling through a pile of squirming wretches. One man straightened, holding up a blood-smeared sword with a crazed laugh. Another cursed as he hacked at a finger that refused to give up its ring.

'Let them have their fun, Al. We'd be doing the same if we didn't have these two,' Paul laughed, shoving his prisoner forward.

But not every English soldier was looting, and not every soldier was English. As we passed the spot where I had taken position at the start of the battle, I saw a lone figure among the fallen. He sat motionless, staring to nothing.

I stopped. 'Emyr?' He didn't react at first, lost in whatever hell he had found himself.

'Leave him, Al,' Paul muttered. 'Just another kid who thought he was a soldier – until he saw the cost.'

He pushed me to keep moving, but Emyr turned his head toward me, his eyes hollow. 'Mae e wedi marw.'

I had spent enough time around Welsh soldiers to understand. His hand rested on the head of his grey-haired father, the fallen archer's face caked in mud, his war bow still clutched in death.

'He was a good man, Emyr,' I said as Paul continued to yank me onward.

'Yeah, we're all good men,' Paul jeered, 'and some of us are still alive. Leave him be, Al – God helps those that help themselves – we have more important things to do than babysit.'

I hesitated but realised we had to continue.

In the distance, the remnants of the French vanguard limped toward the treeline – once-proud knights, now hunted and slaughtered by blood-lusted fiends without pity.

I looked beyond, to the horizon. The sun had long since dipped below, its final light vanishing. Somewhere out there, our allies hunted the last of the French, spilling more blood into the dark earth.

'It's not over yet,' I said, turning to follow Paul

as we made for the prisoners' compound.

'It is for us, brother,' Paul said. 'We're going to be rich.'

CHAPTER 30

We found the makeshift stockade, a ring of wagons and storerooms thrown together in case of retreat. God had favoured the righteous this day – or so Paul proclaimed – so instead of sheltering allies, the stockade now held the damned. The guards, men already laid low by wounds from skirmishes before the battle, leaned on pikes or sat slumped against the barricades, their hollow eyes a stark contrast to the elation of the victors outside.

Inside, the captives sat huddled in the centre, shadows of the warriors they'd been only hours earlier. More were dragged in even as we watched – bloodied, broken, but breathing. These were the lucky ones, though none would agree. Escape was futile. Many bore terrible wounds, but the shame of surrender hurt more than injury. Their lands were stripped, their families cleansed – they had nowhere to run. When asked to pledge their honour to remain, most offered up oaths with bowed heads and trembling voices. The consequences were swift for those who refused, whether out of pride or the wish to spare their families the burden of ransom. Rebellion meant execution. Heads fell without ceremony, their remains left as warnings to any who dared defy. After that, few dared to test the limits of our mercy.

*

We sat across from our two captives. Paul grew restless, dismissing them as "arrogant French peacocks". He was itching to join the celebrations echoing across the battlefield and beyond as the remnants of the French army were driven towards Flanders or cut down. Behind us, the windmill stood as a charred husk, black against the dim moonlight.

Along with the Count of Artois, our other captive was Charles II, Count of Alençon – both men of considerable standing in French nobility. Though bruised and weary from the day's slaughter, they carried themselves with the imperious grace of men who believed themselves born above the mud and blood that surrounded them.

'You may think you have won a great prize in our capture, Monsieur, but the price *you* pay will be ten times your asked ransom.' The Count of Artois leaned back on an empty barrel, glancing at his companion with a raised brow. 'I think the English dog has bitten off more than he can chew.'

They both spoke good English, and from the moment they realised they were worth more alive than dead, they wasted no time in using their words to antagonise us.

Charles of Alençon laughed and looked at Paul. 'The mongrel dressed as a preacher knows his limit, I think – he will run away when the big dog growls.'

The Count of Artois nodded and growled at Paul. 'How do you English pigs say, "His bark is worse than his bite"?'

Paul shifted, but I laid a firm arm across him, handing each of them a mug of ale. They accepted without thanks, sipping only to spit it out theatrically.

'This tastes of cows piss,' de Châtillon spluttered, 'Do you not have wine?'

The Count of Artois wiped his hand across his mouth and nodded. 'And will we be issued a maid and mistress?'

I downed the dregs of my ale and rolled my eyes, already accustomed to their brand of jesting. The two were clearly close friends, using humour to mask the day's horrors. They sat with their heads high, their camaraderie unbroken – a sharp contrast to those around them. The other prisoners, shattered in body and spirit, slumped in the mud, faces hollow and eyes vacant, as though they had already given up on life.

I liked them. Strange, perhaps, but true. Soldiers have much in common, whether they fight as allies or enemies. Only hours earlier, I'd been trying to kill them.

There was a short silence before de Châtillon broke it.

'You two runts were at Aiguillon, were you not?'

I looked towards Paul, who shrugged, bored with the conversation.

'You seem well informed. How did you know?' I didn't expect a courteous reply and wasn't disappointed.

'The Duke of Normandy's mistress told us that the stench of shit came from Aiguillon when she was stationed there.' De Châtillon leaned towards Paul and then me, sniffing. 'And I smell Aiguillon here.'

My mind flashed back to those days of siege: the distant sight of a dark-haired woman in a crimson dress, her movements graceful, her presence commanding.

'I remember her,' I said, looking at de Châtillon. 'Was she as beautiful as we, behind the walls, imagined?' I asked with unguarded excitement. 'Her black hair and body were the subject of every man's alone time.'

'Yes, she was far beyond your station – a woman for kings and princes, though others got their turn when backs were turned.' He glanced at Charles of Alençon, who smirked. 'We brought her from Aiguillon. Gave her hair a trim to mark the occasion.' He laughed. 'The Duke was meant to join us, but the King attacked too soon, misled by a certain tramp…' He faltered as though realising he'd said too much, his smirk vanishing.

Paul looked up. It was the first time he'd shown any interest. 'She was here at Crécy?'

De Châtillon hesitated, exchanging a look with Alençon.

'She was,' he said at last, his tone evasive. 'Perhaps she still is. Or perhaps not.'

I rose from my barrel, exhausted with their cryptic talk and stretched my arms wide. 'I'm tired. It'll be getting light soon, my French friends. We'll see you in the morning.' I turned to leave, pulling Paul with me and glanced back. 'Perhaps one of the guards can act as your maid tomorrow, but I can't promise a mistress.'

De Châtillon laughed loud. 'That's fine, son of an English whore. We've had enough mistress fun for one day, haven't we, Charles?'

The Count of Artois smirked but kept his thoughts to himself.

We left in search of a tent – and sleep.

CHAPTER 31

Here's something that might interest you, Brother Michael. The first thing I notice about someone when we meet is if they listen. Most want to talk about themselves, using the other to raise their own standing. You were, and still are, different. You have so much to tell, but choose to keep it to yourself, preferring my story above your own. Do you know how refreshing that is? No, I did not think so. It is a rare gift, my friend, and sets you apart. Regardless of your reluctance, I will get to the soul of your essence one day.

*

The next day, my entire body ached. I was getting too old for this. How many times have I said that over the years? Too many. I had visited the Chirurgeon on my way back to the tent, who called me a mummy's boy and told me I was at the back of a long queue. He was knee-deep in blood and broken bones, straightening limbs and sawing through others. The air around his filthy table was filled with the stench of cauterised flesh and festering wounds. Rows of desperate men lay waiting, their pitiful moans a far cry from the celebratory scenes within earshot. As the Chirurgeon spoke, he sawed furiously below the kneecap of his patient, cutting away the remaining skin and shards of bone from his shattered leg. The man bit down hard on a thick leather strap as his assistants fought to hold him down. On the next table, another pale and sweating knight clutched his stomach and begged for water as his intestines lay spilt by his side. I took one look at the mangled heap of men around me and decided my ear could wait.

*

'Did you sleep well?'

Both men turned their battered faces toward me but said nothing. Most of the other prisoners sat huddled together for warmth, mist clinging to the ground on that damp new morning. In the grey light of dawn, I saw fresh injuries, unnoticed the night before. Charles of Alençon's eyes were swollen to dark slits, while the Count of Artois's face bore deep bruises and the gap where his front teeth had been.

'Did you two fall out overnight?' I asked, tilting the Count of Artois's chin to get a better look at his swollen face.

He slapped my hand away, scowling, his eyes flickering for a heartbeat toward the grinning guards nearby, who sat nursing mugs of ale and picking at dried fish.

'It is nothing, Monsieur, just the English doing what the English do best.'

I didn't recognise the guards – likely men from King Edward's army, the same we'd only recently joined.

Deciding to introduce myself, I walked over and was immediately blocked by a massive man with one eye.

'You looking to join our guard detail? Hoping to dodge any more fighting?' he sneered, bending forward to pat my torn ear. 'Looks like you've been mortally wounded there, fella.'

The rest of the group laughed.

Ignoring them, I gestured toward my captives. 'Do you know who those men are?'

'I don't give a rat's arse who they are. They're French, and that's enough.'

I nodded and grinned. 'Let me enlighten you. That's Charles II, Count of Alençon, and the other is the Count of Artois, Duke of Brittany.'

He shrugged. 'And?'

'And it means they're worth a great deal of coin to my brother and me.'

He laughed and turned to the rest of his detail. 'Better start watching over your prize bullocks then, lad. Those two look like they're ready for the knacker's yard.'

I nodded. 'The Duke of Brittany, the man you men beat to within an inch of his life, is my brother's ward. Do you know who my brother is?'

His grin faltered, face hardening. 'Your brother could be the Archbishop of Canterbury, for all I care...'

'Not yet, he isn't, but maybe one day – he's the Reverend Paul Christian.' His following words died in his throat as I offered him a knowing smile. 'Ah, so I see you've heard of him.'

'I... I know of the reverend, Sir.' He dropped his gaze, fumbling for words.

'Good. We have an understanding, then. Keep your eyes on these two prisoners – sorry, your *eye*, and ensure no harm comes to them. My brother and I would be most grateful.'

He nodded and gestured towards the other guards sitting ashen-faced. 'Don't just sit there, you lazy bastards, you heard the man. Get some food into these prisoners – and if anyone so much as touches a hair on their heads, they'll answer to the Reverend Paul Christian.'

As the sentries jumped to their feet and rushed to comply, I wandered over and picked up two tankards of discarded ale and returned to the French noblemen.

'My apologies, gentlemen. I am sorry you had to witness that,' I said, handing them the drinks.

They drank the ale without protest this time, downing to the dregs.

'Merci, Monsieur. It would seem you are the only man of principle in the English army,' the Count of Artois said through broken teeth as he returned the tankard.

The beatings and nighttime reflection had dulled the edge of the noblemen's arrogance. They looked genuinely pleased to see me.

'You gave your oath of parole yesterday, so I'll arrange for you to be moved out of this compound and into accommodation more suited to high-born gentlemen such as yourselves.'

'You are too kind, Monsieur,' Charles of Alençon said, bowing. 'You have our word that we will not attempt escape.'

I laughed. 'I believe you, but you only get one chance. Besides,' I glanced at the guards, 'I don't trust them to look after my prize assets – your ransom means a lifetime of luxury when I get home.'

*

I found the Prince of Wales in his lavish tent. I hadn't sought Paul's opinion but knew he'd agree. In truth, I doubted the Prince would object to leniency for our captives either, but I felt it was my duty to ask his consent.

Once the bodyguards permitted me entry, I found him half-dressed, his face drawn from the previous day's trials. In the cold light of morning, stripped of his royal finery, he looked every inch the boy prince. At sixteen, the man in progress was beginning to take shape, though his face, untouched by a razor, bore the faint promise of a beard – more ambition than reality.

As I explained my proposal, he continued to dress. His mannerisms were less histrionic without an audience, and he listened without interruption.

'As far as I'm concerned, these two are yours. Do with them as you will, but remember, they are your responsibility.' He pulled on his final boot, and his pageboy draped a woollen fleece over his shoulders. 'Come, walk with me. I'm meeting with our King and advisors to survey the battlefield and the French positions. We learn much from observing the enemy's discarded possessions and remnants of their defences. It's the small details that win battles.'

'You honour me, my Prince,' I said, scurrying to keep up as he swept from the room.

We were the last to arrive, the King's expression souring as we joined the assembled group. Paul was there, standing close by dressed in his full priesthood robes, his eyes a little blurry but otherwise a picture of saintly goodness.

'Late, as ever,' King Edward sighed. 'Your mother indulged you too much as a child. Right, let us get on with this.'

Apart from Lord Beauchamp's customary look of disdain, the others barely acknowledged me. Sir Thomas and Lord Stafford stood amongst them, both unscathed and pleased to see me.

As we wandered, the King paused occasionally to take notes, enlighten the Prince on tactical matters, or chastise him for his wandering attention.

'You fought well yesterday, Edward, but being a lion in battle is only a small part of victory. I waste my breath if you haven't learned that by now.'

The Prince bowed, his expression contrite but

composed. 'A day will come, Father, when my name becomes the scourge of these nations, and it will be through your guiding hand and example. Rest assured, everything you say is learned and stored here.' He tapped his head and grinned.

The King chuckled. 'If you can manipulate nations as skillfully as you think you manipulate me, England's future is indeed secure.'

The gathered nobles laughed along, myself included. It was always wise to follow the King's lead.

Enemy bodies littered the landscape. Lines of Genoese crossbowmen lay as if left by a retreating tide, cut down by their paymasters – a testament to the French betrayal. Meanwhile, the English, Welsh, and Gascon dead had already been gathered, prepared for Christian burial – an honour denied to all but the most noble Frenchmen.

Sir Thomas de Clare placed a firm hand on my shoulder as we approached a set of half-collapsed tents. I had lingered toward the party's rear, not wanting to seem obtrusive, and he'd dropped back to speak with me.

'If you recall, Ailred, I said I was going home after this battle, and I'll be true to my word.'

'I remember, my Lord. You told us not long before the killing started.' I smiled. 'I'll miss you, if I may say so.'

'You're such an old woman,' he said, removing

his hand with a shake of his head. ‘I meant to say – before you interrupted me with all your sentimental clap-trap – is that I can offer you passage home with me.’

The temptation came and went in the same heartbeat. ‘It’s an offer I’d usually leap at, Sire, but I have custody of the Count of Artois. As you know, he’s King Philip’s nephew and worth a fortune. I'll not want to let him out of my sight for a second.'

He nodded. ‘I understand. Still, I thought I’d give you the opportunity.’ He looked around. 'And where is he at this very moment?'

I shrugged. 'I'm not sure – he should be in the compound, but he might be somewhere...' I caught the gleam in his eye. 'Yes, Lord, I'll keep a closer eye on him from now on.'

We jogged to catch up, reaching the rest of the party as they entered the most prominent tent still standing.

Inside, the tent reeked of damp canvas and churned earth. The Prince stood near a wide table littered with parchment scraps and spilt ink while the King kicked through discarded belongings and bedding left unwanted by looting soldiers.

The King stooped, lifting a battered goblet and turning it in his hands before letting it fall back into the pile with a hollow clang. ‘Rubbish,’ he muttered, kicking a broken shield aside as though insulted by the disorder.

'It would seem this was Philip's command tent, Father,' the Prince said, tapping his fingers on the table before picking up a torn map and turning it around. 'And unless my French betrays me, it appears an entire division of reinforcements was travelling towards our lines before the battle to aid us!'

The King frowned and walked over to join him.

The Prince smoothed the map out and stepped back, giving the King a clear view.

The King ran a finger over some French wording I couldn't understand, frowning deeper. 'No, your French is perfect. It clearly states that the French believed we had…' He paused, pointing to the text. 'Une division de dix mille soldats.' He looked up, astonished. 'They thought we had a division of ten thousand men on the way to reinforce us!'

The Prince's mouth fell open before a broad smile swept his face. 'No wonder they attacked too early – they wanted to slaughter us before the non-existent reserves arrived!'

In the silence that followed, my mind wandered to the conversation I'd had with the two French captives.

'The French might have been fed false information, Your Highnesses,' I volunteered.

Every head in the tent turned toward me.

The Prince chuckled, shaking his head. 'Well, I think we all worked that out, Ailred.'

The tent erupted into chatter as everyone debated the discovery's significance, their voices blending astonishment and triumph.

I cleared my throat. 'If I may, I have a theory.'

No one listened, their conversations carrying on as if I weren't there.

Paul sidled up, his tone low. 'I'd keep it to yourself, Al. Whatever it is. They should figure it out on their own. No one likes a smart-arse.'

I shrugged but understood. Taking his advice, I slipped out of the tent to clear my head.

The morning air was crisp as I wandered towards a small wooded area, stepping over French bodies. I stopped, staring down at one lifeless form, its eyes filled with terror. How had I become so numb? Birdsong broke my reverie. After days filled with the sounds of suffering, the melody caught me off guard. I smiled, glancing up into the trees where the song came from.

A crimson dress caught my eye first – torn and caked with mud, its lifeless folds hanging unnaturally. The body within faced away, pale arms bound behind its back. Where hair should have been, the scalp was shorn, cut, and bloodied. As I stepped closer, strands of jet-black hair lay scattered like fallen leaves below.

'Who's that?'

The King's commanding voice startled me. I spun to find him and his party standing just behind, their faces grim as they stared up at the body.

'I think I know, Your Highness,' Paul said, ever casual in the face of horror, grabbing a discarded French pike. He strode past me, pulled a French corpse over and stood on it to gain extra height, and jabbed the hanging body, setting it spinning.

As it turned, a wooden sign hanging from her neck came into view: Traîtresse.

But it wasn't the word "traitor" that made the world tilt – it was the face.

My heart broke. Those beautiful eyes, once so alive, stared into a distant void.

Paul dropped the pike and vanished behind me as I crumpled to my knees.

'Well, who is it, Ailred?' the King demanded.

Sir Thomas stepped forward, taking my arm and pulling me to my feet.

'It was a spy from behind the French lines, your Grace,' he said quietly.

I turned to him, my voice trembling. 'You... you knew all along that Izelda was working with...?' Words failed me.

He held my gaze but said nothing.

The King's tone softened, a note of understanding in his voice. 'Did you know this woman, Ailred?'

My eyes lifted to her face, frozen in death.

'I did...' The words choked off, leaving me hollow.

Lord Beauchamp stepped forward, hefting the pike to use its side blade against the rope.

'Shaving the head marks betrayal,' he said as

the body slumped to the ground at my feet. 'Whoever did this is either long gone or lying among the dead.'

The pieces didn't fall together gently; they slammed into place with a force that stole my breath. My hands shook as I stared at her, the word on the sign around her neck searing into my mind.

'BASTARDS!' I screamed, trying to run, but Sir Thomas seized me, holding me tight.

'Who, Ailred? Who did this?' His voice was a harsh whisper as I fought to break free.

'Our bloody prisoners, Alençon and the Count of Artois – they killed her.'

The King stepped closer, his voice cold. 'Do not harm them, Ailred. I know your anger, but I need those two alive. Their ransom is worth a fortune – yours for the taking. And, more importantly, they will yield valuable information for our cause.'

I thrashed against Sir Thomas's hold, but he was too strong.

'THEY'RE DEAD!' I kept shouting, over and over, like it was the only truth left in the world.

The King's patience snapped. 'I am ordering you, on pain of death, do not touch those men. Anyone who lays a hand on them will hang.' He moved before me, his gaze a cold, iron lock on mine. 'Do not defy me, Ailred.'

The words were hidden within the echoes of my madness.

I spun around and punched Sir Thomas in the face with all my might. The impact caused him to relax his grip enough for me to break free and run.

'DO NOT DO THIS.'

The King's words followed me as I sprinted away.

*

I did not stop running. Rational thought had long since left, replaced by a single, all-consuming need. Revenge. To hell with the consequences.

The holding pen wasn't far. As I neared, a ring of guards stood watch over the captives. My eyes caught a table where they'd been at rest – a sword, still sheathed, hanging from the back of a chair. Without breaking stride, I snatched it up.

'MOVE NOW!' I bellowed, grabbing the first man I approached and hauling him aside. The next, I shoved out of my way.

And then I stopped dead.

My breath came hard and fast, my grip tightening around the sword.

Paul stood at the centre, grinning, both hands grasping blood-soaked hair. He lifted them high – two severed heads, their faces frozen in terror, still dripping onto the carnage below. The bodies were unrecognisable, hacked apart with savagery only meted out by genuine belief in one's purpose. Two hands lay severed and together, their fingers intertwined as if still begging for mercy. An axe jutted up from a severed leg, its blade sunk deep into the flesh, holding the handle upright like a macabre placeholder.

The one-eyed guard stumbled back as I approached, his voice a whisper. 'We couldn't stop him – he'd have done this to us, too.' He shook his head at the thought. 'He wouldn't stop laughing.'

CHAPTER 32

Paul sat with his back against the tent's central post, his hands bound behind as he shifted, trying to find a comfortable position. This was where King Philip of France had plotted our destruction before Crécy. Philip's body was never found, so we assumed he'd escaped. His plans were in ruins, his nobility decimated, but we knew he would already be scheming vengeance. The one-eyed guard lingered by the tent's flapping entrance, leaning on the pike that had cut Izelda down. With Paul now secured, the guard's fear had melted away.

Lord Beauchamp and Sir Thomas were the first to arrive at Paul's carnage, subduing him with ease – though, in truth, he hadn't resisted. By the time the King and the Prince of Wales sauntered to the scene, Paul was trussed, gagged, and sprawled on a flat-topped wagon.

'Why, Paul?'

It was the first chance I'd had to speak to him. The King and his advisors had kept me away during their preliminary inquiry.

'I knew exactly what you'd do, Ailred.'

'Yes, I'd have slaughtered the bastards, but the King vowed death to anyone who touched them – and you did far more than that.'

'All the more reason to act,' he replied with

a smile. 'I made them suffer for their crimes. You'd have just killed them.' He leaned forward as much as his bonds allowed. 'I gave them what they deserved – and spared you the risk of hanging. Think of it as a thank you for those years of suffering me.'

I stared at him. I should have grown used to his callousness by now – yet it still astounded me. 'And now *you'll* hang for it.'

He shrugged. 'Better me than you. Besides, I'm the King's priest. He wouldn't dare.'

I could understand his logic, but he was playing a dangerous game.

'Did the murdering bastards say anything else about Izelda?' I asked, though the mere mention of her name felt like a blade through my heart.

Paul smiled. 'When someone stands before you with an axe, you'd be surprised what they'll say to cling to life for a few more fear-ravished moments.'

'Did she suffer?'

His gaze dropped. 'You don't want to ask that question.'

I went to press him, but he cut me short. 'Don't ask it, Al.'

'But why? She was just a wench…'

'She was far more, Ailred. She was the leading infiltrator behind French lines.'

I blinked, shattered. 'She was just a go-between who ran messages. She told me herself.'

He shook his head. 'You believed what you

wanted to believe. She was Duke John's mistress outside Aiguillon, the woman we watched from the battlements – but she worked for us. When Alençon and the Count of Artois brought her here, she convinced King Philip that we had ten thousand more men en route. That's part of why he rushed his attack.'

'And they told you this?' I asked.

Paul remained silent.

My voice rose. '*You knew all along*?'

He nodded, eyes lowered. 'I knew some. I wanted to tell you, I really did, but Lancaster, Stafford, even the King all said you were too emotional. They swore me to secrecy. Those two realised her betrayal and killed her as punishment.' He looked up, his eyes cold. 'She could have run at any time, but didn't. She knew the risks. She saved all our lives, Ailred.'

I stood there, speechless, drowning in my naivety. A thousand thoughts fought for control. She knew the risks... but why hadn't she told me? Was I not trustworthy? Had she had genuine love for the Duke?

'She lied to me,' I said softly, though the words weren't meant to be heard.

'She lied to everyone,' Paul said. 'And for good reason. You would've given her away with your yearning – she knew that better than anyone.' His words struck like a slap, but I didn't react. He saw I was crestfallen and beckoned me closer. 'She told me once that you were her safe place.

Those short times she spent with you were her distraction from the hell she lived. Don't let what she's done be for nothing.'

I felt my legs close to buckling, but steadied myself. 'Without me, she might have lived a long, happy life,' I said as guilt brought me close to tears.

Paul shifted as if he wanted to comfort me, but slumped back in his binds. 'You didn't kill her, Alired, they did.' His face changed, all compassion banished. 'And I made those bastards suffer for it – tenfold.'

I opened my mouth to scold him for keeping me in the dark, but the one-eyed guard could hold his tongue no longer. Out of the corner of my eye, I'd seen him itching to add his two-pennies-worth.

'You think you're safe, crazy man? I've heard the King speak to the Prince and Beauchamp – you're getting strung up as an example.' He laughed, mimicking the grotesque convulsions of a man on the gallows.

Still clad in his monk's robe, Paul turned his head with an unnerving slowness, giving the impression it might swivel all the way around. His pupils rolled back, leaving only the whites of his eyes.

'I'll drag you to hell with me – and all your family,' he whispered.

The guard opened his mouth to speak, but no words came. His face drained of colour before he turned and left.

Paul looked back at me, his smile widening. 'A man's soul is easy to unravel when you know which threads to pull.'

I shivered. 'I'm not sure anything like that will work with the King, Paul,' I said, glancing up as the one-eyed guard returned, flanked by a dozen others.

He drew his sword and strode toward me, its point pressing against my throat.

'Leave. Now.'

I looked at Paul, who gave a casual nod. 'They wouldn't dare kill me,' he laughed. 'The Devil has room enough for these future apostles. One word from me and an eternity of flames would seem like an act of mercy.'

I walked out, reassured he was safe – for now.

As I stood and drew a deep breath, taking in this new information, my gaze lifted. Above me, the frayed rope that had held Izelda swung in the stiffening breeze, a stark reminder of the horror I had fought to bury. What was one more death amid the wholesale carnage of this campaign? Yet hers was different – and was now my undoing. Two days on, the ache consumed me, raw and unrelenting, sharp enough to strip away sleep and reason. I was exhausted in mind and body; the longing for home was heavier now than ever. Philippa's arms, warmth, and reassurance felt a world away. I needed her, though I knew Izelda was a secret till my grave.

'Ailred, I want a word.'

It was the distraction I needed, though not one I welcomed.

'Yes, Sir Thomas, I am your servant.'

'Servant?' He scrunched his face. 'You're many things, Ailred, but a servant isn't one. They're useful. I'd rank you somewhere around the dung-beetle level.' He jabbed a finger towards one of the French tents, patched together after the army's ransacking. 'Over there, if you please.'

We entered the tent.

He punched me in the eye.

I regained my feet.

'What would you like to speak to me about, my Lord?'

'Ah, Ailred, good of you to agree to this little chat.'

'It's my pleasure, Sire.'

He pointed at his face. 'You see this black eye?'

'Yes, Lord. I might have one to match.'

He punched me in the other eye. I regained my feet unsteadily.

'Though I think I might have two black eyes to your one, Lord.'

He nodded. 'Now, can you remember how I got mine, Ailred? Think back.'

'I do recall a dung beetle might have slugged you in the heat of the moment, and I'm sure the poor creature regrets it. In fact, Sire, I suspect his two blackened eyes are a stark reminder of his station in life.'

'That seems to be all, Ailred. Nice chatting with you.'

I bowed. 'The pleasure was all mine, Sir Thomas.'

He turned to leave but paused at the entrance. 'Oh, and the offer of transport home still stands.'

*

'Do you remember me?'

The words were spoken without conviction, lost and confused.

I looked up with bloodshot eyes from where I sat, resting, after dismantling my tent and loading my weapons and supplies onto the wagon. It was a bright morning, and I watched flocks of ravens pecking the eyes from the French dead that lay undisturbed on the silent battlefield. I'd had little sleep the night before – my mind constantly shifting between Izelda, Paul, the battle, and Philippa, each thought weighed with guilt.

It took me a second to place the words through the thickness of his Welsh accent.

'Of course I do, Emyr. It's good to see you.' I hesitated. 'I didn't get to say how sorry I was about your father.'

He gave a faint smile. 'He always told me this day would come. Said he'd be happy – wherever he was.' I frowned, unsure of his meaning. 'He said that if he died in battle and I was grieving, it meant I was still alive.' He swallowed hard. 'His greatest fear was for it to be the other way around.'

I nodded. It was a wish I'd heard expressed by most fathers who fought alongside their sons and understood the heartfelt belief.

'I... I buried him where he fell,' he said. 'He is at peace now.'

He looked as if he would say more, but didn't. He stared at me for a moment, then turned to leave.

'Wait,' I called out. 'Are you assigned to a company? Do you have travelling companions?'

He seemed to have no possessions besides his bow and a single arrow in his quiver. He had no mail, his tunic stiff with dried blood, and his mud-caked boots.

He hesitated, then shook his head. 'We served under Sir John Chandos. He paid better than the Welsh, so my father joined him. It was our best chance of steady pay.' He exhaled and looked skyward. 'They never let us forget we were Welsh.'

I understood. As I'd discovered while serving with a Welsh company years before, the animosity between the English and Welsh never let up. With his father gone, any protection he might have offered vanished.

'What will you do now?'

He shrugged. 'I've not thought about it.' He looked down, wringing his hands together. 'Father made all the decisions.'

It looked as though the kid needed to grow up.

Fast.

'You could do worse than join me.'

His eyes lit up for the first time since I'd met him.

'You mean it?'

I smiled, took my muddy boots off and tossed them in his direction.

'Do a decent job cleaning them, and I'll take you.'

Emyr picked them up and threw them into the nearby trees, then turned to leave.

'Clean them yourself. I still have my pride.'

I gave a huge smile. 'If you'd said anything else, I wouldn't want you,' I laughed, as I searched for the boots in the undergrowth.

He stopped and stared back at me, his face softening.

I pulled my boots on again.

'Follow me, Emyr. Come and meet my brother.'

We talked as we walked the short distance to the tent where Paul was being held.

Emyr came from Abertawe. His family had worked most of their lives in the castle there until they were cast out. A spate of thefts had gone unsolved, and Lord John de Mowbray, rather than seeking the culprits, had simply evicted every Welsh employee. With nowhere else to turn, his father, Alwyn, joined a group of English archers sent by Lord Mowbray as part of his obligation to King Edward's claim to the French crown, taking his son with him.

'You shoot well for your age,' I said as we approached the tent, 'I'm sure I can get Lord Stafford to take you on. From what I heard, we're moving on to Calais today. I know many of the men under Stafford and can put a good word in for you. Hopefully, that'll stop them abusing you for your Welshness.'

He raised an eyebrow. 'What about you? Aren't you going, too?'

We stopped short of the tent. Ten armed sentries were standing outside, watching me.

'I'm heading home with…' but the words died in my throat.

'Come no further, Norman,' the one-eyed guard called. 'The King and his advisors are inside, passing judgment on that crazy brother of yours.' He spat on the ground. 'He's going to hang.'

'Stay here,' I muttered, striding forward.

'I'm warning you – stay back,' the guard growled. The others stepped up beside him, blocking my way.

'Just let me speak to the King,' I pleaded. I was in no position to demand, not now. 'Please. He'll want to hear me out.'

They burst into laughter.

'You really are as dumb as they say,' the one-eyed man sneered. 'The King and Lord Beauchamp gave orders to keep you out.' His grin widened. 'You aren't as important as you think, Norman.'

The tent flap parted, and Lord Stafford exited, walking straight to me. He drew me aside.

'It's done, Ailred,' he said. His voice was firm. 'The King has made his ruling. Nothing will change his mind.'

'What ruling? Why wasn't I informed?'

Stafford stiffened. 'Watch your tone, Norman, or I'll have you on a charge.'

I exhaled, trying to compose myself. 'I'm sorry, my Lord, but...'

He raised his chin. 'Beauchamp petitioned for the death sentence. The King upheld it. He owes no one an explanation.' He glanced at the tent, where advisors were filing out. His voice softened. 'Those prisoners were valuable. They were a valuable source of information. The King swore he'd hang any man who touched them. Paul did more than that.' He clapped my shoulder. 'He means to make an example of him. I am sorry.' He removed his hand. 'Go, Ailred, save yourself the pain of watching.'

As Stafford turned away, the King emerged, Beauchamp at his side.

'Your Majesty!' I called. 'Have clemency! He is a man of God – you need him!'

The King didn't so much as glance at me. The guards moved in, shoving me back.

'Better get yourself a good viewing position, Norman,' the one-eyed guard mocked. 'They're hanging the bastard from the same tree they strung that French whore from. Big crowd for this one.'

I lunged, fighting to get past him, shouting, pleading to the King's better nature.

A bright burst of stars. Pain.

The next thing I knew, Emyr was hauling me upright.

'Where... what?' I muttered, shaking my head, my fingers finding the swollen lump at my temple.

'They're taking him to that tree over there,' Emyr said, pointing.

We stood where I'd been left cold, slightly uphill, as they led him down to the gathering crowd. The tree stood about two hundred yards away, marking the place where Izelda had been cut down.

I could see Paul walking without a struggle. He was a proud man, and I expected nothing less. His cassock's hood was pulled up, but one of the guards yanked it back. He turned his head, searching the nearby faces. He was looking for me.

I went to call out but stopped myself. He'd never hear me over the rising chatter of the crowd. The atmosphere was almost carnival-like, with more men gathering by the second. Only then did I realise how many people he had crossed.

I felt so impotent.

Once, he had confided in me that hanging was the worst way to die – to choke, to kick, to flail until the life drained out of you.

I couldn't let that happen. I had to save him. Somehow.

As the King looked on, seated on a canvas chair, Lord Beauchamp threw a coiled rope over the beech tree's branch beside the frayed remains of the previous noose.

Just as panic dared me to intervene, I caught movement in the corner of my eye – two men sprinting across the field, the one in front waving his arms wildly.

'Who's that?' Emyr asked, squinting into the rising sun.

I shielded my eyes. My heart leapt.

'It's the Prince of Wales and Sir Thomas.'

'What's he shouting?' he asked.

The Prince was in the front, but I couldn't hear what he was saying.

A smile came easily to me. 'He'll be stopping it,' I said, turning to Emyr, embracing him and swinging him around. 'I knew Sir Thomas wouldn't fail me.'

As I looked back towards the King, I saw him raise an arm, and Beauchamp stopped securing the rope to his grey destrier's pommel.

On reaching the King, the Prince bent over, hands on his hips, to catch his breath while Sir Thomas ambled up beside him, age taking its toll. The King stood, and I saw him calling across to Beauchamp, who dropped the rope's end and jogged to his side.

I breathed deeply, then held my breath.

The royal pair argued, the Prince shaking his head, but the King silenced him with a raised finger. Then, with a sweeping motion, he gestured toward the stony-faced crowd. The Prince fell silent and bowed. Sir Thomas stood back and looked into the crowd as if searching for someone before staring at the floor.

It was finished. The King had won.

'AILRED...!'

Paul's shout carried across the heads of the now silent audience. It had pain and pleading laced through.

Tears welled as I stared, and the crowd's howl rose.

As Beauchamp returned to his horse, the guards led Paul beneath the rope, his hands bound behind his back. The one-eyed brute slipped the noose around his neck. Beauchamp tugged the rope, drawing it taut over the branch.

'String your bow and give it to me, Emyr,' I ordered.

He hesitated but obeyed, passing it over with his single arrow.

'What are you doing?'

I didn't answer. I moved down the slope, stopping a hundred yards away.

Emyr followed.

'You're not going to try and shoot the rope...' he started to say, but the moment's gravity silenced him.

I knelt, steadying my breath, my fingers tight around the bow.

Paul was silent now, staring straight ahead toward me.

The watching soldiers hushed, showing respect.

Another canvas chair had been brought and placed next to the King, in which the Prince sat, his hands resting in his lap. Behind them stood Sir Thomas and Lord Stafford.

'Do you have any final words before the sentence is carried out?'

I had moved close enough to catch the King's words, clear and distinct.

Paul said nothing, staring straight ahead.

I nocked the arrow and kissed its tip, knowing I had but one chance.

With shaking hands, I stared at the rope and started to draw.

I smiled as I remembered our childhood and the brotherhood that brought us to this point.

I looked at Paul's face, and his eyes widened as he saw me. He smiled and nodded.

As Beauchamp slapped the destrier's flank and the rope tightened, I released the arrow.

Through tear-filled eyes, I watched it fly straight and true, striking Paul in the heart just as the rope snapped taut. His head stayed still, staring at me, and in that silent moment, his smile never wavered. For the first time in his life, he looked at peace.

CHAPTER 33

I see you, too, have a tear in your eye, Brother Michael. That is the first time I have spoken of Paul's death, and the sorrow of that day still presses on me, as heavy now as it did then.

Could I have split the rope? Perhaps. But what would have come of it? It would have ended the same. By then, he had burned all his bridges.

I have learned to live with my choices, trusting that God will judge me kindly. I suspect I will know that answer soon enough.

*

You don't make life easy for yourself, do you, Ailred!'

Lord Stafford shook his head, leaned back on his seat and turned to Sir Thomas. We were inside the Lord's tent later that day. I had been captured by a few of the guards and beaten, though I'd had no stomach to fight back. Emyr did that for me. Despite his years, he fought with a young archer's strength and a Welshman's ferocity. He removed the front teeth from the first guard at the scene and knocked the next unconscious before being overpowered and battered senseless.

Sir Thomas cleared his throat and spoke for the first time. 'May I make a suggestion, my Lord?'

'By all means, Sir Thomas. If you can find sense in his head, you're a better man than me.'

Sir Thomas nodded. 'Normally, I'd suggest whipping or a turn in the stocks.' He gave a faint smile. 'But on this occasion, I feel it might be counterproductive.' He turned to Stafford. 'That was an act of mercy, Lord, and apart from everything he does being wrong, he has a good heart. There are many a man still walking God's green earth because of Ailred.'

Stafford scratched his beard, plucked a louse, crushed it between his nails, and flicked the remains towards me.

'Well, the King's left us free to do as we will.' He looked again at my emotionless expression. 'And by the looks of things, you don't care whether you live or die.' He turned back to Sir Thomas. 'So if the King doesn't care, and Ailred doesn't care either, why should I? Thomas, he's all yours.'

Sir Thomas stood and looked towards Emyr. 'And what about what's left of the lad?'

Emyr tried to straighten but couldn't, his body a mass of bruises.

'Take him too. He's a feisty little chap – he'll make a fine addition. Besides, I think Ailred has his first squire.'

Looking towards Emyr for the first time since being brought into the tent, I forced my mind from the blankness that shrouded my thoughts. Sir Thomas and Lord Stafford had a patience I didn't deserve, and the smile on Emyr's disfigured face made me realise life must go on. Paul would have expected nothing less.

As we were about to leave the tent, Stafford stopped us.

'Oh, and we still hold Jean, the Count of Harcourt and Charles, the Count of Montmorency. As you are aware, Sir Thomas, these two are vulnerable. If, for some reason, your man, Ailred, had a rush of blood to his head and replicated his brother's actions, I will have to...' He let the words hang, the meaning plain.

'Rest assured, my Lord, Ailred will not go near the prisoners. You have my word on that.'

Stafford nodded. 'I will hold you to that, Sir Thomas.'

We left.

*

We joined the rest of Lord Stafford's archers and men-at-arms, many offering quiet words of condolence as they broke camp, readying for the next leg of our chevauchée. Paul had friends as well as enemies – enough so that some had retrieved his body and laid him to rest near the charred remains of the windmill.

Before paying my final respects and seeing his soul onward, I went in search of Izelda.

No one had seen her body since they cut her down from the tree, and I dreaded she had been left to rot in the fields.

I trudged every inch of the battlefield, stepping over bloated, putrefied corpses, the stench thick enough to choke. The crows barely stirred as I passed, too gorged to care. Then, from the edge of the devastation, a man in simple peasant garb approached.

'Are you Ailred Norman?' His voice was unassuming, his English thick with a Gascon accent.

His face seemed familiar, and it took me a moment to place him. He was the man I had questioned when he'd entered Earl Lancaster's camp months ago. I had asked him about Izelda, a conversation that had gotten me into enough trouble to be expelled from Lancaster's company.

My pulse quickened. 'Yes – do you know where...'

'Izelda's body is? Do not worry, my friend. We have her.'

I exhaled, a deep breath I hadn't realised I was holding. 'You don't know how happy that makes me feel...' I stopped. How could I feel happiness? What was wrong with me?

He stepped forward and hugged me. I stiffened, instinctively pulling back.

A faint smile crossed his face. 'I know what you are feeling – the guilt, the pain. We feel it too. It is natural.'

He embraced me again, and this time, I let him.

'Allow yourself to grieve,' he murmured, stepping back. 'We know all about you.'

'We?'

He gestured down the slope towards the

forest. ‘We Gascons who worked for Izelda behind the French lines.’ His face looked drawn. ‘Now that she is gone and the French are beaten here, we must reassess our roles. Some will return to Gascony, start new lives – others continue the fight, maybe go undercover again.’ He nodded and smiled. 'She spoke of you often. She wasn't supposed to, but she couldn't help herself. If it wasn't for you, she wouldn't have...' He stopped himself.

I looked at him in shock, as I processed his pause. 'She talked of me? Even though all the commanders forbade it!'

I couldn't believe what I was hearing. When I had spoken to her, beyond the initial contact, she had been cold and evasive.

He laughed. 'Of course she did. She loved you.' I was speechless. 'She knew you needed shielding, and that was her way of protecting you.'

Then it dawned on me – why he hadn't finished his sentence. 'If it wasn't for me, she wouldn't have taken the risks she did – is that what you were going to say?'

He stared at the ground. 'It is true. She wanted to give you every chance at life in this God-forsaken war. If it meant her risking her life, so be it.' He looked at my face. 'Do not allow yourself to feel responsible. I can see from your sadness that it will take time, but trust me, you are not to blame.' He put an arm around my shoulder. 'Come, I will take you to her. I am one of the few who are leaving and returning home. We are taking her body with us. We will give her a Christian burial in her hometown. It is the least we can do.'

As we walked, he told me of her heroism and the sacrifices she endured. If you know me well, you'll understand my conscience. If not – you don't know me at all.

Amongst the sweet-smelling pine, in the cool of the forest, we were reunited. She was wrapped in linen on the back of a cart.

I stood and stared. 'Can I look at her one last time?' I said, reaching towards the body.

He stepped forward and gripped my arm.' I would not do that, Monsieur. We have used Mos Teutonicus.' He looked at my confused face. 'It is a way to allow us to transfer the body home without the...'

His voice drifted to nothing as I nodded sadly, understanding.

'I will remember her as she was,' I said, stepping back.

'That is as she would have wanted, Ailred.'

Another man, similarly dressed, approached. 'We must go now, Caprasi, we have a long journey ahead.' He glanced at me. 'You must be Ailred? I have heard much of you...' I went to speak, but he raised a hand and smiled. 'Yes, all good. You are a lucky man. You will appreciate that one day, when the fog lifts.'

With one final prayer as they readied

themselves, I said goodbye.

*

I found Emyr at Paul's makeshift grave.

‘I knew I would find you here, Lord,' he said, smiling. 'Did you find her...?'

I nodded, staring at the small patch of ground that would be Paul's forever.

Silence.

A few of Paul's associates gathered around us, none speaking.

Without warning, Emyr stepped forward and spoke. His voice was as I had never heard before: clear, confident and with the warmth of total conviction. 'Grant, most gracious God, that we may love and seek Thee always and everywhere, above all things and for Thy sake, in the life present, and may at length find Thee and forever hold Thee fast in the life to come. Grant this for the sake of Jesus Christ our Lord. Amen.

'Amen.'

As we left, I turned one final time – and smiled.

*

Calais lay three days ahead, though we could have reached it sooner. But with so many wounded from Crécy, the King saw no need to rush.

‘Stop being a martyr, Emyr, and get up on that wagon.’

I was still fighting with Bastard, muttering threats of serving her up as the French liked their horsemeat.

He gave me a puzzled look as he limped along the hard-packed road, struggling to keep pace.

'Martyr, my Lord?'

'You're scarcely staying on your feet. You got those bruises for me – let me do this much. And I'm not a lord.'

He laughed. 'Force of habit, Ailred – my Lord.'

He clambered aboard, shifted a few bundles of arrows to make space, and was asleep within moments.

The march to Calais began in silence, men nursing wounds both seen and unseen. The French were broken, no threat remained, and we allowed ourselves to relax for the first time in weeks. We marched, sang, laughed, and filled the hours with meaningless banter. We became human again.

But hunger and greed are hard to suppress, and soon the beast surfaced. We plundered every town and village we passed. Word spread like the wildfires we left in our wake, and most settlements lay deserted, their people and valuables hidden deep in the forests.

Then we reached Wissant, a fishing port not far from Calais. It was too important and wealthy for the townsfolk to abandon, yet too weak to defend itself.

As we neared, a group of mounted aldermen and a band of friars barred our way on the road ahead. The King was just ahead, leading. For most of the journey, I'd trotted alongside

Sir Thomas. I had learned that Bastard behaved herself in his presence, so I sought his company whenever I could. It felt good to be outsmarting a horse. Emyr was never far behind, either jogging or walking like a shadow. I'd forgotten how quickly the young heal.

'Ailred, with me,' Sir Thomas called as he spotted the delegation blocking our path. 'The King will want my counsel.' He glanced at Emyr. 'And bring the monkey.'

I laughed.

'What's so funny?' he asked, frowning.

'You used to call me that.' I puffed out my chest. 'Does this mean I've risen in value?'

He shook his head. 'You're still a dung-beetle, Ailred. I was referring to his superior standing in God's order.'

I shrugged and nudged Bastard forward to catch up.

The King and Prince of Wales didn't acknowledge me as they greeted Sir Thomas. Beauchamp was already there, along with Lord Stafford and a cluster of advisors and bodyguards. Since Paul's death, Beauchamp's stance toward me had softened. He had hated Paul, and I wasn't enough of a threat to hold a grudge against. After seeing him face Paul in single combat – and witnessing his brutality on the fields of Crécy – it came as a relief. The King looked tired and irritable, his eyes showing signs of days in the saddle and lack of sleep. We all felt it. Food had all but run out, and the King only ate as his men did. It was a gesture not lost on us.

As we drew close to our French reception party, Beauchamp and Lord Stafford moved ahead while the rest of us hung back, encircling the King and Prince. We didn't expect a trap, but we took no chances.

After a few minutes, the King grew restless.

'With me,' he commanded, urging his horse forward to join the group.

As we arrived, Beauchamp steadied his mount and turned to the King. 'We are not wanted here,' he laughed.

The King's eyes narrowed. 'I bet we aren't.' He nudged past Beauchamp, his gaze locked on the man who seemed to be the town's spokesman. He was in his early thirties, draped in a gaudy red-and-blue surcoat over a brown cotehardie. His air of self-importance, the tilt of his chin as he surveyed us, clearly irritated the King.

'Do you speak English?' the King demanded, his voice edged with impatience.

'I do, but you are in my country, Monsieur.' The man's lips curled into a sneer. 'If you are ignorant of our tongue, I will indulge you. I am the Mayor of Wissant. What business have you here?'

The King's knuckles whitened on his pommel. A couple of the aldermen shifted uneasily while one of the friars murmured something in French.

'Do you know who you are addressing?' the

King asked with barely concealed disbelief.

'Of course I do. You are King Edward of England, Monsieur. A man who respects only strength – who has no time for weakness.' The mayor gave a knowing grin. 'I think you and I are very much alike.'

The King smiled and nodded. He extended his hand in greeting.

The mayor leaned forward, shifting his reins to clasp it.

The King's dagger flashed before he even had time to react. The blade punched deep into his neck, cutting off his breath in a wet choke. His eyes flared in shock as his hands clawed at the wound, but the King wrenched the knife free and struck again, slashing across his face and eyes. Grasping the man's hair in his fist, he hauled him from the saddle and threw him to the ground.

Shouts erupted. The aldermen scattered, some wheeling their horses, others sprinting toward the town gates.

The King wiped his blade clean on his sleeve, turned to us, and smiled.

'The town's yours, gentlemen.'

*

Wissant burned.

Word of the King's brutality spread through the ranks, with most taking it as an invitation to do likewise. And they did. Flames ripped roofs from the timber houses that adorned the ancient town, curling smoke into the sky as screams tangled with the sounds of doors kicked in. Soldiers moved through the streets like wolves among sheep, dragging the townsfolk into the open. As night fell and everything of value had been claimed, men played dice in drunken stupors while women and girls were used as currency.

I will not set to words all that was done. Some horrors are best left unspoken. I will not claim innocence either, as I ate heartily that night on plundered food and, after allowing Emyr free rein, accepted a share of the gold coins he looted. I even gave thought to how Paul would have relished the night, so what does that say about me?

But when it was over, Wissant was nothing but ash and ghosts.

As I rode Bastard away the next day, my eyes were still red-rimmed from the smoke, my throat coarse. Guilt ate from within as I passed twisted bodies and abandoned children crawling through the wreckage.

Nothing could bring me lower. But something did.

'Ailred, I have news.'

As soon as I saw Sir Thomas's face, I knew it wasn't good, but I asked anyway.

'If I pray hard enough, might it be in my favour?'

He forced a smile but wouldn't meet my eyes.

'While you gentlemen were making yourselves

rich and drunk last night, I went about sourcing a boat,' he said, nodding toward the seafront. 'There would never be a better time to take possession of a vessel than last night – and that was the case.'

A broad grin spread across my face. I turned to Emyr, who looked sick from the night's excesses.

'Did you hear that, Em? We're going home!' I turned back to Sir Thomas. 'You did just say that, didn't you, Sire?'

He sighed and shook his head. 'Sorry, Ailred. I spoke to the King, but he won't spare you.' His voice held no mockery this time. 'Says every man will be needed for the siege.' He gave me a humourless smile. 'It seems you're worth more than a dung beetle after all.'

I appreciated his attempt at flattery, but it left me cold.

Before I could plead, the King rode past with the Prince and Lord Stafford.

'Move out, people,' Stafford called across, 'next stop, Calais. If you thought Wissant was wealthy, wait to see what awaits there.'

I turned back towards Sir Thomas, but he was gone, striding towards the shoreline and a journey home.

*

I sulked. It made no difference, as Emyr saw a side to me he hadn't witnessed before. He found it funny, which wasn't the idea, but helped me snap out of it.

'And let this be a lesson to you, lad. Don't get your hopes up – someone will always come along and dash them.'

We'd been marching for a couple of hours, and Emyr's colour had returned, although he'd vomited twice along the way. He shrugged.

'Those noblemen are all the same, Lord, been doing it to me all my life.'

'I'm not a lord. And, yeah, you're right.'

I went back to sulking.

I still had a face like a washed-out turnip when the walls of Calais came into view.

This wasn't my first sight of the town, and it brought back bittersweet memories. The last time I was here, I'd been with Philippa and Paul, slipping away from the siege of Tournai.

If you recall, Brother Michael, you scribed it – and yes, you're right, it does seem like a lifetime ago. But don't let us be distracted from this tale.

Emyr stopped dead as he caught sight of the distant defences. 'How the hell are we supposed to take that?' His mouth hung open in wonder. 'Those walls must be a thousand feet tall, my Lord.'

I laughed, shaking off the last of my sullenness. 'I'm not a lord. And your grasp of reality is somewhat lacking, Em, but aye, they're formidable.'

The column behind shoved us forward, and we kept moving. 'You've never been in a siege, have you?' I asked, passing him my water pouch before swinging back into the saddle.

He shook his head.

'Well, lad, sieges are long and dull. Waiting, watching, and starving the bastards out. Now and then, the King throws us expendables at the walls in a futile attempt to scale them. Mostly, we die. Eventually, though, they break.' I looked down at him. 'If the King skipped the part where we get butchered for no reason, it'd be simple.'

And so it proved.

The King had us set up our sea of tents to the west of the town near Nouville, cutting off any chance of relief from that direction. It was the 4th of September, 1346, and sweltering. Within hours, the stench of human waste became unbearable. Lord Stafford requisitioned Emyr, putting him to work with the squires and pageboys digging latrines. It was filthy, back-breaking work, but someone had to do it. Character building was my explanation to Emyr, from bitter experience. He told me he'd prefer to keep his old character if it meant not digging pits.

Calais was governed by Jean de Vienne, a seasoned campaigner, and on day one, the King offered him terms of surrender. De Vienne refused, insulting Edward in his written reply, setting the tone for the siege. From that moment, the King's patience wore thin. De Vienne knew precisely what he was doing, seizing every opportunity to antagonise Edward. The defenders hurled filth alongside their crossbow bolts when the King drew close to the walls. None came close, but the insult landed.

The French could resupply Calais by sea, so when we arrived, English ships began a blockade, running supplies to our army instead. King Philip had no answer. No enemy ships challenged us; our only threat lay within the walls.

Without Izelda's intelligence, Edward was blind – no word of Philip's whereabouts, no sense of his numbers or intentions. She had been worth a thousand soldiers, and the King had vowed to honour her name after the campaign. It rang hollow to me, meant more to ease his own guilt than to commemorate her death – if he felt guilt at all. I doubted she would ever find a place in history beyond the manuscript Brother Michael is writing. The world would forget her, as it did so many, but I would not. I was heartened, knowing she was travelling home to Gascony, her birthplace, where a quiet burial awaited. That was enough for me.

On day one, we started losing men. Every assault on the walls met a storm of bolts from jeering Frenchmen, and for every crossbowman I struck from his perch, we lost ten of our own. We were there to protect the foot soldiers as they probed for weakness, but there was none.

By the second evening, Edward summoned his war council. Lord Stafford brought me along, despite my many faults. He still valued me as an archer and a leader of men, and in the stifling heat of the tent, the King laid out his plan.

'We will break them tomorrow,' he said, slamming his fist into the flimsy table in front of him and scattering its contents. 'I will have that bastard's head at my feet by the day's end.'

We looked at each other in surprise as silence descended. No one was willing to speak, so I did.

'When you say, that bastard, can we assume you mean Jean de Vienne, Your Highness?' That drew pained expressions from the assembled lords and advisors, but I wasn't finished. 'And how are we going to manage to...'

But I stopped. Stafford was mouthing the word "no" and shaking his head whilst everyone else was staring at me wide-eyed.

The King stood and leaned forward, resting his knuckles on the table, looking as though he'd seen me for the first time.

'Remind me – who are you?'

Lord Beauchamp moved to his side. 'This is Paul Christian's brother, Your Majesty, the man who murdered the Count of Artois and Charles of Alençon.'

The King nodded. 'Of course he is – I remember him now. Always doing the wrong thing. Even shot his own brother, as I recall.' He looked towards Lord Stafford. 'And he still hasn't learned anything. Tell me, my Lord, what made you think bringing him along was a good idea?'

Stafford blushed and went to speak, but no

words came out.

Before I had a chance to explain myself or apologise, Beauchamp grabbed me by the neck and dragged me to the tent's exit.

The King's final words followed me out. 'And be sure, whatever your name is, you'll discover my plans soon enough.' He laughed. 'Leading from the front will teach you well.'

CHAPTER 34

It was nighttime. I lay on the ground outside my tent, staring up at Lord Stafford as candlelight twisted his features into something demonic. Emyr stood nearby, uncertain what to do but wise enough to keep silent. I wish I'd been born with that instinct.

'I think you broke my nose, Sire,' I stammered, wiping blood from my face.

He lunged and drove his boot into my stomach, stealing whatever words I might have had left.

'We're done, you fool. You made me a laughingstock back there. Whatever comes of you tomorrow, I don't care – it's of your own making.'

And just like that, he was gone. He turned on his heels and strode out of my life, leaving me gasping for air. As the candle guttered, Emyr came to my aid, lifting me to my feet and helping me towards my tent.

'Beth ddigwyddodd yn ôl yno, Arglwydd?' he asked in a panicked voice.

'You'll have to speak English, lad,' I replied through spasms of pain. 'The only word I understood was Lord, and I'm not one.'

'What happened back there? What did you say to upset him, Lord?'

I stood, tilted my head back and took deep breaths while Emyr took a filthy rag to my nose to stem the bleeding.

'I think it was the wrong thing.'

I spat blood.

'And what did he mean by whatever comes of you tomorrow, Lord?'

I took the cloth from him and felt my nose. It squeaked. 'I wouldn't concern yourself. Just be thankful you're not me.'

He sat down in a heap by my feet. 'I'd love to have no concerns, Lord, but whatever comes of you tomorrow will come of me too.'

I looked down at him. 'I didn't think of that, Emyr. I'm sorry.'

He lay back in the dew-soaked grass and stared at the clear, dark sky, awash with stars. 'I'm beginning to see a pattern to your behaviour, Lord.'

Neither of us said another word. We just crawled into our tents and let exhaustion take its course.

*

I didn't know what to expect the following day. I soon found out.

'Up, you dogs. It's time you earned your pay.'

Lord Stafford's captains repeated Beauchamp's voice as they roused us, kicking those still sleeping and dragging the sluggish to their feet by their collars.

I was already up, sat by the fire, boiling water

and chewing on dried pork and bread. The sun had yet to rise, but a dull glow in the east cast faint shadows. I'd been woken when a dog crawled under my tent flap and stole from my provisions, which surprised me – I thought I was awake. Most of the night had been spent turning over the King's parting words.

'Are we attacking today, Lord?'

I had stopped Beauchamp as he passed, still barking orders.

He eyed me with the first flicker of compassion I'd seen from him. 'Yes, Norman. Be assured, we take the town today. Be ready in an hour.' He glanced toward the makeshift chapel nearby. 'That gives you time to prepare.'

I took a deep breath as I understood his implication. He looked at me, his face blank but his voice soft.

'The King is angry, Ailred,' he said, 'we're going in the front door.'

He went to leave.

'Thanks, Lord. I'll make my peace.'

He nodded and left.

I stared into the fire. The warmth felt good. I tossed the remains of my meat into it and watched it crackle. I'd lost my appetite. I scooped up a handful of dry earth and clenched it.

'What did he mean?'

Emyr's voice startled me. He stood at his tent's opening, a few feet from where I sat.

I looked at his youthful face and the lines of

worry that were already etched into his skin. He was too young to be here today. It didn't seem fair.

I kept my voice as even as possible. 'Oh, nothing, Em, just that we're attacking the walls.'

He walked over, wringing his hands together.

'There's more you're not telling me, Lord.'

Without looking up, I said, 'I'm not a lord, lad, and there isn't anything else to tell.' I nodded towards the chapel. 'Join me?'

There was a long pause before his gentle answer. 'Yes, Lord, I would be honoured.'

*

We seized the bridge over the outer moat on the first day, our speed and surprise catching the French off guard. But before we could reach the second, they destroyed it – along with the wooden causeway that spanned the marshland – forcing us to build our own crossing. Beyond it, the walls and gatehouse loomed, a formidable barrier. Simple – at least in the King's mind.

His fury with Jean de Vienne drove him to order a full frontal assault – rash, unnecessary, and no doubt against the advice of his council. But he had called it anyway. And we would pay the price for his impatience. It was the only decision he'd ever made that I'd doubted. But who was I to question the King?

I was frightened.

As Beauchamp and his captains herded us into position, I realised my home division would lead the vanguard. All around me stood men from my town and county – friends, recruits, people who had once looked to me with trust. Now, they looked for reassurance.

I had none.

Men-at-arms, siege engineers, and light infantry swelled our ranks as we readied to storm Calais. From the battlements, the enemy stirred – thousands of French crossbowmen and men-at-arms, eager to pour death upon us.

Emyr tugged at my sleeve. We had already strung our bows and packed our quivers with as many arrows as they would hold.

'Lord, we might not make it through this.' His voice was low, unsteady. I started to speak, but he silenced me with a shake of his head. 'No, Sire. I know what you'll say, but let me finish.' I breathed out and nodded. 'I never had the chance to say what I wanted to my father. That pain will never leave me. I've learnt you don't always get the moment you think you will – so I'll take mine now.' He straightened his back, eyes firm. 'It has been an honour serving you, *Lord*.' I opened my mouth to correct him, but he pressed on with a small smile. 'Without you, I'd have deserted long ago. I'd be swinging from a rope as a coward or lying dead in a ditch with a French blade in my gut. That is all – thank you.'

I looked down, trying to find words that might match his, but as usual, my mind was blank.

'To your positions.'

Lord Beauchamp pushed through the ranks, directing his captains to chivvy us on, making the final preparations.

'Norman, I'm putting you and the rest of Sir Thomas's men under Captain Ethelbald.' He called over a huge archer I had seen a few times but never spoken to.

'Sire?' Ethelbald had a broad West Country accent that reminded me of my old friend, Godric.

'Take Ailred Norman and the rest of Sir Thomas's men and support the siege engineers while they bridge that second moat.' Beauchamp pointed to its narrowest point, close to the imposing gatehouse. Despite the good weather of the last few days, the area looked covered in marsh water, and wetland birds were picking across its reedy surface.

Ethelbald studied the terrain for a few seconds. 'Aye, Sire. It's a tall ask, getting men and materials across under that tower's fire…' He caught Beauchamp's hardened look and stopped himself. 'But we'll get the job done, my Lord.'

Beauchamp turned to our men-at-arms, his voice unwavering. 'You men will carry the ladders and scale the walls the moment the crossings are in place – no hesitation.' He fixed Ethelbald with a cold stare. 'And I want a steady barrage of arrows – no gaps. Keep them pinned.'

He drew Ethelbald away and called the rest of his captains together, ensuring every man knew his duty.

'Looks like you're one of us now, Ailred. No more special treatment,' one of the archers called in good humour.

He was right. I had burned my final bridge. The King would never forgive me. I should have felt deflated, but I didn't – the weight had lifted.

I looked around at so many familiar faces and smiled to myself. If I were to meet death today, I would meet it among my own. It was a comfort.

As our massed ranks readied, resolved to whatever fate God had written, we waited for that horn to blast – the one that would send us across those sodden grounds and into hell.

I heard shouting from behind. It was the King's voice, deep and commanding.

'HOLD, CAPTAINS.'

I turned to see Edward and the Prince of Wales, shadowed by their lords and bodyguards. Then I spotted Lord Stafford. He was escorting two prisoners – Jean, Count of Harcourt, and Charles, Count of Montmorency – the most valuable hostages taken at Crécy.

'What's going on?' Emyr whispered. He was crouched beside me; his war bow clutched tight in shaking hands.

Stafford strode past us toward the town, flanked by a couple of senior men-at-arms and a lone friar carrying a white flag of truce. By the time they reached the bridge over the first moat, a group of French knights emerged from the partially opened gates of the gatehouse. They, too, bore flags of truce, forcing their mounts through the waterlogged marshland to the edge of the second moat, where they halted, waiting.

Emyr's eyes were still on me, searching for an answer.

'My guess, lad, is they're making a final offer of surrender – hoping the French hostages can sway them.'

'Do you think they'll accept?'

My mind returned to Tournai when Edward had allowed thousands of townsfolk to starve in no man's land after the defenders cast out their "useless mouths".

'If they don't, Edward will show no mercy. And Jean de Vienne knows it. If the noblemen can persuade him that it's better to save the lives of…'

Emyr's young face lit with sudden hope.

'I pray to God they do,' he murmured. 'Dydw I ddim eisiau marw heddiw.'

By the time they reached the far bank, their legs were caked in mud. They had waded knee-deep in places, and every man watching understood what reaching those walls would cost if the negotiations failed.

We watched and waited.

'That's Jean de Vienne negotiating,' Captain Ethelbald said as the lead rider on a jet-black Friesian removed his helmet and shook his long hair loose. Ethelbald nodded to himself. 'That's a good sign.'

As the groups stood on either bank, conversing across the watery divide beyond our hearing, every man held his breath as if the slightest sound might shatter the fragile moment.

At first, it seemed promising. The hostages exchanged pleasantries with their fellow compatriots on the other side, and I even saw Lord Stafford and Jean de Vienne swap courtesies. This continued for a few minutes as the men around me started to murmur. Some even unstrung their bows, though their eyes remained fixated on the scene. It was still on a knife's edge. If words could win the day, perhaps we'd be spared from wading through that death trap after all.

But then it happened. I saw De Vienne stand in his stirrups, look beyond Lord Stafford, and point towards the King, who was looking on with the rest of us. He was waving his arms as if demanding the King should approach. I watched Edward. He was smiling. De Vienne became animated, raising his chin as if issuing a challenge. The King's smile turned to laughter. I could faintly hear frantic taunts in French being bellowed before the King turned his back on the French leader and walked away.

It was over. There would be blood.

*

By the time the engineers reached the moat, we had lost more men than in the entire Crécy campaign. The King should have called the retreat and reassessed, but stubbornness or pride held him fast. The ground swallowed our legs to the knee, each step a desperate heave through the sucking mire. Bolts tore through us, men jerked backwards, thrashing as they hit the ground. For every pavise raised, five lay shattered; their carriers sprawled lifeless.

'To me!' I bellowed at Emyr as he floundered, half-drowned in the mire, clawing for the quiver of arrows he'd dropped. 'Forget it! Just move!'

I had found shelter of sorts beside another archer and his shield, his eyes wild with fear. As Emyr crawled the last few feet, I lunged, dragging him in.

The engineers who had survived the death march across the bog crouched behind whatever wreckage they could, too. On the King's orders, Captain Ethelbald had thrown wave after wave of infantry forward to haul the timbers for a crossing, but now so many lay dead, their materials abandoned in the sludge. Whenever an archer dared to rise, a storm of quarrels met him.

'This is madness!' I snarled, struggling to nock another arrow in the tight space. 'I've loosed a dozen shafts, and not one's found its mark. They have thousands of crossbowmen!'

'Surely they'll run out of bolts at some point,' the other archer said, his cheek pressed against the pavise.

'That they will, but long after we're dead. Just pray the King sees sense and sounds the retreat.'

He rose to shoot. We had been taking turns, each shot answered with a fresh volley hammering into our shield. It had worked – until now. He stood, bow bent to its limit. The string brushed his nose. Then his head snapped back, a bolt buried to the fletching in his eye. He collapsed, a spray of blood covering me as he slumped beside Emyr, his arrow soaring harmlessly into the sky.

Screams howled across the battlefield. The wounded writhed in the mire, their hands clasping embedded bolts. Drenched in mud and blood, men dragged themselves forward, only to be peppered mercilessly. Somewhere in the distance, a horse shrieked, its rider dragged into the quagmire as it thrashed in its death throes.

And still, King Edward threw men forward.

With Emyr kneeling beside me, holding the pavise steady, I fired my last arrow. Breathless, I huddled beside him.

'How the hell are we still alive?' I asked, surveying the field of corpses. Emyr said nothing, lost in fear and regret. 'Damned if I'm moving from here, lad. No one can complain if we stop firing – we're out of arrows.'

He looked at me, finally speaking. 'Yes, Lord.'

I shook my head and laughed, the sound unhinged. 'I'm not a lord, Emyr.'

'No, Lord.'

A shout from behind turned my head.

Across the blood-soaked ground, English

pageboys scurried between the dead, pairs of them working in tandem – one carrying a pavise, the other hauling fresh quivers.

Two reached us. The lad being shielded pressed two quivers into my hands. His face was ghostly pale.

I took them and handed one to Emyr. 'Surely the King isn't expecting us to continue? Hasn't he ordered a retreat?'

The boy shook his head. 'No, Sire. His Majesty commands you to press on.'

The words were a death sentence. I glanced at Emyr. He was frozen, terror striking him silent.

The page swallowed. 'I must return – more archers need resupplying.'

I nodded. 'Go, lad. And may God be with you – because he sure isn't with me.'

The boy turned to leave, checking his pavise, but hesitated.

'Before we leave, Sire – do you know if an archer named Ailred Norman and his squire still live? I've had orders to ask.'

I frowned. 'Orders from who?'

His gaze flicked from me to the safer ground behind. 'I can't say, Sire. I've strict instructions to deliver the message and return at once.'

I seized his arm. 'I'm Ailred Norman. This is my squire. Tell me who sent you, or so help me I'll…'

'Sir Thomas de Clare, Sire.'

I stared, my mouth dry. 'Sir Thomas? He sailed for England days ago.'

'Begging your pardon, Sire, you're mistaken – he has yet to leave.' The lad glanced at his shield-bearer, who gave a quick nod, bracing for the perilous return. 'Follow us, we'll take you to him.'

I turned, placing the battered pavise behind me, shoved Emyr ahead, and crouched low. Resting the shield across my back, we crept forward, inch by inch. Bolts slammed into the wood, the wet earth, and the corpses littering the field, but none found our flesh. We left nothing exposed.

The marsh dragged at our legs, the slow, agonising crawl grinding my body to ruin. My thighs burned, my arms trembled, and by the time we cleared the worst of it, I couldn't stand. I collapsed, breathless, my stomach cramping so fiercely I thought I'd vomit.

But we lived.

I turned back. Men and boys still fell, their bodies twisting as they crashed into the sodden earth. My elation turned to guilt.

How could I walk away from my brothers-in-arms, still trapped in that slaughter?

'I... I must go back,' I said, my eyes fixed on Captain Ethelbald as he fell. A bolt struck his shoulder, spinning him from cover before more pierced him where he lay.

'No, you won't, Ailred. I need you.'

I tore my gaze from the slaughter. 'Sir Thomas, my Lord, I can't just walk away...'

He seized my arm, dragging me back. 'You can,

and you will. Emyr, you too – move.'

He led us through the chaos, past frantic men and dying horses. The air reeked of blood and released bowels.

'Where the hell are you taking us?' I demanded, yanking free. 'I've sworn myself to the King – he demands my service!'

Sir Thomas held my gaze. 'And you're duty-bound to me.' I opened my mouth to argue, but he cut me off. 'Yes, the King comes first, always, but he's granted me two men of my choosing. He knows the value of what I'm doing.' He clapped my shoulder. 'So, like it or not, you're mine now. We're shipping two valuable prisoners back to England – immediately.'

I shook my head. 'The King wouldn't allow it. He wouldn't send me away from this assault.'

Thomas shoved me forward. 'I told him I needed two more hands to crew and knew two experienced sailors. He said as long as I brought the Count of Harcourt and Montmorency safely to English soil, I could take whoever I pleased.'

He stopped, meeting my eyes. 'You and Emyr once swore you knew the sea... *didn't you*?'

I hesitated – until the meaning of his words struck me.

With one last glance at the carnage – the screams, the dying – I turned away... accepting his offer of life.

CHAPTER 35

As we climbed aboard Sir Thomas's requisitioned boat, the Counts of Harcourt and Montmorency were in fine fettle.

'What luck – two English archers masquerading as sailors to ensure we never see land again,' Harcourt mused. 'And is it them or the boat that stinks of fish?'

He bore the look of his lineage – sharp features, noble bearing, and the arrogance to match – though his once-fine clothing was torn and caked in mud. Crécy's loss had stripped him of his dignity but not his wit.

Montmorency was more detached but took to the theme. 'May I suggest we scuttle the boat here in the harbour and spare ourselves the indignity of drowning, Sir Thomas? They say one should never swim after a hearty meal – and I assume you'll be treating us to one before we set sail, no?'

Both Frenchmen sat shackled in the stern, speaking flawless English.

'Right, let's put this crate to sea,' Sir Thomas cried, slipping the mooring rope free before jumping aboard.

With no other crew besides the prisoners, we turned to Sir Thomas for instruction.

He stared back.

Both Frenchmen burst into laughter.

Harcourt wiped away his tears. 'This voyage should be fun, Messieurs, given that no one knows how to sail.'

Montmorency leaned back and put his feet on the railings. Stroking his sculpted beard, he closed his eyes and yawned. 'Wake me just before we wreck.'

Sir Thomas had no time for their theatrics.

'Ailred, Emyr – there. Take the oars.' Sir Thomas turned to the Frenchmen, his gaze as cold. 'You failed to broker a surrender. Now, you belong to me and the King.' He pointed to the benches opposite. 'Sit. Row.'

They laughed but complied, their chains just long enough to let them take their seats. Sir Thomas took the tiller.

'Now row, you sea-dogs. Get us out of this harbour.'

*

'Tell me, do you steer by the stars or by sheer incompetence?'

We had reached open sea under oar power. That had been the easy part. The real trouble began when we raised the sail. For the past hour, we'd done little but drift in aimless circles while Sir Thomas banged his head against the tiller, cursing himself for not selecting at least one competent sailor.

I snapped and turned on Montmorency. 'Are all French noblemen insufferable?'

He smirked at Harcourt. 'The man looks like he's kin to an ape and yet dares to ask if we're all alike.'

Harcourt chuckled. 'I'd wager an ape would handle the rigging better.'

Before I could reply, the boom swung hard across the deck and cracked Emyr across the face, knocking him flat. The Frenchmen burst into laughter.

I hauled Emyr upright, pinching his nose to stem the bleeding. 'I asked,' I said, 'because my brother and I once knew Charles of Alençon and the Count of Artois. They seemed cut from the same cloth as you two.'

Their laughter died. For the first time since boarding, their faces turned serious.

'They are good men, Monsieur,' Harcourt said, watching me closely. 'It eases my heart to hear you speak of them. I had feared the worst. I trust you have cared for their well-being better than ours?' He cast a glance at Montmorency, who nodded. 'As we share their fate of captivity, we look forward to meeting them soon.'

I propped Emyr against the low hull and checked that he was steady before I met Harcourt's glare. 'If you keep on as you are, you'll meet them sooner than you think, *Messieurs*.' They exchanged puzzled looks. 'My brother butchered them and threw their heads to the dogs.'

Silence.

Sir Thomas, having let me make my point, decided it was time to end the conversation. Leaning on the tiller, he called down, 'Enough, Ailred. Get back to work.'

Over the next few hours, we learned from our mistakes, using the warm southern breeze to our advantage. We improved enough to move in the right direction, even daring to believe we might set foot on English soil again.

The Counts of Harcourt and Montmorency simmered in silence. It was clear they'd been close to the men Paul had killed. Their demeanour shifted; the forced humour melted away, replaced by sneers that turned to open animosity.

'Keep her steady,' Sir Thomas called as if he had the slightest idea what he was doing. We had swapped positions, me now on the rudder, and I let myself relax, pushing the horrors of Calais to the back of my mind.

Then, the tension shifted.

'You men are doing a fine job.'

I turned to Harcourt. He was smiling, broad, and easygoing, as if we were old friends sharing a quiet drink.

Montmorency followed suit, his grin no less unsettling. 'You English take to sailing like ducks to water. I believe that's the saying, yes?'

I glanced at Emyr. He looked at Sir Thomas. Sir Thomas stared back at me.

None of us spoke.

But we all felt it.

Something wasn't right.

'SHIP TO OVER THERE!'

Emyr's shout snapped the pieces into place.

As the Frenchmen burst into laughter, I turned to see a large vessel cutting through the waves, bearing straight for us.

'French pirates!' Sir Thomas snapped. 'They've been raiding the English coast for months. We're in trouble.'

No insignia flew, but none was necessary. The sight alone was enough – everyone knew the French had dozens of ships prowling the waters, raiding the coastline, slaughtering entire crews and driving off all but the most ruthless English pirates.

'We look like a fishing boat, my Lord. They might pass us by,' I offered, staring into the spray as the sunlight caught the droplets, turning them into fleeting rainbows. 'We've nothing of value. Surely, we're not worth their bother?'

'Maybe they are hungry, Monsieur,' Montmorency mused, licking his lips. 'You know how we French like fish. Sprinkle them with a little parsley, drizzle with lemon…'

Laughter again.

Harcourt smirked. 'Or maybe they saw us signalling to them while you weren't looking. Either way…' He nodded toward the closing ship. 'They're coming for you.'

'Damn,' I said. It was all I could manage.

Montmorency gestured toward the looming ship. 'You could try to outrun them, my English friends. It's a big vessel – too slow to catch a well-handled boat of this size.'

Harcourt nodded, grinning. 'Oh yes, a good crew would slip away with ease.' He turned to me. 'But alas, we have no sailors, only murdering bastards who butcher French noblemen. So, I think the game is up.' He chuckled. 'That is another quaint English saying, yes?'

We scrambled across the deck, trying anything that might coax more speed from the boat, but we barely knew how to sail in a straight line.

I had heard the stories – English and French pirates alike, their names spoken in taverns with hushed dread. None of them left survivors.

The noblemen were enjoying their sport now.

'They'll slaughter you two as well as us, so don't get ahead of yourselves, you idiots.' My patience was wearing thin, and I wasn't alone.

'You think they'll spare you just because you're French?' Sir Thomas let out a short, forced laugh.

Harcourt feigned shock, clasping a hand to his mouth before grinning. 'Oh, but you, Sir Thomas, are worth a great deal of money. These French peasants won't know how to ransom you, so they'll need someone to guide them. Someone who knows how these things work.' He glanced at Montmorency. 'Do we know anyone like that?'

Montmorency gave an exaggerated shrug. 'Oh, I think I know two good negotiators.' Then his gaze settled on me. 'And I wonder what they'll do to those without value and who stink of fish?'

'Oh, we'll ask them, shall we?' Harcourt chuckled, turning as the ship loomed closer.

'YOU THERE, STOP THAT BOAT AND PREPARE TO BE BOARDED!'

The voice belonged to a massive man standing at the bow, flanked by twenty others armed with axes and swords.

The laughter died in Harcourt and Montmorency's throats, their faces draining of colour.

Sir Thomas shot me a look. 'Either those Frenchmen lost their accents, or they're English.' The noblemen's silence was a brief pleasure. 'Doesn't matter either way,' Sir Thomas muttered. 'The King has a death warrant on every pirate, French or English. They won't care about ransoms.'

Harcourt rattled his shackles. 'You can die with us like this, or let us sail this boat. Your choice.'

We stared at the pair in confusion.

'You can sail this heap of junk?' Sir Thomas exclaimed.

Montmorency nodded at the looming ship. 'Maybe. Can you risk it? They'll kill you as quickly as us. Trust us, or we all die.'

Sir Thomas shot me a look before rushing forward to unlock their shackles.

The counts sprang to their feet. For a

moment, I thought they meant to attack us, but Montmorency bolted for the bow, yanking open a box and pulling out what we'd dismissed earlier as a spare sail. He shouted something in French about a spi to Harcourt, who was already scrambling halfway up the mast.

'What the hell are you doing?' I barked, but they ignored me.

Montmorency unfurled the sail across the deck and grabbed a rope.

'MAKE THIS EASY ON YOURSELVES,' the pirate captain called in amusement. 'WE WON'T HARM YOU.'

The laughter that followed said otherwise.

'Passe vite le spi, ici!' Harcourt shouted. Montmorency flung the rope up to him.

With practised efficiency, Harcourt secured the sail to the mast while Montmorency lashed the other end to a post at the bow.

The wind caught. The boat lurched, almost lifting it from the water.

An axe thudded into the stern, the last act of desperation as we tore away at speed, leaving a chorus of English curses in our wake.

*

A quiet truce held as we came alongside the quayside at Dover. After freeing them, we had armed ourselves, forcing Montmorency and Harcourt to see us home. They had admitted they were seasoned sailors all along, raised on the warm Mediterranean off France's southern coast. They still hated us – me in particular – but the choice had been simple: ransom or butchery at the hands of English pirates. So they raised the spinnaker.

As we disembarked, the King's wardens awaited us – men in royal livery, swords at their hips, their eyes cold. They had little patience for French nobility, but understood the worth of the ransom.

'When this is over, we will come for you, Monsieur,' one of our captives murmured.

I can't recall which one spoke – but by then, I was sick of their voices.

CHAPTER 36

As we neared my hometown of Tonebricge, night was falling, and the rain came down in sheets. Every muscle ached. Emyr and I had walked for four days after Sir Thomas had bought a fine chestnut thoroughbred from a farmstead off the Dover road and ridden ahead. His purchase had reminded me that I'd never see Bastard again, which made the walk home that bit sweeter.

After mooring and unloading our human cargo, Sir Thomas graciously paid for two nights' lodging at a local tavern, saying we'd earned a slow stroll home. It seemed out of character, but we didn't complain as we dined on the best the tavern had to offer, courtesy of my Lord.

That night, after many tankards from the landlord's black barrel, Emyr loosened up. That's an understatement – he was hammered. I learned a great deal about him: devoutly religious, shaped by his father into an archer, with the makings of an exceptional one in time. But his true calling was the church. That explained his impromptu prayer at Paul's graveside, spoken with such conviction and passion. He confided that he'd seen through Paul's masquerade at first glance, then spent the rest of the night apologising in that endless way only drunk people can, once he realised I wasn't ready to hear anything bad about my brother.

As I helped him to bed at the end of the night, besides telling me I was his best friend and throwing up on my boots, he told me he wanted to put down his bow and pull on a cassock. With his father gone, he felt no duty to fulfil his wishes.

The following day, bleary-eyed and apologetic, Emyr insisted on giving thanks for our safe return at St Mary's Parish Church, not far from the port. I let him. He'd earned as much.

Days later, we crossed the town's southern boundary, bypassing the priory, and ambled up the main thoroughfare. I had been away a year, but it felt longer. The first threads of grey wove through my thinning hair, and every morning, I grumbled – too hot, too cold, too wet, too... well, you get the idea. I'd also taken to talking to myself – that and to animals and plants. I'm unsure if that comes with age, but I had to question myself when imagining their replies. I reflected more, much as I'm doing now, Brother Michael. In short, I was grateful to be alive.

A scrawny dog snapping at my ankles brought me back to reality.

'Leave that poor wretch be, Bo.'

I recognised the voice. It was the same voice I heard talking to me every time death's hand clawed me. I'd heard it many times over the last year.

Emyr went to kick it, but I stopped him.

''Tis a fine-looking mutt, my Lady, though its temperament leaves a lot to be desired,' I said, lifting my head and shaking the raindrops from my face. 'A little like its owner!'

'AILRED…?'

Philippa ran towards me, slipped, and skidded to a stop by my feet while the dog renewed its assault on my legs.

I helped her to her feet, brushing the mud from her once-grand clothing while permitting Emyr to drag Bo away.

We embraced, two wet bodies slapping together.

She stood back and glared. 'You could have told me you were coming home.' She saw my look of disappointment and flung her arms around me, kissing me before standing back and spitting out the mud she'd swallowed from my filthy lips.

'Get a room.'

Sir Thomas was trotting his new gelding through the town and stopped at our public show of affection. He looked tired, but was in high spirits, having been home a few days already. I could only imagine how we must have looked.

'Emyr, unless you fancy getting caught in the middle of whatever comes next between these two…' He grinned as Philippa blushed. 'Hop up behind me, and I'll take you to the castle.'

'You're most gracious, my Lord,' Emyr muttered, hauling himself up.

As he settled, Sir Thomas turned his head. 'You could have ridden behind me days ago, lad. You'd have saved yourself all that walking. All you had to do was ask.'

Emyr groaned.

Sir Thomas turned back to us. 'When you're done, come to the castle.' He tapped his flanks and moved off. 'Oh, and for God's sake, wash and change those rags you call clothing.'

I won't trouble you with the details, Brother Michael – your past reactions speak for themselves. Suffice it to say, I was the happiest I'd been in a long time. Flashbacks to Izelda dampened the pleasure somewhat, and for a fleeting moment, as we basked in the afterglow, I considered telling Philippa the truth. Madness, I know. The thought vanished as quickly as it came, but it had been there all the same.

Over the next couple of hours, in between bouts of sexual contortion, only Philippa could achieve, I caught up on her life without me. Unsurprisingly, she had flourished, bringing Kimberly into the fold full-time. Her textile business was thriving, and the taverns supplied enough income for expansion. She told me that, just yesterday, she and Kimberly had returned from Goudhurst, where they'd spent two days negotiating terms to buy out a tavern owner.

She also owned a dog called Bo, who liked to bite strangers' legs.

We had already met.

Some time later, in a silent moment after she'd left my body exhausted and begging for mercy, she asked the question.

'Where's that useless brother of yours? Still out terrorising France?' She shifted her naked body away from my embrace. 'And if you think he's coming back here to stay with us, you can go...'

I closed my eyes. 'He's dead.'

Silence followed – and with it, the buried visions. At first, mere flickers: Paul standing before me, his face vacant, an arrow embedded deep in his chest. Then the visions swelled. Bodies tumbled down like relentless rain, the metallic stench of blood filling the air. Distant moans erupted into screams, growing louder with each heartbeat. Limbs twitched and spasmed as if reaching for me, clawing with broken, curled fingers, while empty eyes stared, unblinking.

My breath came in short, shallow gasps. The candle on the table guttered, and in its wavering light, the dead stirred. Their mouths gaped open – black pits dripping blood – as they whispered incoherent words I couldn't decipher yet somehow understood. I clamped my hands over my ears, but their pleas became a deafening clamour. The air pressed in, thick and suffocating.

Then, as the Devil twisted my soul into final submission, Philippa's voice drifted in – distant, almost unimportant. I fell from the bed with a harsh thud and crawled beneath it.

'I couldn't save him... I couldn't help them... I left them to die.'

*

When I awoke, it was light. I looked up. Gone was the familiar army canvas, replaced by timber beams with thatching stuffed between them. The stench of men's bodily expulsions had given way to lavender and meadowsweet, and it took me several seconds to realise where I was.

'There you are, finally awake.'

Kimberly's voice confirmed it. The joy of being home flooded back.

'I...' I started to speak, but my mouth was dry.

She handed me a tankard of ale, and my eyes focused on the beautiful woman before me.

'You've been asleep for hours, father.'

Her voice was calmer than I remembered, more assured.

I burst into tears.

She took the drink, placed it on the table beside me, and hugged me.

'Welcome home. I missed you so much.'

I brushed away my tears. It was funny how emotions came and went beyond my control. Give me a battlefield of broken men, and I could laugh – but home was a different kind of war. I pulled back, studied her face, and took her hands.

'You've grown.'

It's not my finest greeting, and if I could go

back in time, I could come up with something more heartfelt.

She laughed and brushed a tear from her eye.

'Now look what you've done,' she said, sniffing and wiping her nose with the back of her hand.

'Didn't I always tell you that's not ladylike?'

She punched my arm, then hugged me again.

'Get up, we have guests downstairs.'

Following her downstairs, I expected a welcoming party. Instead, I walked into a reckoning.

Lord John de Cobham stood by the front door, glaring at me. The last time I'd seen him, he'd accused me of killing Terrence Curley's adopted son, Richard. I'd escaped by joining Sir Thomas's division, sailing for France to fight for King Edward. Judging by his face, I hadn't been forgiven.

Beside him stood Sir Thomas, wearing that air of detachment only nobility could master. Philippa fussed with things that didn't need fussing before finally speaking.

'And this is my husband, Lord Cobham – Ailred Norman.'

I stepped down from the final stair and bowed. 'My Lord Cobham, it is an honour to have you…'

'Shut up, Norman,' he snarled. His face was red, and not just from wine. 'It was bloody well you that did it. Own up, or as God is my witness…'

The last time he accused me of something, I'd

been guilty as sin. This time, I hadn't a clue what he was talking about.

Sir Thomas, as ever, intervened. 'Calm yourself, my Lord. Now that he's here, perhaps you might explain what crime you accuse him of?'

Cobham looked ready to burst. 'This man killed my chief hand and bondsman, Terrence Curley.' Sir Thomas's expression darkened, but he stayed silent. 'Tortured the poor fellow to death,' Cobham added.

Sir Thomas turned to me. 'That is a grave charge, Lord. If proved, it will end in hanging. I will not have such conduct in my manor. When and where did this happen?'

Cobham snorted. 'Ask that murdering bastard.'

Sir Thomas's voice remained even. 'With respect, I am asking you as you make the accusation. I need to know when and where his body was found. And in what state it was in.'

Cobham let out an exasperated growl. 'God's teeth, man! Why does his *state* matter? Were you planning to ask him to dance? He was in the state of death – does that clear things up for you?'

Sir Thomas raised a brow. 'I am Sir Thomas de Clare, my Lord. Not "man". I'd be obliged if you referred to me as such.'

Cobham exhaled sharply, temper straining. 'Apologies, Sir Thomas. This... person brings out the worst in me.'

Sir Thomas nodded. 'Apology accepted. And

yes, he could provoke a negative reaction from a stone.' He folded his arms. 'The reason I ask has nothing to do with my next dance partner. I am establishing a timeline.'

Cobham narrowed his eyes. 'Timeline, Sire?'

'Yes, Lord. Unless Terrence Curley was murdered this very day, Ailred Norman could not have done it. He has been travelling from Dover, having attended the King's business. He arrived last night.'

Sir Thomas then detailed our movements, from when we moored to our return to Tonebricge, even suggesting Cobham send men to the Dover tavern to confirm Emyr and my lodging.

Cobham's glare didn't soften. 'He was killed a few days ago in Staplehurst, Sir Thomas. So, admittedly, that casts doubt on this being our man. But this… this creature believed Curley had a hand in his twin sons' murders. He had every reason to kill him – and just happens to return home right after his brutal death.'

I laughed. 'Good. I'll be in the debt of whoever killed the bastard.'

Sir Thomas's scowl deepened.

I met his gaze and sighed. 'But whoever it was, it wasn't me. I swear on the souls of those two little boys.'

Sir Thomas shook his head. 'So this murder happened in Staplehurst? I wish you had mentioned that at the start, Lord. For one, that is not my manor, so it has nothing to do with me. And second, there is no way on God's earth Ailred could have travelled there in the timescale we are speaking of.'

Cobham's face darkened. 'Well, someone with a grudge killed him.'

Sir Thomas exhaled through his nose, his patience fraying. 'I will not be spoken to this way... Lord. His innocence is beyond reproach, and this happened in *your* manor. May I suggest you make your inquiries closer to home?' Sir Thomas turned to me. 'Ailred is as dumb as a post, but even he wouldn't be fool enough to come straight home and murder an eminent man like Terrence Curly on arrival. You've wasted my time – and your own.' He gestured to the door. 'Unless you have anything else, Lord? These good people have endured enough falsehoods for one day.'

Cobham looked fit to burst but swallowed his anger. 'I apologise if I have offended, Sir Thomas, and the other family members are under no suspicion.' He forced a crooked smile at Philippa and Kimberly. 'I will take my leave, Sire.' As he turned to go, his gaze settled on me. 'I'd say you're a lucky man, Norman.'

He left, muttering vague threats under his breath.

'Well, that settles that,' Sir Thomas sighed as Philippa returned from seeing him out.

A silence fell. I saw the glances exchanged

between Sir Thomas, Philippa, and Kimberly.

I broke it. 'I would have killed him.'

Sir Thomas exhaled. 'I know.' He glanced at Philippa and Kimberly. 'We knew.'

'I'll never get the chance now. I needed justice for Timothy and Frederick,' I mumbled, as Philippa and Kimberly were both near to tears. 'We as a family needed it.'

Sir Thomas's voice was quiet, strained. 'They were loved by me too, Ailred.'

I studied all three of them. There was something strange in the air, something I couldn't put my finger on.

'It's almost as if someone knew what I'd do and did it first – to keep the blame from falling on me,' I said slowly.

They held my stare.

'Whoever it was must have hated Terrence Curly with a passion,' Philippa murmured.

'And now you're not a suspect,' Kimberly added.

Sir Thomas set his hat on his head. 'It seemed a fitting punishment to me.'

I kept looking between the three of them.

And then it clicked.

CHAPTER 37

I am tired now, Brother Michael. And old. It is time to put down your quill. These weeks of nostalgia have been both a curse and a triumph. I have much to be thankful for, but, on reflection, I have lost much – yet I have lived.

There were years of love and prosperity following my return, but those tales belong to me alone. I swore to Philippa I would never again leave her to fight in another man's war. I kept that pledge. So what remains to tell? I grew fat, and the years of drawing the bow and life lived in constant battlefield squalor took their toll. My joints stiffened. The body forgets nothing, nor does the mind, though I learned to live with the echoes. But I woke beside her, and that was enough. Philippa and Kimberly became wealthy and successful. Sir Thomas and I would meet occasionally, sharing old stories over too much wine, our memories growing dimmer with each meeting. Then that stopped, and he left to meet Paul and the others we had left behind.

It's been a good life. And despite its trials, I would not have traded it for another. If I died tonight, I would pass with a happy heart.

Tell me, Brother Michael, do you know if Philippa ever read that first manuscript – the story of my early years? She's never said. If she knew about Izelda, I doubt I would be here to narrate this conclusion. Perhaps she suspected but chose not to face the truth.

If you ever read this, Philippa – I am sorry. But I suspect you won't, just as you never read the first. I will never ask.

But before you go, Brother, I have one final request. Humour me. Over the months it has taken to scribe this tale, you have refused to be drawn on what lies behind your recent solemness. Have I offended you in some way? I would hate to think so. No? Well, sleep on it and maybe we can clear the air tomorrow.

*

That night, Ailred left us. It was too late to tell him what lay behind my surliness. It was love. He knew he was dying, and he was saying goodbye. At the start of this tale, it was about adventure – a life lived to the fullest – but as it progressed, I sensed his acceptance of death, his understanding of its inevitability. I had come to know the man, and each session broke my heart.

You have read my initial sentiment on finding him at the beginning of this testimony, so I will not dwell. By then, I had gotten to know Philippa, Kimberly, and Kimberley's twin boys well. Kimberly's husband, Sir Robert Bemborough, had been killed at the Combat of the Thirty early in their marriage, so he never lived to see his sons grow.

We grieved together. His funeral overflowed

Tonebricge Priory, a testament to the respect he commanded. Brother Emyr conducted the service. He had been offered a squire's position under Sir Thomas but turned that down, choosing instead to train as a man of the cloth, joining the seminary at Tonebricge Priory. He was, and still is, a fine priest, and I have no doubt his father would have been proud.

And now, as I prepare myself for life without the man, I wonder if he would be pleased with what I have written or if he would scoff, complaining that I had made him sound too noble and thoughtful. I chuckle to myself, knowing he would never have read the manuscript anyway – the "squiggly nonsense" forever beyond his understanding.

I have given him a voice beyond death, leaving it to you to decide his legacy. He was many things – a soldier, a friend, a fool, and, at times, a monster. But never once was he a man without purpose.

I will miss him.

Printed in Dunstable, United Kingdom